THE GREENYARDS LEGACY

Jane King

In memory of my father

PETER GWYNN

1930 - 2011

HISTORICAL NOTE

For the Scots there are few more bitter periods of history than the Highland Clearances. This controversial chapter in Scotland's past took place relatively recently; the incident at Greenyards in Strathcarron, Ross-shire, which provides the real life background to this novel, occurred in the 1850's. Yet few people outside Scotland have even heard of the Clearances, let alone know anything about them.

It was the battle of Culloden in 1746 that acted as the catalyst. After the battle the parliament in London was determined that never again would a rebellion arise out of the north. They disarmed the clans and prohibited Highland dress, and they took away the clan chiefs' traditional authority over their people. Many of those chiefs who supported Bonnie Prince Charlie at Culloden paid a forfeit in the loss of land. Those who held onto their estates found that the loss of their traditional powers left many of them in a desperate financial state.

The Great Cheviot Sheep came to the hills of the Highlands in the late seventeen hundreds, and it was the answer to the impoverished laird's prayers. A tough and adaptable creature, the Cheviot could weather the Highland winter. Unlike the Highland sheep it didn't require taking in at night. And its yield in terms of wool and mutton was impressive. Nor was there any need to go to the trouble of herding and shearing, when there were any number of Lowland and Northumbrian graziers desperate to lease the land. By 1810 the price of sheep in the Highlands had quadrupled.

But there was one problem. Before the sheep could be brought in, with their shepherds and their dogs, the people had to go. And, with no legal right to the land that they had inhabited for centuries, the people had no choice. They went.

CHAPTER ONE

Anna Sinclair was balanced at the top of a step-ladder, clutching an armful of books to her chest, when the phone on her father's desk began to ring. The sudden shriek of the phone in the quiet room made her jump. As her weight shifted, the ladder wobbled and swayed. In slow motion the book on the top of the pile she was holding slid sideways, teetered for a moment on the edge, and plunged earthwards.

With a crunch the spine cracked on impact and several of the pages detached themselves and fluttered across the floor. The ringing ceased as abruptly as it had started. Through the open door of the room Anna could hear the distant murmur of voices and the sound of the kitchen door opening. Then her stepmother's voice calling down the corridor.

"Anna. It's Richard again. Do you want to speak to him this time? What do you want me to tell him?"

Anna dumped the books she was holding on an empty shelf and began to climb backwards down the ladder.

"Could you tell him I'm still out," she called. "You don't know when I'll be back." She hesitated, relented a little. "Tell him I'll ring him later." She reached the bottom of the ladder.

"Tell him what, honey?"

Barbara had appeared in the doorway. She was holding the phone in her right hand. Anna stood frozen, torn between guilt and resentment.

"Oh," she said, feeling caught out. "Is he there?"

"It's alright," said Barbara in her easy way. "He's gone. I told him you were running an errand for me."

Anna bit her lip. She knew she owed it to her stepmother to explain why she had arrived yesterday alone, and why she was now refusing to take her husband's calls. But while Barbara might have been married to her father for over twelve years, the truth was that they were as good as strangers to each other. In all that time she and Anna had met no more than six or seven times. And, when you fly to Scotland to attend a memorial service for the father you've done your best to avoid for most of your life, how do you begin to explain to someone who is as good as a stranger why your husband isn't by your side?

"I thought if I turned off my mobile he might just leave a message," Anna said, ashamed of the disruption she was causing. "I didn't realise he would keep on ringing the house."

"He sure is persistent," said Barbara dryly. "I'll give him that."

"I will call him back. Later." Anna looked back at the stepladder. "When I've finished in here."

But Barbara waved a hand at her.

"Hey… Whatever. He's your problem, not mine." She glanced thoughtfully at Anna. "For what it's worth. If he was my husband, I don't suppose I'd be in too much of a rush to speak to him either."

Anna was conscious of a strong desire to step forward, lay her head on her stepmother's shoulder, and cry. If she had known her better she would have hugged her.

"You probably think I'm being very childish."

Barbara looked reflectively at her. "I've found it helps not to think anything unless I'm certain of all the facts." She turned to go, then stopped and looked at Anna over her shoulder. "Are you sure you haven't had enough yet? Sorting through your father's books is truly a labour of love."

Anna wasn't sure where love came into it. But what she did know was that keeping busy was a good way to stop her from thinking.

"I'm happy. Honestly. I'm no good at sitting around doing nothing."

"Well, when you're tired of it you just stop."

Barbara went out through the door. Then reappeared.

"By the way. What do you want me to say next time he rings?"

Anna listened to Barbara's footsteps going back up the corridor, and heard the brief burst of voices as the kitchen door opened and closed. She looked at the box of books at her feet. Richard would have been in Moscow a day by now, would have held the crisis meeting with his team, would know what needed to be done, and would be getting on with doing it. He was probably trying to get hold of her to give her the flight details for when he would be joining her. She knew the grown up thing to do would be to switch on her mobile and save Barbara from any more calls. But she couldn't bring herself to do the grown up thing.

What really stuck in Anna's throat was that it had been Richard who insisted that they should go to Charlie's memorial service in the first place. If it had been left up to her they wouldn't have gone.

It had been her mother Jennifer who had rung to tell her the news of her father's death.

"You're telling me he fell off a horse?" Even for Charlie it was hard to believe. "He was seventy-one years old, for chrissakes. What was he doing on a horse?"

"They were staying with Barbara's parents. At their ranch in Texas. I think he was herding cattle."

"You're kidding me. I have never heard of anything so ridiculous."

"You could sound a bit more sad about it, darling."

"Why?"

"He was your father…"

"Well, he never behaved like it."

"Now you're being unfair."

"Come off it, Mum. I was six when he left us. I can't remember the last time I spoke more than a few words to him. We only know what he's up to because you keep in touch with Barbara. Which has always seemed bizarre to me."

"I like her. She's a nice woman."

"She's a nice woman who is - sorry, was - married to the man who walked out on you."

"He didn't walk out on me for her though."

Anna gave up. She had never been able to understand her mother's relationship with Barbara. She could only put it down to the fact that, like victims of the same accident, they shared an experience and understanding that acted as a bond between them.

"There's going to be a memorial service," continued Jennifer. "Barbara said Charlie was very specific about it. Started planning it several years ago. Left clear instructions. She said she would have preferred it to be a bit more low-key, but it's what he wanted."

Anna snorted. "There was never anything low-key about Charlie."

"Darling…" Jennifer was sounding pained. "Do you have to be so antagonistic?"

Anna bit her lip and said nothing. There was no point.

"So we can all go together. Fly to Inverness. Barbara's offered to put us up for a few days. And we can see something of the Highlands while we're there."

Jennifer was making it sound like a holiday.

"You are joking."

"What do you mean?"

"There is no way I'm going all the way up to the north of Scotland for the memorial service of a father I never saw."

"Anna… Darling… Of course you must go."

But Anna was adamant.

When she told Richard that she wasn't going the last thing she expected was for him to react badly. He had always left her to make her own decisions when it came to her father. But on this occasion he had surprised her.

"What do you mean you're not going?"

He had been standing in the doorway to the kitchen, suitcase in hand, on his way upstairs to unpack, having arrived back from Japan twenty minutes earlier, when she told him about Jennifer's phone call.

"Of course you must go," he said, echoing her mother. "You'll regret it if you don't."

"I can promise you that I won't."

She had followed him from the kitchen, and watched with her hands on her hips as he went upstairs.

"I think you will," he said firmly, looking down at her from the landing. "We'll go together. We can fly up to Inverness with your mother."

"Hello... Can you hear me? I'm telling you that I don't want to."

He turned and came back down the stairs towards her.

"Anna... Come on. He was your father."

She felt her breath catch in her throat and glared at him

"Well, it never felt like it."

He stood in front of her and put his hands on her shoulders. "Come on," he said. "The girls are both away for the summer – we don't have to involve them. We can take Barbara up on her offer to put us up, and be back home again in no time. We could even stay up for a bit longer, find a nice hotel, see more of the Highlands."

She looked fiercely at him. Had he been speaking to Jennifer?

"I have no desire to see more of the Highlands."

He put his arm around her and gave her a gentle shake.

"You know it's the right thing to do. You're his only daughter, his only child. I don't want to hear another word about not going."

Anna kicked her foot against the box of books at her feet. Turn on her phone? The way she was feeling at the moment there was a good chance of hell freezing over before she was willing to open a text from him, let alone take one of his calls. She had a job to be getting on with. Richard would just have to wait.

She knelt down and restacked some of the books in the box to free up more space. As she straightened up she caught sight of the bent spine and scattered pages of the book she had dropped from the top of the stepladder when the phone rang. She had forgotten all about it. Absent husbands and unwanted phone calls had combined to put it completely out of her mind. Anna bent down and rescued the book from under the desk.

It was a slender volume with a cover of stained brown leather, which gave off a musty smell that caught at the back of her nostrils when she turned it over in the light from the window. It was a relief to see that most of the damage must have been there long before she dropped it. The book was clearly pretty ancient. Along the tattered spine she could make out the faded gleam from the remains of gilt lettering. The words were barely legible. Was it some sort of a logbook? She opened the front cover. From the title page she saw that it was a Fishing Journal. On the flyleaf written in bold, black ink, was the name of the man to whom it must have belonged – Robert Gillespie.

Anna stared. One of her ancestors - was it her great great grandfather? - had been called Robert Gillespie. The reason she knew this was because her father had written a book about him. Not that she had read it. But she remembered the name. She leaned weakly against the desk. What if this logbook had been an important part of her father's research when he was writing his book? What if she was responsible for the destruction of a vital source of information? For one guilty moment her strongest emotion was relief that at least Charlie was no longer around to tell her if she was.

She began to flick through the journal. Maybe it was possible to replace the pages that had become detached without anybody noticing what had happened? Perhaps she could get away without confessing to her crime? But a considerable number of pages had disconnected themselves in the fall. It was going to be difficult to patch them up. She thought guiltily of Barbara. Why did she have to be so likeable? It made owning up so much harder.

But there was no need to worry. As she turned the pages it became clear that this journal had never been used. Each page was made up of columns with headings: Date, Location, Weather Conditions, Species, Fly. But no record had been made of any catch. The columns were empty of information. It must, thought Anna with gratitude, have been a poor year for catching fish.

As neatly as she could she tucked the loose pages into the back of the book, and was about to put it in the box with the others when she caught sight of what looked like another page, one that must have escaped and come to rest against the leg of the table under the window. She stepped round the desk to retrieve it.

When she picked it up it was immediately apparent that this was not, as she had assumed, a page from the book. For a start it was folded in half; and the paper was thicker than the other pages. And, while the others contained nothing apart from the column headings, this was crossed with handwriting; a faded scrawl of black ink filled both sides. It had not been on the floor before Anna dropped the journal – she would have seen it. It must have been tucked between the pages and slipped out when the book fell.

Anna rubbed the edge of the page between her fingers. It felt dry and flaky like parchment, its edges curled with age. When she unfolded it, there was the suggestion of resistance, a stiffness in the paper, a barely perceptible cracking along the crease, which made her think that it must have been a long time since anybody else had opened and read it. With careful hands she flattened out the sheet of paper and peered at the writing. It was hard to make out the words. Was that a date at the top? It looked like April 20th. And the year… could it be 1854?

Anna stared. Whatever it was – a receipt, a thank you letter, a shopping list – it was more than a hundred and fifty years old. It was impossible not to feel excited.

She read the opening line.

My dearest one, my darling Fiona,

Not a shopping list or a receipt. Nothing so ordinary. This was a love letter.

The faded words on the sheet of paper danced in front of Anna's eyes. Her great great grandmother had been called Fiona. Anna might not know much about her father's side of the family. But she most definitely knew that. When she was a little girl her father had told her that she had an ancestor called Fiona who was the daughter of a Highland chieftain. Anna remembered that she had been full of questions. Did a chieftain's daughter wear a crown? Did she live in a castle? When she went to parties did she wear a tartan ball gown? But her father knew frustratingly little of the essential details.

One thing though… "I always wanted to call you Fiona," she remembered him saying. "But your mother wouldn't have it." Anna had been furious when she heard this. Imagine the sublime good fortune of being named after a Highland princess. How could her mother have been so mean? It had taken a long time to get over her disappointment.

Now she re-read the opening line of the letter. '*My dearest one, my darling Fiona.*' To address your wife in such a way. Anna felt a pang of something close to jealousy. She read on eagerly.

My dearest one, my darling Fiona,

Words are inadequate. I am in a frenzy of love and torment. You will not come to me. I know you will not come. And yet I write and beg you to reconsider.

You know that I loved you from the moment that I first saw you. Now that I have seen your courage in the face of danger, now that I have watched helpless while you suffered bloody assault and injury, now that I have felt the pain of your wounds as if they had been my own, now, if it is possible, I love you even more.

I watched you hold your battered head high, when they dragged you off to prison with the others, as if you were common criminals instead of heroines. Then the agony of my love for you was like a dagger twisting in my heart.

Now you hold that heart in your hands. You know that I have to go away. The love I bear for my country will not allow me to stay. To see what I have seen, to know what I know, makes it impossible. But you must also know that, after what we have been through together, I cannot leave you. You love me, I know. Come with me. Come with me. You must come with me.

I will wait for you at noon tomorrow. You know where to find me.

The letter was signed with a flourish.

Forever yours
Iain

Anna had to read the letter through several times for the full impact to sink in. Because it wasn't from Robert after all. Not from Fiona's husband, but from somebody else all together.

Who was Iain? Had he and Fiona been lovers? Did Robert know anything about it? She laid the letter down on the desk in front of her, struck by the strength of feeling, by how much she wished – for perhaps the first time in her life – that she knew more about her family's past. Who could she ask? Who would know? She stared blindly out of the window, pierced by a sudden and unexpected sensation of loss. Charlie Gillespie - her father - he was the obvious person. Had he been alive she would have asked him.

The sound of voices from outside in the corridor reminded her of where she was. There were footsteps on the parquet floor, and Barbara's clear tone calling goodbye and thank you to the team of local ladies who had been with her from first thing that morning, helping with the preparations for the wake the following day. Barbara's distinctive drawl stood out against the softness of the local voices. Anna heard car doors slamming, tyres crunching on gravel, then Barbara's voice calling down the corridor to her.

"Tea, Anna? You wanna call it a day?"

Anna stared at the letter in her hands. What was the best thing to do with it? Show Barbara? Own up to dropping the book? She hesitated, then tucked it back in its original hiding place between the covers of the journal, opened a drawer in the desk and slipped the book inside. Then she made her way up the long corridor that ran the length of the house towards the kitchen.

CHAPTER TWO

Barbara was pouring boiling water into a teapot when Anna entered. As Anna came in she lifted her head and smiled.

"Take a seat. Tea's just brewing."

Anna hovered in the doorway.

"Can I do anything?"

"You can sit down and take it easy."

"If you're sure?" Anna took an uncertain step towards the table. "I feel I should be doing more to help."

Barbara nodded her head at her.

"Go on. Sit. You've done plenty to help already."

So Anna pulled out a chair and sat down, while Barbara took mugs from the cupboard in the dresser and put biscuits from a tartan-patterned tin onto a plate. Anna watched her. "You've had so much to do," she said guiltily, aware that having an unfamiliar stepdaughter to stay at such a time was an additional burden. "You must be exhausted."

"But I've had so much help. Everything's been done for me. All I really need to do is show up." Barbara set the plate of biscuits on the table in front of Anna. "It always amazes me - the way people step up to the mark when the occasion requires it."

"Not everyone," said Anna, thinking of Richard.

"In my experience," said Barbara, giving Anna a glance that was full of compassion, "most people do the best they can. But how about you? How did you get on with that heap of books I set you to sort out?"

Anna opened her mouth to tell Barbara about her discovery. But then she hesitated. There was something so intensely personal about the letter. It felt as if she had been trusted with a secret that had been kept hidden for a very long time. She wasn't sure if the right thing to do was to share it.

"I've cleared most of the shelves behind the desk," she said instead.

"Good job. For that you deserve a cookie to go with your tea. Go on, take one. They're home-made."

While Barbara Gillespie poured the tea she watched her late husband's daughter out of the corner of one eye. Anna sat upright on the kitchen chair with her hands tightly clasped on the table in front of her, watching out of serious eyes that were precisely the same green as her father's had been. At this moment the likeness was uncanny. Turning her back on Anna to get the milk jug out of the fridge, Barbara found herself having to brush away tears with a fierce hand. It was a tragedy, she thought, that it had taken his death to get Charlie's daughter to visit.

"Here we go," she said, wheeling round to face Anna with a bright smile. "You don't take sugar, do you?"

Anna took the jug from her outstretched hand. In the grey light from the window Barbara could see that she looked tired in the way that people who are more than just in need of a good night's sleep look tired. Barbara would have liked to clear the air and ask outright what was going on between Anna and her husband. But she didn't know how to go about it.

"I was wondering about my great great grandmother - "

In the middle of pouring tea, Barbara stopped and looked at Anna in surprise.

"You were?"

"And about Robert Gillespie? About their marriage?"

"Well, that's really great…" And really unexpected, thought Barbara privately, considering the determination with which Anna had always gone out of her way to avoid anything to do with her father's side of the family.

"Those books… Charlie's books… " Anna spoke quickly, seeming to feel the need to explain. "It got me thinking."

"Uhuh…?" Barbara nodded her head, at a loss to know what to say. "Well… As I said… that's great."

"It's just that I know so little," cried Anna, sitting up even straighter in her chair and pushing her hair back from her face. "Nothing at all really."

"Your father would have been delighted to see you showing an interest," said Barbara. Delighted and perplexed. She sat down opposite Anna.

"So what about your father's book? Didn't that help?"

She asked this knowing that Charlie had sent a copy to Anna, with a note saying that he hoped very much that she would enjoy reading about a great man whose blood ran in her veins. "After all," he had said to Barbara, "look at all those websites for people to trace their ancestors. Everyone's at it these days. Most people would give their eyeteeth to discover someone like Robert Gillespie in their family tree. I can't believe she won't be interested."

But it looked like Charlie had been wrong. Anna's face was bent over the table, but Barbara could see that the rush of pink in her cheeks had darkened to a deep crimson red.

"Hey," she said gently. "I guess you didn't get round to reading it, huh?"

Anna lifted her head, and looked Barbara straight in the eye for what felt like the first time since her arrival.

"I'm really sorry," she said.

Barbara's eyes widened. "My dear girl - whatever for? He wasn't my ancestor. From the little I've managed to learn about my ancestors, they were all scoundrels and villains. I try not to think about them unless I absolutely have to." She smiled at Anna. "Why would you apologise to me?"

Anna shook her head and said she didn't know. And she sat back in her chair, and it was possible to see the tension easing from her shoulders, and the muscles in her jaw relaxing. Barbara sipped her tea. She was conscious of a profound sense of relief. It felt as if an important hurdle in her relationship with her stepdaughter had just been cleared.

"Is there a spare copy of Charlie's book I could borrow?" said Anna stiffly. "Maybe I could read it while I'm up here."

Oh Charlie, thought Barbara. I hope wherever you are, you can hear this. She put down her mug.

"Would you like to see his picture?"

"His picture?"

"Robert's picture... His portrait. It's in the living room."

"I'd love to," said Anna.

"Come on then. Bring your tea." Barbara led the way.

"Here we are."

Barbara waved Anna through the door into the living room. Anna went ahead of her. She stood in the centre of the room and said something that Barbara couldn't hear.

"Sorry I missed that?"

"I said, does it ever stop raining?"

It had been raining the first time Barbara came to the house that was to become her home for the twelve years of her marriage to Charlie Gillespie. Charlie had brought her to see Rowancross House on her first visit to Scotland. It was lucky for him, she sometimes thought, that it wasn't her last.

The house, a long sturdy building with lime washed walls and a roof of grey slate, had been lived in by members of the Gillespie family for generations. It was set in an acre of land on the edge of Loch Broom, the narrow stretch of water that threads its way inland between the purple brooding mountains of the north-western Highlands. From the outside it could not be considered beautiful. It reminded her, said Barbara, while she and Charlie sheltered under an umbrella on the weed-infested drive, waiting for the agent to arrive to show them around, of nothing more than the shed her father used to store his tractors. Only the shed was in rather better condition.

What made the house exceptional was its location. There wasn't a window that didn't look out on a spectacular view. That first day the view was hidden under a blanket of cloud. You'll just have to believe me, Charlie told Barbara. She was not convinced. Passing through the front door into a dilapidated entrance hall, she was disheartened to discover that the outside appearance had been a fair indication of the state of the inside. The house was in a bad way. It had been sold in the sixties by an uncle of Charlie's to pay off a tax bill, and used as a hostel for years. It was in desperate need of money and attention - a daunting prospect for anybody, let alone a newly married couple with one partner broke and heading into his sixties, and the other younger, wealthy, but entirely unconvinced about living in the UK, let alone the Scottish Highlands.

Luckily for Rowancross, Charlie's enthusiasm was infectious. He persuaded Barbara that restoring the house was a good use of a relatively modest proportion of the very immodest fortune left to her by her first husband when he died. And, although it took some time to get used to the weather, and the midges, and the long dark winters, over the years Barbara grew to love it almost as much as he did.

By the time Anna had arrived the previous day it was too late to do more than conduct a stilted conversation over supper in the large, comfortable kitchen that functioned as the heart of the house, and go early to bed. Anna had spent most of the day in her father's study. So this was the first time she had been into the room that offered the best opportunity to appreciate what made Rowancross House so special. The living room stretched the entire width of the house, with a stone fireplace at one end flanked by windows looking towards the steep rolling hills at the back, and a picture window with a window seat taking up the whole of the opposite end, looking out across the ever-changing waters of Loch Broom.

Today, as on that first day when Barbara came to Rowancross, the spectacular view was in hiding.

"I said, does it ever stop raining?"

Anna had to shout to be heard, as a sudden squall threw rain against the windows so that they rattled like castanets.

Barbara smiled. "It does... I promise. But I know how you feel. When I first arrived I struggled to see what all the fuss was about." She crossed the room to stand alongside Anna. "You can imagine. Hailing from my part of the world, I was used to light and space and heat. This came as quite a shock."

"I bet it did," said Anna vehemently, gazing at the rain.

Barbara took her by the hand.

"Come and meet your great great grandfather."

She drew Anna towards the fireplace, above which hung a dark portrait in an ornate gilt frame. Together they looked up at a dark haired man who stared across their shoulders into the distance. He stood legs astride in the heather, an iron bridge rising up behind him across a rushing river. He was wearing tartan trousers and a short jacket, with a stretch of plaid slung over one shoulder. His face was strong and handsome, with a long straight nose above firm lips and a square jaw. He looked watchful and controlled.

Barbara glanced at Anna. "What do you think?"

"He's nice-looking..."

She sounded surprised. Barbara laughed.

"He is rather a dish, isn't he? Although he doesn't look to me like he's blessed with a great sense of humour. In my experience they rarely are – these silent driven types."

She knew what she was talking about. Her first husband Ray had been a driven man. Driven to pursue her and persuade her to marry him when she was only just out of school; driven to build the airfreight business he had inherited from his father from nothing into a company worth millions; driven to put work before pleasure; driven to an early grave. Barbara wondered if Anna was thinking about Richard. She was prepared to bet that he was the driven type too.

Barbara was right. Anna was thinking about Richard. About what exactly he was he doing at that precise moment? About what was so important that he had to drop everything and fly to Moscow? About why he wasn't there with her? She stood beside Barbara, in front of the portrait of the great great grandfather she knew so little about, and hoped that her stepmother couldn't tell how difficult she was finding it to hold it together.

It was by no means the first time in their marriage that Anna had had to handle important family occasions without her husband. The question, she told herself bitterly, was why she should be surprised? After all this was the man who had missed the birth of his second daughter Ellie, because he was delayed in New York when Anna went into labour. This was the man who had to rearrange their trip to Venice to celebrate their tenth wedding anniversary because he was needed in Prague. She should have been used to it by now.

She had lost count of the number of trips they had made - laughingly referred to as family holidays - when she and Rose and Ellie waited for him to join them, from whatever country he happened to be in at the time that wasn't the one they were in. While other fathers splashed their children in the pool, dug elaborate sandcastles on the beach, relaxed over a glass of wine with their wives, Richard rang from hotel rooms to say that he had just one more meeting to get through, and then he would be on the next flight to join them.

Then there were the times - was it five in all? – when, because of his job, they had been required to move house, more often not with a change of country thrown in for good measure. And - more often than not - he had left her to manage the whole thing without him. His presence at school plays, concerts, sports days and parents' evenings was as rare as snow in August. His suitcase was never in one place for long enough to be put away in the attic with the others. Anna's mother Jennifer said that it was all part and parcel of being married to a successful man. Anna supposed that she should have grown used to it by now. So why hadn't she?

Barbara was looking at her speculatively.

"I'm guessing that you'd like to see Fiona?"

"Fiona?" said Anna, not understanding.

"Robert's wife? Your great great grandmother."

Thoughts of Richard were banished. She remembered the letter she had found. "There's a picture of Fiona?"

"Not in here," said Barbara, laughing at her eagerness. "Upstairs… In our…" She stopped laughing and corrected herself. "I suppose I should say 'in my' bedroom."

The look she gave Anna was defiantly upbeat, but the catch in her voice was unmissable. Anna felt sadness and guilt in equal measures. How selfish of her? At least she still had a husband, even if he was in the wrong place. She would have liked to have offered comfort to Barbara, but didn't know how to go about it.

"Come on," said Barbara, holding out her hand and smiling in the fiercely determined manner of someone who is doing their best to hide a deep, dark sadness. Anna hesitated, wondering if maybe now was the time to come clean about the letter. Would it be a distraction from, or an intrusion into, Barbara's grief? She couldn't be sure, and didn't want to appear insensitive. So instead she allowed herself to be led upstairs, feeling slightly awkward to be hand in hand with this openhearted woman, but not wanting to offend her by disengaging.

Barbara's bedroom was directly above the living room, and shared the same double aspect. Above a smaller fireplace was a smaller portrait, inside a carved wooden frame. Like Robert's, this was in oil. It showed a girl standing against a backdrop of moorland, with a stretch of water gleaming in the distance behind her. As they approached the fireplace, Anna could see that she was dressed for cold weather, in long skirts, with an overcoat nipped in at the waist and edged with fur. Her hands were small, encased in leather gloves, and one was resting on the head of a great dog that stood obediently beside her. She was gazing straight out of the painting, a smile lifting the corners of her mouth, laughter in her expressive eyes.

"Is this Fiona?" Anna dropped Barbara's hand. There was something so intensely familiar in the eyes, the set of the jaw, in the arched brows and determined mouth, that for a moment Anna couldn't quite believe what she was seeing. She turned to Barbara. "She looks just like Ellie."

"Doesn't she?" Barbara nodded, smiling. "Quite a girl, isn't she? Put her in jeans and a t-shirt and she and your Ellie could be twins."

Anna stepped closer to the painting to have a better look.

"Isn't it the darndest thing?" said Barbara's voice behind her. "The way family likenesses pop up in such a random manner. I'm surprised your father never said anything about it to you. The few times we met Ellie it was all he could talk about."

Anna was pierced by another dart of guilt. Her father hadn't seen his granddaughters more than a dozen times. Now that it was too late, she wondered if it had been fair of her to keep them apart. She looked over her shoulder at Barbara and saw that a shadow had crossed her face.

"I don't know what's wrong with me today." Barbara rubbed a hand across her eyes. "I keep on forgetting he's gone. And then I remember, and it hits me like a ten ton truck."

The huskiness in her voice was back. Looking away, Anna thought that her father had been a very lucky man to be the subject of such deep love.

"You know," said Barbara after a few minutes silence, "when I look at the pair of them, I struggle to put them together. Robert and Fiona, I mean." She had reverted to her customary composed self. "He looks so stern and serious. And she looks so full of fun."

It was true, thought Anna. They did seem a mismatched pair. She glanced at Barbara. Maybe now was the right time to tell her about the letter? But what if she was making a big deal about something insignificant, mistaking it for something more important than it really was? She had seen the way Barbara looked at her when she mentioned her interest in finding out more about the family history. Shock would be the best way to describe her reaction. The last thing Anna wanted was to draw more attention to her recently awakened curiosity if it turned out she was making something out of nothing.

Barbara was contemplating Fiona's portrait. "It just goes to show that appearances can be deceptive," she said. "By all accounts theirs was a long and happy marriage. You know he had this house built for her, in her favourite place by the edge of Loch Broom, so that she could watch the boats heading out to sea from Ullapool."

"He did?" Anna's immediate reaction was disappointment, but it was quickly overtaken by relief. She had been right not to say anything. She must have misinterpreted the letter. Got overexcited and read more into it than was actually there.

"Lovely to have a husband who thinks so much of you that he builds a house just so you can watch the ships go by," she said.

"Well, it certainly beats garage flowers and a box of After Eights." Barbara was laughing. "Although from what I gather he wasn't around that much to enjoy it with her. Always away doing business somewhere or other." She glanced at Anna. "Sounds familiar, huh?"

Anna turned and met her gaze.

"Tell me about it," she said.

CHAPTER THREE

B ack in the kitchen, Anna sat at the table folding paper napkins around sets of knife, fork, spoon, while Barbara prepared their supper. When the basket in front of her was full, Barbara handed another pack of napkins across the table. Anna received it with good grace, but Barbara could see her expression and read her mind. Barbara experienced her own moment of doubt. Was she overestimating the numbers likely to attend Charlie's memorial? Anna clearly thought so.

She opened her mouth to suggest that Anna take a break from napkin folding, and instead open a bottle of wine so that they could have a glass with their meal, when the phone rang. She crossed the kitchen to answer it. There was a familiar voice on the line.

"Barbara?"

"Richard –"

"It's me again."

"So it is."

"Is she there?"

Barbara looked doubtfully at Anna who shrugged and nodded, holding out her hand for the phone with a resigned smile.

"It's Richard," said Barbara unnecessarily. "Do you want to take it in the other room?"

Richard's voice sounded to Anna's ears just a little too loud. He didn't ask her to explain why she hadn't called him, and she understood him well enough to know that he was speaking in that hearty exaggerated manner to hide how he really felt.

Instead he asked about her journey. How was the flight? And how was Barbara? He hoped she was coping all right. She sounded in good shape. He was expecting that he should be able to join them in a couple of days. Was looking forward to seeing the Highlands, and spending some time with his wife. Should be wonderful, just what they needed, didn't she think? He paused, waiting for her to agree with him.

Anna could hear the suppressed guilt in the uncomfortable silence, and knew that he was miserable. Rain lashed the window. Outside the surface of Loch Broom glistened like wet concrete. It was as if the grey waters of the loch had entered her soul and washed her clean of compassion. She was brief and polite.

"There you are," said Barbara when Anna returned to the kitchen. "Everything ok? Let me get you a glass of wine? Or a cup of tea? What would you prefer?

"Wine would be good," said Anna thinking that she needed it. She started to say that she was happy to get it for herself. But Barbara was on her feet. And Anna realised with a sudden flash of understanding that playing the role of hostess was her stepmother's way of keeping her grief at bay. So she sat down at the table, while Barbara went to the large American fridge and took out a bottle.

"Thank you." Anna accepted the glass that Barbara handed to her, grateful for the tact that Barbara showed in not inquiring about her conversation with Richard. Instead Barbara asked about the girls and what they were up to. Anna explained about Rose and the gap year that had started in Richard's offices in Prague, and would continue with a flight to Australia in September where she would stay until Christmas. And how Ellie was on a hockey tour. Of schools in and near Boston.

"That's where they go to for tours these days?" exclaimed Barbara.

Anna laughed and told Barbara that Ellie had really fallen on her feet, because, after the tour was done she was staying on for the rest of the summer, visiting with a friend whose parents owned a house in Cape Cod.

"What a lucky girl," said Barbara, drizzling olive oil onto salmon fillets before putting them onto a hot griddle where they sizzled and spat. "Any tour I went on at her age started and finished in my own back yard."

The kitchen was warm and comfortable. Barbara had turned on the lights, and the soft glow they cast banished the grey light back outside from where it had come. Anna sipped her wine while Barbara moved quietly from oven to sink, draining new potatoes, slicing bread, spooning mayonnaise into a glass bowl and setting it on the table. Lulled into a state of relaxed weariness, Anna watched her almost dreamily, thinking that it had been a long time since she had felt this tranquil.

"Here you go." Barbara set a plate in front of her and sat down in the chair opposite.

Anna picked up her knife and fork, realizing with a start that she was hungry for what seemed like the first time in days. "It looks delicious," she said, full of gratitude for more than just the food. They ate in companionable silence. Anna was struck by how much the atmosphere had changed between them in the course of an afternoon. It had been when they were looking at the paintings of Robert and Fiona that the ice really began to thaw.

Anna made a snap decision. "Barbara?" she said, setting down her knife and fork. "I don't suppose you know... Has there ever been any suggestion that Fiona and Robert's marriage was in trouble?"

The forkful of food that Barbara was raising to her mouth stopped in mid air.

"I found a letter," said Anna quickly. "This afternoon while I was sorting the books. It's probably nothing."

Barbara lowered her fork to her plate. "What kind of a letter?"

"Wait there. I'll get it."

Within minutes Anna was back with the letter in her hand. "Here." She handed it to Barbara.

Barbara read slowly. When she had finished she looked up at Anna with wide eyes. "Well," she said. Then she read it through again. "This is quite a thing now, isn't it? Wherever did you find it?"

Anna told her about Robert's journal.

"It must have slipped out when I dropped the book. Do you think it was Robert who hid it there? I wonder if Fiona ever actually saw it."

Barbara read it through for a third time.

"It's certainly hot stuff," she said, sitting back in her chair. "Doesn't quite fit with the happy marriage story, does it?"

"What about the bit - ?" Anna came round the table to look over Barbara's shoulder. "Here. Where it talks about '*bloody assault and injury.*' What could that be about?"

Barbara frowned. "It's certainly the first I've heard of anything like that going on. I'm sure Charlie knew nothing about it, or he would have checked it out."

Anna sat back against the edge of the table. "Do you have any idea who Iain might be?"

"The only Iain I can think of was a journalist. Robert had dealings with him over the Clearances."

"The Clearances?"

"You don't know about the Clearances?" Barbara sighed. "It's a long story. I'm really the wrong person to explain."

But Anna wasn't interested in the Clearances. Whatever they were, they were a distraction. It was Iain she wanted to know about.

"So this Iain…?"

"The journalist, yes. His name was Iain Mackay. He and Fiona certainly met each other - several times, I think."

Anna leant forward.

"They did? So you think it could be him?"

Barbara looked regretfully at her. "Oh sweetie… I really couldn't say." She handed the letter back to Anna. "You know what I would suggest? There's some stuff of Fiona's - journals, letters, that sort of thing. We found a box in the attic when we moved in. After tomorrow is over I'll dig it out for you. It's all packed away." She reached across the table and picked up Anna's plate. "I'm pretty certain Fiona mentions meeting Iain Mackay in one of her diaries. I just wish I could remember the details."

Anna sprang up to help. Barbara might not be able to remember much, but it didn't matter. There were diaries, diaries in which Fiona had written about meeting Iain Mackay. It gave her a place to start. In the time available to her before Richard arrived she would try and get to the bottom of this mystery.

⟨+ +⟩

On her way up to bed, Anna stopped off in the living room. She twisted the head of a desklamp so that its beam lit up the bookcase beside the fireplace. Searching along the shelves, she found what she was looking for. With soft footsteps she padded up the wide staircase and across the landing to her bedroom.

When she opened the door she found that Barbara had been in before her and pulled the curtains shut and turned down the bed. The pillows were plumped up high, and there was a warm woolen throw folded across the bottom of the bed in case she felt cold in the night. Anna pulled the door shut behind her, pausing to appreciate how good it felt to be on the receiving end of such thoughtfulness.

She was quick to get ready for bed. Settling herself against the pillows, she picked up the book she had taken from the bookcase downstairs. She looked at author's name - Charlie Gillespie. Her father. How delighted he would have been that she was finally showing some interest in her family's past. As she opened the cover she had the oddest sensation that, although he might not be around in the flesh to help her, he was guiding her towards the answers she sought.

It didn't take long for her to appreciate how wrong she had been to believe that the story of her great great grandfather's life would contain little to interest her. She had grown up knowing that one of her ancestors was a politician who made a fortune out of jute. She had never been bothered enough to find out anything more about him. As she began to read her father's book she realised that there was lot more to Robert Gillespie than she had ever imagined.

He was born in 1814, the son of James Gillespie, a sheep farmer of Ayrshire, and Isabella, daughter of a miller from Dumfries. From the start he was an unusually bright and quick-witted boy who stood out from his friends at the local school. His father was an astute man who made sufficient money off the backs of his sheep to send his son away for a gentleman's education. Robert went to Rugby, and from there to Cambridge. At Christ's College he worked hard enough to get himself a first class degree, but he also found the time to take a keen interest in college politics and play cricket for the university. It was here, rubbing shoulders with the sons of the landed gentry, that he began to appreciate that it was the ownership of land that conferred both profit and status upon those who understood how best to make use of it.

He was intelligent and he was ambitious. He came back to his father's house from university full of ideas for improving the land that would be his inheritance. His father - delighted and a little overawed at the way his son was turning out - stepped back and allowed him free rein with his ideas. Robert experimented with breeding, crossing the Cheviot sheep with other hardy breeds, searching for the ideal combination to deliver maximum profit. He introduced the latest techniques of land management, draining marshland to create conditions for his sheep to flourish. And he combined the land of the smaller tenant farmers into one large farm, placing it under his direct control. He took his father's modest success and turned it into something much more substantial. Failure was not a word in his vocabulary.

When it came to marriage, however, things were not so straightforward. His mother chose a local girl for him, the daughter of a wealthy corn chandler from Kilmarnock. It was a good match, but Robert showed no desire to comply with his mother's wishes. He concentrated all his energies on his business interests, and it seemed that marriage was well down his list of priorities. Until he met Lachlan Mackenzie in Edinburgh, where he was introduced to his daughter, Fiona.

It was at this point in the story that Anna began to get irritated with her father. And it was just like being a little girl all over again. Because Charlie didn't seem very interested in Fiona. It was hard for her to understand but he seemed concerned with Robert's marriage as a business transaction and nothing more. He introduced Fiona Mackenzie in an entirely unexceptional manner, as the daughter of a man in whose land Robert was interested.

It was, according to Charlie, *'a judicious alliance, an eminently sensible match for both parties. He brought his wealth, his energy, his business acumen and his ambition. She bestowed the ancient lineage of her father's clan, together with the great house at Kildorran, and the acres that went with it.'* So much for romance.

Anna flipped through the pages, looking for more: a description of their courtship, the wedding ceremony, anything to put flesh on the cold bones of this business arrangement. All she found was that Fiona was a '*handsome girl, with beautiful manners*'. That she was apparently a '*fine horsewoman and graceful dancer*'. And that '*she encouraged her husband in his political ambitions.*'

Sighing with frustration Anna glanced at her watch. It was well past midnight and she had a funeral to go to the next day. She could have gone on reading all night, but, if she wanted to look her best when she met people who had known her father better than she had, she needed to get some sleep.

She lay the book down, switched off the light, and closed her eyes.

'*I'm in a frenzy of love and torment.*'

It was as if the words had been spoken out loud somewhere on the edge of her hearing. Anna sat up. It was no good. She had to find out who had written that letter. Just a couple more pages of Charlie's book. Maybe the answer lay there.

She switched on the light, picked up the book again, and turned to where she had left off.

When Robert Gillespie married Fiona Mackenzie he turned his attention to the Highlands. Would he have done so had marriage not focused his attention on the north, it is hard to say? But the market for wool and for mutton was expanding rapidly, as the great towns of the south embraced the industrial revolution. It was men such as Robert who recognised the opportunity to exploit the Highland pastures, by introducing sheep that were able to weather the Highland winters, were less subject to disease, and would yield a greater degree of wool and mutton; sheep such as the hardy, coarse woolled creatures that Robert had been breeding in Ayrshire.

As with everything he did, Robert took very seriously his duty to improve the land which marriage had brought him. In his eyes the ownership of property bestowed an obligation that took precedence over everything else, the obligation to make improvements for the general good. Robert used the pages of the Inverness Courier to give voice to his opinions, having become an occasional correspondent for this journal when it appeared to him necessary to correct some of the more sentimental views with regard to land reform, which he felt did more harm than good.

Robert took issue with those who would stand in the way of progress, arguing that a willingness to abandon the traditional ways in favour of modern methodology was sadly lacking in the Highlands. The people must recognize that change was inevitable. The system of land tenure was working against the interests of those who lived there. It was time to embrace the future and leave behind the old ways, the blind adherence to which delivered little but starvation and poverty.

The appearance of Robert's letters in the Courier generated a great deal of comment. He was not the first, nor would he be the last, to recognize that change was both essential and inevitable. However this was a region that had suffered, within the memory of too many, the notorious evictions instigated by the Duke of Sutherland, when the inhabitants of the county of Sutherland were cleared from their homes in their thousands with a degree of ruthlessness that defied belief. Now people were understandably nervous of what change entailed.

One man in particular took it upon himself to express the fears of the people. Iain Mackay, a young man whose father had experienced the horrors of the Clearances in Sutherland, was at that time working as a journalist for the Courier. He used the letters page of the newspaper that paid his wage to present the opposing view.

'My respected friend, Mr. Robert Gillespie, is absolutely right,' he wrote. 'The question of land reform in the Highlands must indeed be the subject of consideration by all who have an interest. But it cannot be addressed without taking account of the interests of those most affected as the central issue. I am talking of the real Highlanders, the men and the women and the children who were born and live in the hills, who work the land, who fish the rivers and the lochs, whose fathers and fathers' fathers are buried beneath the heather. These are the people to whom we must listen. It is their views that count.'

His argument was well penned. Iain Mackay was an articulate advocate for the people. His writing generated a groundswell of opinion in the area against Robert

Gillespie. Some argue that it was the negative response to Robert's opinions, fuelled by Iain MacKay's writing that led to Robert's ultimate abandonment of his plans to undertake major reforms at Kildorran. Others, myself included, believe that Robert made the decision based on the economics of the situation, and hastened by his emerging interest in the opportunities in Dundee for building a business out of jute. Whatever the cause, it is undeniable that Iain Mackay had considerable impact upon a man who was rarely moved by another's views. Robert once said that he honed his skills of representation on the stone of MacKay's opinions. He even went as far as to thank him for it.'

Iain Mackay. He certainly sounded like the sort of man who might have written so passionately to the woman he loved. Anna skimmed through the following pages, searching for further mention of his name. But she could find nothing more about him.

She laid the book down on the bedside table and reached over to turn out the light. Lying in the darkness, she smiled to herself. Already she had a clearer picture of Robert Gillespie. And she had the name of someone who might conceivably turn out to be the mysterious writer of Fiona's love letter. It was a good start.

As she drifted into sleep an image of Richard, getting ready for bed in a Moscow hotel room, slipped into her consciousness. He seemed far away, separated from her by more than distance. But now it didn't seem to matter quite so much.

CHAPTER FOUR

The next morning Anna woke up to the sound of rain against her window. In the grey light of day her positive mood of the previous night had drained away. Now all she could think about was what lay ahead of her. The prospect of going to her father's memorial made her turn in her bed and pull the duvet over her head.

But there was no escaping it. She took a deep breath and got out of bed. On her way into the bathroom she knocked her father's book from the bedside table. Bending to pick it up it was hard to believe that she had got so excited about the lives of people who had lived such a long time ago. This morning Robert and Fiona were nothing more than ancient history. It was hard enough dealing with the present, without getting worked up about the past.

On her way downstairs Anna caught sight of her reflection in the long mirror that hung on the mid landing. She paused, suddenly seized by doubt. Her outfit - was it sufficiently sober? The jacket was entirely sensible. But the skirt? It was frivolous and fluted, falling to the knee in a swirl of magenta and khaki. And the shoes? Magenta slingbacks with kitten heels – christened the 'red hot mama shoes' by her daughters. She had bought the suit the year before, egged on by a friend and in a moment of impulse, and it was hardly worn. Being in no mood for compromise when she packed, the muted green khaki had seemed suitably austere. But now? Was it a mistake? The last thing she wanted to do was offend Barbara.

Barbara was in the kitchen with her team of helpers. She looked up as Anna entered.

"Now don't you look great," she said warmly, looking at Anna with admiring eyes. "You put us country girls to shame."

Since she was looking white faced but immaculate, in a simple black jersey dress of such understated elegance that there could be no doubting that it must have cost a serious amount of money, Anna didn't take her too seriously. But Barbara's approval allowed her to relax a little.

"You'll be Charlie's daughter, then," said a woman, introduced by Barbara as Minnie, the butcher's wife. Minnie was standing by the open door of the fridge, gazing at Anna with unashamed curiosity. She was waiting to receive the several large packs of butter that were being decanted from the depths of the fridge by another helper.

"There's no missing the family connection, is there?" Minnie was addressing the room at large. "That hair. And those eyes."

"Is it really that obvious?" It was a worrying indication of what to expect for the rest of the day.

"Well, for heaven's sake," laughed Minnie, carrying the butter across to the kitchen table. "Have you looked in the mirror lately? Aren't you just like him?"

It had been a very long time since anybody had pointed this out to Anna. Not since she was a little girl. She tried to conjure up her father's face in her mind's eye. And couldn't.

Barbara was counting out loaves of bread on the draining board, trying to occupy her mind with the mundane details of the day ahead. She glanced at Anna and saw that she was looking lost. She pushed the bread to one side and wiped the crumbs into the sink.

"You don't mind if I leave you to it, do you ladies?" She took hold of Anna's hand. "I need to sit down and have a bit of a breather before we leave for the church. Will you join me, Anna?"

Anna was happy to oblige. The prospect of the church service, of all those people she didn't know but who would know her, had caused her to spend a troubled night. And now, when she thought of the ordeal ahead of her, her stomach turned over and she felt rather sick. She couldn't stop herself from thinking how much easier it would have been if Richard had been there with her. It kept on reigniting her anger, which in turn made her feel more anxious. Barbara's calm presence was just what she needed. And she hoped that in return she could be of some help to her stepmother. Although, from her outward appearance of steady good humour, it seemed that Barbara was coping with the situation rather better than her stepdaughter.

They sat at either end of the window seat in the sitting room. Anna peered out at the grey sky. There was no sign of an improvement in the weather. Wind whipped the clouds into disarray, as pulses of rain swept in from the sea. The surface of the loch shifted and heaved, as if beaten by an unseen hand.

"It's hard to escape the view in this house," she sighed, feeling the impact of the grey sea and sky like a weight bearing down on her. Barbara smiled her understanding smile.

"It does look rather gloomy at the minute, I'll grant you. But give it time and you'll find it grows on you. It's always changing, literally from one moment to the next. And it's always beautiful, whatever the weather."

"Beautiful?" Anna peered out through the window. "It just looks bleak to me."

It was as if somebody had heard her and wished to prove her wrong, for as she spoke a gap appeared in the clouds, and a shaft of light sprung from the sky and cast a shimmering path across the water. A sailing boat was cutting its way over the loch, and, at that moment, it slipped through the sun's rays, white sails gleaming like mother of pearl in the light. Anna gazed at the little ship struggling against the wind, as it tacked out towards the open sea.

"I suppose there is a certain sort of dramatic wildness about it," she said grudgingly, as the boat changed direction. "But it just makes me feel relieved that I'm not out there. That little boat looks so vulnerable."

"You know the thing that always gets me?" Barbara was watching the boat bobbing valiantly across the waves. "If that little guy was to keep going west for long enough, eventually he would wind up in Canada. Can you imagine what a hellish journey that must be?" She turned to Anna. "But folk from around here have been doing it off and on for centuries."

"Surely not in a boat that size?"

"Bigger than that. But not a lot. Ullapool was the starting point for hundreds of Scots who decided... Or rather, had it decided for them... that they were better off starting a new life somewhere else. A whole heap of them ended up in Canada. Some moved west to the prairies, but quite a few went further south, across the border into the United States. There's a gang of us who can trace our roots back to this part of the world. You guys with your family trees laid out for you in the churchyard down the road take it for granted. But it means a lot, I can tell you."

Anna had a vision of the little boat heading out to take on the wild waters of the Atlantic. She shuddered. Why would anyone do it? Things must have been pretty bad at home for people to undertake such a journey.

She thought about the letter she had found the previous day. The mysterious Iain, whoever he was, had written that he was leaving. *The love I bear for my country does not allow me to stay.* What could have happened to make him feel that way?

She stared out of the window. The boat had disappeared around the headland, but the image it had conjured up in her mind remained. She imagined the people lined up on the deck, waving goodbye to the land they loved. She glanced sideways at her stepmother.

"I found Iain Mackay in Charlie's book last night."

Barbara swung round in her seat to look at her.

"You did?" Her satisfaction was plain to see. "You know, I've been thinking about him too. And it occurred to me that I've got just the person for you to meet. A writer called Fin Maclean. Who just happens to have written a book about Iain Mackay."

Anna stared at her. "I'd love to meet him."

"Fin was a big fan of your father's - he'll be there today." Barbara looked at her watch. "He's the guy to tell you about Iain Mackay." She squared her shoulders. "Are you ready? We should be going."

They stood up in unison.

They left the house in the charge of Barbara's ladies, who were still busy making sandwiches in the kitchen, churning them out with the efficiency of an assembly line. Barbara had asked Anna if she minded driving, and Anna was glad to be given something to do. She backed Barbara's Volvo out of the drive. It was the first time she had left Rowancross House since her arrival the day before yesterday, and she glanced back at the house with longing as they turned out of the gate. When she had arrived it had seemed drab and unwelcoming. Now it felt like she was leaving a safe haven.

She swung the steering wheel and pulled out onto the main road. The rain had eased to drizzle, but the cloud still lay heavy over the hills, and the temperature gauge on the dashboard indicated a temperature outside that was more akin to a winter's day than midsummer. Anna shivered and hoped she wasn't going to be too cold in the church.

Barbara was gazing out of the window with a bleak expression on her face. She looked like she needed distraction from what lay ahead, thought Anna.

"This writer? Does he live up here?"

Barbara turned and shook her head.

"He lives in London. But he comes up here whenever he gets the chance. And he's up for the summer, working on a new book, a novel this time. He's staying with his aunt while he writes it. Sarah's a good friend of mine; she'll be there today as well."

"So what makes Iain Mackay worth writing a book about?"

"Well you know The Mackay Group? You've heard of them?"

Anna nodded. Who hadn't heard of The Mackay Group? It was hard to ignore them, particularly at the moment. The vast Canadian media enterprise had been buying up publications in the UK and was getting a lot of coverage in the press.

"When Iain Mackay left the Highlands he went to Canada. And when he got there he set up a newspaper. Which was the foundation for what was to become The Mackay Group." Barbara smoothed her skirt over her knees. "So they asked Fin to write this book to celebrate the centenary of Iain's death. And it's just about to be published. If anyone can tell you about Iain Mackay, he's the one."

The caravan in front of them swung over the brow of a hill. They followed it down the other side as the road took them towards the little town of Ullapool. To their right a golf course curled around the edge of the loch, its tees and greens empty of people. They went past a row of ugly modern bungalows as they entered the back of the town. Anna had driven through Ullapool when she arrived. It had been raining then as well.

"Remind me again, Barbara," she said, as she slowed down to allow a couple of walkers swathed in green waterproofs to cross the road in front of them. "What exactly was it that made you want to live in this place?"

Barbara smiled.

"Your father wouldn't consider living anywhere else. When he heard that Rowancross had come on the market, he knew it was meant to be. He was always a great believer in fate."

The walkers nodded their thanks. Anna accelerated away.

"What did fate have to do with it?"

"Well by rights Rowancross House should have been your father's all along. Originally it was left to his grandfather Neil – Fiona's youngest son – and should have been passed on to Neil's son Charles, and from him to his son."

"My father?"

"That's it. But apparently there was some mix up with the will, and the house ended up going to Neil's older brother Robert instead. Who left it to his son… also called Robert."

She directed Anna towards the road that led them out of town, heading south along the edge of the loch.

"By all accounts this younger Robert was a bit of a no-hoper. He managed to gamble away pretty much all of the fortune that the original Robert had built up. Your father used to visit the house when he was a boy, in the days when his uncle still lived there, and it used to make his blood boil to see the way he was letting it go. The family had to sell it to pay the death duties when the old man died in the sixties. It was a youth hostel before we bought it.

"The house was in a pretty terrible state when we took it on. We couldn't move in for over six months. And, when we finally did, the rooms on the attic floor were still blocked off. The staircase was completely rotten. Getting up there wasn't exactly top of the list of priorities. There was so much to be done in the rest of the house. So it was more than a year before we got round to fixing the stairs, and when we finally made it up there we found a whole heap of junk. Furniture, clothes… all kinds of stuff.

But what was really exciting was that we found a small leather case containing letters, newspaper cuttings, sketches. And Fiona's journals – that was the best of all.

So then we had these great descriptions of her life when she was growing up, information about her life with Robert, letters from friends, that kind of thing. Charlie used bits and pieces for his book, although for his purposes there was too much domestic detail."

She paused. They were past the end of Loch Broom.

"But you know, when I think about it, I can't remember that there was anything there to suggest anything untoward in their marriage." She looked over at Anna. "It sure is a mystery. I am just longing to know what that letter of yours is all about."

They turned off the main road and along a narrow lane at the end of which was a church. The church was square and plain and simple. It stood in the middle of a graveyard beside a grey loch. Parked along the road, for as far as the eye could see, were vehicles of all shapes and sizes. They lined the verges on both sides, perching on banks, double parked in lay-bys, tucked into wherever a space could be found.

"What on earth are all these people doing here?" Anna backed up to allow a car coming from the opposite direction to squeeze past her. Barbara shot a glance at her.

"Your father was a popular man around here. People thought a great deal of him."

There was an edge to her voice that Anna hadn't heard before, and she felt her face grow hot. She hadn't meant to sound rude. She opened her mouth to apologise, but Barbara was pointing out a parking space beyond the church, and Anna decided that it was better not to say anything. She had spent most of her life seeing her father in a negative light and it had become a habit. She would have to watch the way she spoke about him in future.

She edged the car slowly towards the church, following a minibus full of people. Beside her a gleaming black Audi with darkened windows had pulled up on the verge, and the passenger door swung open suddenly, so that she had to brake hard to avoid hitting it. From the other side of the car a tall man with a suntanned face strode round to push the door back out of her way. Seeing her glaring at him through the windscreen, he grinned and jerked his head at his passenger with an expression of resignation. Then he saw Barbara beside her and lifted his hand in greeting. From inside the car a woman in a black hat was checking her face in the rearview mirror, oblivious to the fact that she had nearly caused an accident. Anna drove slowly past.

"That's Cameron Gillespie," said Barbara. "He's a second cousin of your father."

Anna glanced in her wing mirror. Cameron was still waiting for his passenger to emerge.

"Is that his wife?"

Barbara laughed.

"Cameron doesn't do wives. That was Laura. I suppose she's what you would call his housekeeper. She looks after him. Has done for years."

"Well he ought to have a word with her about looking out before she opens a car door."

In front of them the minister had come out of his church and was standing in the gateway, his robes flapping in the breeze. He caught sight of Barbara and raised his hand. Barbara waved back.

"Would you mind dropping me off here, Anna, before you park the car. I need to have a quick chat with David before we go in."

Anna pulled up at the gate and let Barbara out before moving slowly on to find a space big enough to fit the Volvo. There were still cars arriving, queuing behind her for places to park. Having seen the quantities of food and drink that was being prepared back at the house, she had suspected that Barbara might have overestimated the numbers. Now she began to think that there might not be enough for everyone.

She found a space to park the car on the brow of the hill, several hundred metres from the church. As she switched off the engine she heard her mobile phone ringing from somewhere deep inside her handbag. Anna fumbled among the lipsticks and biros, cursing under her breath, until she found the phone and managed to answer it just in time, before it passed the caller on to her messaging service.

"Hello darling."

It was Richard.

Anna could see Barbara moving towards the church door with the minister.

"Are you there? Can you hear me?"

"Yes, yes," said Anna. She was exasperated by his timing. It wasn't deliberate she knew, but it just served to highlight his lack of involvement.

"I tried the house, but they said you had left already."

"I can't really talk now." She undid her seatbelt with her spare hand. "I'm just about to go into the church."

"I thought you might be," he said. "That's why I wanted to catch you. I just wanted to apologise... I know I've really let you down this time."

Anna stared through the windscreen at the rain and didn't say anything.

"Are you coping alright?"

What would he do about it if she said she wasn't?

"I'm fine."

"Good… That's great," he said in a hearty voice.

"I've got to go," she said.

Anna switched off her phone and slung it back into her handbag. She got out of the car with her head bent against the rain and opened the umbrella that Barbara had given her. The wind took it and played with it, trying to turn it inside out. She pulled her scarf up over her hair and picked her way between the puddles towards the church, trying not to mind too much about the damage being done to her appearance by the weather. It was, she knew, a superficial and unworthy concern for a funeral, but at this particular moment her appearance was an essential part of the armour she needed to cope with what lay ahead of her.

There was a crowd of people standing in the shelter of the porch at the front of the church. Anna couldn't see Barbara and guessed that she must have gone inside. The thought of entering alone filled her with dismay. She hesitated, in spite of the wind and rain, steeling herself to go in.

Afterwards Anna remembered very little of the service. But what did stay with her was the obvious affection with which those who had known him spoke of Charlie Gillespie. She wasn't used to hearing her father talked about with such warmth. Again she found herself wishing, this time with a touch of resentment, that she had known him better. In the presence of all these people who had been his friends she felt that in some way he had cheated her.

Barbara stood straight as a ramrod throughout the service, her eyes fixed on a point above the altar. She spoke the responses clearly; she sang the hymns without looking at the words. When a stocky man with bushy eyebrows stood up to give the address, her eyes didn't leave his face. She was the epitome of the dignified widow. Only Anna could see that her knuckles were white where she gripped the prayer book, and hear the tremor in her voice as she sang.

The service ended with a lament, played on the bagpipes by a giant of a man wearing a kilt that could have doubled as a small tent. The music swooped and swirled around the rafters as the congregation stood up and began to shuffle slowly outside. Anna, who had grown up hating the bagpipes, was moved beyond anything she could have expected. Her eyes filled with unanticipated tears, and she let Barbara go ahead of her and stood with her head down.

Most of the congregation had filed out by the time she followed them. As she made her way down the aisle she could see Barbara talking to a group at the back of the church. She walked past, nodding and smiling politely, hoping that Barbara wouldn't stop her to make introductions. She needed some fresh air.

For a moment, stepping out into the daylight from the dim interior of the church, she was disoriented. It was as if somebody had gone ahead of her and switched all the lights on. In the forty-five minutes or so that they had been inside the wind had blown itself out, taking the rain with it. Now the surface of the loch beside the church reflected a sky as blue as a field of cornflowers. On either side of her the mountains tumbled down to the water's edge in pleats and folds the colour of green silk splashed with purple. It was hard to believe she was in the same place as when she had gone inside.

She was aware of people speaking in low voices around her, and wondered if Barbara had come outside yet. There was a sound behind her.

"Enjoying the view?"

Anna turned to find the tall man with the suntanned face standing beside her.

"It's stunning," she said. "I'd been told it would be. But up until now I didn't believe it."

"It certainly looks a lot better when the sun's shining," he said, holding out his hand. "I'm Cameron Gillespie. The one whose door you nearly removed."

He was immaculately dressed in an expensive suit, with a navy shirt that exactly matched his eyes. First impression, when she had seen him before the service, was that he was handsome. Up close he wasn't as good looking as she had first thought. But his handshake was firm and his smile was wide, even if he did seem a little too pleased with himself. And she was grateful for his company. It saved her from standing alone in a crowd of people who all seemed to know each other.

"I'm sorry for the loss of your father," he said. "Charlie was a one off. They don't make them like that any more."

Anna nodded and smiled, and wished that hearing other people say nice things about her father didn't make her feel so uncomfortable. She changed the subject.

"I understand from Barbara that we're related."

"First cousins. Once removed." Very precise. He let go of her hand. "Are you up here for long?"

"Only a few days."

"Shame," he said. "You really need more time than that to get to know this place better."

Over his shoulder she saw that Barbara had come out of the church.

"You're staying at Rowancross?"

Anna nodded.

"It's a great house, isn't it?"

"It is –"

"You don't happen to know what Barbara's planning to do with it, do you?"

Anna glanced at him in surprise.

"I know it's probably a bit premature."

It certainly was.

"It's not something I've discussed with her," she said.

"No... of course – " He hesitated. "The thing is... I'm hoping she'll let me know if she's thinking of selling up and moving back to America. It's rather a delicate subject, but by rights the house should really be mine."

Anna's eyes widened. He shook his head. "Forgive me. I'm overstepping the mark."

He sounded like he was trying to be light-hearted, but Anna could see that he was bitter about it.

"The thing is that it was my side of the family who originally had the house - and my bloody useless Dad who lost it for us. My plan was always to buy it back, once I had the funds. But Charlie got there before me, so I missed out."

His eyes were narrow slits as he stared out across the loch.

"That must have been very annoying for you," said Anna stiffly. Out of the corner of her eye she saw Barbara wave at her.

"Excuse me." She turned away from Cameron with relief. "I've got to go. Barbara needs a lift back to the house."

"I'll see you later then," he said.

Not if I see you first, was what Anna was thinking as she walked away.

"It was a nice service, don't you think?" said Barbara from the passenger seat, as Anna backed the car out of the parking space.

Anna nodded. "It was lovely."

"Charlie would have been pleased that so many people made the effort to come."

They drove in silence for a while.

"I see you met Cameron."

"I certainly did."

Barbara glanced at her.

"You weren't impressed?"

"Not enormously."

"That's a shame."

Anna negotiated her way round a group of cyclists.

"Why a shame?"

"I was going to suggest that you show him Fiona's letter."

"Now why would I want to do that?"

"Because for one thing he's an expert on the Clearances. Which could be helpful… But he's also obsessed with the family history. He's made researching the Gillespie family his life's work. So if there was even a whiff of a scandal involving Fiona there's a chance he might know something about it."

"I thought Charlie was the expert."

Barbara smiled.

"Charlie's obsession was with Robert. Cameron's interested in the whole crowd." She sighed. "Poor Cameron… He was mightily pissed off when Charlie got his book published. He's being trying to do the same thing for years without success."

They had reached Ullapool.

"I did get the impression that there was a bit of resentment there," said Anna, wondering if Barbara knew the way Cameron felt about Rowancross.

"Cameron's got a major chip on his shoulder about who owns what and who lives where," said Barbara, suggesting that she did. "But he's not a bad guy for all that."

"Really?" Anna wasn't convinced.

"So I'm getting the feeling you wouldn't be happy showing him the letter?"

Anna shook her head.

"I may have got him wrong, but I get the impression that he's not the sort of man who likes to share. He'd try to take over. And that's the last thing I want." She turned into the track to Rowancross. "I'm only up here for a few days. But while I am I want to find out what I can in my own way. Without someone like Cameron trying to run the show." She looked at Barbara. "This will probably sound silly to you, but I think it's the way Charlie would have wanted it."

Barbara smiled her warm smile.

"It doesn't sound silly at all," she said, her huskiness returning. Anna found to her surprise that she was feeling a little husky herself.

"Who needs Cameron anyway?" she said. "Maybe this Fin Maclean guy will be able to point me in the right direction. I've got a good feeling about him."

CHAPTER FIVE

Barbara had been uncertain about how many people would want to come back after the service - it being a weekday, and most of them with work to do. But it seemed like everyone did. Within a short space of time there wasn't a room at Rowancross that wasn't crammed with people, and the noise of their conversation and laughter was almost deafening.

Barbara's helpers had to squeeze their way round the guests to serve them. First with the sandwiches: ham and mustard, beef with horseradish, egg and cress. Nothing too fancy - this was a crowd with simple tastes. The appreciative guests held out their plates for mushroom vol a vents and sausage rolls, miniature quiches filled with smoked bacon and onion, cheese straws, shortbread and ginger snaps, and wedges of treacle tart. There was chocolate cake, coffee cake and rich, dark slabs of fruitcake laced with whisky. Eating vied with talking as the favoured occupation.

To drink there was wine and whisky and beer. For the non-drinkers there was elderflower and cranberry juice, and tea served in quantity out of vast silver urns borrowed from the church. The whisky flowed freely, particularly amongst those who had had the foresight to come by minibus. These, Anna discovered, included the members of the Ullapool Golf Club, and the regulars at the Ferry Boat Inn – mostly fishermen, and the people who ran the ferries and boat trips to the Summer Isles. They were quick to take up position by the window in the sitting room, with their faces turned to the loch, as if a view of the water was essential to their well-being.

Everyone Anna spoke to had a story to tell her about her father - an anecdote, a joke, one of his far-fetched tales of outrageous events and unlikely coincidences. And they told them to the accompaniment of great gusts of laughter and good-natured banter. It quickly became clear to her that Charlie had had many friends, true friends, people who liked and admired him, and were genuinely and profoundly sorry that he was not around any more to enliven their lives.

It was exhausting. And frustrating. And the one person she wanted to meet was the one person who it seemed hadn't turned up. It appeared that Fin Maclean and his aunt had had to stop in Ullapool on their way back from the church and were yet to arrive.

Anna was relieved when one of Barbara's ladies, squeezing past with a harassed expression on her face, accepted her offer of help. It freed her from the necessity of pretending to everyone she spoke to that she had known her father better than she had. She hastened into the kitchen where she made herself useful, pouring cups of tea, and stacking used glasses into boxes. Until Barbara came and found her.

"You shouldn't be doing that."

Anna was standing at the sink washing plates. She had taken off her jacket and was up to her elbows in soapsuds.

"I needed a breather," she said apologetically. "Do you mind?"

Barbara smiled. "Of course not. But stop now and come with me. There's somebody I think you might be interested to meet."

She held out her hand. Anna peeled off her rubber gloves and left them on the draining board.

"By the way, Cameron's been looking all over for you," said Barbara, as she led the way out of the kitchen. "He was worried you might have disappeared before he had a proper chance to talk to you."

"Really?" Anna's heart sank. The last thing she felt like was having a heart to heart with Cameron Gillespie.

"Here we are." Barbara drew Anna towards the fireplace in the dining room, where a woman in a navy blue dress stood next to a fair haired man wearing an open neck shirt and a dark grey suit.

"Sarah… Finlay… Here she is. This is Anna."

The woman smiled warmly, taking Anna's hand in hers.

"My dear… How like your father you are. Don't you think so, Fin?"

Fin Maclean held out his hand to Anna. "Aunt Sarah sees family likenesses wherever she goes," he said dryly. "You'll have to forgive me if I'm unable to pass comment. I lack her vision."

Anna shook his hand. She had the feeling that he disapproved of her, although she couldn't for the life of her think why.

"Anna's interested in finding out as much as she can about her family's history while she's up here," said Barbara. "I told her you might be able to help."

"Certainly," said Fin politely. "If I can."

Anna hesitated. He was gazing at her with his head tilted to one side. She wondered what she had done to deserve this level of scrutiny? Barbara had moved away with Sarah towards the window, and they had their heads together discussing the service. Anna glanced uncertainly up at Fin.

"So," he said. "Let me get this straight. You want to know about the Gillespies?"

"You sound surprised?"

"I am. I got the impression from your father that you weren't interested in that kind of thing."

Anna lifted her chin.

"And what kind of thing would '*that kind of thing*' be?"

"Oh you know," he waved a hand, "the past, your roots. Charlie told me you didn't care where you came from."

Anna frowned. "My father knew very little about me."

"I see," he said, scratching his head. "I suppose… You've never been up here. Never came to visit. How could he know anything about you?" He looked sideways at her. "Shame really."

Anna stared at him. "Forgive me," she said coldly, "but I really don't see what my relationship with my father has got to do with you."

She looked for Barbara over his shoulder and saw that she had gone. It was time to go back to the kitchen.

"I'm sorry." Fin put his hand on her arm. "It's just that I really liked your dad. And I know how sad it made him that he didn't see more of his family."

She plucked his hand away.

"Not that I have any desire to discuss my private life with you… But that was his choice."

"Look here. Anna…"

She glared at him. He shook his head despairingly.

"It is Anna, isn't it? I haven't got that wrong as well."

She didn't reply.

"Please don't take offence," he said. "I think it's really great that you're interested."

Now he was patronising her. "You'll have to excuse me," she said through gritted teeth. "Barbara needs my help in the kitchen."

Fin stood and watched Anna walk towards the door. His aunt joined him by the fireplace.

"What a very good-looking girl', she said following the direction of his gaze. "Charlie would have been very proud of her."

Fin turned to look at her. "Terrified of her more like," he said. "And she's hardly a girl, Sarah. She's got to be in her early forties."

His aunt made a tutting noise.

"My dear boy, that counts as a girl to me. You wait until you get to my age. And whatever did you say to upset her? There was a point while she was talking to you when she looked positively livid."

Fin shrugged and did his best to look innocent.

"I think she might have taken something I said the wrong way. I'm not sure that the good-looking girl and I are destined to get along."

Anna was loading used glasses onto a tray in the dining room, and wondering whether anyone would notice if she slipped away to her room, when she spotted Cameron's dark head weaving through the crowd towards her. She looked for a way to escape, but he was upon her before she could do anything about it.

"There you are," he said. "I've finally tracked you down."

She forced a smile.

"How've you been getting on? Saw you talking to Fin MacLean back there. So what did you make of him?"

Anna was too tired to be polite.

"I thought he was a patronizing git –"

Cameron raised his eyebrows.

"Oh Fin's alright," he said in an expansive voice. "Can be a bit arrogant at times, but he's OK."

Anna placed a couple of empty wine glasses on her tray and didn't comment. She was in no mood to get drawn into a discussion with Cameron about Fin Maclean. But Cameron wasn't going to be put off.

"So I suppose he was telling you all about this book he's written," he said. "The one about Iain Mackay."

"Please don't talk to me about Iain Mackay."

Cameron laughed. "Fin been banging on a bit, has he? Say no more. To be honest with you the whole thing's a bit ridiculous. Him being handed that book on a plate. It's not as if he can call himself an expert."

Anna put another glass on the tray. "I don't want to sound rude," she said. "But I'm really not terribly interested."

"He has upset you, hasn't he? But you mustn't tar us all with the same brush. We're not all like Finlay Maclean, you know."

"Well, I suppose that's something to be grateful for," said Anna, glasses sliding and rattling together as she picked up the tray.

"Here. Let me take that for you." He held out his hands.

"Thanks." She handed the tray to him with real gratitude.

"So what are your plans while you're up here?" he said over his shoulder, as she followed him across the room to the door. "Are you a walker?"

"Yes, I like walking," she said, uncertain if this was a sensible thing to admit to.

"Good. You should make the most of the fine weather and see something of the countryside while you've got the chance. Why don't I pick you up in the morning and show you some of the sights?"

"I'm not sure what Barbara –"

"Barbara will be busy clearing this lot up."

"But she'll need my help."

"I'm sure the last thing Barbara will want you to do is spend the little time you're here clearing | up."

She was too tired to argue with him.

"Have you got something sensible to wear on your feet?" He glanced down at her ankles. "You can't walk in those."

She made a face at him. "I'm not a complete idiot you know."

"Fair point," he said. "Stupid comment." He stood back to let her go through the door ahead of him. "Now you're going to think I'm just another. ... how did you put it... 'patronising git' wasn't it?"

"There's a very good chance," she said. But she was laughing.

In the doorway, Fin MacLean was searching for Barbara to say goodbye. From across the room he caught sight of Anna with Cameron and saw the way her face softened as she laughed. She hadn't been laughing while she was talking to him.

He found himself staring. Aunt Sarah had been quite right. There was no getting away from it. Charlie Gillespie's daughter was most definitely a very good looking girl.

He was not the only one to notice. Laura McBride, Cameron's housekeeper, stood with the group of fishermen by the window, an untouched glass of wine in her hand, listening to a discussion about the return of sea trout to the River Broom. She smiled and nodded with the rest of the group, but anyone watching closely would have seen that her attention was somewhere else. She was watching Cameron carrying the tray for Anna. And she didn't look happy.

⇒⊢ ⊣⇐

It was nearly ten in the evening by the time the last glass had been washed and dried and put back in its box, the last plate stacked in the dishwasher, the last empty bottle put out for recycling. Barbara and Anna stood on the drive and watched as the little red post van carrying the last of the helpers headed back towards the main road, headlights glowing in the dim light of the Highland dusk.

Barbara turned to Anna.

"It went well I thought," she said in a matter of fact voice.

Anna glanced at her face.

"Are you OK?"

Barbara drew in her breath. And then she gave a quick fierce nod of her head and took Anna's arm. Standing together in the fading light they looked up at the sky. High above them the new moon shone like a piece of priceless jewellery against a swathe of satin. It was very quiet. It seemed to Anna as though the world was waiting for them, watching for their next move, wondering how they would choose to go on.

Her back ached from standing up all day, and her feet in the magenta slingbacks were pinched and sore. She was ready to drop, but Barbara had gone a stage further, to a place where she seemed unable to think clearly. Anna saw it in the blank expression in her eyes. She took her by the arm and led her inside. At the foot of the stairs Barbara stood and squeezed her stepdaughter's hand. There was a tremor in her voice as she spoke.

"It is wonderful to have you here, Anna. I wanted to tell you that it has helped me enormously."

Anna wrapped her arms around Barbara and hugged her. "I'm so glad," she said in a soft voice. "Now, go to bed".

Barbara put her foot on the bottom stair. Then she thought of something and paused. "Fiona's diaries," she said. "You wanted to see them."

"Don't worry about that now," protested Anna.

Barbara shook her head.

"You're not here for very long. Every day counts. There's a box on your father's desk. I asked one of the guys to get it down from the attic for me when they were here moving furniture this morning. Why don't you go and have a look now. If you're not too tired."

Anna watched her climb the stairs and then made her way down the corridor to the study. She was feeling numb with exhaustion, but the thought of Fiona's journals was impossible to resist.

Through the study window the sky was darkening to a deep indigo blue. Anna went to her father's desk and sat down in the leather chair, flicking the switch on the desk lamp. The lamp's beam lit up the collection of photos next to the phone. When Anna was sorting through Charlie's books she had barely glanced at them. Now she reached out and picked up the one nearest to her. It showed Charlie and Barbara, arm in arm, standing in the doorway of a hotel. Charlie was smiling at Barbara as if he couldn't quite believe his luck. Barbara held a small bouquet of flowers in one hand, and she was looking back at Charlie with an expression of such tenderness that Anna couldn't tear her eyes away.

She remembered with a pang that she had been dismissive when the wedding invitation arrived, and had written a perfunctory note saying that she and Richard were away and would be unable to attend. Now she was filled with regret that they hadn't been there.

She picked up another photo, of her with Richard and the girls, taken while they were on holiday in France. She hadn't realised her father had a copy – Jennifer must have sent it to him. The four of them were grouped together, she and Richard behind Rose and Ellie, sitting on stone steps that ran down from the terrace of the farmhouse they had rented. Richard had his arm across her shoulders, the girls were smiling; they looked the perfect happy family. But Richard's white skin showed pale beside the tanned faces of Anna and the girls, and she remembered that he had only just flown in that morning from Budapest to join them.

The grandfather clock in the hall chimed, reminding her that it was getting late. She was glad for the interruption. Best not to think about Richard. She bent forward and opened the door of the small cupboard in the back of the desk. Inside were a box of envelopes, a copy of the local Yellow Pages, and an old leather chest. Anna lifted out the chest and set it on top of the desk. With trembling fingers she struggled with the catch. Swearing softly with impatience she pressed and pushed, until with a click it sprang open and she lifted the lid.

The chest was crammed with papers. At the top was a bundle of letters tied up with tattered ribbon. She could make out words written in faded blue ink: '*I was so happy to see you and Robert in such good spirits...* '*shame that inclement weather interrupted our picnic...* '

In her mind's eye she saw women with slender waists in hooped skirts, wicker hampers, umbrellas raised against the rain. It was tempting to untie the ribbon and read more. But she was looking for Iain Mackay, and from the little she knew of him he didn't sound the sort of man who spent much time at picnics.

She set the bundle of letters down on the desk and took out a folder crammed with sheets of thick white paper. She pulled out one of the sheets. It was covered in scribbled sketches of seabirds. Fiona's work, Anna assumed. The sketches were good; the birds swooped and tumbled across the page. She slipped the sheet back into the folder and put it next to the bundle of letters. Again she peered into the chest. Stacked side by side in the bottom were Fiona's diaries.

There were six of them in all. Anna lifted them out one by one and laid them on the desk in front of her. Three out of the six were badly damaged; the covers curled back to reveal crumpled brown pages with ink so faded it was impossible to make out what was written. Anna picked up one of the undamaged books and opened it. There was a date written on the flyleaf: 1844. And a name written in green ink - Fiona Mackenzie.

Anna put the journal down and inspected the others. There were three in sequence for the years 1844, 1845 and 1846; the last in such a sorry condition it was barely intact. There was nothing for 1847; one for 1848 and for 1849; and then nothing until the last for 1853.

Anna held 1844 against her chest and stroked the faded leather. For the moment she wasn't impatient to read what was inside. It was the promise of insight into another life and time that held her. Was this how her father had felt when he looked through Robert Gillespie's papers? Did he hold his breath as she did, and marvel at the thought that here was a direct route to the past? Not the dry facts contained in the pages of the history books, but the musings and ponderings of a living human being who had been made of flesh and blood just like him. She felt in her bones that this was exactly how he would have reacted, and the thought drew her close to him.

Anna glanced at her watch. It was near to midnight. She picked up the diary for 1853 and headed upstairs. She made a half-hearted attempt to clean her face and brush her teeth, and climbed into bed. The sheets were cool against her skin. Tempting to go straight to sleep, but she didn't have that much time before Richard arrived to join her and reading a few pages wouldn't hurt. She leant back against the pillows and picked up the diary.

May 28th 1853
My father's funeral

The diary fell open of its own accord, and it was as if Fiona had reached out across time to her. Anna stroked the page with the tip of her index finger. She had to remind herself that it had most likely opened where it did because this was the section of most interest to recent readers such as her father and Fin Maclean. But she couldn't shake off the idea that Fiona was showing her the way.

Dear diary! Poor diary more like. It has been far too long since I wrote anything at all in these neglected pages. Robert laughs at me. He tells me that I like the idea of keeping a journal but lack the application to keep up with it.

But I mean to write regularly. I really do. I love to read back and be reminded of what I have done, and how I felt about the things that have happened to me. But I get out of the habit, and then I feel bad about it. And then there is too much to catch up with, and too much I've forgotten, and it becomes a chore rather than a pleasure.

But certainly for the past weeks and months I have been unable to find myself in the right mood to write anything. And it is only now – with more than a month since the funeral and six weeks from the day that my father died – that I have found the inclination to put pen to paper. The move to Kildorran has used up all of my time and, indeed, all of my energy. And if I am honest I have been happy for it to be that way, for it has saved me from the pain of remembering that Father is gone and that I will not see him again.

I do remember that it was a fine spring morning, with the mist lying in the valley like milk in a saucer, when we heard the news of his death. John arrived at the house before breakfast. When I heard the clatter of hooves outside on the drive I thought it might be Robert come back early to surprise me. But I should have known better. When I went down to see who it was that had arrived in such a hurry it was John that I found standing in the entrance hall, with such a look on his face that I knew immediately that something was wrong.

I think John did not know how to tell me, even though I have known him all my life. He has been factor of my father's estate from when I was a little girl. I can never forget that it was he who taught me to ride and to fish and to row a boat. When I was small he would take me and wrap me up in the plaid he wore, and tie me against his back to carry me into the hills to see a stag. My nurse, who was old and always cross, would scold him. She was of the opinion that it was not right for a young lady to take part in such activities. But John simply laughed at her and told her that it was what the Laird wanted for his daughter. And he was quite right. My father was never a soft man, and after my mother died he required me to stand up in place of the son he would never have. And I was glad to do it, for I was never one for frills and dolls and suchlike.

It is more than two hours ride from my father's house at Kildorran, for our house at Drummond is but seven miles north of Inverness. John could have sent one of the boys with the news but he chose to make the journey himself. On his way down to dinner the previous evening, my father had tripped on a worn piece of rug, and fallen down the main staircase. He broke his neck in the fall.

When John told me I did not know what to say. All I could think was that it seemed a pale kind of death for so colourful a man. I remember that John stood close by me, as if he thought I might fall into a faint, or have hysterics, or at the very least break into a fit of crying. He knew the bond that had always existed between my father and me. But the truth was that I struggled to know how to feel. For many years after my mother died we were everything to each other. We looked to each other for love and support. But he had become weary and bitter in the years since I grew up. There was a distance between us that had never been there before.

As his only child it was down to me to arrange everything. I told John I would come as soon as Robert returned from the south. And I was able to ride back with him that very afternoon for Robert arrived soon after. I left him to arrange for the boys to be brought over to join me as soon as was possible. My dear Mary insisted on coming with me, to look after me as she has done for the past three years, although I knew that Janet would be waiting to welcome me.

I knew exactly how my father wished for things to be arranged. His funeral was a substantial affair, for we are proud to call ourselves Mackenzie, and although it has been some time since we could claim to be one of the great families of our clan, yet nor are we so diminished that we do not know how these things should be done. Everybody knew the laird of Kildorran, and many wished to come and pay their respects. We had to allow sufficient time for word to be sent out to all who wanted to attend. They came from many districts, and we had to be very careful to arrange things so as to prevent the fighting that all too often breaks out when too much whisky is taken and old feuds are rekindled.

My father's body was laid to rest in our family mausoleum, in the graveyard at the top of the loch. The coffin was carried on the shoulders of the men of our clan, with the piper in front playing the lament. Robbie wore the dress of the Mackenzies and walked with the coffin, managing to keep up very well, while Robert carried Angus in his arms.

I was proud of my little boys. Robbie can be very wilful at times - he has his father's determination. But he did not let us down once by misbehaving. Both of my uncles took their places at either side of the coffin and looked suitably sorrowful, although I think they were looking forward to the whisky.

Afterwards we gathered on the lawn at the front of the house. There were too many to count, but I think it must have been well over one hundred. I was worried that there would be insufficient to feed everyone, but Robert had thought to arrange for the provision of extra crates of whisky and an additional supply of cheese and oatcakes, and even with so many people it was not a problem that anyone went hungry.

It was a great relief for me to see that my father's family treated my husband with the proper respect and courtesy. There have been times, particularly when we were first married, when this was always not the case.

There was a strange thing that happened after the service. I had been standing on the steps looking out onto the lawn at the crowds of men who had gathered there. From the east the sky was growing dark, and I was very much hoping that it would not rain, there being insufficient shelter for such a large number of people, when Robert arrived by my side and said there was somebody he wished for me to meet.

I turned and saw a young man standing beside my husband. He was tall, more than six feet I should say, and broad shouldered with a fierce look in his eyes. When I held out my hand to him there was something about the way he looked at me, almost glaring I should say, that made me feel as if I had done something wrong, although I had no idea what it could be.

Robert told me that the man's name was Iain Mackay and that he was there to write about the funeral. He explained that Mr Mackay was a journalist for the Inverness Courier. He said that they had been enjoying a most interesting talk. It turned out that Mr Mackay had read some of Robert's letters.

Robert has been conducting an ongoing but one-sided correspondence with the editor of the Courier, outlining the economic improvements he believes are necessary to bring prosperity and change to the region. But he has been growing increasingly frustrated by the lack of response. Apparently Mr Mackay had some strong views of his own and he agreed with Robert that it was most disappointing that his letters had not met with more of a reaction. Robert was delighted because Mr Mackay had offered to discuss with his editor the possibility of including a written reply in the letters page, in the hope that it might generate greater interest.

I was pleased for my husband, but I couldn't help feeling that it was an inappropriate occasion to be discussing such matters. Mr Mackay must have seen my expression, for when Robert paused he offered his condolences and said in a low voice that he was sorry for my loss.

I thanked him and asked if he had known my father, but he said unfortunately he had not had that pleasure.

His tone was polite but I couldn't shake off the feeling that in some unaccountable way he was angry with me. Robert had been taken hostage by my uncle who was, needless to say, in search of more whisky. Iain Mackay and I stood together, and did not know what to say to each other. Finally he spoke.

"This is certainly a great occasion," he said, looking out at the crowds on the lawn below. "Your father was known to be a good man. Those of us who remember the old ways regret his passing."

I thanked him again for his consideration and made a move to leave him, but he put his hand on my arm to stop me. Now I looked into his eyes and saw that they were blazing with a kind of ferocious energy.

"Sir," I said, looking at where his hand lay on my arm, "I wish you will tell me if I have done something to offend you."

At this he stepped back and looked regretful, and apologized in a most profound manner for his impertinence. I could see that he was troubled and asked him for an explanation. He replied by inquiring of me if I knew the ploughman, Donald MacLean, who was a tenant of the Kildorran estate. I did know the man, remembering that he had been away and had returned to the estate a year or so back when his father Roderick died. Iain told me that one of his sisters was married to Donald. He said that she was very much afraid that with the old laird gone and a new laird in his place there would be changes. And with changes there would be evictions.

I was stunned by his words. I told him that such a thing would never happen at Kildorran. I told him that, like my father, my husband was a man of integrity and honour, a man whose commitment was to improving the lot of the Highland people, not making things worse for them.

"Your concern is unwarranted," I finished. "It is many years now since people were forced to leave their land. Are not things a great deal better than they were?"

He looked at me with his fierce eyes as if he thought I was very foolish.

"You are fortunate to have such a wealthy man for your husband," he said. "You are protected from the realities of life."

I was filled with indignation at his words. "It has been hard for all of us," I told him. "Do you think I have not been touched by it? I am not so young that I cannot remember how we all suffered when the harvest failed and famine followed so close behind. It was the cholera that killed my mother, perhaps you did not know it?"

He had the good grace to look ashamed.

"I am sincerely sorry for that," he said. "But perhaps you do not realize that things continue to be very difficult for many people."

I told him that I was neither blind nor stupid. Added to which my husband had strong views about what was happening which he shared with me on many occasions. "You must know it," I said, "if, as you say, you have read his letters in the paper."

"Mr Gillespie thinks he knows what is best for the Highlands," said Mr Mackay, looking me straight in the eye. "But what he considers progress is, to my way of thinking, the very opposite."

I could not believe what I was hearing. "But you have offered to write on his behalf," I said. "Why would you do such a thing if you do not believe there is any value in what he has to say?"

He looked at me, and his eyes grew darker still.

"Because I hope that I may be able to convince him to see things differently," he said.

"You are overstepping the mark, sir," I said, and I turned to leave him. Again he put his hand upon my arm.

"So your husband has no plans to bring lowland sheep to the Kildorran estate?"

I swung round.

"Certainly not. And even if he did - which I promise you he does not - I would not allow it."

"I am glad to hear it," he said in his curt manner. "But it won't stop me trying to convince him that his views are misguided." He paused. "And perhaps you also could do with a little education."

With these words he walked away.

I was left speechless. I could not believe that a lowly journalist had spoken to me in such a way. Who did he think I was? The ignorant wife of a misguided lowlander. I went in search of Robert and found him preparing Robbie for the procession, which was about to start.

"*I think you will find that man of little help to you,*" *I told him through gritted teeth, as I bent down to straighten Robbie's collar.*

"*What man is that?*"

"*The journalist -*"

"*You are upset?*" *He looked at me in some surprise.*

"*His intention is to convince you that your views are wrong.*"

Robert patted Robbie on the shoulder, pushing him forward to take his position, and laughed.

"*He can try. But he won't succeed. He is an intelligent man. He will soon come round to my way of thinking, just you wait and see.*"

CHAPTER SIX

"Still with us then. Not heading back to London just yet?"

Fin MacLean, reaching for his wallet in his jeans pocket, glanced up at the assistant behind the counter in the bookshop and smiled briefly. She was a plump girl with an eager expression. He had been aware for some time that she had been watching him, and now he was trying to remember if he was supposed to know her.

"Not yet," he said, unable to place her.

"Working on your next book, are you?"

She was somehow managing to punch keys on the till without taking her eyes from his face. He smiled and nodded. Didn't want to appear rude. It was quite possible that she was a friend of Sarah's; she seemed to know a lot about him.

"I'm certainly trying."

"Not going so well?" she said sympathetically. "Finding it tough?"

It seemed unlikely, but you never knew, perhaps she was a writer too and understood what it was like to stare at a blank page with no idea of how to fill it.

"I don't know how you make yourself do it all day. Sit there and write I mean. I find it hard enough writing a postcard. I'm much happier sending a text."

So not a writer then.

"Haven't seen your girlfriend around much recently."

Fin pulled out a twenty pound note and laid it on the counter beside the book he was beginning to wish he hadn't come in to buy. It was unnerving the way people up here seemed to know more about his life than he did.

"She's always so friendly when she comes in here. She showed me your books - and told me all about the new one. A novel, she said."

Fin sighed. Now he understood; Allie had been in. She could never resist a bookshop. She liked having a 'famous writer' for a boyfriend. Had been known to reposition his books on the shelves so that they could be seen more easily. He supposed he should have been grateful.

He considered saying that she wasn't his girl-friend any more. But decided against it. This stranger knew more than enough about him already. Backing out of the shop at speed he collided with Cameron.

"Fin." Cameron's smile was wide. He nodded in the direction of the bookshop. "Checking out your facings? Haven't seen your name around that much recently."

Fin's smile was equally false.

"Moving off the shelves too quickly, Cameron. Like greased lightning."

Cameron nodded his head. "Glad to hear it, mate," he said. "I'd hate to think you were losing your touch. Wondered if you wanted me to put a good word in for you with my people."

Fin ground his teeth. It shouldn't get to him, but Cameron's habit of talking to him as if he was an incompetent hack never failed to rile him. You wouldn't think that this was a man who was strug-gling to get anything into print. From his manner you'd suppose he was fighting off the publishers.

"So when can we expect to see something from you, Cameron?" he asked smoothly.

Cameron shrugged.

"Hard to say, Fin mate. I'm working on a couple of things at the moment. It's really a question of de-ciding which to go with."

"Really? So who's handling -"

"Good day yesterday, didn't you think?" Cameron switched gear without pause. "Charlie would have enjoyed it."

Fin felt a moment's reluctance to let him off the hook, but let it go.

"He would. They'd have needed a deal more whisky though."

They both laughed.

"Bit of a surprise meeting the daughter." Now Cameron was sounding positively friendly. "Not at all what I was expecting."

"What were you expecting?"

"From the way Charlie talked about her I always thought she sounded a bit too good to be true. The way he used to go on - that proud father routine he used to pull even though he never saw her. You could have knocked me down with a feather when she came into the church."

Fin gave a rueful smile.

"We didn't exactly hit it off."

As soon as he had made the admission he knew it was a mistake. He saw the beginning of a grin that was close to a smirk lift the corners of Cameron's mouth.

"Now that's a shame. What went wrong?"

"Oh," Fin gave a careless wave of his hand, "I misunderstood something she said. Got the wrong end of the stick. Turns out she's really interested in finding out more about the family history."

Cameron looked surprised.

"I got the impression from Charlie that she had positively gone out of her way to avoid having anything to do with his side of the family. Not in the slightest bit interested, he said."

Fin shrugged.

"That's not the way it sounded yesterday.

"Well good for her," said Cameron. "Sounds like the woman's got brains as well as looks. So what exactly did you say to upset her?"

Fin gazed at the ferry coming alongside the jetty.

"I think I might have given the impression that I disapproved of her. At least that's the way it must have seemed."

Cameron was shaking his head. "Sounds like bad form to me. Forgive me for pointing it out, but I can't help feeling that it's possibly not the best way of getting into her good books."

Fin tucked the book he had just bought under his arm. "To be honest with you, Cameron, I have no particular desire to get into her good books."

"Really?" Cameron's voice was smug. "I on the other hand rather like the idea. In fact I'm on my way to see the lovely Anna right now. We've got a hill to climb together."

Fin, watching Cameron stride down the street to-wards the harbour, fought the desire to go after him and punch him on his self-satisfied nose.

***

At Rowancross House Anna had been woken by Barbara, who knocked softly on her bedroom door, before coming into the room with a mug of tea in one hand and a pair of walking boots in the other. This morning she looked a completely different person from the one Anna had watched go upstairs the night before.

"You found the diaries," she said, nodding her head at the book on the bedside table. "Did you man-age to come across anything to help?"

Anna reached out for the mug of tea. "I read the bit about her father's funeral. About when she met Iain Mackay for the first time." She took a sip. "It was great to read. But not much help. They seemed to re-ally dislike each other."

"Well, don't give up. You know what they say about opposites attracting." Barbara waved the boots in the air. "I thought you might like to borrow these. If I know Cameron it won't be a gentle stroll he's plan-ning to take you on."

Anna shut her eyes and groaned.

"What was I doing when I said I'd go walking with him? I don't even like the guy."

Barbara set the boots on the floor by the chair and crossed over to the window.

"I did wonder," she said, pulling back the curtain to let the sunshine flood into the room. "But it's a beautiful day, and Cameron's OK when you get to know him. And he really knows his stuff. Not just about the family, but the bigger picture as well. If you really want to get to the bottom of whatever it was that Fiona got herself involved in, you need to understand what was going on up here at the time. And Cameron can help you. You don't have to tell him about finding the letter."

Anna looked at her over the rim of her mug. "How did you get to be so wise?"

"I'm not sure about that," laughed Barbara, "but Cameron's your man. You'd better get yourself up and ready. He's just rung to say he's on his way."

Anna grabbed her watch. It was nearly ten. She couldn't remember the last time she had slept so late.

Barbara laughed at her. "Don't worry. I told him not to rush. He's stopping off in Ullapool to buy supplies. Apparently he's planning a picnic." She gave Anna an old fashioned look. "He's quite a one for the ladies, is our Cameron. I'm sure I don't need to tell you to watch out for him."

Anna sat back against the pillows and laughed.

"That's the last thing you need to worry about."

⊷ ⊶

Half an hour later, as she walked towards the kitchen, flexing her toes in the unfamiliar boots, Anna could hear Barbara's voice.

"You did warn her about the climb, didn't you Cameron? It's not going to be too much for her?"

"She looks fit enough. It will be good for her."

Anna checked in the corridor. Cameron was sounding disturbingly hearty. She considered retreating back to her room and feigning sudden illness. But Barbara must have heard her footsteps, because she called out to her, and there was nothing for it but to keep going. She squared her shoulders and went into the kitchen to find Cameron leaning against the counter, mug of tea in his hand, looking very much at home. He was wearing khaki trousers, and another shirt that emphasised the bold blueness of his eyes. But Anna wasn't interested in his eyes; she was looking at his feet which were clad in hiking boots that made the ones Barbara had lent her look like trainers.

"You're not taking me up a mountain, are you?" she said suspiciously.

He laughed. "Not quite a mountain."

She poured herself a cup of coffee, and wondered what *not quite a mountain* entailed.

Outside the air tasted of salt. Above Anna's head seagulls rode the breeze. She followed Cameron towards the black Audi.

"Got everything you need?"

She nodded. The sun was shining, the setting was breathtaking. And, while in an ideal world she would have preferred to spend the day with someone other than Cameron Gillespie, Barbara had been right when she said that he knew what he was talking about when it came to the Gillespie family. She didn't need reminding that time was short. Richard would be arriving within a day or two. And, if she wanted to get anywhere nearer to the truth about her great great grandmother before it was time to leave, she needed to make the most of every opportunity that came along.

They drove through Ullapool without stopping, and took the Inverness road along the side of Loch Broom. In the lea of the town, sheltered from wind and tide, the surface of the loch was flat and shining like glass. The water threw back a replica of the hills to the sky. The few cars that sped along the road seemed tiny, out of all proportion to their surroundings, like toys in a make-believe world where the scale was out of kilter. Anna was grateful for Cameron's silence. It left her in peace to appreciate the beauty of her surroundings.

They left the loch behind, and after a mile or so, turned right onto a concrete bridge over a brown, tumbling river. The road took them down an avenue of lime trees, whose branches met over their heads to form an archway of bright green leaves. Where the road joined with another they took a right turn between low stone walls and headed back in the direction of the loch. Cameron pulled over into a layby and parked the car, just up from a small stone church. Anna could see where a narrow path made its way between blue irises and tall foxgloves, winding upwards until it turned a corner and lost itself in the bracken and heather. She got out of the car.

"Is it very steep?"

"Not really," said Cameron, coming round to join her. "The path winds about a bit. And it's rocky in places. But it's actually more difficult on the way down. That's why the boots are a good thing." He was looking at her legs. "They support your ankles."

It was amazing, thought Anna, as she squatted on her heels by the side of the path, how deceptive appearances could be. Cameron's well-groomed appearance hardly suggested a life spent in the great outdoors.

And yet above her he had just climbed a particularly steep section of the path with as little effort as if he was strolling across a road in Knightsbridge. She, on the other hand, was struggling.

They had been following the path upwards for an hour or so, and the warm day and her lack of fitness had combined to leave Anna out of breath and feeling the strain. When she looked down in the direction from which they had come she had the alarming sensation that if she leant forward she would topple away from the hillside and plunge to her death. And to make matters worse ahead of her Cameron climbed steadily upwards without waiting, giving her no time to catch her breath.

Now, with muscles that protested at every step and blisters ballooning on her heels like bubble gum, she struggled up to join him. He glanced at her with amused eyes as she reached him, and handed her a piece of chocolate.

"Here you go. Do you think you can manage the last stretch?"

Anna heard disdain in his tone for her southern frailty and lifted her chin.

"Of course."

The path took a turn to the left and slipped over a hillock, and finally the summit was ahead of them. Anna didn't dare look behind her. They were a long way up. She fixed her eyes on a tumbled down wall of grey stone, a hundred yards or so below the point where the brow of the hill touched the sky, and forced her legs to carry her across the rough heather towards it.

Needless to say, Cameron got there first. He was watching her as she stepped gingerly across a patch of boggy ground to join him. Now Anna had arrived she could see that the pile of stone was - or rather once had been - a house; a small stone house, with little left standing, apart from a section of the front wall with a rectangular gap where the window must have been, and a crumbling wall at one end with a chimney stack pointing up to the sky like a finger. At its base was the remains of a fireplace with nothing left but blackened stones to show where fires had once been kindled to provide warmth and solace during the long nights of winter.

"Somebody lived up here?" she said disbelievingly.

"It was built for the minister. Sometime at the beginning of the last century." Cameron leant his shoulder against the wall. "There is a story that he was banished up here for misbehaving with one of his parishioners. Poor sod. Imagine having to slog up here every night after you've had a few too many in the Ferry Boat Inn. And all because of a woman." He waved one arm across the landscape. "Still the view's not bad -"

Now that Anna had recovered her breath she found the courage to turn round and look in the direction in which he pointed. Far below them the loch shimmered in the sunlight, flecks of silver sparkling on the surface like stars. The water was a deep blue against the greens and browns and purples of the hills. She could see all the way to Ullapool and beyond, out to the open sea. On all sides the hills folded back and away towards the far horizon, the landscape changing colour as clouds slipped in and out of the sun's path. She felt that if she reached up she could touch the sky. She turned back to Cameron.

"It's breathtaking," she said.

He smiled and nodded, proudly, as if he'd had a hand in its creation. "Hungry?" he asked her.

She realized that she was ravenous. But it appeared that the minister's house was not their final destination. Once more Anna found herself clambering behind Cameron across heather and rocks, until they reached a place where a great lump of granite jutted out of the hillside, its surface worn smooth by the wind and the rain. Cameron swung the rucksack from his back, while Anna lowered herself down onto the ground with a groan.

In the lea of the rock, sheltered from the wind, the sun was warm on her face. There was no sound, apart from the calling of a bird somewhere behind them. Cameron opened his rucksack and took out a couple of cans. He handed one down to her.

"Comfortable?"

She took the can from him. "I am."

"You sound surprised."

"Yes… well… It's the last thing I expected after that climb. I thought we'd be perched precariously on a rockface somewhere, at the top of the highest mountain."

He grinned at her. "You should have said. I could have arranged it for you."

"I'm extremely glad you didn't."

"You see An Teallach over there behind us." He waved his hand in the direction of the horizon. "Three and a half thousand feet, nearly twice as high again as we are here. Plenty of rockfaces to perch on there."

Anna shivered. "I'm perfectly happy here, thanks very much."

"Ok, so maybe if you want something a little less challenging you could have a go at Ben More Assynt." He pointed across to where the distant peaks bit a chunk out of the horizon beyond the hills on the far side of Loch Broom. "A mere three thousand three hundred feet; and as welcoming a mountain as you'll find anywhere. Or Suilven… She's one of my particular favourites. And of course there's always Stac Pollaidh."

There was a warmth in his voice Anna hadn't heard before. "You talk about them as if they were people."

"I've known them all my life," he answered simply. "Walked these hills and mountains since I was a boy. They're like part of my family."

"I can imagine they're a lot less trouble."

He gave a shout of laughter.

"You can say that again. They're not that great about Christmas presents. And I can't remember the last time one of them brought a round in the pub. But they're always there for you when you need them. And they never let you down."

She laughed with him. This more relaxed Cameron was a lot easier to like. He noticed her gaze and looked away. She had a feeling that he was embarrassed at having shown a side of himself that didn't often get seen. Maybe she had misjudged him when they first met.

⇥ ⇤

When Barbara initially suggested showing Fiona's letter to Cameron Anna had been quick to pour cold water on the idea. She was aware that she needed help if she was going to make any progress with getting to the bottom of what had happened. And she knew that she had very little time before Richard arrived and she returned to her old life. But she felt a ferocious kind of possessiveness about her great great grandmother's letter, and the last thing she had wanted was someone like Cameron taking over. She had been hoping that Fin Maclean would be the one to help her. But that was before she met him. Now Cameron was showing signs of being rather more human than she had at first thought. And he was family, which was more than could be said of Fin. She decided to trust him.

"Barbara was telling me that when it comes to the Gillespie family you're the expert."

Cameron raised his eyebrows. "Your stepmother is a very perceptive woman," he said. "I've always liked her."

Anna laughed. "The thing is," she said, "while I've been staying with Barbara I've... well I've discovered something which I think might be rather interesting."

Cameron looked sideways at her.

"A little bird told me you were dabbling in a bit of family history."

Dabbling? Was it dabbling? Anna felt a surge of irritation.

"So, come on then. Spill the beans. What is this great discovery of yours?"

He was watching her with the same smug expression she remembered from when they first met, looking at her as if she was a morsel of food he was about to swallow up. She bit her lip. Suddenly she found that she didn't want to confide in Cameron after all.

But now his attention was caught.

"You're looking very secretive. Come on... Tell Uncle Cameron. What's it all about?"

"Well..." she said, thinking fast, "one of the women helping Barbara was very scathing about the fact that I had never heard of the Clearances."

"I'm not surprised."

"But when I asked Barbara about it she said she wasn't the right person to explain. And then I found Fiona's journals. And started reading about her life. And the more I read, the more I realised how little I know about what was going on up here at the time." She gazed at him wide-eyed. "And I thought you were just the man to help explain it all to me."

"So your big discovery was Fiona's diaries?" He sounded disappointed. "Well of course I'm familiar with them. But you've touched something of a raw nerve there. Whenever I think about those diaries I'm reminded that if Rowancross had been in the hands of its rightful owner, it would have been me rather than Charlie who found them."

Cameron glared across the hillside, his good mood of a few moments ago gone. Anna picked at a patch of lichen on the rock she was resting against and watched him out of the corner of her eye, wondering how best to move the conversation on.

He cleared his throat. "I'm sorry... I'm being churlish. These are old grievances. Not your problem." He turned to her and managed a smile. "If it's the Clearances you're interested in you've come to the right man."

"Good... I know... I mean that's what I thought."

He took a long sip of beer from his can.

"So... What can I tell you?"

"Well, what exactly happened I suppose. How they came about –"

"Well, it's a big subject. I'll assume complete ignorance, shall I?"

Anna gave him her sweetest smile. He set the can down on the rock beside him.

"You're probably not aware of it, but around about the time Robert and Fiona met – so we're talking the middle of the nineteenth century – life was pretty bloody impossible for a majority of the people living in this part of the world. You had a situation where the population had grown to the point where the land could no longer support the numbers living on it. Which inevitably meant poverty, famine and disease. And you had landlords who were notable primarily for their absence. By the end of the eighteenth century three fifths of the clan chiefs had left the Highlands. You also had a great tide of emigration as those poor bastards who were left behind to get on with it looked for a better life somewhere else. It was pretty obvious to anyone with a modicum of intelligence that things would have to change, that the old ways were no longer viable. But it took men like Robert Gillespie to recognize that change was essential and try to do something about it."

Anna settled herself more comfortably against the rock. She might not trust Cameron enough to share Fiona's letter with him, but he knew what he was talking about, and there was so much to learn.

"You have to remember," he continued, "that relatively speaking we're not talking about a very long time ago. This was the eighteen hundreds. Across Britain the Industrial Revolution was in full swing. Small market towns were being transformed into great cities, dominated by factories. You had mass-produced goods being sold at prices low enough to make them accessible to everyone. You could climb on a train and travel to pretty well anywhere in the country you wanted to go. But in the Highlands it was a very different story. Compared with the rest of Britain Highland society was stuck in the dark ages, still organized along feudal lines, until relatively late in the day."

"Are you talking about the clans?"

"Absolutely. Now the thing you have to understand about the clans was that, although we hear about them fighting each other all the time, in fact they provided a stabilizing force with a clear structure that everybody recognized. So you had the chief at the top of the pyramid, and immediately below him you had what were known as the tacksmen - they tended to be members of the chief's family, the people bound most closely to him by blood - and they leased their land from him. These tacksmen in turn leased their land to sub tenants, and at the bottom of the pile you had the cotters, the men without land, the serfs if you like.

"The important thing to remember is that none of these guys paid rent for their land with money. It was their services they provided. At each level the tenants owed the kind of service that was most appropriate to their status. So if you were a miller you ground the chief's grain for him; if you were a ploughman you ploughed his land; if you were a carpenter you built his barns. But more often than not the services provided were of a military nature. Gaelic society honoured the warrior and set great store by the art of war. A high value was placed on such activities as hunting and the like, while those who worked the land were held in low esteem."

Anna shook her head. Wasn't it always the way? Go out and kill things and you get all the glory. Stay at home and dig the garden and do the dishes and see who notices.

"Am I boring you?" Cameron was quick to notice that her attention seemed to have wandered.

"Oh no… not at all. Go on, please."

"OK," he said. "Well the whole point was that none of this was ever put down in writing. And the only one with any legal right to the land was the chief. Which was fine in the old days, when the chiefs saw themselves as the custodians of their people and were bound by an incredibly strong sense of duty to maintain the clan and its lands for posterity. But the problem was that when the clan system began to break down, there was nothing to replace it."

"But why did the clan system break down? What happened?"

"You could say that it all began - or perhaps it would be fairer to say that it all came to an end – at the battle of Culloden. You've heard of Culloden?"

Anna was embarrassed to admit that she knew the name but little else. Cameron shook his head.

"Outrageous," he said. "The last battle to be fought on native soil, and you know nothing about it. Are you quite sure you're Charlie's daughter?"

He was teasing her, but only just.

"Right," he said. "Basically Culloden was where the clans got hammered. The Young Pretender – Bonnie Prince Charlie to you - landed from exile in France in July of 1745, and conjured up an army out of the Highlands to march on London and reclaim the throne of the United Kingdom for the exiled Stuarts." He glanced at her. "But it wasn't as simple as it sounds. I should point out that at Culloden only a small proportion of the Highland clans were actually involved in the battle. And there were more than a few who fought against Charlie rather than for him. But they all suffered the fallout after it ended.

"Bonnie Prince Charlie and his men reached as far as Derby on their way to London. But having got all that way south, they lost heart. They turned round and marched all the way back to Inverness, pursued by government forces, and they made it as far as Culloden. Poor buggers, they didn't stand a chance. They were outnumbered two to one by an army who had seen how close a Highland rebellion could come to overthrowing the established monarchy, and were damned sure they weren't going to let it happen again. And it was after Culloden that the destruction of the clan system began in earnest.

"After Culloden the estates of those who had died - and of those who survived but who forfeited their lands as a result of their involvement - were handed over to be managed by men who had absolutely no bond between them and the people. There were still many of the great estates that remained in the hands of the original landowners. But unfortunately those chiefs who still held onto their ancestral lands got a taste of what life was like down south. And they no longer wanted to live the way their fathers had done. They headed for the bright lights and left their agents in charge.

"Which was all very well. But the big problem for the new type of chief was that they found that it was no good being rich in land when they were poor in cash. So very simply they began to demand payment for their land in money rather than services, from people who had none and had no way of making it. And, with nothing in writing to protect those who had lived on the land for centuries, it was no problem for the chiefs when they decided to lease it to people who could pay for it.

"So you've got a new breed of Highland chief, who is beginning to find it impossible to fund his lifestyle out of a barren land that is incapable of supporting the population let alone deliver profits. So what does he do? He turns to a very different kind of tenant - a woolly one. The Great Cheviot Sheep was the answer to every laird's prayer. Here was an animal capable of putting up with pretty much anything the Highlands could throw at it."

"So you're saying they got rid of the people and replaced them with sheep?"

He nodded.

"That's about the long and short of it."

"But what about men like Fiona's father?"

"Ah," said Cameron, "now Lachlan Mackenzie was an honourable man, a chieftain of the old school - but he struggled as much as anybody. The Kildorran estate couldn't support the number of people living there and things got pretty desperate. The arrival of Robert Gillespie on his doorstep must have been a godsend."

"But Robert was a sheep farmer -"

"Lachlan Mackenzie saw that Robert Gillespie was a man with the funds and the inclination to invest in the land. And the commitment to improving the lot of the Highland people."

"So Iain Mackay got it wrong when he told Fiona that he believed Robert was planning to evict the people at Kildorran to make way for his sheep?"

Irritation flared in Cameron's eyes.

"That man was a bloody nuisance. All that hero of the people crap. He was a know-nothing guy taking cheap shots in the press at a man who had the intelligence to recognize that things needed to change.

And then, having stirred things up, what did Mackay go and do? Did he stay at home and try to make things better? Did he hell. He buggered off to Canada at the drop of a hat. And just because he set up some little paper when he got there, now he's the next best thing since sliced bread. And that cheapskate Fin MacLean gets to make a tidy sum writing a book about him."

Anna drew in her breath.

"Not a big fan then? Of either of them."

Cameron glowered at her. Clearly she had touched another nerve; he seemed to have quite a few. There was a moment of uncomfortable silence between them, and then he uttered a short laugh. "You must be bored rigid. I do have a tendency to go on a bit. Laura's always having a go at me about it."

"It's fine. I was interested."

He reached into his rucksack and handed her a sandwich.

"I've gone on far too long," he said. "Let's have some lunch."

The walk down was – as Cameron had promised – even worse than the walk up. Every step jarred. Anna's ankles twisted and cracked as she skidded and slid down the path. At one point she slipped on a loose patch of shale and fell. A pair of sheep in the bracken beside the path started and jumped with fright, and dashed away from her, their grubby white bottoms bouncing in protest, as if they were ashamed to be seen with her. There were moments when it required a massive effort to stay cheerful in the face of Cameron's amused gaze.

It was a relief to get back to the car. She fell into the passenger seat and sat back gratefully, stretching out her aching legs in front of her.

"I hope it wasn't too much for you."

Cameron got into the driver's seat beside her. She glanced across at him.

"You know something... I loved it." She was surprised to find, now that it was over, that she meant it.

"Well, if you make any more discoveries... You know who to come to."

CHAPTER SEVEN

Barbara was writing letters at her desk when Anna got back to Rowancross. She looked up as Anna came in.

"How was it?"

Anna flopped down in the corner of one of the sofas.

"It was good. We climbed up to the minister's house. Or rather Cameron climbed, and I sort of scrambled and staggered and fell over a lot."

"You were lucky."

"I was?"

"He's been known to drag people up far worse than what you went up today."

"Well thanks for warning me."

Barbara laughed.

"So was it helpful?"

Anna thought for a moment.

"You know something... It was," she said. "I know a lot more now about the background to the Clearances. And I'm beginning to understand why it was such a big deal for everyone. But it was a bit like reading Charlie's book; more about the politics than the people. And my big problem is that so far I've got Fiona and Robert in a marriage that seems to be pretty solid, and I've got the letter from Iain. And the two just don't seem to go together."

"Frustrating, huh?"

"I just wish I had more time."

Barbara took off her glasses.

"That reminds me. Richard called an hour or so ago. Said he'd tried your mobile but it was switched off. He sounded very stressed. Wanted you to ring him as soon as you got back."

Anna's face darkened.

"What's the betting he's been delayed? By the time he finally makes it up here there won't be much point. We're meant to be flying south on Tuesday."

"That still gives you several days." Barbara got up. "I'll go and make us some tea while you ring him."

Anna heaved herself up from the cushions and found her phone. When she dialed Richard's number he answered immediately.

"Barbara said you rang."

"Darling... Yes... Look, I don't know how to tell you this, but I'm not going to be able to make it up to join you after all."

Anna sighed.

"Tell me something I hadn't guessed already." She sat back down on the sofa. "So, when will you be back?"

"Hard to say. We haven't found anybody to replace Sergei yet, and I can't leave until things have been sorted out. The guy we thought we had, who was supposed to be shadowing me, has turned out to be a disaster. It's a pain, I know. But the thing is that once we've found the right person I should be able to stop these trips. So it's worth hanging on and doing the job properly, don't you see."

"How long?"

"It's going to be at least another couple of weeks. And it could be a month. Maybe more. It's hard to say at the moment."

Anna closed her eyes.

"I'd better cancel the hotel booking then."

"You don't mind?"

"I gave up minding a long time ago."

✥

Barbara, coming into the room carrying a tray with mugs of tea and a plate of homemade shortbread, found Anna slumped back in the sofa with her arm across her eyes. She set the tray down on the low table and sat down.

"Is everything alright, honey?" She stretched out her hand and touched Anna's knee. "The girls? Richard?"

Anna spoke from behind her arm.

"They are all fine. The girls are fine. Richard is fine. Everybody is absolutely fine."

Barbara sighed.

"Apart from you. You're not fine, are you Anna?"

Anna's face emerged from behind her arm. Her eyes were wet.

"Is it too much to expect?" she asked Barbara in a low voice. "Is it too much to hope for? To have a husband you actually spend some time with. One you actually get to see once in a while. I've had enough of managing on my own. I don't want to do it any more."

Barbara looked like she was trying to think of something encouraging to say - and couldn't.

"He's not coming," continued Anna miserably. "And not only is he not coming, he's got to stay in Moscow for at least another month. That's practically the whole summer. And what am I going to do? The girls are gone until the end of August. Everybody's away. This is when people go on holiday with their families. And I'm going back to an empty house." She shook her head angrily, brushing away tears. "It's hard to see the point of this marriage of mine. I might just as well be single." She looked at Barbara. "I'm sorry," she said. "I'm being pathetic. This is the last thing you need right now."

Barbara took her hand.

"Listen to me, sweetie. You are precisely what I need right now. I couldn't have got through the past few days without you." She paused. "In fact, why don't you stay on? The last thing I want is to be on my own at the moment. You could chill out with me, get to know the area. And it would give you time to find out more about Fiona, and see if you can get to the bottom of that letter of hers."

Anna stared at her. It seemed too obvious a solution to be possible. There were so many reasons she could think of for staying it didn't seem right. It couldn't be that easy.

"Well, my job's not a problem," she said slowly. "It's the great thing about being a classroom assistant. School doesn't go back until the beginning of September."

"There you go then," said Barbara.

"But I haven't got enough clothes with me."

"There's a thing called a washing machine. They have them up here you know. And you can borrow anything you like of mine - we're about the same height. And there are shops in Ullapool, and in Inverness. We haven't got a Harvey Nichols on the doorstep I grant you, but we can fit you up, don't you worry."

"I can't leave the house empty for that long."

"Why ever not? You've got a cleaning lady? Ring her and get her to keep an eye on things for you."

"The garden."

"You were going to spend the summer gardening?"

"My mother will think I'm completely mad."

"So? I'll ring Jennifer. By the time I've finished with her she'll think it was her idea."

"There must be something else I've forgotten."

"For crying out loud, what?" Barbara raised her eyes to the ceiling. And then she hesitated. "Unless you don't want to."

Anna took hold of her hands and squeezed them tightly.

"I can't think of anything I want more."

It was an extraordinary summer to be in the Highlands. While in London people huddled under umbrellas and wondered if it would ever stop raining, on the west coast of Scotland day after day dawned blue and clear and full of promise. Nobody could remember a year quite like it. The summers of childhood paled by comparison.

It didn't take Anna long to slip into a more gentle rhythm of life - going to bed more often than not before it was properly dark, rising early. She walked every morning before breakfast along the edge of the loch with Barbara, while her stepmother pointed out seabirds and slippery black seals, and the occasional glimpse of a porpoise lifting and rising out of the water, like some mythical creature out of a folk story. In the clear light of early morning her troubles with Richard seemed a million miles away.

She quickly changed her mind about the little town of Ullapool. She loved to wander along the edge of the harbour, watching the ferries coming and going, carrying passengers to Stornaway on the Western Isles. She was charmed by the shops that faced out across the loch, selling their tartan and their whisky and their woolly jumpers, making the most of the summer custom before the long winter set in again and the town emptied of visitors. The local people were invariably good natured and courteous, more than happy to pass the time of day, in no hurry to be on to the next thing before the time was right. She found she even liked the tourists, the Germans and the French and the Scandinavians.

They seemed always to be smiling. Most had come expecting rain and were therefore doubly appreciative of the sunshine.

She stayed in touch with her daughters by email and spoke to them occasionally on the phone. She spoke as often as necessary to her mother to keep her happy. And Richard rang every few days to keep her up to date with developments in Moscow. Their conversations were brisk and business-like. And they steered clear of discussing when he might be coming home.

Cameron was a frequent visitor at Rowancross, and more often than not she was happy to see him. When he wasn't being pompous he was an entertaining companion, and more importantly he was immensely knowledgeable about the history of the region.

One day he drove her along the coast to the gardens at Inverewe, travelling he told her by the road once known as 'Destitution Road', because it had been built with the proceeds from a grant made to relieve distress in the tough years of the late nineteenth century. On the way back they stopped at the wide horseshoe beach in Gruinard Bay and walked along the shoreline together. As they walked back up the narrow steps from the beach they had to stand back to allow a man with his dogs to pass them. Cameron put his arm around her shoulders and pulled her against him for just a little longer than was absolutely necessary. With her back pressed against his chest she could feel his heart beating. His breath was hot on her neck. She tugged herself away and strode back to the car. And was wary afterwards of spending more time alone with him than was absolutely necessary.

Most days she divided her attention between packing up her father's things for Barbara and continuing with her research into Fiona's life. She spent hours in Charlie's study filling black plastic bags with the debris left behind after his death, trying to come to terms with the person he had been, and the growing regret that she had not made more of an effort to find out more about him while he was alive. The principle effect of going through his things was to remind her more than ever that he was a stranger to her, a stranger whose personal effects she handled on a daily basis, but whose face she struggled to remember. And it served to emphasise the fact that he was never coming back, and that this meant a great deal more to her than she had expected.

This sadness, the sense of having missed out on an opportunity, was countered by her growing interest and increasing pleasure as she read Fiona's journals and letters, getting to know her great great grandmother better as the days passed. The more she learnt the clearer and more rounded grew the picture of Fiona in her mind's eye. At what point she ceased to be a historical character and became a real person Anna couldn't say, but tucked away on her own for so many hours, talking to nobody, Fiona began to seem almost more real to her than her father had been.

Fiona's reminiscences gave a vivid impression of the life of a laird's daughter in the mid nineteenth century. The early diaries contained lively accounts of her teenage years, and were full of the kind of domestic detail that gave Anna a real feeling for the way her ancestor had lived. Fiona described the novelty of coming back to a coal fire after a day out on the hill. Cameron had told Anna that until the opening of the Caledonian Canal in 1822 people had to rely on peat and wood for heating and cooking, but with the linking of the North Sea to the Atlantic the way was opened for the provision of those luxuries into the Highlands which were taken for granted further south. Fiona wrote that at Kildorran her father was suspicious of what he saw as new-fangled, southern ways, but eventually he bowed to the inevitable and there was great excitement in having a fire which didn't emit clouds of damp smoke that smelt like old socks burning.

Without a mother to care for her it seemed that Fiona was allowed a degree of licence that Anna suspected was unusual for the highborn daughter of a Highland chief. There was a housekeeper and a nurse who had the care of her, and she wrote with frustration about the days when she was prevented from going out to ride across the glens on Derry, her pony, and instead was made to attempt the conversion into accomplished needlewoman, moving from the darning of stockings and mending of clothes onto embroidery and tapestry work. The only thing that made this chore acceptable to her was that they sang the old songs while they worked. Janet, the housekeeper, spoke only Gaelic, as did most of the household. She and the factor, John, taught Fiona the ballads and poems of the past, rich with tales of ancient kings and clan wars, of the brave deeds of legendary warriors, of stones that talked, and giants that walked the snowy mountains in days of old.

Fiona received her education at home, her father going to great lengths to ensure that she acquired the necessary skills to attract a good husband. She was tutored in dancing and singing, played the piano, and at seventeen spoke both French and Italian. That Fiona wrote in English was something Anna took for granted, until she read how reluctant Fiona's father had been for his daughter to speak the language of the mistrusted South. That she did was thanks to his recognition that the acquirement of English was a necessary evil, the precursor to finding a place in the new world that was advancing upon them. Anna was grateful to him. These diaries would have been completely inaccessible to her had Fiona written them in her native tongue.

May 21ˢᵗ 1844 was Fiona's sixteenth birthday.

After today I am truly a grown up, she wrote. *This morning when I awoke I was still a child. But now everything has changed.*

Calum came yesterday to Kildorran with Flora and my aunt and uncle, and he greeted me in the usual way, pinching my cheek and tugging my hair. We arranged that we would go riding together before breakfast as we always do when the families stay together. I woke early and went and knocked on his door, and he called me inside so cheerfully that I thought he must have a birthday present waiting for me. But I should have known that he meant mischief. For when I opened the door he had placed a jug of water so that it fell and soaked me. And when I went to scold him he laughed so that he could not speak. I had to tell him to be quiet, for I knew Janet would say it was not the right thing for me to be in his bedroom.

We crept out of the house together – Flora would not come, sleepy head - and took our horses and rode up to the head of the valley. There was a solitary stag on the hillside who stood and watched our passing, and I swear we saw an eagle high above our heads although Calum said it was a buzzard. But, eagle or buzzard, I knew that there was no better place to be. When we came back we sneaked in through

*the back way and Calum's deerhound, Dugald, pushed in
beside us and escaped into the hall where he found a fur
tippet belonging to Aunt Alice and tore it into shreds. I was
laughing so much to see Calum in a tug of war with his
great dog.*

*Sometimes you do not see what is under your nose.
Tonight there was a dance in the great hall, held in honour
of my birthday. My father had allowed for material to be
ordered from London, blue silk the colour of a spring sky, for
a dress to be made up for me. When I spun around on my
toes the skirt flowed all around me like water. I wore my hair
pinned up on my head like a lady, and when I looked at myself in the glass before I went downstairs I did not know for
certain that the face that looked back at me was really mine.*

*When I came down the main staircase into the great
hall people turned and stared. Calum laughed and pinched
my nose and told me to take off the fancy dress. But I swear
he looked at me as if he had never seen me before.*

*Oh how I danced. I flew, I was a bird. The piper played,
the people laughed and sang, and I danced until my head
was spinning. And Calum danced with me, and made such
a whooping and a crying that I thought the rafters would
come down on our heads. And when we stopped and went
outside to cool down that is when he told me that I was
beautiful. And then he kissed me.*

*What words are there to describe his kiss? First his lips
were soft against mine, no more than the brush of a bird's
wing. But then he slipped his arms around my shoulders*

and held me tighter. And then there was nothing soft about the way he kissed me. Nor about the way I kissed him back. I closed my eyes and the stars span above my head. And the only thing I wished was for time to stand still and nothing ever to change, so that I might stay in that moment forever.

We had to go inside. They were looking for us. And I did not get the chance to be alone with him again. But it does not matter. Because now I shall marry him and we will always be together, for that is how it was meant to be, although we did not realize it until today.

Now Fiona's journal became the repository for the outpouring of her passion for her cousin. The depth of her love for him, the agony of not seeing enough of him, the black misery when she received a letter from him telling her that he was being sent south to finish his education – it was all there. But with Calum at school in England their meetings were few and far between. And passion's flame needs fuel. As time passed his name began to appear less frequently. Until eventually it petered out altogether.

It wasn't until Anna was several pages into 1848 that Calum reappeared.

This morning, wrote Fiona, *when I came down to breakfast, Father told me that Calum was to be married. I have not seen him more than four times over the past three years, so I could not be too unhappy about it. And Flora had already written to warn me - after her brother came back from the south - that he was spending a great deal of time with the daughter of a merchant in Inverness. So I knew what to expect. Father could not look me in the face when he told me, but I was proud to be able to smile when I heard the news, and say that I was glad for Calum. For a long time I believed that he and I were destined to be together. But I was a child then and I didn't understand. Calum had to marry a woman with money. As I too must find a rich husband. It is the way things have to be.*

Afterwards I did not feel in the mood for talking to anybody very much, so I did something I have not done for years. I went and found the cap and the breeches that Calum had outgrown and left behind for me when he was a boy. And I tucked up my hair and took a rod and went out through the woods behind the house to the river. With the terrier Kyle for company, I made my way along the bank to the Kennel pool. I wanted to see if I could catch the big old cock salmon that John told me had been teasing him for the past few days.

But the strangest thing happened on my way there. I was crossing the river at the drain, to go through the wood where the wild orchids grow, and there were three men there. They shouted at me to stop. But I ran, and they came after me. When they caught up with me I hid my face from them, and they must have thought I was a boy, for they were threatening to beat me. Then I took off my cap and shook out my hair and asked them in as haughty a tone as I could manage what they were doing on my land. They were more respectful then, although not in the way that they should be. They said it was fine for me to be there, but that I should be careful to stick to the path. I told them that I had played in these woods all my life and had no intention of sticking to the path. And this is where it was strange, because the tall one said that it would be best for me if I did what I was told, and that he didn't want to have to throw me off the land. I thought perhaps they had not heard me the first time, so I said more loudly that it was my land and they could not throw me off. And they looked at one another in a strange way, and then the tall one said that it might have been my land once, but it wasn't any more.

I could not believe what I was hearing and went immediately home and searched for father. But he was nowhere to be found, so I went up to the cottages to look for John. He was feeding his dogs in the backyard. He would not meet my gaze when I told him about the men I had seen. I said he would find it amusing when he heard what had happened, although in truth I did not feel much like laughing. John did not laugh either, but looked angry and worried at the same time. He said it was for my father to explain, but that the men had paid for the lease of the wood and the deer moor, and that we no longer had the right to use it.

I could not believe my ears. Why had my father said nothing about this to me? I know that things have been bad for some time, that we have not been always able to pay the bills on time. And there have been times when the tenants

*on the estate have struggled to feed their families, and fa-
ther has stayed up late into the night trying to work out
how best to manage things. Only a month ago John's son,
Thomas, came to say that he had taken passage on a boat
from Ullapool for himself and his wife and his brothers,
because they could not see a way to make a living for themselves at Kildorran. I don't know if Father was more sad or
more angry. I do know that he thought they were deserting
us. But Thomas took me to one side and told me that father
did not understand that there was no other way for them.*

*I wish that father would explain to me what is going on.
I know that he is doing his best and wishes to protect me.
But no matter how bad things have become I cannot believe
that we should give up our land, which in the end is all we
have. It appears that he has had to go away at short notice
so I can't ask him about it, but John said it was to tide us
through a particularly difficult time, and that he had no
doubt that the forest would be restored to us very soon.*

*I went home and crept up the back staircase to my
bedroom, and I sat for a long time before I felt able to go
downstairs.*

It was this incident with the men in the wood that
really aroused Anna's curiosity. Because here was the
first indication that conditions in the Highlands were
having an impact at Kildorran. It seemed to be pav-
ing the way for the appearance of Robert Gillespie
on the scene. It was clear that Fiona was going to

have to marry money. But what Anna really wanted to find out was if there was any room for love as well?

The biggest obstacle facing Anna was the condition of the diaries that dealt with the years in question. Years 1848 and 1849 were in a fragile state. The pages for most of the second half of 1848 were moulded together into a solid wedge, and it was impossible to prise them apart. There was hardly a page for 1849 – the year in which Fiona and Robert got married - where the damp hadn't blurred the writing to the extent that it was almost completely illegible. What Anna was able to decipher proved unenlightening. Frustrated by her failure to find anything that helped shed light on Fiona's courtship and marriage, Anna turned to the bundle of letters that had been in the chest with the diaries.

Fiona had kept the letters that meant most to her, so there were letters congratulating her on the births of her sons. There were letters from those same sons sent from boarding school in England, a number containing desperate pleas to be allowed to come home. Anna read these with tears in her eyes. It brought back unhappy memories of the time when Rose and Ellie had to be sent home to boarding school while they were living overseas. There were long chatty letters from friends, updating Fiona on births and marriages and deaths. And there were letters of condolence, written around September 1888, commiserating with Fiona for the loss of her husband. There was nothing from Robert himself.

A number were from Calum's younger sister, Flora. And it was these letters that gave Anna something a little more concrete to go on. Flora's parents had taken a house in Edinburgh, and she wrote regularly to her cousin in the Highlands about life in the city. In the autumn of 1848 it appeared that Fiona paid her uncle and aunt a visit, because after she left them to return to Kildorran Flora wrote to say how much they all missed her.

Dearest cousin, wrote Flora,

I was never more sad to say goodbye to anyone. Edinburgh will be most horribly dull without you. Now the evenings will drag by while Mother goes on about Margaret and what a wonderful wife she will make for Calum, and Papa pretends to fall asleep to avoid having to listen to her. It is almost enough to make me wish I was returning to the country with you. I think it most likely that I shall go mad and they will have to carry me off to the asylum.

How was your journey home? I know how pleased you must be to be back at your beloved Kildorran. You will be amused to hear that Mr Gillespie called round to see you and looked most put out to hear that he had missed you. I saw from his face that he was most anxious, and he looked heartily relieved when Mother explained that it was because your aunt Eliza had been taken ill and it was felt necessary for you to be there in case her condition grew worse. After that he didn't stay long and when he had gone I heard Mother tell Mrs Jessop, who was taking tea with us, that it was obvious which way the wind was blowing, and that it was an ill wind that blows nobody any good. Which I have never understood, have you?

Will you see him again do you think? I think he must like you very much. I remember the first time I saw him, when he came to the ball that Mother arranged for you. I was sitting on the landing in the upstairs hall, feeling very cross because Mother had said that I was too young to join in, when everybody knows that fifteen is plenty old enough. I peeked through the banister rail as the guests arrived, and I saw the fuss that everybody made of Mr Gillespie when he was announced, which I cannot understand because he is quite old, don't you think, thirty or so at least, and he doesn't smile very often. I know they say he is very wealthy, and Mother thinks he is handsome, even if he is a Lowlander and she doesn't really approve

I crept downstairs to watch the dancing from the door-way, and that is when I saw Mother introduce Mr Gillespie to Mr and Mrs Andrews. But, although he shook hands and bowed and appeared to be listening to their conversation, I could see that his attention was somewhere else altogether. And, when I followed the direction of his gaze, I saw immediately what it was that had attracted his notice. Dear cousin, it was you. You were dancing with Mr Ogilvy, and I think he must have said something to amuse you, for you were laughing in such a merry way and your eyes were shining, and you didn't look at all like so many of the other girls who make it their business to appear bored all the time. Mr Gillespie couldn't take his eyes off you. It was hard to believe that you could be unaware of it, for truly it seemed as if his gaze must burn you. He stopped talking to the Andrews and stood impatiently waiting for the dance to finish. And then he practically dragged Mother over to be introduced to you.

Do you like him, Fiona? Mother thinks that you do. He was certainly the most frequent visitor out of all your admirers. But if you liked him that much I think that you would have been happier to stay in Edinburgh, and not missed the countryside as much as you did. For although I know you have enjoyed your time with us, you cannot pretend that you were not delighted to have an excuse to go home.

I have decided that I shall never fall in love and get married. Instead I will have lots of lovers and go to parties and dance and eat all the things that Mother tells me are bad for my figure. And I won't take a bit of notice of doing the right thing, or putting the family first, or choosing the right husband. Or any of the other tedious duties that seem to be expected of one.

Will you write back to me, dear Fiona? I miss you already.

Your loving cousin,
Flora

There was another letter written a few months later in the spring of 1849.

My dearest of dear cousins,

Your letter arrived this morning, and the first moment I could I sat down to write straight back to you. Because I am so excited for you I could die. For everybody in Edinburgh is speaking of Mr Gillespie, don't you know. He made such an impression when he was here last year, and when he visited us again in January the only topic of conversation was who he would choose to be his wife.

I knew there was some mystery when Mother met him recently at the Lyalls. He had been out of town for nigh on a month, and everybody was curious to know where he had been and what he had been doing. Katherine Baillie was at the Lyalls with her mother, and she spoke to Mr Gillespie of the rumour that the reason he was so uninterested in any of the girls in Edinburgh was because his heart was already attached. Mother thought Katherine's behaviour most forward and brazen, and indeed I think your Mr Gillespie thought so too, for according to Mother he looked very cross. He coughed and frowned and looked as though he would have escaped if he could.

Mother went over and rescued him, and he looked most gratefully at her. And, when she mentioned your name to him, she says that he went a little red in the face and stared at the floor, and said in a quiet voice so she could barely hear him that he was praying that you would have him.

She said she trembled to hear him. That his voice was full of passion. (At least I think that is what she said, for she was telling Papa about it and it was difficult for me to hear through the door.)

And so my very dear cousin, you are to be married. It comes as something of a relief to hear that you are happy about it, for if I am honest I have been afraid that you may have been carrying a torch for Calum all these years. But from your letter it sounds to me as though you are very glad to be marrying Mr Gillespie.

I hope you will ask me to be your bridesmaid, for it is something I have always longed to be but nobody has ever asked me. Mother said not to mention it, that it would be bad manners of me to ask, but I knew you would want to know how much it would mean to me.

Write back soon and tell me what you think of my idea.

Your hopeful cousin,

Flora

CHAPTER EIGHT

Anna was in her father's study, sorting through stacks of old magazines, when she heard voices from down the corridor, and a few seconds later Barbara called out to her that she was making coffee and did Anna want her to bring her one. She was glad for the interruption. It was a tedious job, and the weather was humid, so that even with the windows open the room was stuffy. She slung an armful of magazines into the cardboard box beside the desk and called back that she would come and get it for herself.

When she went into the kitchen she found Fin Maclean sitting at the table, coffee cup in hand, long denim-clad legs stretched out in front of him.

"Fin dropped by to return some books I lent him," said Barbara, handing her a mug. Anna looked sideways at him. She was tempted to take her coffee and go straight back to Charlie's study, but the truth was that the sight of Fin wasn't as unwelcome as it might have been. The past few days spent reading Fiona's diaries and letters had brought with it a mixture of enjoyment and frustration. While she had been able to build up a reasonably clear picture of Fiona's life at Kildorran, she had found absolutely nothing so far to connect Fiona with Iain Mackay.

Fin smiled, and said hello in a friendly manner that suggested that he, if not she, had decided to set aside the circumstances of their first meeting. So she decided she could be generous and do the same. She took the coffee handed to her by Barbara and sat down opposite him.

The truth was that Fin MacLean was not nearly as relaxed as he seemed. Something about Anna Sinclair had got to him. The expression in her eyes when she thought he disapproved of her kept on replaying itself in his memory. He had thrown her enthusiasm back in her face, and he felt bad about it. He told himself that the reason she kept on sneaking into his thoughts was because he was struggling with his writing and looking for distraction. But he was uncomfortably aware that he had said the wrong thing, and he wanted to find a way of proving to her that first impressions could be misleading.

That morning Sarah had mentioned casually over breakfast that Charlie Gillespie's daughter was still at Rowancross House, after deciding to stay on with Barbara for the summer. Fin had been fully intending to settle down and concentrate on working his way through the writer's block that was making it impossible for him to make any real progress with his novel. But he told himself that Barbara would be missing the books she had lent him a while back, so he decided to go into Ullapool and do some errands for Sarah, drop in at Rowancross on the way back, try and make amends with Anna, and settle down to work on his book after lunch.

Fin's desire to repair the damage done during his first encounter with Anna had nothing – or not much - to do with the fact that she was an attractive woman. He appreciated that she was – to quote Aunt Sarah – a good looking girl; he wasn't blind. But even if he had been interested in her in that way - which he wasn't - she was married. Which put her out of the picture as far as he was concerned. He had come up to the Highlands to escape from the complications caused by the women in his life. Not add to them.

Ten years earlier, when Fin was struggling to find a job that would allow him to earn a living out of writing, he met and married within three months the features editor of the newspaper whose offices he was haunting in the hope of being employed. There was no ulterior motive in his decision. Amy was intelligent and beautiful and more focussed than anybody he had ever met before. They embarked on married life together with a rose tinted picture of themselves as principled journalists on a mission to enlighten the world. But while Fin remained true to his ideals, and as a consequence found it difficult to make any money, Amy sold her soul to the devil (as far as he was concerned), and accepted a job as deputy editor of a TV magazine devoted to publicising the gory details of celebrity life in all its glory.

They agreed that they were heading in different directions, and divorced with the minimum of fuss, since the only property to divide between them was hers, and there was a surprisingly small amount of emotional baggage to divvy up. Fin embraced bachelor life with enthusiasm. But recently he had begun to feel envious of his married friends, of their built in togetherness and mutual support systems. When he boarded the plane for Inverness at the beginning of June he was waved off by Allie, a struggling actress he had met at a New Years Eve party. Over the past few months he had become very familiar with the bedroom of her Fulham apartment, and he said goodbye to her with the appropriate show of affection. But the truth was that he was relieved to be putting some distance between them. He was looking for commitment. But not with her.

Allie had flown up to stay for a couple of weekends, but it had not been a success. Her flimsy prettiness, and taste in jeweled sandals and gossamer caftans, so appealing in the West End of London, seemed ridiculous and out of place in the Highlands. And the way she paraded their relationship in front of everyone she met infuriated him. He had promised to fly down for her birthday in July, but Charlie's funeral had come up, and he was ashamed to admit that he had fallen on it as an excuse not to bother.

Allie appeared to have got the message. Her phone calls and text messages had gradually petered out, and Fin told himself that it was all for the best. He needed to concentrate on his writing without a woman around to make life complicated for him. Which was why - as he tilted himself back on the kitchen chair at Rowancross, and took a gulp of his coffee - he was struggling to understand why it was so important to him to demonstrate to a woman he barely knew that he wasn't the bigoted halfwit she believed him to be.

"So, how's the book going, Fin?" said Barbara, sitting down between them.

He pulled a face.

"Don't ask… I'm struggling a bit at the moment. Don't seem to be able to concentrate."

"It's such a great subject," said Barbara with her customary enthusiasm. "One that's very close to my heart."

Fin looked across the table at Anna. She was watching him over the rim of her mug, but it was impossible to tell if she was interested.

"It's about the Scottish settlers who went to the New World," said Barbara. "Sounds intriguing, don't you think, Anna?"

No response beyond a raised eyebrow.

"I'm hoping you're not the only one to think so, Barbara," said Fin, more to fill the silence than for any other reason "I got the idea when I was over in Toronto doing some research for the last book. Some of the stories I came across were just incredible. You wouldn't believe the conditions these guys had to face when they arrived. I mean Jesus it was tough enough living in the Highlands, but that was nothing compared to what they found when they got there."

He was talking too much, he knew it. Usually he didn't like to give too much away when he was writing. But now, faced with Anna's cool gaze across the table, he was jabbering like a nervous schoolboy.

"I'll be honest with you, though." He frowned into his coffee cup. "I'm beginning to wonder if fiction is really my thing. I'm fine when I'm dealing with fact, but, as soon as I have to invent stuff, I literally find myself losing the plot."

What was he saying? He hadn't known that this was how he was feeling until the words slipped out of his mouth. But if he was going to do vulnerability, why did he have to do it in front of Anna Sinclair?

"Maybe it's just a phase you're going through," said Barbara, pushing a plate of biscuits towards him, as if feeding him up could release the blockage. "It happens to all writers at some time or another. If it was easy everybody would be doing it." She took a biscuit for herself. "When does your book about Iain Mackay come out?"

Fin flashed a glance in Anna's direction. She was inspecting the tracery of lines in the palm of her right hand, and appeared not to have heard her stepmother.

"It's out in Canada already. Over here it's due some time in October."

"I'm really looking forward to reading it," Barbara said. "I've always thought he sounded like an intriguing character." She looked across the table at Anna. "Did Anna tell you about her interest in him?"

Watching her out of the corner of his eye Fin knew that Barbara thought she was helping, but wished she wouldn't. The fact of the matter was that

Anna looked bored stiff. He opened his mouth to change the subject, but Barbara was in her stride.

"Didn't Iain get involved in some kind of dispute with Robert Gillespie?"

Fin took a deep breath.

"He did. It was while he was working for the Inverness Courier."

"Remind me. What happened?"

There was no escaping it. The only thing to do was plunge right in. "Ok…" said Fin, thinking that if medals were being handed out for giving the impression of not giving a damn, Anna deserved the gold. "Robert had strong ideas about what he believed should be done to improve conditions in the Highlands. His letters were published, but nobody seemed prepared to take issue with him over his views. Except for Iain. He wasn't the sort of man to sit by and listen while some Lowlander talked about transforming the countryside. So he jeopardized his whole career to stand up for what he believed in."

"If you talk to Cameron he says that Iain Mackay was nothing but a troublemaker." Anna's cool voice cut across him.

Fin snorted.

"He would."

"You know," said Barbara, "I've never understood why Iain disappeared off to Canada, just when he was about to make a name for himself over here."

"You and me both," Fin said, shaking his head. "It's the black hole in the Iain Mackay story. What was it that made him go?"

Barbara stood up.

"It would be a great coup to find out what really happened, wouldn't it?" She looked from one to the other. "Needs a bit more investigation, don't you think?" She went over to the kitchen counter and picked up her wallet and phone. "I'm going to have to love you and leave you. I've got some errands to run in Ullapool."

Fin and Anna leapt up in unison.

"I'd better be off too," said Fin.

"Not on my account." Barbara put her hand on his shoulder. "Stay and finish your coffee. Anna will be glad of the company. She's been stuck in her father's study all morning."

Fin caught a glimpse of Anna mouthing a silent protest at her stepmother.

"There you go, Anna." Barbara crossed over to the door. "You've got an expert on Iain Mackay all to yourself. I'd make the most of the opportunity if I were you."

Barbara left the room, and Fin and Anna stood across the table from each other, and listened to her footsteps as they faded away along the corridor. Neither of them spoke. A bee was buzzing frantically against the window, making a sound like a miniature drill. Fin went over and lifted the sash, releasing it, then turned to face Anna. She had sat down again at the table, and her head was bent over her coffee cup, as if something fascinating lay at the bottom of it. All he could see was the crown of her auburn hair.

"This is awkward, isn't it?"

"You could say that."

"I didn't impress you much last time we met, did I?"

"Nope."

"Would you be willing to give me another chance?"

Anna raised her head and gave him a look which wasn't unfriendly, but neither was it very encouraging. He sat down opposite her and wished – for the first time in months - that he hadn't given up smoking.

"So," he said. "You're interested in Iain Mackay?"

Anna shrugged.

"I know he met my great great grandmother several times. It just occurred to me to wonder what kind of relationship they would have had."

"It's an interesting question."

"Is it?" She looked suspiciously at him.

"Well, if you think about it, Iain and Robert were sparring partners, but they seemed to respect each other, even if they didn't agree with each other. But I wouldn't be surprised if Iain had little time for

Robert's wife. In fact I reckon there would have been a fair bit of antagonism between them."

"Why do you say that?"

"Because I can't imagine Iain would have had a good opinion of a Mackenzie woman who married a man like Robert Gillespie. And I don't suppose Fiona thought much of him either. After all, he was out to shoot down her husband's opinions in public. It's not going to make her love him, is it?"

Anna frowned.

"But they were both from the Highlands. Wouldn't that act like some kind of a mutual bond?"

"Different clans," he explained. "Mackay's and Mackenzies. At Culloden they fought on different sides. But I don't think it would have been clan rivalry that set them apart. I reckon Iain would have seen Fiona as the ultimate traitor. She was a woman of Highland blood, from one of the great old families, who married a Lowlander. And, to make matters worse, he was a Lowlander who had made his fortune out of sheep."

"But Iain must have recognized that Robert had a point about things in the Highlands needing to change?"

He raised his eyebrows. She had been doing her homework.

"Absolutely he did. But there's change and change. And Iain had very good reasons for understanding that one man's idea of improvement could be another's idea of devastation."

"What reasons?"

"You really want to know?"

She tossed her head impatiently.

"Would I be asking if I didn't?"

"OK," he said, putting up his hands. "Iain's reasons for being suspicious of Fiona Gillespie's marriage to Robert were good ones. Because he had seen for himself what happens when an outsider with big ideas for making so-called improvements marries a Highland woman, and takes control of her land.

"Iain's family were victims of the most notorious of all the Highland Clearances; those were the evictions that took place in the early eighteen hundreds in Sutherland. And it was all because an English Marquess – who just happened to be the richest man in England - married the Countess of Sutherland – who just happened to own most of the county.

"It was the Marquess of Stafford who, after the wedding, came up with a cunning plan to 'improve'..." Fin mimed quotation marks with his fingers. "... his wife's estates.

"Which meant the land was sold. Which meant that, within a matter of months, those people who just happened to have lived there for centuries had to leave it all behind and head for the coast.

"After what his family suffered, Iain must have seen Fiona's marriage to a man like Robert as the ultimate betrayal."

He looked across the table at Anna. She had let go of her earlier stiff watchfulness and was leaning forwards on her chair, hands clasped round her coffee cup.

"It sounds like ethnic cleansing," she said.

"It was ethnic cleansing. We hear a lot about it these days, but it's always somewhere else - somewhere a long way from home. Well this was ethnic cleansing taking place right on our doorstep. There was a guy called James Loch who was Commissioner for all of Lord Stafford's estates. He made it his life's work to clear the interior of its people. He wrote that he wanted to completely change the character of the whole of the population. I can quote him for you. He said that it was his intention that the 'children of those who are removed from the hills will lose all recollection of the habits and customs of their fathers."

Anna stared at him.

"But that's terrible. I had absolutely no idea that anything like this went on."

"It's OK," he said. "You're not the only one."

"But I'm half Scottish."

"So are lots of other people who don't know anything about the Clearances."

She pulled a face.

"You don't have to be kind."

He grinned at her.

"After our first meeting I think I probably do."

＝⟨⟩＝

Anna got up to make them both a fresh cup of coffee. It felt like the air had cleared between them, and she was pleased that she'd stayed put rather than escaping back to Charlie's study. Fin clearly knew his stuff.

"So what happened to Iain's family?" she asked, sitting back down opposite him. "When they were evicted?

"Their house was torched over their heads, while they scrambled to save what they could - they were lucky to escape with their lives. Iain's father must have told him all about it in detail, because several decades later he wrote an account of what happened for the Courier. I know your father had a copy of it somewhere in his files, because I gave it to him. You should read it. Then you'd really understand why he was unlikely to be a big fan of Fiona Gillespie."

Anna sighed. This wasn't what she wanted to hear. She could feel Fin's eyes on her and wondered if she should tell him about the letter. But she still wasn't sure if she could trust him. She needed to know more.

"So Iain wasn't actually there when it happened?"

"It was before he was born. They were in Helmsdale by the time he came along. And Iain never knew the place that had been home to his family for several generations.

"He was a bright boy, destined for great things, and his family pinned all their hopes on him. There was an old lady in Helmsdale with a bit of money to spare and no children of her own - she took an interest in him. She paid for him to go to university in Edinburgh where he studied to be a lawyer.

"So he's in Edinburgh, and he's preparing to join the legal profession. He's chosen the law because he believes it's the best way to fight for the rights of the dispossessed. But he finds that the reality is a lot more restrictive than he expected. So when he meets a man called Thomas Mulock, an Irish journalist whose stated aim is to expose the injustices suffered by the people of Scotland, he gives up the law to join him.

"Together Iain and Mulock toured the Highlands, seeking out evidence of the suffering caused by the evictions. And they didn't have to look too hard. Everywhere they went they were confronted by people who had lost everything, trying to eke a living out of nothing. Famine had been followed by cholera, followed by more famine. Whole families were found starved to death in the makeshift huts that they now called home.

"By the time Mulock eventually left the Highlands in 1853 Iain had seen enough to know that what his family had suffered wasn't an isolated incident. By then he had established his own credentials. When Mulock left Iain took a job at the Inverness Courier, with the intention of demonstrating to its readers that there were two sides to the story of the Clearances."

Fin looked at Anna.

"Now you appreciate why men like Robert Gillespie weren't exactly top of his Christmas card list. And why it's hard to imagine him having anything but a pretty poor opinion of Robert's wife."

"But Robert wasn't planning to evict anyone at Kildorran, was he?"

Fin spread his hands on the table in front of him.

"I'm sorry to disappoint you, but I think you'll find that he was. After all he'd done it before."

"He had - ?"

"Didn't you know? It is rather glossed over. Charlie barely mentions it in his book. Your family don't like to think that the great Robert got himself involved in such things. But it's pretty clear that his initial reason for getting to know Lachlan Mackenzie had as much to do with his interest in the

Kildorran estate as in Fiona. You have to remember that he was a business man and a pragmatist, as well as her husband."

"But he never actually evicted anyone, did he? Not at Kildorran?"

"Not at Kildorran, no. But it certainly looked at one point as if that was his intention."

"So what made him change his mind?"

"Nobody really knows for sure. It's a bit of a mystery."

"Another mystery?"

"What do you mean?"

"Iain leaving. Robert changing his mind. Is there any way they could be connected?"

Fin frowned. "I don't see how." He looked thoughtful. "Although now I think about it…"

"Think about what?" asked Anna, her eyes fixed on his face.

"Robert ditched his plans for evictions at Kildorran only a matter of weeks before Iain left the country. It's probably a coincidence, but it kind of makes you wonder."

"I've got something that will make you wonder even more," said Anna. And she stood up and left the room.

When she returned she was holding a plastic wallet, which she handed to Fin across the table. He took it from her and slid out the sheet of paper that was inside.

"It was tucked into the back of a book in Charlie's office," she said, as he unfolded the letter. "It must have been there since… well I don't know how long. Since it was written maybe."

She came round the table to stand beside his shoulder while he read. When he finished he looked up at her with a stunned expression on his face.

"Do you think it could be from him?"

"From Iain Mackay?"

Anna nodded.

"The handwriting certainly looks like his."

"So it's possible?"

He rubbed his hand across his jaw.

"I suppose it is."

"Is there any way of checking?"

"I've got examples of his writing at home," he said slowly. "I can see if they match."

Anna took a deep breath. "You can take it away with you if it would help."

"Are you sure?"

"I wouldn't be offering if I wasn't sure," she said with a touch of her earlier impatience.

"I promise I'll be incredibly careful with it."

"You'd better be. I haven't shown it to anybody else. Apart from Barbara that is."

He got up from the table. "If I were you I'd keep it that way for now. You don't want everyone jumping on board before you've got to the bottom of what this is all about." He slipped the letter back into the plastic wallet. "You never know. This could be really big."

CHAPTER NINE

Fin drove away from Rowancross House with the precious letter locked in the glove compartment of Aunt Sarah's car. He drove as fast as the ancient Renault and the winding road allowed. If it turned out that it was Iain Mackay who had written the letter, then Anna's discovery opened up the possibility of shedding light on the one aspect of Iain's life that had always eluded him. Why had Iain emigrated? What made him leave the family and country he was so passionate about? Nobody had ever come up with a satisfactory explanation.

It could also go some way to explaining why had he never married. It had always struck Fin as curious that a man like Iain had never found himself a wife. Could Fiona Gillespie be behind it? Had he been harbouring a life long passion for the woman he had left behind? Stuck behind a caravan on the single track road to Alchitibuie Fin drummed his fingers on the steering wheel in his impatience to get past. He had to remind himself to stay cool. There was always the chance that the letter was from another Iain altogether.

Fin Maclean had grown up knowing there were family connections in Canada, and that he was distantly related to the man who had set up the Mackay Group. But it had meant very little to him. So when he found himself in Toronto to promote his second book he had no idea that a distant ancestor whose existence he had barely considered was about to play an important role in his life. He met the editor of the Eastern Courier at a publisher's party. It was Fin's North American agent, Della, who mentioned to Jimmy Blake as she introduced him, that Fin was related to the original Iain Mackay.

"You're kidding me –"

Jimmy Blake had round eyes like a goldfish. Now they narrowed to slits, and he looked at Fin with a great deal more interest than he had originally felt for a man who wrote books about the great train journeys of the world. Della was explaining to Fin that the Eastern Courier was owned by The Mackay Group.

"You must be proud to have such a guy for one of your ancestors," said Jimmy.

Fin felt the point of Della's elbow against his rib-cage. He got the message.

"Yeah, yeah… Really proud," he said, wondering where this was going.

"And is this your first book, Mr. Maclean?"

"His second. The first did very nicely," said Della, leaping in. "This latest one's looking even better. There's talk of a TV series on the back of it."

"Is there?" said Jimmy, looking Fin up and down with his expressionless eyes. "Maybe we should talk, Della…"

Della beamed at him.

"That would be great, Jimmy."

Fin left the party none the wiser. But before he flew back to London he was briefed by Della on what Jimmy Blake wanted from him.

Initially, the prospect of writing a book based on the life of a distantly related ancestor he knew little about didn't fire him with enthusiasm. He was still gripped by the travel bug, and wanted to explore more of the world before looking closer to home for inspiration. But it hadn't taken very long for him to realise that in Iain Mackay he had found the subject of a lifetime.

Iain quickly stopped being a name on the Maclean family tree and sprang into life as an all action hero. From the first moment of reading about the manner of his arrival in Newfoundland Fin was hooked. The boat that brought Iain to the New World - along with several hundred other emigrants - was a leaky old bucket, with a rotten hull that had to be tied up with rope to stop it from falling apart. That it held together for the Atlantic crossing was a miracle. There were many other more seaworthy vessels that were unable to withstand the battering of wind and waves, and abandoned their miserable passengers to a watery grave.

But Iain's boat didn't quite make it all the way. A mile or so out from shore it split at the seams. The tragedy was that having made it this far many on board were drowned. But, out of those that survived, a good few had Iain Mackay to thank for it. He managed to save at least fifteen, lashing a makeshift raft together, and paddling them to shore.

The ones who did survive must have wondered at times if they were the lucky ones after all. For this new territory was most definitely not for the faint-hearted. But there were fish to be caught in the rivers and streams, there were deer and rabbit to be hunted in the forests, and, for a resourceful and determined character like Iain, the civilization that was being carved out of the wilderness offered many opportunities. He made his way to the nearest town, and offered his services to the local paper to help record the daily progress of this fine new land.

Fin discovered that Iain Mackay had the integrity and the objectivity it takes to make a fine reporter. Plus he had wit and he had courage. In his ancestor's writing Fin found passion and the occasional burst of brilliance. Iain recorded the growing pains of his adopted country with a perceptive eye, and, as he read, Fin felt that for the first time he truly understood how hard it must have been for the early settlers. Besieged in their homeland by speculators and ship masters who saw them as a profit opportunity, they suffered terribly on the crossing to their new land. They arrived with the promise of the bare essentials to make a life for themselves, and all too often found nothing but inhospitable weather, harsh conditions, poverty, and disease.

Those who came in the early days fought with the indigenous people of their new land, the tribes of native North America. Those that came later begged and starved in the streets of the new cities. Iain Mackay was an articulate witness to the suffering of his fellow emigrants. And the record he made of what he saw still had the power to move a hundred and fifty years later.

It was a great story that unfolded, and the more he discovered the more Fin became fascinated by the man who reported the events with such clarity and understanding. But everything he had been given or directed to by Jimmy Blake related to Iain's life in Canada. When Fin went back to the UK he began to research Iain's life before he emigrated. Which was when Sarah introduced him to Charlie Gillespie. Fin found more than enough to give him a good understanding of Iain's family and background. But at no point did he come across anything to explain why Iain made the decision to leave the Highlands. The detail and the interest of those who had commissioned the book lay with Iain's time in Canada, and it was on this period of his life that Fin was required to concentrate. But something was missing. And he knew it.

⤚◆◆⤙

When Barbara returned from her shopping trip she found that Anna had prepared lunch for them both.

"Wonderful girl," she said, settling herself down on one of the kitchen chairs. "I'm going to miss this when the time comes for you to leave. Which – by the way - I'm hoping won't be for a good while yet."

Anna laughed. "You and me both."

She sat down opposite Barbara.

"By the way," she said. "I've got a bone to pick with you. Thanks for dropping me in it with Fin this morning."

Barbara had the good grace to look guilty.

"I thought it was only fair to give him the chance to redeem himself."

Anna shook her head at her.

"Thanks for warning me."

"So how did you get on this time?"

"This time it was OK."

"So you showed him the letter?"

"I did." Anna raised an eyebrow at her stepmother. "Wasn't that what you wanted me to do?"

Barbara laughed.

"I didn't want you to do anything. But I'm glad that you did."

She was silently congratulating herself. Inviting Anna to stay on had been a masterstroke. She was deriving great satisfaction from watching as Anna discovered more about the family she'd spent so long trying to avoid. But she would be kidding herself if she didn't recognise that having her there gave Barbara a reason to put off the moment when she would have to decide what to do with the rest of her life. With Fin on board Anna was likely to make more progress in her quest to discover the truth about Fiona. And the more involved she became the less likely she would be to think about going home.

"You should have seen his face when I showed him the letter." Anna's voice cut through Barbara's musing. "He'd always assumed that Fiona and Iain Mackay were on opposite sides, so he was stunned."

"I'll bet he was."

"At first I don't think he couldn't quite believe it. He's taken the letter away to check the handwriting. Then we'll know for sure if it really was written by Iain Mackay."

Fin's arrival back at his aunt's whitewashed cottage was announced with a screech of brakes and a slammed car door. Shouting a quick hello to Sarah, who popped her head out of the kitchen door as she heard her poor car protesting at its harsh treatment, he went straight to the desk in front of the wide window that looked out across the bay to the island of Tanera Mor. This was where he had been struggling with his novel for the past few weeks. Now the novel was forgotten. He opened the lid of his laptop and switched it on.

He searched through the files until he found what he was looking for - extracts from the journal that Iain Mackay had written during his journey to

Newfoundland, after he had set sail from Aberdeen. Fin had taken photos of the original and download-ed them onto his computer, so that he could look at them whenever he felt in need of inspiration. It never failed to give him a thrill when he thought about Iain sitting crouched on his bunk while the ship tossed and pitched about him. But now Iain could have been writing about the price of mutton for all Fin cared. This time it wasn't the content he was interested in.

He unfolded Anna's letter and held it up to the screen, checking the handwriting. There was no doubting the similarity. The downstrokes on the capital letters were significantly thicker than the upstrokes. In both letter and journal the writer had crossed the e in the same distinctive style. There was the same elongated stroke on the f and the t.

Fin stared out of the window. A fishing boat was making its way out between the mainland and Tanera Mor to the open sea, trailing its wake behind it. He thought about phoning Anna, but what if he was wrong? Silly to get her hopes up until he was absolutely certain. He took another look at the let-ter. If Iain Mackay really had written it they could be on the brink of something very exciting. But Fin wasn't an expert, he couldn't be sure. The only way to be one hundred per cent certain was to get Jerry Baldwin to take a look at it. Jerry was a handwriting

analyst who had worked with Fin in the past. If anyone would know he would.

━⊱ ⊰━

After she and Barbara had finished lunch, Anna decided that it was far too nice an afternoon to spend
shut away in Charlie's study. She took a picnic rug
and a couple of cushions with her, and went outside
to the bench by the edge of the loch, in the shade of
a couple of ancient pine trees. The scent of pine in
the salty air was pleasantly sharp in her nostrils. She
spread out the rug on the bench, and settled herself
against the cushions.

With all the research she had done she was yet
to find the hard proof to show that Fiona and Iain
had been more than just acquaintances. But Fin had
taken the letter and perhaps even now was making
the connection between it and the samples of Iain
Mackay's writing he already had in his possession.
She wondered how he was getting on. It was frustrating having to wait for him to call. But she was going
to have to be patient.

Before Barbara had settled down to catch up on
her emails she had gone and dug out Iain Mackay's
account of his father's eviction from Strathnaver.
Anna knew that in order to properly appreciate quite
how extraordinary it would be if it did turn out that

Iain and Fiona really had been lovers she needed to know more about what Iain's family had suffered in the Clearances. Now she picked up the photocopied sheets of paper that Barbara had found for her and turned to the first page.

There was a note written in her father's distinctive scrawl across the top of the page. It said that this was written when Iain was editor of the Eastern Courier. The article appeared in January of the year 1874.

So - another hard winter. And, as we bid farewell to the old year and celebrate the birth of the new, I speak to those of you who value the past and call upon you to preserve your identity and maintain links with your fellow countrymen. All of us who come hither to this land, from wherever and with whatever reason, must embrace it as a place of adventure and opportunity, with all the fervour and optimism it deserves. But we must not forget from whence we came.

At a party to celebrate Hogmanay I spent some time in conversation with the granddaughter of a man from Sutherland. She was proud to tell me about her grandfather. He was one of the band of brave men who first came to the trading post on the Red River in the early years of this century. He came with his wife and son. The family sheltered from their first savage winter in a log cabin he built with his bare hands. And when April came he was one of the forty or so who travelled overland for nigh on two hundred miles through the ice and snow, with handmade sledges to drag their belongings, looking for a place that they could call home. He brought his family to the settlement that was to become Winnipeg, and there they restarted their lives.

This young lady knew the full story of her grandfather's bravery. The family was justifiably proud of his courage in the face of terrible hardship. But I was sad to discover that she knew nothing of his life before, nothing of the land from whence he came. She said that her grandfather would not speak of it.

We must not forget the suffering that led so many of us to choose exile. It is who we are, and what has led us to this place. Which is why I share with you this story close to my heart, the story of another man of great courage and dignity.

My father, William Mackay, was born and bred in the township of Rhifail, one of a dozen or so small settlements that once stretched along the beautiful valley of Strathnaver, in the northwest corner of the Scottish Highlands. This long narrow glen reaches down from the Atlantic to trail a fingertip in the waters of Loch Naver, deep in the heart of the county of Sutherland. It is a wild and desolate region, ruthless with its inhabitants, showing them no mercy. But my readers, you of all people will understand when I tell you that the inhabitants of Strathnaver were happy to be there. For this was the land of their fathers, and their fathers' fathers before them. It was the place they called home.

In this inhospitable location Mackays had lived for many centuries, sharing with the rest of the people of Sutherland the tendency towards insularity and hardiness that meant they relied on nobody but themselves. For they had plenty of what mattered to them. From the black cattle of the Highlands they had their milk and their butter and their cheese. They kept flocks of goats and Highland sheep. There were the tough mountain ponies - garrons suited for farm work in the hilly countryside of the north. There were potatoes and kail to be had from the land. There was meat to be taken from the hillside, fish to pull from the rivers and lochans. And this was plenty enough for the Mackays. They needed nothing more.

As the century turned on its tail, and the call went out for men to fight in the Napoleonic Wars, the Great Lady of Sutherland - the Countess Elizabeth - came up with a novel method of raising a regiment from amongst her people. She did not follow the example of the beautiful Duchess of Gordon who, in 1784, had encouraged recruitment into the Gordon Highlanders by donning a particularly fetching version of their uniform and kissing each man as he enlisted. Our lady Elizabeth did not ask for volunteers at all, but rather made it a choice between losing a son and losing a tenancy.

My father was just fifteen at the time. His mother wept and cried and raged at the cruelty of the Countess, and declared that she had to be a monster to make mothers choose between their sons and their homes. But young William went willingly with a song on his lips, relishing the opportunity to fight for his clan.

He did not see his home again for many a long year, returning for good in 1814, as the war in Europe began to see its way towards a conclusion. A musket ball in the shoulder put paid to his intentions to see the war out to its bitter conclusion. But he was pleased to return to the land he loved. When eventually he strode down the hill towards the collection of houses that clustered on the banks of the River Naver, beside the brown waters where he had fished as a boy, he did not find the welcome he had hoped for.

Back in January, blown in with the snow, had come a man called Patrick Sellar. Speaking no Gaelic he had enlisted the minister to speak for him, and thus it was from their own man of god that the tenants of Strathnaver learnt that, not only had Patrick Sellar acquired the land upon which they had lived for many years, but he was expecting them to have left it by Whitsuntide. He was also good enough to let it be known that within four years the whole of Strathnaver, from Altnaharra at the very tip of Loch Naver to Dunvedin towards the sea, would be completely cleared of its people.

When William asked his father where they were expected to go his father replied that Lord Stafford, Sellar's employer, husband to the Countess, and the man behind all of this, would provide land for everyone on the coast. Everybody knew that the daily grind of life in Strathnaver was a picnic compared to the challenge of making a living out of the cliffs and crags of the coast of Sutherland, so it was difficult to believe that anything positive would come out of the enforced move.

Since it was now getting on for the end of May, William suggested that maybe the whole thing had been a misunderstanding, and that the threat had gone away. His father could not reassure him. A surveyor had turned up as the snow melted, and begun the job of parcelling out plots of land on the coast. His family grew ill and he was forced to leave - a fact that had been seized on by William's mother as a good omen, since it suggested that the good lord was on their side. However the surveyor had reappeared earlier that month to continue with his unwelcome work.

Another discouraging sign was that significant areas of land had been put to the torch as Mr Sellar's shepherd, a weasel faced man called John Dryden, prepared the hills for pasture. Worst of all, the news had reached them that - unlike earlier evictions in other regions of the Highlands, where the people had been allowed to take away with them the timbers that had provided the framework of their homes (a small but important gesture in a land so short of trees) – this time the timber was to be burnt along with everything else, and the people would be paid its value. Which everybody knew was worse than useless in a land where it didn't matter how much money you had if there was nothing of what was needed to buy.

So the joyful homecoming was not to be. William spent the first few weeks after his return trying to find out what was going on, but nobody seemed to know very much about what was likely to happen or when. A man accustomed to action, he grew increasingly frustrated, and when his father came to him and suggested that they might head into the hills, up to the shielings, to look for the small herd of black cattle on which their livelihood depended, he was happy to do something useful, for the cattle had wandered further than usual in search of pasture that was not under fire.

He and his father were gone for a couple of days. They knew, well before they reached home, that they had chosen the wrong time to be away.

My father told me that he wasn't sure at what precise moment he smelt smoke, but the bitter tang of it was in his nostrils and at the back of his throat when they were still several miles from home. He and his father did not need to speak. With a glance at each other they broke into a run, striding across the heather and bracken, leaving the hard sought cattle to their own devices. As they drew nearer they saw great billowing clouds of smoke rolling up into the sky, and could hear the sound of shrieks and cries, of dogs barking and the hoarse sound of men cursing.

Years of soldiering meant that William was fitter than his father, and he was the first to reach the boundary of the township. On his way between the houses he passed scenes that made him wonder if he was back in France. A young boy, naked and shivering, stood and waited, wide eyed with fear, as a girl handed clothes to him from the doorway of a house whose roof was on fire. Next door an old woman sat in a crumpled heap on the bare earth, her skirts spread out around her, wailing and sobbing as she watched the only home she had ever known crumble in the flames and crash to the ground before her. Around about them men carried torches to set fire to houses from both ends, ignoring the pitiful protests of the inhabitants. If William had not been intent on reaching his own house he would have stopped and waded in to try and prevent the worst of the destruction, but he had his family to think about.

He reached his home just in time to see his mother being dragged from the house by an evil looking ruffian, who swore at her as he pulled her through the open doorway. She was struggling for all she was worth, clinging to the doorframe, kicking and crying out, and as William rushed forward he saw why. Inside the doorway he caught sight of his sister Grace, ashen faced, her body bent double in pain, crying out that she would never leave her home alive.

"Then ye'll die there, lassie," called out one of the other men, waving a flaming torch in the air, so that sparks fell all around him. "This house will be the bonfire for your funeral pyre."

He bent to the ground and touched his torch to a pile of faggots that had been laid against the wall of the house. William heard his mother cry out, begging with the men to help her carry Grace away from the flames. But they laughed and mocked her cries. Can you not see, called poor Mary Mackay, she is about to have a baby. But the men stood back and did nothing as the flames began to lick up the wall of the house.

William leapt through the door, and picked up his sister in his arms. Carrying her outside, he set her down beside his mother and turned back. Flames were billowing out from the walls. With his bare hands William tore at the stone, trying to save as much of the precious wood as he could, before it was consumed by fire.

But there was little he could do. His hands were bleeding and blistering within seconds, but he managed to drag several good lengths of timber away from the walls and, as the roof began to collapse, he was able to seize a few more. He pulled away all that he could, and then he turned to look for his mother and sister. His father had reached them and had picked up his weeping daughter, and was carrying her away from the flames towards a stand of gnarled trees on the hillside.

It was a pitiful sight. William felt a wave of anger surge in his chest, and tears well up in his smoke filled eyes. He brushed at them angrily with a blackened hand and turned back to his task, and as he did he caught sight of a man standing motionless in the middle of the chaos, a man made conspicuous by his lack of action, a spectator in the midst of hell. And he knew, without having to be told, that the man was the new landowner, Patrick Sellar, and that he watched the proceedings with approval.

William carried the salvaged timber to the river and began to fashion a raft out of it. For he had come up with a plan to float the wood downstream, and find a suitable

*place where he could dismantle his craft and build a hut
to provide shelter for his family. He was forced to return to
the houses to find something to secure the wood for the short
journey he had in mind. And came back to the river to find
the same evil faced devil that had set fire to his home watching and laughing as the sorry craft crackled and burned.
William would have murdered him where he stood. But the
coward was surrounded by companions, and William could
see that at least one of them was armed. Good sense pre-
vailed, and he went away to find his family and do what he
could to help them.*

*They stayed in the hills for several days, while the ruins
smouldered, and the people exchanged sad stories of all they
had suffered and everything they had lost. At last, when
they realised there was nothing else to be done, several of
them began to make their way towards the coast, and the
new lives that had been assigned to them.*

*My family did not go east, but went towards Alnaharra
at the head of the loch, where they found a home with Grace's
husband and his people. They felt themselves the lucky ones
when they heard of the conditions faced by those who wound
up on the coastal allotments handed out to them. For who
could be expected to grow anything on narrow strips of land
on the cliff's edge, where the seed blew away in the high
wind, and salt and seawater destroyed anything that did
manage to find a foothold.*

*For William and Mary it was not the end. They
were to face eviction twice more, before finally they gave*

up, and left the valley that had been home to more than five generations of our family. In 1815 they moved to Grummore, after facing eviction for the second time. In 1819 a posse of men approached the valley, giving the people an hour to evacuate their homes. My family ended up in Helmsdale. But many others chose to emigrate, rather than face a life on the coast. Along the Red River Valley, here on the plains of Canada, are the descendants of the people of Strathnaver – Mathesons, Gunns, Macbeths, and Mackays.

It is hard to believe, but when they went they were accused of treachery. "The idle and lazy alone think of emigration," said James Loch, one of the architects of the Clearances. By god he should have seen what these 'idle and lazy' folk have achieved out here.

But my father was beaten. No longer the brave soldier, proud father, loving husband; he became a shadow of his former self. He never truly recovered.

Anna finished reading and leaned back against the cushions. She stared out across the loch. In the peace of a summer's afternoon it was hard to imagine such terrible events taking place not so far away from where she sat. Of course Iain Mackay had been anxious and angry when he met Fiona for the first time at her father's funeral. He must have been terrified that the fate that befell his family in Strathnaver was about to be inflicted on his sister at Kildorran.

Anna was swept by a wave of sudden doubt. It wasn't a promising start to an affair. Fiona must have seemed like the enemy.

CHAPTER TEN

Why hadn't Fin rung? What if it wasn't Iain Mackay who wrote the letter after all?

The sun had disappeared behind a cloud, and the loch was suddenly grey. Doubt, unbidden and unwelcome, had lodged itself in Anna's mind. She had seen a name in her father's book and leapt on it. But it was a common name in the area. And pretty much everything she had discovered so far suggested that, far from being potential lovers, the reality was that Iain and Fiona were more likely to have loathed each other. Fin was playing along with her. He probably felt guilty at the way he had behaved when they first met. He had only taken the letter away with him to be kind.

Anna shivered, suddenly chilled to the bone. Without the sun the wind was cold against her skin. If the letter wasn't from Iain Mackay she was back at square one, in other words nowhere. Maybe the time had come to consider going home, going back to her old life. The thought of it made her feel breathless. Which came as a shock to her. How had this unwelcome situation crept up on her without her noticing?

She gathered up her things and went inside. The sound of the radio drifting down the corridor told her that Barbara was in the kitchen.

"Everything OK?"

Barbara was cleaning shelves. Activity was one of her strategies for dealing with difficult emotions. Anna envied her.

"Don't suppose Fin has called, has he?"

Barbara shook her head. Anna sat down at the kitchen table.

"You know what it means?" she said, dropping her head into her hands. "It's not from Iain Mackay. The letter. He would have rung straight away if it was."

Barbara peeled off her rubber gloves.

"Give the guy a chance, Anna."

"He must think I'm a complete idiot."

Barbara looked mystified.

"What's brought this on?"

"That letter could have been from anybody. There's absolutely nothing to suggest that it was Iain Mackay who wrote it?"

"Yes there is," said Barbara calmly. She ticked the points off on her fingers. "We know for sure that they knew each other. The letter said that he was going away. We know Iain Mackay left the country at that time. And didn't you say that Fin recognised the handwriting?"

"He thought he did -"

"There you go then."

"It's not much to go on."

"It's quite a lot to go on if you ask me."

"So why hasn't Fin rung then?"

Barbara wrinkled her brow.

"Maybe he has. I think I heard your mobile ring a couple of times. Perhaps it was him."

"He doesn't have my number," said Anna. But she went to look just in case.

But it wasn't Fin who had been trying to get hold of her. It was Richard. She frowned at his name on the screen. Did she want to speak to him? Not at that precise moment, no. But when did they last talk? Thursday… Or was it Wednesday? It might even have been Tuesday. Damn him. She pressed ring-back and waited for him to pick up, hoping that he might not.

"So how's life in 'bonny Scotland'?"

His attempt at a Scottish accent was atrocious.

"It's fine. What about you?"

"Good. I'm good. Ready to come home though. Hotel living is beginning to really get me down."

Anna wandered into the sitting room and sat down in the corner of one of the sofas.

"I suppose it must be," she said, finding it hard to feel any sympathy for him. A hotel was her idea of bliss; people to wait on her hand and foot, no cooking, no washing, no cleaning. Although to be fair Moscow hotels probably left a bit to be desired. But she was in no mood to be fair.

"You must be about ready for home as well," said Richard.

"What makes you say that?"

"You've been up there for quite a while. Aren't you getting a bit bored with it by now?"

"I'm not in the slightest bit bored."

She knew she was being defensive, but couldn't help herself.

"I'm glad to hear it," he said, although he didn't sound like he meant it.

"So what about you?" Anna wasn't letting him off the hook. "When are you coming home?"

"I'm not absolutely sure yet. Soon I hope." A pause. "How about you?"

"I'm not sure either."

Another silence.

"You must have some idea -"

"You haven't. I haven't. I'm having a great time up here. If you're not ready to come back yet, there's really no reason for me to leave, is there?"

"I suppose not. I just don't like the thought of the house being left empty for so long."

"You're saying I should go back and make sure the house isn't lonely," she said in a tight voice.

She heard him sigh.

"Now you're being ridiculous."

She took a deep breath.

"I'll come back when you do. Just let me know when that is likely to be."

She hung up.

⚊⧺ ⧺⚊

It was as if a hand had taken hold of her heart, and was squeezing it. Suddenly everything – the future, her marriage, Fin's silence - felt too much for her. She couldn't face Barbara. She tossed her phone onto the sofa, and went out through the front door and into the garden.

The sky had cleared and the loch had settled back to the blue she was used to. But the sight of it failed to weave its usual magic. Tears of anger were clouding her vision. She brushed the back of her hand across her eyes, and stumbled across the gravel drive and over the grass to the old grey bench where she had sat and read earlier that day. The wooden slats were warm with the sun's rays. Anna leant back and closed her eyes. Her heart beat loud in her ears. Just breathe, she told herself. Just breathe.

How long did she sit before she heard a car turn into the driveway and crunch over the gravel to the front door? However long it was, it wasn't enough. She sat without moving, hoping that whoever it was wouldn't notice her.

But they did.

"Hello there."

It was all she needed. It was Cameron. He called through the window as he pulled up and switched off the engine. There was no escape. The car door slammed, and he was striding across the grass towards her.

"Haven't seen you for a while. Wondered how you were getting on. Just on my way back from Lochinver. Thought I'd pop in."

She dipped her face so it was hidden by the curtain of her hair. If she had to choose the last person she wanted to find her crying Cameron would be at the front of the queue. He arrived beside her.

"Hey." She didn't look up. All she could see of him was his feet. "What are you doing out here on your own? Are you feeling alright?"

Anna held her breath. Go away, Cameron.

"Anna…?"

"I'm fine. Just enjoying the view."

"I can see that. Grass looking good, is it? It's one of my favourite views too." He made a move as if to sit down beside her.

Comedy. Just what she needed. She didn't shift to give him space to sit.

"Anything I can do to help?"

She waved a hand at him, still not looking up

"No… Thanks."

"Are you sure?"

He really wasn't going to give up, was he?

"It's nothing… Honestly… A silly argument, that's all."

"Not with Barbara?"

"Oh no."

He crouched down in front of her.

"Anna." His voice was surprisingly gentle. "I know I'm just a blundering male, and probably the last person you want to share your troubles with."

Got it in one, Cameron.

"But you look really down in the dumps sitting out here all on your own. And you know what they say about a problem shared. Anyway…" He began to straighten up. "If you need one, there's a shoulder here for you to cry on."

It was amazing, thought Anna, the way he could transform himself into a genuinely nice person when the occasion arose.

"That's really thoughtful of you, Cameron," she said, looking up at him.

"It is, isn't it?" he said, laughing. "Sometimes I surprise even myself."

Anna laughed too, and felt the gloom lifting a little. She made space for him to sit down.

"You don't have to tell me what's upsetting you if you don't feel like it." He tucked himself in beside her. "Let's just sit and enjoy that view of yours."

She was pressed against his shoulder. The citrus tang of his aftershave mingled with the salt and pine. He shifted slightly to make more room for them both. They watched as the sun began to slide towards the horizon. The occasional bleating from the sheep on the hillside only served to emphasise the silence, until Cameron stretched out his arms, and sighed, and dropped his arm along the back of the bench behind her. It was such a schoolboy trick she couldn't quite believe he was trying it. Maybe he wasn't. But then he dropped his arm across her shoulders and edged closer.

Anna stood up.

"I think that's enough view for one day. Barbara will be wondering what's happened to me."

He stood up beside her.

"Don't go," he said, taking her hand. "Stay and talk to me. You still haven't told me what's upsetting you."

Anna slid her hand from his grasp.

"Thanks Cameron. But I'm fine. There's really nothing to talk about."

"Was that Cameron?" asked Barbara. She had stopped cleaning shelves and was sitting at the kitchen table reading the paper.

"Yes," said Anna.

"Has he gone?"

"He has."

"What was he after? Didn't he want to stay for a drink?"

"What he wanted, amongst other things, was for me to pour out my troubles to him."

Barbara stared.

"You've got troubles? I wondered why you'd disappeared." She frowned at Anna over the rim of her reading glasses. "Anything I can help with?"

"I wish you could. But no… Thanks."

"Well, whatever they are, don't share them with Cameron."

"Don't worry. I'm not going to." Anna sat down opposite her. "He was being a little bit… overfriendly."

Barbara shook her head. "He is a boy, isn't he? He tried it on with me once, when I first got up here. I never told Charlie. He would have gone round and challenged him to a duel or something crazy like that."

"Really?" Another side to her father she didn't know about. "Didn't it make things rather awkward?"

"Oh, I didn't take him seriously. I don't think he can help himself. He's one of those men who can't rest until he has proved to himself that he is irresistible to every women he meets. Even ancient old birds like me." She folded her newspaper. "The person I feel really sorry for is Laura."

"Laura?"

"His housekeeper –"

"The girl with the hat?"

"That's the one."

"Why do you feel sorry for her?"

"Because she's the one who sits at home and waits for him to notice her. And she's not even his wife, for crying out loud. He pays her an absolute pittance, to wash for him and clean for him and cook for him. And probably you know what for him. And he hasn't got the decency to marry her."

"Why does she put up with it?"

"Because she adores him. And because presumably she believes that one day he will open his eyes and realize what's under his nose."

"She's a fool."

Barbara glanced at her.

"You're very unforgiving. What's brought this on? Is it anything to do with what's bothering you? Do you want to talk about it?"

"There's no point. It won't change anything."

"Fair enough."

"Nothing from Fin I suppose?"

Barbara shook her head.

In the bar at his hotel in Moscow Richard Sinclair called a waiter over and ordered himself a drink. At the table next to him three men in matching grey suits sat opposite each other drinking iced vodka. Their conversation was muffled by the thick carpets and low hum of the air conditioning. Richard settled back in his chair and watched the door, waiting for his colleagues to join him. The waiter brought him a gin and tonic in a long glass beaded with condensation. He took a sip, and felt better as the alcohol began to take effect.

He was strung out and exhausted. The irritation he felt after his conversation with Anna hung over him like a cloud. He took another swallow of gin, hoping that it would help. What the hell was she playing at? She hadn't wanted to go to Scotland in the first place, so what was she still doing there? She should be at home. He wished he was back there now. He hated to think of the house being left empty for so long. He imagined rooms disappearing under layers of dust, grass growing out of control, the post piling up unopened in the hallway. Life was difficult enough for him at the moment, without having to worry about things at home. The Moscow office was proving more troublesome than he had envisaged when they first set it up. The last thing he needed right now was for Anna to make things more complicated.

"Hey Rich…"

His junior manager materialised in front of him. Richard ground his teeth and wondered whether it was worth reminding him for the umpteenth time that his name was Richard.

"I brought Yelena with me. Thought you wouldn't mind. Jonathan's just taking a leak."

A pretty dark eyed girl was standing in Andrew's wake, wearing a very short skirt and too much make up. Richard remembered that he had met her before somewhere, but he couldn't think where. She was something to do with PR. She held out a manicured hand.

"Hello Richard. So good to see you again."

Her accent was not unattractive. He smiled.

"What can I get you to drink, Yelena?"

In all the years that Richard had spent traveling it had never happened before. It must have been the alcohol. He couldn't remember how much he'd had, but it had been a lot. There were several large gins in the bar, and then wine with the meal. After dinner they went to the club in the basement of the hotel, where they played drinking games with Russian vodka. He had been rather pleased to notice that both Andrew and Jonathan showed the effects of the alcohol well before he did. At about one in the morning Andrew slid sideways off the bar stool, stumbled, almost fell, heaved himself up, and disappeared. Jonathan stayed put, leaning against the bar with his bleary eyes just open. But in every other sense he might just as well have been unconscious. Yelena showed no outward sign that she had been drinking at all. The noise in the club was deafening. The lighting was so dim that it was difficult to see much. Richard and Yelena sat side by side on a velvet bench seat.

"You are married?" asked Yelena, taking his left hand in her cool palm and stroking his ring finger with the tip of her index finger. He had to lean close to her to hear what she was saying.

"Yes," he replied, watching her moving finger.

"Your wife is at home?"

"No she bloody well isn't..."

Yelena's eyes widened.

"With you? Here?"

He shook his head.

"No, no… I don't really know where she is. Somewhere in the wilds of Scotland. God knows what she's doing up there."

"Ah," sighed Yelena into his ear. Suddenly she was sitting even closer to him. "You are lonely. It is hard to be lonely."

At his aunt's house in Achiltibuie Fin was finding it hard to settle to anything. He had rung Jerry and explained what he needed. Jerry had suggested that he email a copy of both examples of the handwriting, which he had done. Now all he could do was wait. But it was the waiting that was so difficult. Because, now Fin had time to think about it, he was beginning to wonder if he might have jumped to the wrong conclusion about Iain Mackay being the author of the letter. If Fiona and Iain had become romantically involved while Fiona was married to Robert, and if they had got themselves mixed up in some kind of trouble, wouldn't it have come out somewhere? Fiona was the wife of a famous politician; Iain Mackay was making a name for himself as a journalist. Somebody somewhere must have known about it.

Fin sat down in front of his computer. Perhaps he had missed something. He opened the file containing pages from Iain's account of his voyage across the Atlantic. If Iain and Fiona had been romantically involved, then the ship was carrying him away from the only woman he ever loved. Surely in his writing there had to be some clue to how he was feeling about it.

Day fifteen, read Fin, *and today Janet Campbell died. She had been a friend of my sister Maggie from our days at Helmsdale. I remember her from when they were girls. She used to come and call for Maggie when the summer herring came to the waters off the coast and the woman were called upon to go and help with the catch. Even at fifteen she was a strong brave girl. I went with them to watch the men go out, and I remember seeing her wade out through the choppy water to her father's boat. Beside her was her mother who carried Janet's father upon her back, keeping him out of the water so that he might set forth for the night's fishing in dry clothes. Janet carried the provisions, holding them high above the waves; a keg of water and a supply of oat bannocks for each man.*

I had not seen Janet for some years, but we met again on the jetty at Aberdeen, the day before our boat was to set sail. I would not have noticed her if she had not called out my name. All around me was hustle and bustle, but I didn't see any of it. All I could think of was what I was leaving behind me. And I was like a blind man.

Janet had to tug at my arm before I noticed her. But when I recognised her I was shocked. Hunger and deprivation had left their mark upon her, and the once blooming and bonnie lass was a shadow of the girl I remembered. She told me that she had married the previous year, and that she and her husband Murdoch had made the decision to emigrate after the failure of the potato harvest. She said that they were prepared for a hard voyage, but considered that it would be worth it if it meant they could escape from the hardship they had faced at home to a better life in a new land.

Seeing Janet that day was a good thing. Because the truth was that my resolve had been weakening. But the sight of Janet's gaunt face and wasted body reminded me of the horrors I had seen. I could not stay in a country that placed so little value on its own people. I had made the only decision I could. Which was to leave. No matter how much pain it brought me.

Janet died because she had no strength left to fight. She was one of seventeen to die this day, and her death brings the total fatalities to thirty-one since our voyage began. Cholera and typhus have made their contribution, encouraged to breed in the dire conditions under which most of the passengers of this vessel have been forced to travel.

I paid pretty much all I had for my passage. I was in no mood for being sociable, and wanted the privacy of my own quarters so that I might properly mourn what I was leaving behind me. My accommodation is vastly superior to that endured by the passengers in steerage, although the partition I had been promised by the captain never materialized, so the privacy I sought is denied me

Yesterday I saved some bread and meat to take to Janet. When Murdoch took me down and showed me his berth I could not credit that this space was considered fit for a human being for even one day, let alone the five to six weeks of the journey. It was hard to believe that these poor souls had paid good money for this degradation.

When I saw the terrible conditions under which they travelled I was ashamed of the way I had been wallowing in my own unhappiness. One man's misery counts for nothing compared to what these people are being forced to endure. The stench alone is enough to make one ill. There is no possibility for fresh air to enter, and no provision for the basic requirements of human sanitation. Combine this with the fact that the swell of the ocean had rendered many of the passengers unwell and you can imagine the effect.

In the bowels of the ship there are several hundred passengers unfortunate enough to be traveling steerage. They are expected to live cheek by jowl, men and women, old and young, on long shelves of coarse pinewood. These shelves are no more than three feet wide and maybe six feet long, and they are positioned in such a way that there can be no more than two feet of headroom. To add insult to injury even this meagre space has to be shared with another. I have spoken with the captain about the situation, and he is a reasonable enough fellow. But I think he had no idea of the numbers he would be called upon to carry. Unfortunately he has no Gaelic, and the people cannot understand him when he comes to explain and find out what needs to be done.

I could see immediately that Janet was in a bad way. I found the poor soul lying amidst the squalor and filth, with the other passengers, men, women and children, feeding and sleeping and fighting and crying all about her while she lay dying. I saw that there was little to be done for her. Murdoch spoke to her and wiped her brow and told her to be strong. But I think he knew that the journey for her was nearly over. I turned away and left them to their sorrow and returned to the fresh air on deck.

Later Murdoch came and joined me as I stood by the rail and stared across the waves at the distant horizon. He stood beside me and didn't look at me as he told me that Janet was gone. "To a better place I hope,' said I. Tears sprang into his eyes and he wiped his arm across his face. 'It's together we were supposed to be… going to that better place. That is why we are on this godforsaken ship.'

I put my hand on his shoulder while he hung his head and wept.

"It's knowing that I'll never look on her face again that I cannot bear," he said.

And his words struck a chord deep within me, and I felt the ache in my heart as I thought of what I had left behind and would never see again.

"You're up late."

Sarah walked past the open door on her way to bed. Seeing him still working she came in and rested her hand on his shoulder.

"Book going well?"

He looked up. His hair was tousled and his eyes were tired. She was reminded of when he was a little boy, and he used to come up to stay with her, and she would find him in bed after midnight still reading.

"I'm not working on the book. This is something else."

She glanced over his shoulder.

"Iain Mackay? I thought you'd finished with him."

"So did I. But I was wrong."

CHAPTER ELEVEN

It was only just past five thirty when Anna woke the next morning. She lay for a while, listening to the seagulls shrieking outside her window. She had spent an unsettled night. At some point, in the long hours between one and three, it had become blindingly obvious that she had been wrong about Iain Mackay. In the light of day this conclusion still seemed the only possible explanation for Fin's failure to call.

She got out of bed, slipped her feet into a pair of moccasins, and pulled on her robe. Padding softly past Barbara's room, she went downstairs and let herself out through the front door. At this time of day the air outside was cool and soft. Trails of mist hovered above the surface of the loch like smoke. Anna walked across the dew-soaked grass to the water's edge. As she looked out towards the far side of the loch she thought of her father. Barbara had told her how he used to like to get up early and walk beside the loch; she wished he was there with her now.

She thought about how, when she was a little girl, he used to come and sit on the edge of her bed at night and tell her stories. One of her favourites was about a magical land where the air tasted of honey, and the mountains were so tall that they pierced the sky. In this place deer roamed the hills, seals played in the sea, red squirrels hid in the forests, and the fish jumped out of the water onto the rods of the fishermen. Then she had thought that it was a fantasy, conjured up out of her father's imagination. Now she understood that he had been telling her about the Highlands.

It was going to be hard going back to her old life. She felt that a door had been opened for her to a place that had always been there; she just hadn't been able to find it. Now that it looked like the door was going to close, she was frightened she might never be able to discover it again.

She pulled the robe more tightly against her. It was colder than she thought, and the dew on the grass was seeping into her moccasins. She turned and went back inside, checking the clock in the hall as she let herself in. It was still early. Barbara rarely got up before eight, so Anna went back to her room to take a shower. As she stood under the stream of hot water she made a decision. If she hadn't heard from Fin by the end of the day, she would ring Richard and let him know that she was ready to go home.

She wrapped her towel around her and went back into the bedroom. As she was pulling on her jeans she noticed out of the corner of her eye that the glass of water she had brought upstairs with her the night before was lying on its side on the bedside table. In her restlessness she must have flung out an arm and knocked it over. Next to the upturned glass was one of Fiona's journals. She could see a dark stain on the cover where water had seeped into it. Wrapping her towel around her she went quickly to the side of the bed and picked up the diary. Water dripped off the spine into the puddle left behind on the table where it had been lying.

It was the diary for 1853. Anna had been going through it the night before, looking for anything that might link Fiona with Iain Mackay or suggest that her marriage to Robert was in trouble. But this was one of the diaries where a large section of the pages were stuck together, and she hadn't been able to prise them apart. In the end she had been forced to give up and try to get some sleep.

Now she turned the diary over in her hands and attempted to soak up the damp with the corner of her towel. It was hard to tell how much damage had been done. Had that tear been there before? Were those pages coming loose? She was horrified by the evidence of her own carelessness.

But hold on… That page wasn't torn. Where previously a number of pages had been moulded together, now an edge had risen. Anna laid the diary down on the bed and picked gently with the tip of one finger. As the page lifted away from its neighbour words became visible. She stared. The soaking the book had received had worked a miracle. As the page peeled back Fiona's handwriting appeared as fresh and clean as if it had been written yesterday.

July 12th

So today was the day for us to move back home. The boys and I set off in the carriage after breakfast. Robert had gone on ahead of us, and I was pleased that he was not there to see that I was not unhappy to leave the house at Drummond, even though we have been very comfortable there.

About half way to Kildorran we stopped to feed the horses and get some food for ourselves at an inn by the roadside. The woman who served us was very kind and made us a meal of mutton and bread which Robbie fell on like a little wolf cub before the rest of us had even sat down at the table. I had to take him to one side and ask him to remember his manners. He has the same fierce appetite as his father. When his mind is set on something there is no stopping him.

We arrived to a warm welcome. John stood at the gate to greet us with a smile so wide I thought his face would split in two. I had arranged for Mary, who has been house-keeper for me at Drummond, to meet with Janet in advance of our arrival and offer her assistance in the preparations. I was relieved to see that the two of them seemed on the way to becoming friends. Janet is getting old and I think will not be able to manage with the whole family in residence. It was different when it was just my father, but we have had to open up rooms that have been closed for many years, and Robert is very particular in his requirements. So I am pleased that Mary was able to come with us.

When the boys and I passed through the great door into the hall at Kildorran I swear that my ancestors in the paintings that hang on the walls were smiling to see us. A meal was waiting for us and Robbie made no mention of the fact that he had already eaten that day but fell on it with the greatest enthusiasm. Robert laughed and said that we would all end up as fat as English lords if this was an example of how we were to be looked after at Kildorran.

My boys seemed happy to be there. They will have to work hard on their Gaelic for there are some here who speak no English, but they are comfortable with it already and will grow more accustomed to using it as time progresses. It is Robert who will have to make more of an effort if he wishes to be truly accepted.

July 25ᵗʰ

Now that we are here I think Robert wishes to show off a little as the new laird for he has already invited guests to visit us, some of his business associates from the south who will bring their wives with them. He has given us little warning, so I hope we will be ready to receive them in the style they no doubt expect.

I have been doing my best to think of ways to amuse them while they are here. My second cousin Catherine has recently married a southerner. The wedding took place in Shropshire but the couple are to travel north next week and the occasion is to be marked with a festival of Games, to which our guests and we have been invited. After the Queen attended the Games at Braemar it seems that everybody wants to follow her example so I think they will like it. We are also to host a dinner for our guests in the banqueting hall, where we have arranged for a piper to play during dinner and afterwards. Robert tells me that the ladies have taken this very seriously and have been taking lessons in Highland dancing.

Anna skipped through the description of the rest of the preparations Fiona was planning. She would go back to them when she had more time, but now she was looking for any mention of Iain Mackay.

August 11th

I wish I could say that I enjoyed our trip to the Games. I have so many happy memories of attending such occasions with my father when I was a child. Seeing Robbie this morning reminded me of how it used to be. But I couldn't share his excitement. I had woken up with a sinking feeling, and couldn't look forward to the day ahead with anything other than dread.

Our guests have been with us now for three days, and it feels like a lifetime already. We have gone out of our way to offer the best hospitality we can provide, although I am aware that Kildorran is lacking in many of the luxuries to which they are accustomed, but I get the impression that the women in particular view me as some kind of quaint but ignorant savage.

Certainly, when they arrived, they declared themselves enchanted to be staying in such a place, as if it was something out of a fairy tale. The men seem to be enjoying themselves. They go out with Robert each morning, and we see nothing of them until late. But the novelty of staying in the Highlands seems to have lost its appeal for the wives, and I have overheard them complaining to each other on a number of occasions – about the cold and the damp and the plain food. They make a great fuss of the wild nature of the countryside and the harshness of the weather, even though it has been quite pleasant for the past few days. I catch them staring at me from time to time, so that I begin to wonder if there is something wrong with my dress, or my hair, or my entire being. Sometimes they whisper behind their hands when I pass a comment, so that I begin to feel that everything I do is wrong, and cannot relax even when I am alone in my room.

One thing that does seem to please them is the prospect of going to the Games, and there has been much playful conversation over dinner as they ask us about what to expect. Sometimes they laugh so loudly when I explain to them about the caber tossing or the sword dancing, that I wonder if they think I am making a joke of some kind. They are particularly interested in seeing how their husbands fare against 'the natives' (as they insist on calling the local men) and are keen to see our local boy, Donald, the son of one of the ghillies, who is competing in the hammer throwing contest and is expected to do well.

I had hoped to ride with the men on the journey. But Robert was short tempered with me when I suggested it and insisted that I travel in the carriage with the other ladies. I was already angry at the insistence of Marjory that we take her carriage - as if ours was in some way inadequate - so it was with reluctance that I took my place alongside them.

We had a journey of some ten miles. We set off in a group and the party travelled together, the men and the boys on horseback alongside the carriage. There was a deal of eagerness as we made our way; much boasting of challenges to come, bets laid between those of the men who were intending to try their hand at some of the sport on offer. There was also great excitement at the prospect of seeing Auld Angus, a famously gigantic man from the neighbouring estate who, it was rumoured, could toss a caber a full twenty feet further than anybody else. The atmosphere was jovial, the women all in good spirits, behaving in a most friendly manner towards me, and I began to feel that I might have misjudged them. After a while the men grew tired of staying beside us and they rode on. Then the atmosphere changed, and my companions grew dissatisfied and began to complain - at the state of the roads, the warmth of the sun, even the shrill sound of the birds in the trees.

Marjory urged her man to make the horses go faster, and we went along at a good pace, until we turned a corner and came upon a man who stood at the roadside with his wife and children. At first I thought there was pile of rags in the dust beside the woman, but when we drew nearer I saw that it was a child. I made the carriage stop to see what help we could offer. The woman, poor creature, turned her face up to me and put her hand on the side of the carriage as if she would fall to the ground without the support it provided her. Immediately I called to the man – who must have been a fine, strong fellow at one time, but now his bones jutted out under his skin and there were circles of black beneath his eyes. I asked him what was their trouble. He spoke low and fast, so it was difficult to make out the words, but I gathered that they were on their way from a township some twenty miles away, having been recently evicted to make way for the sheep of a Lowlander, a Mr James Boyd, who had recently bought the estate.

The man said that the land they had been forced to abandon was good land. He and his family had raised sheep and cattle, grown vegetables and corn, and made a good living. But the previous owner, a Mr MacDonnell, had wished to *rid himself of responsibility for his tenants. Two hundred people had been thrown out of their homes, and those who refused to emigrate were forced to hide in the hills.*

This poor fellow told me his wife had been preparing their meal when MacDonnell's men arrived. They took the door off while the water in the pot was coming to the boil, emptied the pot onto the fire, and ordered the family outside to watch while their house was destroyed in front of them.

Now they were making their way to Ullapool to board a ship bound for the New World. He told me that his wife was suffering from consumption, that they had been sleeping in the open air, and he was afraid that the damp weather had made her condition a great deal worse. Were it not for the children he whispered to me that he almost thought it would be a blessing if she were to die.

I was close to tears by the time he had finished telling me his story, but, while I wondered how they could be helped, I heard Marjory make a sound behind me, and she put a hand on my arm and urged me to leave them to continue their journey and allow us to get on our way. I was taken aback at her lack of feeling, but the other ladies insisted that it was the best thing, and Marjory's manservant looked in a stern way at the poor husband and told him to stand back. Before I could stop him we had moved off and left them behind us.

I was so much upset by what I had seen and heard that I could think of nothing else for the rest of the journey. The

*other ladies soon fell to chattering and laughing as if noth-
ing untoward had happened, and they all but ignored me
until Marjory smiled at me in her condescending way, and
told me that it was a sad thing to see folk in such a state,
but it was in all likelihood brought on by their own failure
to manage things as they should. I had to bite my tongue to
stop myself from crying out at her for her ignorance. I knew
that Robert would be angry with me if I lost my temper with
our guests. So all I could do was stare out of the window
of the carriage and wonder why I had not known that such
terrible events were going on so close to home.*

*The journey could not be over too soon. Before long we
heard the sound of cheering and shouting, and soon we
could see the flags and the tents and the crowds of people.
The other ladies were greatly excited and cried out to the
driver to go faster, but I was quiet and could not share
their elation. As soon as we arrived I left them to search for
Robert, for I was desperate to tell him what I had seen and
ask him if he could send somebody back to offer help to the
poor man and his family.*

*But I did not find my husband. As I made my way
across the field past a group of people who stood in the shade
of a great oak tree, I caught my shoe on a tussock of rough
grass and stumbled. I would have fallen had it not been for
someone beside me who put out an arm to hold me up. As
I straightened up and turned to thank my rescuer I found
that it was Iain MacKay who was gazing down at me. He
had taken hold of me around my waist to stop me from*

falling, and his arm still held me as he asked me in his deep voice if I was all right.

I was already upset - by the shock of nearly falling, by the rude and unfeeling behaviour of the ladies in the carriage, by the sad sight of the evicted family, and by the absence of my husband when I needed him - and I found that I was trembling and it was difficult to answer him. I had to turn my head away, so that he would not see how close I was to shedding tears.

He realised that I was in some distress and gently, almost as if I were a child, he drew me over to where a fallen tree provided a seat. He made me sit down while he went to fetch me some water to drink. When he came back I had managed to regain something of my composure, so that when he asked if I was feeling a little better I was able to reassure him. He was watching me with such a look of concern in his eyes and he asked me in the kindest way if there was anything that he could do to assist me. In my shaken state I found myself suddenly filled with a strong desire to tell him the whole sorry story.

I am not by any means given to spilling my heart out to strangers, but before I knew it I had told him all about what had happened. Not just about the sad family and their terrible situation, but about the dreadful women who had come to stay with us, and how they had spoken of the poor people on the roadside as if they were little better than animals. But after I had said this I wished that I had kept quiet, for in an instant his manner changed. The look in his eyes was almost murderous, so that I felt quite alarmed and stood up to leave him.

Then he looked full of remorse and begged my forgiveness. He said that it was very hard to hear of the suffering of his fellow Highlanders, and that it made him very angry to think of people being thrown out of their homes. I was reminded of our first meeting, so I said that I was looking for my husband to tell him what I had seen, and felt sure that he would do something to help the poor family.

I spoke in earnest, but Mr Mackay gave a scornful shake of his head as he listened to me. When I asked him what he meant by this he shook his head again and told me that it was no concern of mine. At this it was my turn to grow angry, for I was weary of all the dissembling and double meanings. I'm ashamed to say that I stamped my foot and tossed my head and accused him of being ignorant and impertinent, for he seemed to be suggesting that he found me foolish, and I had been hurt and humiliated enough for one day already.

Then he took me by the hand and drew me to sit down beside him, and he apologised for insulting me. He said that he owed it to me to deal honestly with me, but that he thought I was misguided about my husband's intentions. At this I sprang to my feet and demanded that he explain himself

"It is not for me to explain," he said in a low voice. "I leave that to your husband."

"*You appear to have a very poor opinion of my husband, Mr Mackay,*" *I said.*

He frowned. "*If that is the way it appears I am sorry.*"

"*I think that you are not being straight with me –*"

"*I'm trying to protect you.*"

At this I was even more incensed.

"*I don't see how refusing to answer my questions is protecting me?*" *I said.*

"*Mrs Gillespie,*" *he answered, in a weary voice.* "*If you are unable to see what is going on in front of your own eyes, then it is not for me to open them for you. There are people on your very own land who go in fear of losing their homes and their livelihoods. I wonder how it is that you do not know what is happening on your own doorstep.*"

I could not believe what I was hearing. I told him that while there was a Mackenzie living at Kildorran nobody needed to live in fear of eviction.

"*But you are no longer a Mackenzie. And that is not what my sister and her husband have been led to believe,*" *he said.*

"*Who has told them such a thing?*"

He shook his head. "*It is being whispered. Nobody knows for sure where it started. But people are scared.*"

"*They have no need to be. The daughter of Lachlan Mackenzie promises it. You must tell them.*"

"*Why should they believe me?*"

I gazed at him.

"*Because you have my word.*"

Anna tried to turn to the next page. But the water spill had stopped working its magic; the remaining pages were stuck fast.

She leaned back against the pillows. It was so frustrating. To be left hanging in mid air, not knowing what happened next. She wondered if there was any way of prising the rest of the pages apart without damaging them. But when she tried to peel a corner away, all that happened was that the tear that was already there threatened to get worse.

Outside her bedroom door she heard Barbara's bedroom door open, and footsteps heading along the landing and downstairs. She looked at her watch. Already past nine o'clock; Barbara must have overslept. There was nothing for it. It was time to get on with the day ahead, time to face up to the decision she had been avoiding, but knew she was going to have to make.

She decided not to mention what she had discovered. Apart from anything else she wanted to wait for the journal to dry out properly, before confessing to Barbara about the accident with the glass of water. But she also had a feeling that Barbara might use the discovery of new information as an excuse to try and make her change her mind about leaving. And Anna knew how easily she could be persuaded.

When Barbara asked if she was interested in joining her on a trip into Ullapool, she decided to go with her, buy stamps for all the postcards she'd bought a while back and written but not posted, and then come back to the house and think about booking her flight home.

Barbara dropped Anna off in the centre of town, promising to pick her up from outside the Ferry Boat Inn in forty-five minutes. Anna browsed the shops in the back streets, looking for presents for the girls, then wandered towards the jetty. She turned the corner into the road that ran along the harbour's edge, pausing to look at the tartan scarves and fluffy green Loch Ness monsters in the windows of the shops that faced south down the loch. When she reached the newsagent she went in and queued for her stamps, picking up a couple of magazines for Barbara and a newspaper for herself.

She was scanning the headlines as she headed for the door and didn't see the woman coming in from outside. It was only when they collided and, apologizing, she took a step backwards that she recognized Cameron's housekeeper.

"It's Anna, isn't it?"

Anna nodded, feeling embarrassed.

"Yes. I'm sorry… your name… terribly rude of me -"

"It's Laura."

"Laura… Of course. How nice to see you again." Anna was aware that her response was probably more enthusiastic than the situation demanded. "You work for Cameron, don't you?"

"I do."

"You're his housekeeper?"

Laura gazed at her. "You could call it that, I suppose."

There was an awkward silence which Laura did nothing to break, and yet she showed no sign of moving aside to let Anna pass.

"Well, it's nice to bump into you. Cameron told me what a great job you do looking after him."

"He did?"

Laura continued to gaze at her.

"Absolutely." Why was Anna lying? This woman was a complete stranger to her. "He said he didn't know how he'd manage without you."

Laura snorted.

"Is that so? Well I suppose I should be grateful. After all it's not often we get the recognition we deserve, is it?"

We? What was she suggesting? Anna resented the implication that she and Laura were somehow in the same boat.

"I suppose not." She folded her newspaper under her arm. She'd had enough of this bewilderingly one-sided conversation. "Well I must get going. Barbara will be waiting for me."

Laura seemed not to have heard her. She narrowed her dark eyes at Anna.

"You've been here for a while now."

Anna sighed. Now what?

"Wasn't your husband supposed to be joining you?"

Anna thought about telling Laura that it was none of her business. But while Laura clearly had no qualms about being blunt to the point of rudeness, Anna was not going to be goaded into adopting the same approach.

"Unfortunately he couldn't make it. Business commitments he couldn't get out of."

Laura nodded.

"I see."

What did she see? Anna tucked the newspaper under her arm. "Don't let me hold you up any longer. I'm sure you're on your way to something important." Like clearing up after Cameron.

Laura stood her ground.

"I'm on my way to see my great grandmother. Just stopped in for peppermints. She likes Polos."

Anna sighed again. She was desperate to get away from this trying woman who for some unfathomable reason seemed determined not to let her go.

"Amazing to have a great grandmother who is still going strong," she said, moving sideways and taking a step towards the door.

Laura's lip curled.

"The sweets would be wasted if she wasn't."

Anna had had enough.

"Well, I'm sure she'll be very grateful," she said. And, yanking open the door, she walked out onto the street without looking back.

Anna strode along the pavement towards the Ferry Boat Inn, dodging shoppers as she went. Her encounter with Laura had stirred her up. What was wrong with the woman? Or was that how she behaved with everybody? Anna could imagine that working for Cameron must be a trial at times. But it wasn't like anyone was forcing her to do it.

There was no sign of Barbara outside the pub, so Anna crossed the road and sat down to wait for her on the low wall that ran along the edge of the harbour. She was angry with herself for letting Laura get to her. But she couldn't help it. Laura's comment about not getting the recognition that was deserved had touched a nerve.

At the far end of the loch the light was changing. Anna watched clouds gathering over the distant hills. There was a sudden shriek of excitement from beside her. A woman sitting along from her on the sea wall had caught sight of a seal in the murky waters by the jetty and was calling to her family to come and look. In an instant Anna was surrounded by excited Swedes, chattering incomprehensibly to each other and pointing at the sleek charcoal head that turned to stare at them for a moment before sliding beneath the surface.

Anna heard a voice calling her name. She turned to find Barbara leaning out of the car window, waving to her. She stood up and crossed the road. Barbara was laughing as she cleared a space for Anna on the passenger seat.

"I swear that seal is an escapee from Disneyland. Or he's on the payroll of the guys who run the tourist boats here."

The seal's head had popped out of the water again and he gazed at them out of sad brown eyes, as if he had heard and was wounded by Barbara's suggestion. The Swedes called to him, waving and laughing. Barbara grinned.

"Come on. It's like an Abba convention here. Are you ready for home?"

Anna nodded. Barbara's words were closer to the truth than she knew. She had nearly finished Fiona's journals, the ones that were legible; she had been through all the letters and newspaper articles in her father's study; she had even finished his book. In a matter of weeks autumn would be upon them, and the girls and Richard would be home. The time was fast approaching for her to return to the real world.

CHAPTER TWELVE

Back at Rowancross, Anna unloaded the shopping and handed carrier bags through the kitchen window to Barbara, who had gone inside and was waiting to take them from her. When she joined Barbara in the kitchen she found her checking messages on the answer phone. Anna began to unpack the bags.

"Nothing from Fin I suppose?"

Was that offhand enough? Barbara wasn't fooled.

"He must be tied up with something else," she said reassuringly. "Probably something to do with that novel he's writing."

Anna put milk and butter into the fridge. Not that it mattered much now she'd made her decision. But…

"All he had to do was check to see if the writing was Iain's. He must have done that by now."

Barbara was silent. Anna guessed she was struggling to think of something encouraging to say.

"Perhaps he didn't realise it was so important to you."

Anna closed the fridge door and turned to face her.

"But he did… I know he did. He hasn't rung because he's discovered that the handwriting isn't Iain MacKay's after all, and he doesn't want to be the one to tell me."

Barbara frowned.

"I'm sure it's not that."

"What other explanation could there be?"

Laura McBride drove through the level crossing at Garve, the little town south of Ullapool that offered the first sign of approaching civilization, after the stretch of rough country between Ullapool and Inverness. The rumble of the tyres, as she drove over the railway tracks, shocked her into the realisation that the last thirty miles or so had gone past in a blur. She was

irritated by this evidence of her own feebleminded-
ness. It was all the fault of Anna Sinclair. Speaking to
her in that patronising way, telling her that Cameron
had been singing her praises. It was an insult.

There were times at night, lying in bed after
Cameron had paid one of his visits to her room and
returned to his own to sleep, when Laura considered
leaving him. She knew a couple of people who would
happily employ her, and offer considerably greater
perks than Cameron – more money, her own flat,
holidays in exotic places. But she couldn't bring herself to take them up on their offers.

Once, after Cameron had downed a greater
quantity of whisky than was usual, he lashed out at
her when she accused him of being drunk, catching
her on the chin and cutting her lip. She had waited
for him to leave the house the next morning, then
dialed the number of the nice lawyer in Edinburgh
who was looking for a housekeeper. But, when a
friendly female voice answered, she had hung up
without speaking. She couldn't do it, couldn't bear to
think of Cameron managing without her. Or worse,
getting someone else in to replace her. And so she
had bathed her lip. And spent the day shopping for
and cooking his favourite meal – smoked salmon
from the Achiltibuie smokery, beef Wellington, and
chocolate mousse. And they had both pretended
that nothing had happened.

But now Laura was concerned. She knew Cameron well enough to know that he was interested in Anna Sinclair. She had been pinning her hopes on Anna's husband joining her. But Anna had given no indication that this was about to happen, or when she was planning to leave. It was entirely possible that a woman of her age would welcome the attentions of a man like Cameron. She was at that dangerous stage. A woman of a certain age, neglected by her husband, desperate to rekindle her lost youth. What wouldn't she do to inject some excitement into her life?

Laura was sunk so deep in her thoughts that she almost missed the entrance to the nursing home. Just in time she swung into the driveway of a large house and backed the car into a parking space. She switched off the engine and sat for a moment breathing deeply. She had missed her last visit, and it was more than a fortnight since she had visited her great grandmother. It wouldn't be fair to arrive in a bad mood.

━◈ ◈━

Barbara finished unpacking the shopping and made lunch for both of them. She laid a tray with bread and cheese and a bowl of apples and ordered Anna into the garden. Far away to the south clouds were gathering, but over the loch the sky was still blue, and although the breeze was shifting up a gear it was still pleasant to be outside. They sat on a rug in the shelter of the stone wall that ran along the back of the garden, and Barbara tore off a hunk of bread, spread it with butter and laid a wedge of cheddar and homemade chutney on top. She handed it to Anna who nibbled at it, trying to ignore the sinking feeling in her stomach that reminded her of the way she used to feel as a child, at the end of a holiday when the time to go back to school loomed. Barbara was watching her out of the corner of her eye. Aware of this Anna made an effort to be sociable.

"I bumped into Cameron's housekeeper in Ullapool," she said.

"Laura… Did you? How was she?"

Anna gave a short laugh.

"Difficult would be the best word to describe her."

"She's not the easiest person to talk to –"

"You know what really got to me? She pretty much suggested that she and I were in the same boat. That being a wife and being a housekeeper were one and the same thing."

Barbara selected an apple from the bowl.

"You don't want to take too much notice of Laura," she said. "She's trying to convince herself that being Cameron's housekeeper is on a par with being his wife. She looks after him; he takes her for granted. She's got to find some way of squaring the circle."

Anna glanced at her.

"You could say the same about me and Richard."

Barbara twirled the apple in her hands and thought about this for a moment.

"But you're married to Richard."

"That makes a difference?"

"Of course it does," said Barbara. She paused. "And Richard loves you."

Anna took a deep breath.

"He certainly used to. But I don't know anymore. And you know, when Laura was talking to me, I couldn't help thinking that I might just as well be Richard's housekeeper. It's the way he makes me feel sometimes."

"I'm sure he doesn't see it that way."

Anna closed her eyes. Barbara watched her face.

"You mustn't let Laura get to you, you know. The women in her family have been looking after Gillespies for centuries. She's got several lifetimes of resentment built up inside her. It would be enough to make anybody bitter and twisted."

Anna opened her eyes and looked at Barbara. "Her family has always worked for Gillespies? I didn't know that."

"Absolutely. It goes back several generations."

Barbara was so pleased to see Anna perk up and look interested that she went inside and found the notes that Charlie had made detailing the connection between the McBrides and the Gillespie family. She came back outside and sat down beside Anna.

"Here we are," she said, flicking through the sheets of paper in her hand. "Laura's mother cooked for Cameron's family when he was a boy. Her grandmother was nursemaid to Cameron's father, Cullum. Laura's great great great – wow that's a lot of greats... her three times great grandmother, Mary, was nursemaid to Fiona's youngest boy, Neil."

"You mean my great grandfather?"

"That's the one," smiled Barbara. "Jean... She's the great grandmother Laura was on her way to visit when you bumped into her, worked for Neil after he grew up and had a home of his own."

"She must be ancient?"

"She's ninety two," said Barbara, checking Charlie's notes. "Let me see.... She started as a housemaid for Neil when she was fifteen. And she worked for assorted Gillespies until she retired. She was shuffling though the papers. "Here we are. She was with Neil until he died - which was in the early forties. Then she went to work for Cameron's grandfather, Cullum. He was Fiona's grandson, the son of her oldest son, Robert."

"The Robbie who marched in the procession at his grandfather's funeral?"

"That's the one. But I don't think things worked out with Cullum. I remember Charlie telling me that he was a bit of a bastard. So Jean left him and went to Charles Gillespie, your grandfather. He tried to get her to go south with him as a cook, but she wouldn't leave the Highlands. So in the end she took her girls and went and worked for Alice."

Anna was getting lost. "Where does Alice fit in?"

So Barbara went inside again and got the family tree. "After all," she said, as she rejoined Anna in the garden, "it's important we get this right."

The Gillespie family tree was set out on a thick roll of parchment, the names and dates written in an elaborate hand by Charlie. He had started at the top of the page with Robert and Fiona, their names in thick black ink. Their marriage in 1849 resulted in the birth of three sons. Robert and Angus, the boys Anna had read about in Fiona's journals. And a third son, Neil.

Anna stared at the year of Neil's birth.

"1855… That means he was born a year after the letter was written."

Barbara sat back. "You're absolutely right. I hadn't given it a thought before."

"Which suggests that things must have been OK between them - Robert and Fiona, that is. For them to go on and have another baby." Anna frowned. "Although maybe it was an attempt to patch things up between them. Unless…"

She paused. Barbara stared at her.

"You're not suggesting…?"

Anna stared back.

"If she had an affair… It's not impossible, is it?"

"Goddammit." Barbara swore softly. Anna turned to look at her.

"What is it?"

"Why the hell hasn't Fin been in touch?"

⊷ ⊶

"Here you are, Jeanie. Here's your granddaughter to see you."

The nurse laid a hand on the old lady's arm and shook it gently. Faded blue eyes the colour of washed denim opened slowly, a face wrinkled as a prune smiled, showing empty gums and a moist pink tongue. Laura sat down beside her and took her hand. It lay in hers, light and papery as a dried leaf.

"How are you feeling today, Gran?"

The old lady nodded her head.

"Grand, dear. Just grand."

She was always grand. Laura expected that she would say she was grand on the day she died. The old lady peered at her.

"But you look tired, girl. Has that man been working you too hard?"

Laura sighed.

"No, Gran - Cameron treats me very well, you know that."

But the old lady frowned and tutted and shook her head. Laura knew that her great grandmother disapproved of her set up. Ever since Jean had worked for Cameron's grandfather she had mistrusted this particular branch of the Gillespie family. She was always happy to remind Laura that Cameron had been a spoilt and demanding child. And although it was several years since she had last seen him she refused to believe that he had improved. She was worried that the girl was throwing her life away on a good for nothing chancer, who would never marry her no matter how much she hoped for it. His grandfather had been just the same. Sleeping with the servants as if it was his right.

Laura sighed again. She could see Jean's thin lips set firm, the wrinkles etched like crevasses in rock. It was always the same when Cameron's name was mentioned. She needed to change the subject.

"I bumped into Charlie's daughter on the way here."

She knew that Jean had always had a soft spot for Charlie. Jean's eyes brightened.

"You did?"

"She came up for Charlie's memorial service. She's staying with his wife."

The old lady's face was suddenly sad.

"Oh yes," she said softly. "He died. That dear bonny lad…" She was silent for a moment. But then her eyes grew bright again. "His daughter, you say. She has come to the Highlands. She was never here before, was she? I never heard that she was here before. I would have heard, don't you think? Someone would have told me…"

She was growing agitated. Laura began to wish she hadn't mentioned it.

"I don't know, gran."

Jean struggled up in her chair and reached out her hand to her great granddaughter.

"You must bring her to see me."

Her fingers clutched Laura's arm in a grip that was surprisingly firm. Laura was taken aback.

"You want me to bring Charlie Gillespie's daughter to visit you? What on earth for?"

Jean's grip on her arm tightened.

"It's not your business, Laura. I just need you to bring her to see me."

Laura tightened her lip. What was the old woman thinking of? There was no way in the world that she was going to seek out Anna Sinclair to pass on an invitation to visit her grandmother.

"You promise you will bring her to me." The old voice was fierce.

"Yes, gran," said Laura in a soothing tone. "I promise."

━━╪ ╪━━

After Laura had gone, Jean sat in her chair and gazed out at the neat garden with its clipped box hedging and mown lawns. But she didn't see it. Instead she saw her mother, a year or two before she died.

It was just after the war. Her mother was still a young woman, only just in her fifties, but she must have sensed that old age was not for her. Jean had come to visit for a few days, and her mother had taken her up to her bedroom, and made her sit on the little wooden chair that her father had made when he was a young man, while she rummaged in a chest at the foot of the bed.

"Whatever are you looking for?" Jean had asked, for her mother was muttering under her breath as she searched.

"It's not for you to know, Jeanie." She glanced at her daughter. "It must remain a secret until it goes to the rightful owner."

Jean had no idea what she was talking about and thought that maybe her mother had gone a bit mad. Her mother continued her search, then uttered a squeak of triumph and held up a small flat parcel, wrapped in brown paper and tied with string.

"Here it is -"

"Here what is?"

Her mother got stiffly to her feet. She came over to Jean and knelt down beside her.

"It's up to you now," she said, placing the parcel in her daughter's hands. "She gave it to me before she died, and made me promise to keep it safe for the right person. A blood relative, she said, but it had to be a woman. She said only a woman would understand." She shook her head. "But there have been none - it's been all boys. All Gillespie boys. So now it's for you to take on. You must decide who to give it to, Jeanie."

So Jean had taken the package and promised her mother that she wouldn't let her down. But as the years passed Jean began to worry that she was not going to be able to keep her promise. Gillespie boys grew into men, who fathered more Gillespie boys. There were no girls.

It came as a huge relief to Jean when Charlie's daughter was born. But when Anna failed to materialise in the Highlands, it began to look hopeless. She did think about going south to find her. But old age and infirmity made this impossible. She broke her hip, moved into the home. And began to think about choosing someone to take on the task for her. The problem was that there was nobody she could trust.

But now the time had come. Charlie's daughter was finally in the Highlands. She would be able to keep her promise to her mother after all.

CHAPTER THIRTEEN

Anna and Barbara ate supper together in the kitchen. Outside the clouds had been gathering all day. Now they were tipping out their contents in a steady grey drizzle. Anna pushed her food around her plate and tried to persuade herself that the gloom she was feeling was down to the change in the weather. But when the phone rang and Barbara got up to answer it, she didn't even bother to look up.

It was Barbara's mother calling from Texas. Anna began to clear the table, while Barbara took the phone into the other room and settled down for a long conversation.

The kitchen was as warm and comfortable as ever, but Anna was in no mood to appreciate it. She filled the sink with soapy water and began to wash saucepans with a clash and a clatter, as if by making as much noise as possible she could chase the gremlins away. But how inconsiderate. Barbara was trying to have a conversation down the corridor, and here she was bashing and crashing as if she was the only person in the world with problems. She set the saucepan she had just washed gently down on the draining board and told herself to stop feeling sorry for herself.

She had just made herself a cup of tea, and was sitting down at the table waiting for Barbara to finish, when her mobile rang. It was Ellie - calling from Cape Cod. She had arrived there the night before and had just woken up for breakfast. And she was bubbling over with excitement. The house on the coast - where she had been invited to stay for a fortnight with her best friend's family - was awesome. The bed she had just slept in was big enough for the entire hockey team. Today they were going out on a yacht, and tonight there was a barbeque, and tomorrow they were going to a beach party. The people were awesome. The American boys in particular were awesome. In fact pretty much everything you could think of was awesome. Anna sat back in her chair and smiled. Thank goodness for Ellie. Her high spirits were a tonic.

"I'm so glad you're having a good time, darling. It sounds… Well it sounds awesome."

"So how about you, Mum? I can't believe you're still stuck up in Scotland. You must be bored out of your mind."

"I'm not at all bored," said Anna. Had Ellie been talking to her father? "I'm having a great time. I've been finding out about Fiona Gillespie. She's the one that looks just like you. I told you all about her in my email."

"Did you? Oh yeah…"

Not terribly interested. No surprise really.

"It sounds great, Mum. I'm glad you're having a nice time."

That was something at least.

"So when are you going home? I spoke to Dad yesterday –"

Aha. Thought so.

"He said to check with you, but he thought you would be back by the weekend."

"Did he?"

"Yeah… the thing is my hockey stuff was sent back with the others when they flew home. So I wouldn't have to lug it around with me while I'm here. And Jenny said her mum would drop it round, so she wanted to know when somebody would be there."

Anna frowned.

"I hadn't exactly decided yet. I was going to wait until Dad knew when he was due back."

"He said any day to me."

"So he could be there for Meredith's mother to drop off your stuff?"

"Mum…" Ellie laughed. "This is Dad we're talking about. When does he ever know if he's going to be at home?"

Anna did her best to laugh too. But it was hollow laughter of the worst kind.

When Barbara reappeared the dishwasher was humming quietly in the corner, and Anna was sitting with a cup of tea in her hands, gazing into space.

"You'd think that old age would quieten a woman down a bit, wouldn't you?" said Barbara, joining Anna at the table. "But it just means she repeats herself even more than she used to do. My father's feeling a lot better, I'm glad to say. But how he puts up with her I really don't know."

Anna snorted.

"If he's anything like most men he probably gave up listening years ago."

Barbara shot a glance at her.

"Now who's rattled your cage, honey?"

Anna put down her cup of tea and apologized for her short temper, and told her about the conversation with Ellie, about Richard's assumption that she would drop everything and go home.

"It makes me wonder if it's my fault," she said. "That I've allowed them to walk all over me. To treat me as if what I want doesn't matter."

Barbara sighed.

"Aren't you being a little hard on yourself? I think it's more likely that you've done such a great job of looking after your family all these years, and made it look so easy, that they rather take it for granted."

"But I don't want to be taken for granted anymore. I want all the hard work to be recognized. I want trumpets and fanfares and the godamned Victoria Cross. I want Richard to ring me up and tell me that he doesn't know how I've coped all these years. At least Laura gets paid for being a housekeeper. I don't even get that."

"You do get all their love," said Barbara gently. "They might not be very good at putting it into words, but they couldn't manage without you, you know. Not one of them."

Anna stared at her.

"I know what you're saying is true," she said. "And it matters a lot to me. But what I don't know is if it matters enough anymore."

⊰⊱

Barbara sent Anna to bed early that night.

"You need a good night's sleep," she said at the door to Anna's bedroom. "Things will look a lot better in the morning. They invariably do, you know."

Anna looked doubtful. Barbara kissed her on the cheek and headed towards her own room. Anna watched her, and then went into her bedroom and shut the door behind her. She closed the curtains, took off her clothes, and slid under the duvet without washing her face. The early start that morning meant she was more exhausted than usual, but sleep felt a long way off.

She shifted and turned onto her side. As she did so she noticed Fiona's diary on the bedside table, where she had left it to dry out on a folded towel. Had it recovered from its early morning soaking? She hoped so. She reached over and picked it up to see if there was any lasting damage. When she opened the front cover she saw that, where it had dried out, it was possible to peel back more of the pages. She sat upright in bed. Suddenly she no longer felt so tired.

Those terrible people are still with us, she read. *I begin to feel that they will never leave. I swear that I can feel my father's spirit shaking with rage at the way they treat our servants, the way they talk about our house, the countryside, the people, as if we were some kind of strange throwback to a bygone and barbaric age. I overheard one of them in the hallway suggesting that the only explanation for the way we lived was that we were backward looking people who didn't have the wits to appreciate what was good for us. This from the woman who expressed such delight upon her arrival at staying in a fairy tale castle.*

Robert tells me not to mind them. He says that they are merely ignorant rather than cruel. But he does not have to suffer them as I do. He rides out with the husbands each morning and is not closeted with their wives all day. I am unable to understand what the men should find to interest them in our little estate. But they seem happy when they return in the evening. Which is more than I can say for the ladies.

For a day or so after the Games the talk was of little else but the feats of strength and skill that we witnessed while we were there. The ladies were particularly taken with the antics of Donald, our local boy, who won three out of the four events in which he competed. From the way they talked I think their interest is more to do with the fact that Donald is 'as tall as an oak tree, and as blonde and fair as a Greek god' – as Mrs Bailey put it – as to do with his success in the competition, for they showed little interest in his skill, and a very great deal in his physique.

On one particular morning, when the gentlemen had risen early and gone out before breakfast, the ladies came up with a plan to take the carriage and drive past the cottages where Donald lived, in the hope of catching sight of him. I think that they spoke in jest but nevertheless I wished that they would not. For it was impossible not to feel that in some way they were laughing at us.

I could have wished for Robert to show a little more understanding, particularly in view of the fact that these people were his friends. But he explained to me that they were important to him from the point of view of developing his business interests, and that he would be most grateful if I would support him by putting up with them. I still hadn't had a chance to speak to him about what happened on the way to the Games, and I was in no mood to put up with them, or him for that matter. But I had little choice. I counted the days until it was time for them to leave, and I could talk to him in private about my concerns.

At last the day arrived for our guests to depart. I was delighted to think that my home would be returned to me. However my delight was tempered when I learned at breakfast that Robert was to travel with them to Glasgow, and then on to Yorkshire where he had some business to attend to. I wished that he might have told me when we were alone together, when I would have asked him to stay a few days before leaving.

We have spent so little time together since we came from Drummond, and there is a great deal that I wish to discuss with him. In particular I wish to speak with him of the matter raised by Iain Mackay, this rumour that evictions are to take place on our land, which must be dealt with before it does any further damage. It would make much more sense for Robert to be the one to visit and reassure our tenants that they will not lose their homes. Then they would have no choice but to believe it. But I have not had a chance to speak to him alone, and now he has gone away with the others, and he was unable to say exactly when he would return.

Still it felt good to have the house to myself. Jean and Mary came to find me as I stood in the doorway to wave goodbye. They could not agree about which should have first claim – the overhaul of the linen cupboard after the departure of so many guests, or the restocking of the pantry and game larder – and they wished for me to direct them. I had no desire to get involved - they were looking to score points off each other and wished for me to stand as umpire - so I escaped from their clutches and went in search of John to arrange for Drummer to be saddled up so that I might go for a ride and taste the fresh air again.

With the departure of my unwelcome guests I felt as I had when I was a child, and had escaped from my governess. In a spirit of playfulness I went upstairs to the chest in my old bedroom, and found the breeches and shirt and waistcoat that I used to wear when I wanted a break from skirts and petticoats. As I changed I couldn't help thinking that the last time I wore these clothes was when I rode in the woods, and was chased by the men who had taken a lease on our land. It had caused my father such pain to be forced to stand by and watch while somebody else took control of the land that had belonged to his family for so many hundreds of years. I found myself thanking heaven for Robert, that he had the money to take back the lease and restore the land to us.

I pushed my hair inside the cap and looked at myself in the looking glass. The clothes still fitted me just as they had when I was a girl. With the cap pulled over my face it would have been difficult to recognise the woman I had become. Indeed I think that even Robert himself would have been hard pushed to know me. Although I did not wish for him to have the chance, for he would find little to amuse him in the sight of his wife riding out dressed as a boy.

I called to my dog, Teal, and slipped out of the house through the back way. There was nobody in the stable yard but Drummer was waiting for me. We set off in the direction of the river, and I kicked Drummer to a gallop. As we sped across the heather I couldn't stop myself from shouting out loud at the sheer joy of being free again.

I had no real thought in my mind of where to go, except that I would prefer to stay away from anyone who might recognise me. So, when I found myself heading down the glen in the direction of the houses at East Kildorran it was not with the intention of going anywhere near where people might see me. Usually if I rode in this direction I turned off before the lodge and headed up the track towards the bridge. But today there were two men standing in the middle of the track looking in my direction, so I could not go that way. And, when I would have turned back, I saw John with his dogs coming along behind me, and I knew he must not catch me like this.

So, I pulled my scarf around my face and drew near to the low stone houses with their roofs roughly thatched with heather. I could see that a woman stood at the side of the nearest house hanging washing out on a line. I knew, of course I knew, that this was the house where Iain MacKay's sister lived. But it had not been my purpose to spy on her, although I can see that it might be seen as rather strange that the lady of the manor should dress up in the clothes of a boy in order to go past the house. But of course I had no intention to be discovered, and was hoping to ride by without notice.

But Teal had other plans. He caught sight of a little yellow dog who stood by the gate and barked loudly at him. And, without taking any notice of my command to stay, he leapt over the wall and took it upon himself to engage in a ferocious battle. The woman, Iain's sister, came running, and I did not know what to do since I was very unwilling to be recognised. I was tempted to turn Drummer away and ride off. But Teal would not come away, and so I had to dismount and approach, and, with my head bent and a voice as gruff as I could make it, I did my best to call him off. The good woman and I shouted to our dogs to no avail, and I saw that a man had come out of the cottage with a pail in his hand, and now he strode towards us and flung the water across the dogs, and we were able to drag them apart.

Now that I had Teal's collar in my hand I was anxious to escape before they could see through my disguise. To my relief the woman went inside with her washing. But the yellow dog lunged forwards as I backed away and nipped

Teal on his leg, whereupon my own dog, much enraged, turned back to defend himself. He dragged me with him, so that I stumbled and fell, and, to my very great embarrassment, the cap I was wearing tumbled off. I took some time picking myself up from the floor, because I could not bear to see the astonished look on the man's face when he realised who it was that grovelled in the dust before him. But my embarrassment was nothing to the shame I felt when I finally stood up and turned to apologise. The man I had assumed to be the husband of Iain MacKay's sister was Iain Mackay himself.

Oh, that the ground could have opened up and swallowed me right there and then. Oh, that I could have turned back the clock and gone a different way. Oh, that I had not chosen to dress in the clothes of a boy. I did not know where to look. When eventually I summoned up the courage to face him I found that he stood and watched me, and that his face wore a smile so wide I thought it might split in two. I could see that he was struggling to stop himself from laughing out loud. My face felt so hot I could have burnt my hand upon my cheek.

"What must you think of me?" was all I could say to him. "I am so ashamed." Whereupon his laughter broke from him in great gusts of mirth. He bent down to retrieve my cap, and he dusted it off and handed it back to me. I forced myself to look at him in order to thank him and take my leave of him as quickly as I could. But when I met his gaze his dark eyes were shining with such

amusement that it was impossible not to smile back at him. And that made him laugh some more, and then I found that I was laughing along with him. And all of a sudden it didn't seem quite so bad that he had caught me out in such a way, and we both laughed together, and I felt a very great deal happier than I had before.

"You must come inside so that we can clean you up," he said.

At this I backed away, for the last thing I wanted was for his sister to see me dressed in such an inappropriate way.

"Thank you, but that's not necessary. I must go home and change before anyone else catches me like this. I will pay a visit to your sister when I am more suitably dressed," I told him hastily. And, before he could stop me, I leapt onto Drummer's back and rode home as fast as I could.

Anna turned to the next page and her heart dropped like a stone. It was blank. She turned to the next. It was the same. So was the next. And the next. She flipped through the rest of the pages to the end. All empty.

It was a bitter blow. She had been completely caught up in Fiona's story, had shared her embarrassment at being caught out in boy's clothing - by Iain Mackay of all people, had felt her relief as she laughed with him. Anna had been aware of a growing sense of elation as she read. It was impossible not to be aware that the relationship between Fiona and Iain was changing gear.

Now, with an empty diary and nothing else to go on, there was no way of finding out what happened next.

CHAPTER FOURTEEN

"Is there anything you need me to do this morning?" asked Anna over breakfast. "Because if there isn't I might as well get on with sorting out my flight home."

Barbara was reading The Daily Record and chewing on a slice of toast. She and Anna, both still in their robes, were sitting opposite each other across the table, catching up on the newspapers from the previous day, in what Barbara had assumed was companionable silence. She had just been thinking about how comfortably they had grown into each other's company. Now she unhooked her reading glasses from behind her ears and looked at Anna. She had known the time would come sooner or later, but still it was a shock.

"I'm so sad to hear it," she said. "I've got so used to having you here, I'm not sure how I'll get on without you."

Anna's face was pale under the tanned skin, but her expression was determined.

"You know I've loved being here. But I can't stay on indefinitely. And I reckon I've got as far as I can with Fiona. I haven't heard from Fin - which means there's no way of proving it was Iain Mackay who wrote the letter. If I had more time there would be more research I could do. But, whatever happens, I need to go home soon. Richard will be back any day now. And Ellie will be home in less than a fortnight. There really isn't any good reason for me to stay."

Barbara could feel the future closing in on her.

"How about because you're having a good time?"

Anna gave a wry smile.

"If only life was that simple."

"Isn't it? You're enjoying yourself up here, aren't you?" Barbara wasn't going to give up without a fight. "Nothing has happened to make you want to leave? Not that silly conversation with Laura yesterday?"

"It's got nothing to do with that. It just feels like everything is coming to an end. That there's nothing more for me to do up here."

Barbara reached across the table and took Anna's hand.

"Anna, my dearest girl," she said. "When are you going to let go of this idea that you have about being useful all the time? Sometimes it's good just to go with the flow."

"But that's just what I've been doing. And it's been wonderful. Only now it's time to get back in the boat and start paddling again." She was avoiding Barbara's eye. "I've had the best time. Getting to know you. Getting to know my father. Getting to know Fiona. I've loved every minute of it. But Richard is in a state because I'm not at home looking after everything. And Ellie obviously thinks I'm going a little bit mad. I just feel that I need to get back and take stock of things."

"Is that what you really want?"

Barbara sounded doubtful.

"To be honest with you – " Anna spoke so softly Barbara had to lean in to hear her. "I'm not sure I know what I want anymore."

Anna was looking up flights, when she heard the crunch of gravel outside as a car came up the drive. There was an impatient knocking on the front door by somebody who was in too much of a hurry to use the bell. She heard Barbara's footsteps, and then her greeting whoever it was in a warm voice. As Anna selected her flight more footsteps went along the corridor to the kitchen. While she looked for her credit card she was trying to identify the deep voice murmuring in response to Barbara's lighter tone.

She wondered if the visitor might be Cameron. She had managed to avoid him after he had found her crying in the garden. But she would have to see him before she left, and this could be the opportunity to say goodbye.

She booked her flight for the following afternoon, texted Richard in Moscow to let him know her plans, and made her way back up the corridor to join Barbara.

But the visitor wasn't Cameron. It was Fin.

"Here you are," said Barbara as Anna came through the door. "I was just telling Fin that we are about to lose you."

Fin glanced across the room at her.

"I must have got the wrong end of the stick," he said. "I thought you were here for the rest of the summer."

Anna scowled at him.

"Not all of us are lucky enough to have a life that allows for that kind of freedom. Some of us have responsibilities."

He looked taken aback. She hadn't meant to sound quite so bitter, but the way he was just sitting there at the kitchen table, as if he didn't have a care in the world, made her want to shake him.

"Well now," he said slowly. "That's a real shame."

Anna went to the sink and stood with her back to him, running the cold tap. She filled a glass with water. Yes, it was a shame. It was a shame that he seemed to have forgotten that the last time they met he had taken her letter away with him. It was a shame that he seemed to have forgotten that he promised to check the handwriting and get back to her. It was a shame that he had told her it was a big deal, and now he was acting like it had never happened.

"I came by because I've got some news," he said. "That letter of yours. I wanted to be one hundred per cent sure before I told you. Didn't want to get your hopes up -"

She swung round.

"Hopes?"

"I sent a couple of lines to a mate who analyses handwriting for the police. That's why it's taken me a while to get back to you. He rang this morning. Says there's absolutely no doubt. I came here the minute I'd put the phone down on him."

"No doubt?"

"It was definitely Iain Mackay who wrote your letter."

Anna took a step forwards and gripped the back of a kitchen chair. Suddenly the room was spinning around her.

"Are you OK?"

"I'm fine." She raised her head and stared at him. "You're absolutely sure?"

"Absolutely sure. I had a gut feeling about it anyway. But it's good to have it confirmed." He glanced from Barbara to Anna. "Of course you realise it raises all sorts of interesting questions. Now we just need to decide how to go about following it up."

Anna pulled the chair out from the table and sat down heavily. "Not we. You. I'm going home. I've booked my flight."

"You can change it, can't you?"

"I wish I could. But I've texted Richard to tell him. I can't change my plans now." She looked across the table at him. "You'll just have to carry on without me."

Barbara, looking from one to the other, wished she could think of some way of making Anna change her mind and stay. She hated the idea of sending her back to an empty house, to wait for husband and daughters to come home and take her for granted all over again. Particularly now that there was such a good reason for her to stay. She went to Anna and put an arm around her shoulders.

"You've booked your flight?"

Anna nodded her head.

"For tomorrow afternoon. I was going to ask if you'd mind giving me a lift to the airport. Otherwise I can get a taxi."

"You wouldn't think about putting it off for a few days? A lot can happen in a few days."

"I really wish I could. But it's too complicated. I'm going to have to go soon anyway. It might just as well be tomorrow."

Anna's face wore a stubborn look that Barbara guessed was a disguise to cover uncertainty. She wanted to reason with her stepdaughter, but didn't want to push it with Fin there. Fin was staring at the floor.

"Well I can see that you've made up your mind." Barbara spoke as cheerfully as she could. But the shadow of loneliness that had been lurking for the past weeks and months took a step closer. Empty house, empty heart. It was a frightening thought. Best not to indulge it. The thing to do was concentrate on the present moment.

"So how are you going to spend your last day, honey? Any ideas?"

Anna bit her lip. "Does it matter?"

"Well, how about this for a plan?" Barbara was thinking on her feet. "Fin was just saying that he's got to go and pick up some fishing gear that a friend of his left over at Loch Naver. So why don't you go with him?" She was making 'is it ok?' faces at Fin behind Anna's back. "It's a beautiful drive. And you could go and take a look at Rossal together while you're there."

Anna was making 'are you mad?' faces at her behind Fin's back.

"I should pack -"

"That's not going to take you all day."

"There must be stuff you need me to do before I go."

"Nope." She could try all the excuses she liked. "You'll regret it if you don't go."

"Will I?" Anna wasn't convinced.

"You will. Rossal is one of the townships that were cleared around about the same time that Iain's family were being evicted. It's an extraordinary place. You really don't want to miss it."

Anna gave Fin a sideways look. "I'm sure Fin doesn't want me tagging along."

Barbara held her breath and put her trust in Fin being too much of a gentleman to let her down. He smiled and shrugged his shoulders. "You won't be tagging along. It'll be nice to have the company."

Anna turned to Barbara.

"You're coming too?"

"Oh no, honey, I can't," said Barbara. "The thing is…" She searched for inspiration. "I've got to stay in and wait for the people from Inverness to pick up Charlie's books, the ones you've spent so long sorting out for me. They promised to come around lunchtime."

Barbara held her breath, while Anna looked from Fin to Barbara to Fin again. Then back to Barbara.

"I'm sure Fin's got better things to do."

"You're going that way anyway, aren't you Fin?" said Barbara.

He shrugged.

"Certainly am."

Barbara turned to Anna.

"And you don't want to spend your last day in the Highlands stuck inside with me, when you could go visit this amazing place that you will remember for the rest of your life."

And maybe discover something to make you change your mind about leaving tomorrow. She didn't say it, but it was what she was hoping for.

Anna shook her head and laughed. "You're not going to give up on this one, are you?" She looked at Fin. "Are you sure you're happy to go to this Rossal place? You don't mind taking me with you?"

He squinted at her.

"It is quite a challenge."

She looked suspiciously at him.

"A challenge?"

He grinned.

"Are you kidding me? Barbara has set me the task of making sure your last day in the Highlands is one you'll never forget. What if I fail?"

Fin drove with casual efficiency along the winding road that led north towards Lochinver. To someone who didn't know him well he might have appeared to be his customary laid back self. But the truth was that he was struggling to know how to deal with the silent woman in the passenger seat beside him.

Up until now Fin had believed that he knew pretty much everything there was to know about Iain Mackay. He had assumed that the lack of evidence relating to his dealings with women meant that he hadn't been that interested, that he had had other priorities. But here was proof of secret passion, of desire, of a dangerous liaison with the wife of an adversary. The prospect of uncovering a previously unknown chapter of Iain MacKay's life was electrifying. He couldn't wait to get started. So why was Anna ducking out?

He stole a glance at her profile. She was staring out of the window, apparently deep in thought, and had hardly spoken since they set off. He didn't like to intrude. But he was itching to know why she wasn't as excited as he was. He wished he knew her well enough to so ask what was going on. But the set of her jaw said don't push it, and, after the awkwardness of their first meeting, there was no way he was going to risk upsetting her again.

Fin turned off the Lochinver road and headed inland through Glen Oykel towards the village of Lairg. The road wound between rolling hills. Pockets of dense green pines dotted the landscape. Here the light was softer than on the coast, the contrast between land and sky less intense. The hills lifted and fell away to the far horizon, like the waves of a shifting sea. It was soothing to the soul. And, with Anna sitting silently beside him, his soul was in need of some soothing.

"I owe you an apology."

Anna's voice sounded low beside him. He looked across at her.

"You do?"

"For being such lousy company."

"You don't have to apologise."

"I do. I've been foisted on you."

He thought about this for a moment. "You know?" he said. "You're absolutely right. I don't mind a bit of foisting, when the foisted one tries to make up for it. But while silence is all well and good, at this precise moment it's not very relaxing."

"I really am very sorry." At least she had the good grace to smile. "You must be wishing you'd said no to Barbara."

He snorted. "You're joking aren't you? Say no to Barbara. Nobody says no to Barbara. She's the epitome of the iron hand in the velvet glove if ever I saw one."

"You know I've never thought about her that way before," said Anna. "But of course you're right. It's just that she's so charming about it you don't realise what she's up to until she's got you."

"And you find yourself trapped in a car with a monosyllabic woman and nowhere to hide."

He heard her chuckle. Thank the lord. Maybe now they could both relax a bit. He saw that she was smiling at him.

"Whatever did you do to deserve such a fate?"

He shook his head. "I don't know. But whatever it was, it must have been pretty bad."

Fin drove with one hand on the steering wheel, while he gestured to left and right with the other, telling her what he knew about the land through which they passed. Anna knew that he was desperate to discuss Iain's letter with her. But, when he tried to raise the subject, she made it clear that it was the last thing she wanted to talk about. He was considerate enough to respect her wishes, and she was grateful at the way he changed tack and told her instead about his passion for the Highlands, about how he was hoping to buy a place up here, if the sales of his books ever delivered the necessary funds.

Time passed more quickly than she could have imagined when they set out, and before long they were driving along a narrow street through a cluster of small houses, and he was pointing out the sign for the Altnaharra Hotel. They sat opposite each other in the pretty lounge of the hotel drinking coffee and eating homemade biscuits. There was no sign of any other guests, and Fin explained that they were probably all out on the river, since the hotel was famous as a haven for fishing fanatics. He left her for a moment while he went to find the manager and collect the rod and fishing bag left behind by his friend. She sat and nibbled on her biscuit and looked out of the window, and wondered if there was anywhere else in the British Isles where it was possible to be more isolated. It was hard to believe that the next day she would be back home in the south. It was going to feel like returning from another planet.

They got back in the car and headed towards Loch Naver. There were no other vehicles on the single-track road. Anna had the strangest sensation that they were the only people left alive.

"It's so peaceful," she said, turning to look at Fin. "It's hard to believe that such terrible events took place here."

"That's why I'm taking you to Rossal," said Fin. "So you can see for yourself what was left after the evictions." And he explained that Rossal was one of the dozen or so small townships that had once lined the valley through which they were driving, and which included Rifhail – the place where Iain MacKay's family had been so brutally forced from their home.

Driving along the narrow road beside the water's edge, with only a solitary fisherman casting his fly across the silver loch, and a few sheep scattered across the hillside, it was hard to imagine that the glen had once been home to so many. But Fin told her that in those days they would have been passing long stone houses roofed with turf, with dry stone barns and outhouses and drying kilns dotted amongst them. And in Rossal itself, if they were lucky, they might have come across a stonemason by the name of Donald Macleod, who had been born and bred in the township. And maybe if they had offered him a shot or two of good whisky he might have told them his story.

"Donald Mcleod trained as a mason, but he should have been a journalist," said Fin. "It's thanks to him that such vivid accounts of the clearances were made known to a wider audience.

It's shocking to think that on just one day in 1814 all the people of Rossal - together with the residents of at least four other townships including

Rhifail – were evicted from their homes. By night-fall every one of more than twenty houses in Rossal were burnt to the ground. And the same was true in the other townships. In total twenty-seven families were made homeless that day."

Anna stared out of the window at the empty hills. She was silent for a while. Then she said suddenly, "Do you think that was what Robert Gillespie was planning for Kildorran?"

Fin contemplated her profile. It was the closest she'd come to mentioning the subject all day.

"It certainly looked that way for a time."

"So what made him change his mind?"

"Impossible to say." The car juddered as they crossed a cattle grid. "It's another piece of the jigsaw."

"Well," she said, "I just hope you manage to piece it all together."

She had withdrawn into herself again.

A few miles after leaving Loch Naver behind them Fin drove past a squat stone church by the side of the road, and turned into a winding track just wide enough to allow a car to pass along it. They bumped their way towards a dark stretch of pine forest. After several hundred yards he pulled up and parked on the verge.

Anna got out of the car and stretched. She had been uncommunicative for the last few miles, and he had left her to her thoughts, frustrated, wishing he could read her mind, but unwilling to pry.

He locked the car and joined her. Above her head the sky was blue with a scattering of clouds. They walked side by side along a track that took them between the vibrant green fronds of summer ferns. Trees crowded round the path so thickly that it was impossible to see very far in any direction. The approach was blind, which was not, Fin explained, the way it would have been all those years ago when the eviction officers came. Then they would have come up through the heather, in the sight of everyone. Now the remains of the little township were cloaked in deepest darkest green. Hidden away in the midst of alien forest.

There was a claustrophobic feel to their walk through the woods after the openness of the moorland through which they had driven. After half a mile or so Fin ducked to the left, and led the way along a narrow pathway that wound upwards from the side of the track. As they went up the incline the trees thinned a little and allowed the sunlight to pierce through the canopy. Fin passed through a gap in a low stone wall and stood in front of a stile. Anna came up to stand beside him.

"This is it," he said.

Spread out in front of her was a large clearing, rising and falling with the contours of the land, until it met with the line of trees on the far side. A narrow path, barely visible in places, meandered through the heather and bracken. Anna could see where stone plinths had been positioned at strategic intervals carrying information for visitors. They were standing by the first one, which introduced Rossal and informed them that the stone dyke through which they had just passed was the boundary of the township. It told them that the Forestry Commission had kept the eighty acres clear of trees, but that the shielings - the five thousand acres of summer grazing for the cattle - had been lost to the forest.

Anna went behind Fin over the stile and followed him along the pathway. It led up the side of a rise, and passed by a low circle of stone boulders tumbled upon the ground. Then, a few yards further on, past another circular pile of stones, with several more in the distance. These stone circles, Fin told her, were what was left of the town.

It was utterly quiet. All around them the forest and the hills were still and silent. Anna stood and gazed across the clearing. It made her sad to think that this barren patch of land had once been the location of a thriving little community. Fin came and stood beside her.

"So what do you think?"

"I'm trying to imagine the way it must have been when there were people actually living here. It's hard to believe that it was less than two hundred years ago. It seems more like the ruins of some stone age encampment."

Fin looked around him.

"I know what you mean," he said. "But you have to remember that up here it was a very different existence to the way people were living in the rest of the country. The inhabitants of these townships were used to putting up with the most basic conditions. They were experts at making the most of the limited materials available to them. They didn't have any choice. These houses provided warmth and shelter to people who were accustomed to spending their days out of doors. They had very few possessions, and they got on by living close to their families and supporting each other. It wasn't the most sophisticated of lifestyles. You can imagine that to men of no imagination like Patrick Sellar, it must have seemed that they were doing these people a favour by moving them on."

They continued along the path. Fin pointed out furrows in the soil, curved ridges that showed evidence of where the land had been ploughed.

"They followed a system of joint cultivation or 'run rig'," he told her. "The best land was known as the 'infield', and the whole town worked on it and planted it up with a constant succession of grain crops. All the available manure would be spread on this land, so if you were looking for the best crops this is where you'd find them. The land that wasn't so fertile, or so accessible, was the 'outfield'."

He explained that in addition each of the towns-people would have the right to a share in the common grazings and the shielings in the summer. The implements they used were so primitive, and needed a large amount of labour, which was why they all mucked in together. The lack of transport meant that everybody had to rely on his own produce, and because the quality of the land varied so much it was important that everybody had a share of land that could produce a living.

Anna, following in Fin's footsteps along the narrow path, decided that she liked his way of imparting information. It was conversational, casual. It didn't seem like he was lecturing her, which was how Cameron sometimes made her feel. Half way round he pointed out a small hillock. He strode to the top of it.

"Bronze age burial mound," he said, squinting down at her. "Just shows you that people were living here for a very long time before the landlords got greedy and started burning down their homes."

Anna stared up at him. Did the landlords include her great great grandfather? Was this what he had been planning for Kildorran? It was the question that was haunting her, an uncomfortable thought made even more uncomfortable by the knowledge that she might never know the answer. She walked on.

"Hold on there," called Fin.

She stopped by another circle of stones and waited for him.

"Was it something I said?" he asked, catching up with her.

"No. I was just thinking."

"You think too much," he growled. "Thinking is forbidden." He took her by the hand and led her towards the stone circle.

She frowned. "Now what are you doing?"

"'Homes Are Us' at your service, Madam" he said. "No client too difficult." He grinned at her. "Even you."

"Am I missing something?"

"Just step this way, Madam. I have the perfect property for you."

He directed her through a gap in the stone circle. Following her inside, he offered her a chair, and she laughed and sat down on the stone boulder he was pointing towards and waited to see what he was up to.

"Now, Madam," he said with an extravagant wave of his hand, "I can see by your expression that you think this residence is a wee bit on the primitive side. But let me demonstrate to you the practicality of its design. Starting with the floor – what we in the business like to call the bare earth effect. It's absolutely the latest thing - hardwearing, easy to sweep clean and so affordable." He indicated a non-existent roof. "The latest in divot design for the cottage-effect thatched roof provides great protection from the elements. Of course, we are talking about the latest in air conditioning technology here. Drystone walls allow in just enough air to keep us – well maybe a bit on the chilly side in the winter. But in the summer it works a treat.

I'll grant you that the rafters do have a tendency to become covered in thick black peat soot, which can make things a little gloomy inside. Particularly when it has rained heavily – as we all know it can in these parts - and the drips of inky black water splash down on our heads and run down our necks."

Anna shivered. "Sounds perfectly dreadful."

"Ah, but we're a practical race, and we have a word for the rain that comes through the roof of our homes. It's 'snighe'. So we can warn each other about what to expect."

"How very reassuring."

"And just imagine a raging gale outside. And think how snug and cosy it feels, with a fire burning, and the children and animals safe inside."

Anna looked doubtfully at him. "Snug and cosy?"

"OK. So maybe not on the really cold nights."

"Aren't there quite a few of those up here?"

"Yes," admitted Fin. "But we all have to compromise." He led her out through the doorway. "Would Madam care to see around outside?" They walked down the hillside a little way. "Notice how the house is built on a slope, with the byre for the animals at the lowest end, so that the odour and the dirt and the shi...."

Anna held up her hand. "Too much information."

"Sorry Madam – should I say animal excrement - is kept well away from the living quarters. Maybe you don't care for the idea of living under the same roof as your pets? But consider for a moment. Your dear little cow will be providing you with the milk and butter and cheese that are a staple part of your diet, and this way you have it on tap without having to go outside. As we've already mentioned, it gets pretty cold around these parts in the winter. And you don't want your animals getting frostbite and dying on you. And since it is you lucky ladies who get the job of feeding and caring for all the animals, just think how much nicer it is to be able to look after them without having to brave the elements every time you want to feed a chicken or milk a cow."

Anna frowned. She wasn't sure about this division of labour. But he hadn't finished. There was a holiday home to go with this charming residence.

"In the summer," he announced, "you and the other women get to take the cattle up to the shielings, where the sweet grass grows lush on the hillside. Up in the sheltered hills of this lovely glen you will get to enjoy the pleasure of staying in luxury huts built of stone and turf for about six weeks, while your animals graze on the fresh pastures, and give the grass closer to home a chance to recover for the rest of the year. And, while you are up there, you will get to pass the time milking, and making the butter and the cheese that will feed the whole community for the winter."

Anna folded her arms across her chest.

"Sounds to me like it's the women doing all the hard work around here. What exactly are the men up to while all of this is going on?"

"They are probably away fighting. And when they are home they have to supplement their incomes in order to live, so they have to go out and find work. Inevitably a great deal of the grafting at home falls to the wives and daughters. These Highland women worked incredibly hard. They had no choice."

When did they ever have a choice, thought Anna? But she said it under her breath. Because he was working so hard to entertain her. And Barbara had been quite right; this place was extraordinary. As Fin described it, it had come alive for her. She could imagine that she saw women with bowls of grain feeding scrawny chickens that scratched in the earth around the house. She could hear children shouting and laughing as they ran across the ground chasing the dogs. She pictured men with young boys clearing stones from an area of ground, ready to start the construction of a new barn.

Anna thought about Iain Mackay and his father, coming back from the shielings to find their village under siege. She saw the houses in flames, and men with cudgels breaking down the doors. She imagined the air filled with the sound of people shouting, dogs barking, children screaming for their mothers. It was terrible to contemplate in the midst of the peace and quiet on this empty hillside.

Something moved in the corner of her eye and she jumped. Was it the ghost of one of the dispossessed returning to the scene of desolation? But it was the grubby rear end of a sheep, bobbing away from them down the hillside, where it joined several of its companions and they all turned to stare back up the hill at the intruders with their cold, mistrustful eyes. She turned to Fin.

"It's rather ironic, isn't it?" she said sadly "That now the only things living here are the sheep."

The fresh air was making Anna feel hungry. Fin had picked up sandwiches and drinks for them at the hotel, but eating a picnic in this silent sorrowful place seemed inappropriate, so they made their way back to the car and found a sheltered spot in the lea of a stand of tall trees. Fin spread out a waxed jacket from the back of the car for them to sit on. He lowered himself to the ground, stretched out his legs, and opened a can of beer. Anna sat cross-legged beside him, with her elbows on her knees, and ate a chicken salad sandwich while he told her about the struggle he was having with his novel, and how he reckoned that writing fiction was not going be his thing.

In the shelter of the trees the sun was warm. An easy silence fell upon them, and they leaned back and looked at the sky, watching the clouds drifting across the sun. Anna had rolled up her jacket and tucked it behind her. Now she lay on her side with her head on her arm and her eyes closed, her hair falling across her face. Fin watched her. She looked so peaceful he didn't have the heart to disturb her. As quietly as he could he folded his jacket and collected the cans. Hearing him move beside her Anna opened her eyes. She sat up and stretched, comfortable in the warmth of the afternoon.

"Sorry to wake you," he said.

"I wasn't asleep –"

"So the snoring was just heavy breathing then."

"Was I snoring?" She looked mortified.

He laughed. "Just teasing. You were very ladylike."

She threw a sandwich wrapper at him. He caught it and put it with the rest of the rubbish.

"So will you be sad to leave?" he asked her, tipping the last dregs of his beer onto the heather. She watched him packing the empty cans into his canvas fishing bag.

"Yes, I will. Thank you so much for bringing me here. It's been wonderful."

"I meant tomorrow."

She was quiet for a moment.

"I don't really know how I'm going to feel. None of this has felt quite real to me from the day I arrived. More like a dream I suppose. Something I know I'm going to wake up from at any moment."

"A good dream I hope."

She didn't answer him.

"You know something," he said, as they walked side-by-side back to the car. "Finding that letter wasn't a dream. It really happened."

"I'd rather not talk about it," she said.

"I wish I understood." He stopped in the middle of the path. "I thought you were desperate to find out what it's all about. I know I am –"

But Anna carried on walking. She reached the car and stood beside the passenger door waiting for him to unlock it.

"I thought I'd explained," she said when he caught up with her. "I've got my daughters to think about. And my husband. I can't stay here forever."

He unlocked the car.

"I don't understand what your daughters and your husband have got to do with you not wanting to find out more about Fiona and Iain and what happened to them?"

She looked at him over the roof of the car. "It's not that I don't want to find out what happened. Of course I do. But I've been away too long." She opened the door. "And the longer I stay, the harder it is to leave."

On their way back Fin suggested stopping off at Kildorran. He sounded hesitant. Anna guessed that after the conversation before they left Rossal he wasn't sure how his suggestion would be received. But she was delighted. The site of Fiona's first home held a particular fascination for her. How could she not want to go there?

Barbara had told her that after Neil was born Fiona chose to spend most of her time at Rowancross House, with Robert commuting between the west coast and Dundee where his jute business was based. So the house at Kildorran stayed empty and was allowed to fall into disrepair. After Fiona died it was uninhabited for several years, and in the early part of the twentieth century the original house was destroyed by fire. Now holiday chalets lined the banks of the river, and, where once there were farms and outhouses, now only a couple of stone cottages looked out across the hills and fields. Barbara had said that there wasn't much to see. But Anna would have been disappointed to leave without going there, and Fin was happy to oblige.

They turned off the main road and drove along a narrow track for several miles, following the course of the river as it snaked its way between green fields and wooded gorges. Fin drove slowly, the car dipping and bumping over and around the many cracks and potholes. Anna, looking out of the window to her left, caught sight of a couple of deer on the hillside, and imagined for a moment that she saw Fiona, bare headed and dressed as a boy in breeches and shirt, riding a chestnut pony between the trees. Fin looked in the same direction and noticed that the stone walls were crumbling, that gates were broken, and that the holiday chalets were in dire need of new roofs and a lick of paint.

"This is as far as we can drive." He pulled onto a verge and stopped the car. "We walk from here."

The ground beneath their feet was punctuated with slabs of stone, camouflaged by moss and tufts of grass. There were trees growing out of ancient brickwork. They stepped across the foundations of the old house. Fin pointed out the blackened stones where the fireplace in the great hall would once have burned.

"The most powerful chiefs tended to live in castles, but for the rest of them it was a little less grand," he told Anna. "You'd be surprised at how simply some used to live. Single storey stone houses, not many rooms, and a turf roof, would have been quite normal in the old days. Kildorran was more of a mansion than many."

"Is this all that's left of it?"

Anna couldn't help feeling disappointed, even though she had known there would be little to see. Fin nodded.

"This is all there is. Same as Rossal really. Nothing left standing. But the big difference here is that when the residents moved out, it was their choice."

They walked down towards the river, between clumps of bracken that grew waist high under the trees. Anna noticed tiny purple orchids growing beside the path. In the shadow of a group of pines the ground was thick with needles, so that it seemed that they walked across a fragrant carpet. When they reached the river bank Anna squatted down and took off her shoes and waded out, feeling the way with the tips of her toes, the swirl of water cool against her ankles and shins.

Fin watched her. Her head was down as she negotiated her way across the submerged stones. She had rolled up her jeans, and he could see her calves gleaming below the surface of the water. Her white cotton shirt was tucked into her waistband and she had twisted her hair up and tied it in a knot on top of her head. In the dappled shade from the trees she could have been mistaken for a girl half her age.

"Fin, Fin." She was calling out to him, excited, breathless. She pointed downwards to her feet.

"Fish. There are tiny fish. See."

Slivers of silver, dappled, quick as light, slipped through the water. He took off his shoes and paddled out to join her. As he approached she wobbled and took hold of his arm. He steadied himself beside her.

"Do you really have to go?" he asked on an impulse.

She lifted her head to look at him, her eyes full of regret.

"Yes," she said. "I really do."

CHAPTER FIFTEEN

The next morning Anna and Barbara took their coffee outside and sat side by side on the bench looking out across the loch. The air was mild, but clouds were gathering over their heads. Barbara glanced at Anna's profile and wondered how she was going to manage without her. Feeling herself observed, Anna turned and smiled.

"Home then?" said Barbara in as light a tone as she could manage.

"Looks like it."

"Richard sounded pleased."

He had rung the previous night. Barbara had picked up the phone and spoken to him before Anna.

"Yes."

"When is he due back?"

"Tomorrow morning. I'm going to the airport to pick him up."

"You'll have a lot to say to each other."

"I suppose so."

They finished their coffee and returned inside. Anna had the departure day jitters; she couldn't settle to anything. She had packed the night before, she had stripped the bed for Barbara, she had loaded the dishwasher with the breakfast things. Now she checked the rooms for a second time to make sure she had left nothing behind.

"Not that I brought much with me," she said, finding Barbara in the laundry room, where she was loading towels into the washing machine. "After all, I was only expecting to be here for a few days."

Barbara bent to fill the tray with washing powder and slammed the door shut. Anna looked at her watch.

"Still a couple of hours until we need to go. Why does time drag when you know there's so little left of it?" She turned suddenly. "I know what I've forgotten. I didn't put the last diary back with the others. I'll go and do it now."

"Don't worry about that." Barbara switched on the machine. "Leave it in your room. I'll do it when you've gone."

But Anna was already on her way upstairs. She had put the journal for 1853 out of harm's way in the drawer of the bedside table, intending to put it back with the others at another time. Thank goodness she'd remembered it before she left. Otherwise it might have stayed where it was, abandoned in the drawer and forgotten about. Perhaps only discovered years later, when Barbara moved, or sold the table, or gave it to somebody else. That was how these things often worked, wasn't it? You didn't come across things by design but by accident. That was how she had found the letter after all.

She opened the door of the bedroom that had been hers for the past few weeks and crossed over to the bed. The empty room felt like it was accusing her. She sat on the bare mattress and opened the drawer of the table. She lifted out the narrow book with its faded cover and ran a hand over the worn leather. She wasn't just saying goodbye to Barbara, but to Fiona as well.

She took the diary downstairs and went past the kitchen along the corridor to the study. Lifting the old leather chest from the shelf in her father's cupboard, she set it down on the desk and opened the lid. She wanted to put everything back exactly the way she had found it. The journals had been stacked, one on top of each other, beneath the bundle of letters. She lifted the letters and placed the remaining journal with the others. But when she put the letters back and tried to close the lid, she found that it wouldn't shut. It was like trying to close an overstuffed suitcase; the edges wouldn't come together. She raised the lid, took out the letters, and stacked them into a neater bundle. Then she tried again. Still the chest wouldn't close.

The only thing to do was to take everything out and start again. This time she was particularly careful to make sure that each item went back in just as it had come out. But still there was something preventing the lid from closing. Glancing at her watch she took everything out again and felt carefully with her fingers along the bottom of the box, in case something had become wedged and was getting in the way of its closing. But there was nothing. She couldn't understand it.

She was about to go and ask Barbara if there had been problems with closing the chest in the past when she noticed that the paper lining covering the wooden base appeared to have lifted in one corner. Perhaps this was the cause of the problem. She pushed at the base with the tips of her fingers. There was a slight give which didn't seem right, just by an edge where the lining had come away. She inserted one finger under the lifted edge and pulled gently. The lining came away easily to reveal a narrow cavity, hidden under a false bottom. Anna held her breath.

Nestling in the cavity was a flat package tied up with string.

With trembling hands Anna lifted it out. She could feel her heart beating in her chest as she plucked at the string with her fingers. Age had set the knot solid. She looked around her for scissors, a knife, anything that would cut through it. There was a Swiss army penknife in the desk drawer. She seized it and teased out the little scissors with her nails. The string fell away in limp folds as she cut. She pulled at the brown paper wrapping. Inside was a bundle of letters, neatly stacked, each one carefully folded in half, tied in a parcel with red ribbon. Anna untied the ribbon and unfolded the first letter. She had seen the bold swooping handwriting before.

Dear Mrs Gillespie, she read. *I hope that you will not think it impertinent of me in writing to you, but I have been unable to forgive myself for the graceless way in which I spoke to you.*

Anna turned quickly to the end. The letter was signed *Yours most penitently, I A Mackay.* She picked up the next one. The handwriting was smaller, neater, less flamboyant, but full of quirks and individual touches. Again, the writing was familiar.

My dear sir, It was gracious of you to write. It would be wrong of me not to recognise... And at the end a signature, *F. Gillespie.*

Anna flipped quickly through the pile.

My dear Mrs Gillespie... Dear Fiona... My dear friend...

And the replies.

Sir... Dear Sir... Mr Mackay... My friend... My very dear friend...

They were signed -

Yours truly... yours very truly.

And finally just –

Yours...

Anna ran up the corridor, calling out to Barbara. Barbara's anxious face appeared in the doorway. Anna grabbed her arm and half pulled-half pushed her back down the corridor to Charlie's study. Once inside the room Barbara stood with a bemused expression on her face as Anna handed her the letters.

"Look at these... I found them... They were in the chest... Under the lining..."

"What is it, honey? What have you found?" Barbara didn't know whether to be excited or alarmed.

"Letters... From him... From her... From them both... To each other. They were hidden in the bottom of the box."

Barbara stared at her.

"You mean from Iain and Fiona?"

Anna nodded.

"Go on. Look at them -"

Barbara slipped her glasses from the top of her head onto her nose and unfolded one of the letters.

"*Dear Mrs Gillespie,*" she read out loud. "*Would it pain you to learn that since meeting with you again I have thought of little else?*"

She lifted her head and looked at Anna.

"Oh my word -"

"I know." Anna's voice was barely more than a whisper. She disappeared through the doorway and began to run up the corridor.

Barbara called after her. "Where are you going?"

"To ring Fin."

⊨⊨ ⊨⊨

"So what do they say?"

Anna could hear the excitement in Fin's voice.

"I've only just found them. There are too many to read quickly. I've just glanced at them. I thought I'd wait for you. So we can read them together."

"I'm on my way."

Anna went back to her father's study.

"Fin's coming straight over," she said to Barbara. "I'm going to wait until he gets here. I thought it would be better if we read them together." She had a sudden thought. "Do you want to…? Would you like to be the first to read them? They were found in your house."

But Barbara shook her head, laughing. This was Anna's discovery, Anna's find.

"I shall look forward to hearing what they say."

She turned to go.

"There is one thing -"

"What is it?"

"This flight of yours that leaves in a few hours time. Do I presume that you are not going to be on it?"

While she waited for Fin to arrive Anna tried to ring Richard. But his phone kept passing her on to his messaging service, and she found she didn't know what to say to it. So she sent him a text. 'Have 2 stay few more days. Will ring & explain. Have arranged taxi 2 pick u up from airport. Sorry.'

Fin announced his arrival in the driveway with the sound of gravel spraying out from under his tyres. Anna heard the car door slam. She went to meet him at the front door. When she opened it he was there waiting for her, bouncing on his toes like an impatient child at the start of a party. She led him inside and down the corridor. The letters lay on the desk. Fin approached them cautiously, as if they were a mirage and likely to disappear at any moment. He picked one up from the top of the pile and read it.

"This is extraordinary." He turned to Anna. "Do you realise how extraordinary this is?"

"Why do you think I rang you?"

He pulled back the chair for her to sit down.

"Shall we get started?" He stopped. "What about this plane you've got to catch? How long have we got?"

She waved a dismissive hand.

"I've cancelled it."

He raised his eyebrows and nodded. "Good."

She looked across the desk at him.

"Do you honestly think I'm going to leave when I've just found these?"

He grinned at her. "I said good, didn't I? You don't have to defend yourself to me. I'm delighted you're staying. I couldn't understand why you were going in the first place."

They sat opposite each other on either side of Charlie's desk, Anna in her father's leather chair and Fin in the armchair that he dragged over from the window. Anna held the letters on her lap while they decided the best way to proceed.

"I don't know what you think, but it seems fairly obvious to me," said Fin. "You take the letters from Fiona. And I'll take the letters from Iain. If we read them aloud to each other then we'll both be at the same stage all the way through. Neither of us finding out something before the other."

Anna looked a little blankly at him.

"Unless you've got a better idea…"

"No. It makes sense." She gave her head a shake. "It's just that I can't quite believe that this is happening to me. I was supposed to be on my way to the airport. This is going to sound completely mad, but I can't shake off the feeling that Fiona didn't want me to leave. That somehow finding these letters was meant to happen."

CHAPTER SIXTEEN

The first letter was from Iain. Fin cleared his throat and read.

Dear Mrs Gillespie,

I hope that you will not think it impertinent of me in writing to you, but I have been unable to forgive myself for the graceless manner in which I spoke to you when we met at the Games. I allowed my anger to get the better of me, behaviour for which I cannot apologise enough.

I would have said something when we met again the day that your dog escaped, but you vanished before I had the chance. Now I learn from my sister that you have been gracious enough to pay her a visit, in order to reassure her that her family's tenancy at Kildorran is secure and that she has no cause for concern, and I am even more aware that my treatment of you that day was inexcusable.

I have a tendency to blunt speaking and a quick temper, which gets me into trouble on more occasions than I care to remember. I struggle to keep my feelings in check, but I am aware that all too often my passionate outbursts come across as boorishness. I realise that this must have been the case when I spoke to you at the Games. Your story of the unfortunate family evicted from their home and left to starve ignited the flame of my wrath. And you were unlucky enough to be present while it burned.

My sister has told me of your kindness when you called upon her. I understand that she introduced you to my father. He has been living with Anne these past few years, since our mother died. You will have seen for yourself that he is frail and suffers from ill health, and matters of the slightest concern weigh heavily with him. The experiences he suffered as a young man haunt him to this day. But Anne tells me that your visit did much to revive his spirits.

So may I once again apologise for my rudeness. I would not for anything have offended or upset you, and I very much fear that I did both. My only hope now is that this letter has not given further offence.

Yours most penitently,
I.A. Mackay

My dear sir, read Anna.

Please, I beg you, do not punish yourself unnecessarily. I am as much to blame for what happened between us as you. I have been guilty of shutting my eyes to what has been going on all around me and, truly, I am ashamed of my blindness. You were quite right when you said that I have been sheltered from the truth. Had my family suffered in the same way as yours I would have felt the same anger at my lack of awareness as you did when we first met.

Your sister treated me with such kindness when I called upon her. I am mortified when I think that it took harsh words from you before I made the effort to visit a tenant in need. I have been away from home for too long and have forgotten my duties.

I will admit to you that I was a little worried that your sister might have recognised me from that day when I rode past and my wicked dog got me into so much trouble. But if she had seen she was good enough not to mention it, and she made me feel so comfortable to be in her home, and insisted that I take some tea with her and try one of the excellent scones that she had been making on the open fire when I arrived.

I was very pleased to be introduced to your father. At first I think he was a little confused. He seemed to think that I was your sister Maggie come to visit. But Anne explained that I was the old laird's daughter. Then he spoke to me in a bitter voice. Now it appeared that he believed I had come to see how the family were reacting to the news that they were to be turned out of their homes. *Your poor sister blushed red with embar-rassment, but I was glad to be able to reassure him.*

When he understood that I had not come to warn of im-pending eviction, and was in fact there to reassure him of the opposite, he was most upset with his mistake and was anxious to recount his own experience of eviction in order that I might understand his reaction. Your sister told him not to bother me, but it seemed to me that I owed this gentle good man the honour of listening to him. I had to make my excuses, for my boys were waiting for me up at the house, but I made a promise to return and when I do I am looking forward to hearing the whole story.

Will you try and think more kindly of a foolish woman who is doing her best to make amends for her ignorance? I very much hope that you will.

Yours truly,
F. Gillespie

Dear Mrs Gillespie,
Your generosity and openheartedness do you great cred-it. To repay my churlish treatment of you in such a way is more than I deserve. I hear from Anne that my father is very much looking forward to your next visit, and that the thought of it is keeping him in good spirits. I will be paying my sister a visit myself in a couple of days to see how my father goes on. If it would be convenient for you to call upon her at that time, I would hope to thank you in person.

Yours truly,
Iain Mackay

Dear Mr Mackay,

I am unable to rest until I write this letter to you. You were quite right to chastise me when we first met. I pride myself on my Highland roots and yet I know nothing.

When I called upon your sister the first time I went because I did not - and still do not - wish for any of the people of Kildorran to feel concern or worry about the possibility of losing their homes. But now that I have heard from your father of the terrible treatment meted out to your family, and see how that kind man has been reduced to such a state, I am ashamed to call myself a Highlander

.

I think it must have been clear from my face how shocked I was, as your father told me about that terrible day in Strathnaver, when the burners came. I had heard of the evictions. I knew that people had been moved on from their land. But I had not properly appreciated the cruelty of it, the utter callousness of the men who inflicted such hardship upon their own kind.

Now I can quite understand - how could I not? - that the slightest suggestion of the same thing happening again must have you all up in arms. I am not surprised that you were angry with me. Although the rumours you have been hearing about my husband's plans for the estate are without foundation, yet I can quite appreciate that any change in ownership for those who have suffered so must bring with it a great deal of concern.

And you, Mr Mackay. Will you contrive to forgive my ignorance? You and your family have opened my eyes. For that I can only be grateful.

Yours in turmoil,
Fiona Gillespie

My dear Mrs Gillespie,
It would be dishonest of me to pretend that I was anything other than pleased to receive your letter. But do not I beg you be too hard upon yourself. There are many entirely understandable reasons for your lack of awareness. Your father, a good and honourable man, strove, as any father would, to protect his only daughter from the harsh realities of a world that was changing in ways that must have made him afraid for your future. Your husband does not share your background and sees things differently. No doubt he wishes to protect you also. If I had a wife perhaps I would wish to shield her and protect her in the same way.

My sister has been greatly reassured by your promise of security of tenure for her family. And my father cannot speak highly enough of the graciousness of the daughter of Lachlan Mackenzie. I think you cannot know how much your visit meant to them. And may I add, to me also. I wish I had known your father. If the kindness and generosity of spirit his daughter displays is anything to go by he must have been quite a man.

I leave Kildorran the day after tomorrow. I am pleased to take with me the memory of a generous woman with an honest heart.

Yours very truly,
Iain Mackay

Dear Mr Mackay,

How can I begin to thank you for what you have done for me and my son? I had hoped to be able to express my gratitude to you in person, but when I called upon your sister she explained that you had returned to Inverness. And so the written word must suffice.

You will be pleased to hear that my little boy is now fully recovered. I will never forget that it was your prompt action that saved him. It was fortunate for Robbie that you were riding by, otherwise I dread to think what might have happened to my dearest boy. You made light of it. But I know how treacherous the water can be and cannot thank you enough for your quick reaction.

I blame the unexpected warmth of the sun that saw me close my eyes for what can have only been the merest second, but in that moment Robbie must have tipped forward and slid into the water, without so much as a splash to warn his mother of impending disaster. It was your shout from the bridge that drew my attention to the danger.

Before I really knew what was happening you had plunged into the river to save him. My little wretch was barely even shaken, while his poor mother was in a terrible state, and had to rely upon the kind attention of one who must have had far more important business to attend to.

Robbie thought it a great adventure to ride back to the house upon your horse. He is more likely to remember the ride than the soaking he received! Whereas his mother will never forget what you did for us that day. I was too over-come to say much at the time and you were gone before I could thank you properly.

I am forever in your debt,
F. Gillespie

Dear Mr Mackay,

I write to you in haste because there has been some talk that there is to be an increase in the rents at Kildorran and I wished to let you know, before the rumours reached you, that there is no truth in them.

As soon as I heard what was being suggested I thought immediately of you and your family. I have heard Robert say on several occasions that to ask for money from people who have so little is the last thing any man of sense or compassion would consider. He thinks ill of men who take this route. On this occasion the rumour mongers are quite wrong.

I knew how much the thought of rent increases would worry your sister and took it upon myself to call on her to reassure her that the story is untrue. She received me with great kindness and consideration.

At first when your father saw me he seemed not to re-member me and took me again for your sister Maggie. He became rather distressed, and cried out that what they had feared had finally come to pass. But Anne managed to reassure him, and he soon recovered his composure and remembered me from my last visit.

Anne walked a little way back with me, and explained that your father is worrying for your sister, because of rumours that the people of her village are to face eviction in the near future. He expects her to arrive with her family at any moment, and frets constantly as to how they will contrive to live when they have lost everything. I said that I was sorry if my visit had contributed to his anxiety, but she told me not to worry, that when your father realised who I was he had been happy to meet me again.

You will be pleased to hear that Robbie is fully recovered, and talks of little else but his great adventure and the big black horse.

We are teaching him to swim!

Yours,

Fiona Gillespie

Dear Mrs Gillespie,

It was good of you to think of my sister. I had not heard the rumours of which you write but am delighted to hear that there is no cause for concern. You will be aware that we have much to worry about in the case of our dear sister Maggie, so it is good to know that at least Anne is secure.

I am delighted to hear that your son is well. And glad that I was able to be of service. He is a brave lad and seemed

to recover very quickly after his adventure. I would welcome reassurance that it is not just your son who is fully
recovered, but that his mother is also restored to good health
and humour. I could not help but notice that you were very
pale when we said goodbye, and that your hand trembled
in mine. Would you do me a great favour? Put my mind at
rest by writing to let me know that you are well.

Yours as ever,
Iain Mackay

Dear Mr Mackay,

It is very good of you to worry about me but completely
unnecessary. Let me reassure you that I am absolutely fine
and very much ashamed of my feeble behaviour. It is the
vulnerability of motherhood. I can assure you that it is not
my usual habit to succumb to such displays of frailty.

I hope that you will not think it impertinent but Robbie
has been asking about the man on the big black horse who
jumped into the river on his account. He has asked me when
he will see you again. I like to believe it is so that he may
thank you properly for saving his life, but I have a feeling
that he is more interested in seeing your horse.

Is there a chance that when you next visit your sister
you might call upon us so that my little boy can thank you
in person?

Yours,
Fiona Gillespie

Dear Mrs Gillespie,

I am pleased to hear that Nero made such a lasting impression. My family are gathering to celebrate my father's sixty fifth birthday at the end of the month. I am hoping to bring my sister Maggie with me to join in the celebrations. If I may I will call on you then.

Yours truly,

Iain Mackay

My good friend,

I so enjoyed our conversation this last time we met. And if we have fallen into 'some kind of a friendship' then I am glad of it, for I am learning a great deal. There is so much to know about this country of ours, and it seems to me that I have a lot of catching up to do.

I would have been fascinated to meet your Mr Mulock. He sounds a great character and an interesting companion in your travels around the Highlands. I can appreciate that it must have been most frustrating to deal with his inconsistencies. But I am sure that you are right and without him you would not be in the position to understand the situation as clearly as you do.

I very much hope that your fears for your sister Maggie prove unfounded and that the rumours of evictions at Greenyards come to nothing. I think it entirely understandable that a brother would worry so for his sister, particularly when she and the women of her village are planning a campaign of resistance. But I have to tell you that in her situation I would do exactly the same.

You were quite right about Mary. I was in her bad books after you left. How frustrating it is to be forced to abide by social convention, when our relationship is closer to that of a teacher and his pupil than to anything else. Would it be frowned upon in the same way if you were visiting to teach me the verbs and vocabulary of the French language? What does she imagine we are doing? Is she worried that you are behaving improperly towards me? I think she would be greatly surprised if she knew the subject of our conversation.

Please dear sir, I beg you, don't stop now. I would not wish to put you into a difficult position for all the world. But there is still so much I don't know. And as a Mackenzie of Kildorran I owe it to my people to make sure I am properly informed.

Yours hopefully,
F. Gillespie

My dear Mrs Gillespie,

It seems that we have no option but to be sensible. Anne has written to tell me that it has been mentioned to her on more than one occasion that her brother and the old chief's daughter seem to have a lot to say to each other. Several people from Kildorran, who noticed us talking together at the Games, have heard how I rescued your son and seem to know all about my calling upon you. Let us not give those *who look for trouble any reason to cause it. It is my honour to call you friend. I think we must leave it at that.*

My best wishes for your future happiness.

Sincerely yours,

Iain Mackay

Mr Mackay

Forgive me, my dear sir, but I had to write. I know you think it unwise for us to correspond, but I find myself in a most dreadful situation with no option but to pass news on to you which I know will cause you and your family distress.

It is hard to know where to begin to tell you what has happened. Indeed I am in such a state of shock that I can hardly think straight. But there is no avoiding it. The truth will come out all too soon.

This morning I received a visit from my father's factor, John. It was immediately obvious to me - from the way he bit at his lip and would not look me in the eye - that something had happened to cause him great anguish. He stood in the doorway, turning his cap over and over in his hand and would not come inside, even though I invited him in. When I asked him to tell me what it was that was troubling him he looked so upset that I was immediately worried that something had happened to one of my boys. But then he explained that he had just come from the office of Duncan Grant, the land agent recently appointed by my husband to manage the estate for him. While John waited to see him he noticed a letter on the man's desk. He hadn't intended to pry, but he couldn't help noticing a list of names beside the letter, and that the list of names included his own.

As you might imagine, the sight of his name was a matter of great concern to him. So much so that he leant across the desk and read the letter. I don't have to explain to you his shock when he discovered it was a letter advising all tenants of my husband's plans to transform Kildorran into a sporting estate.

When John first told me this I would not believe him. I insisted that he must have been mistaken. But he took out a sheet of paper from his pocket onto which he had copied the words, and when I read it for myself there could be no misunderstanding it.

'The people will be allowed to remain in their cottages, but they will not be permitted to graze their animals upon any land belonging to the estate, nor will they be able to sow or harvest any crop, and they will be required to work for the estate under the terms laid down by Mr Gillespie.'

My dear Mr Mackay, what else can I tell you? I cannot bring myself to believe that my husband has authorised such a thing. And without discussing it with me. I know he is concerned that the estate has to pay its way, but this goes beyond anything I could ever have imagined.

He is away from home for the next week or so, but when he returns I will do what I can to persuade him to change his plans. Nevertheless, it might be wise for you to warn your sister and her family.

Yours in despair,

F. Gillespie

Dear Mr Mackay,

I have spoken to Robert. He believes that the best opportunity for making Kildorran profitable lies in its development as a sporting estate. He is confident that when I have given it proper thought I will agree with him. It is like talking to a stranger.

I begged him to reconsider, told him that what he is intending goes against everything my father would have wanted. But there seems to be no common ground between us, and I cannot imagine how we are to resolve this.

I have been to see your sister Anne, who told me that she has already heard rumours of what Robert is planning. I told her that I would do everything in my power to try and persuade him to change his mind. But the truth is that we are too angry even to speak to each other, and I think he would not listen to me even if we did.

I am ashamed to admit it, but for the past few days I have been laid low with feelings of helplessness and despair. Until this morning John came to see me, and he told me to pull myself together and remember that I am a Mackenzie of Kildorran and that our family motto is 'Courage against the odds'.

My husband has gone away to Edinburgh to meet with his business partners. The letters to the tenants will not be delivered until his return, so we have some time. I keep on thinking of your sister Maggie and the women of Strathcarron. Their brave plan to resist the evictions is a source of inspiration to me. Be assured I will not sit by and let this happen without a fight.

Yours,
Fiona Gillespie

Anna finished reading and sat back in her chair. Fin gazed at her.

"That's it?"

She nodded. "That's it."

He let out his breath. "It rather leaves us hanging. At least we know a bit more about the situation at Kildorran. Although the letters raises more questions that they answer. There's still so much we don't know."

Anna pushed her chair away from the desk and stood up.

"I simply refuse to be beaten by this. We are going to find out what happened next if it kills us."

He raised his eyebrows.

"I'm rather hoping it won't come to that."

He was laughing, but she couldn't help wondering if he was beginning to lose patience with her. Even she could see that her behaviour was inconsistent. He leant back in his chair, watching her with the suggestion of a smile in his eyes. His expression was hard to interpret. Feeling rather foolish, she sat down again.

"You think I'm being impossible, don't you?"

"I think you're…" He stopped himself.

"What? You think I'm what?"

"Doesn't matter."

"It matters to me."

"OK… I think your enthusiasm does you credit."

She had a feeling it wasn't what he had been going to say.

"Are you patronising me again?"

He shook his head. "What were you saying about being impossible?"

She had the good grace to laugh. "I'm sorry. I'm all over the place, I know. It must be a nightmare trying to keep up with me."

"It's quite a challenge…"

Their eyes met and held, and then he dropped his head, and frowned at the pile of letters on the desk in front of him. "Let's go through these again. See if there are any leads we can follow up."

He was suddenly serious.

"Good idea," said Anna. "But, before we start, there's one thing I wanted to ask about. Fiona mentions the women at Greenyards, that they were planning a campaign of resistance. What exactly happened there? Do you know anything about it?"

Fin frowned.

"When I was doing the research for my book, it was the Strathnaver evictions I was most interested in. I do remember reading something about the women over at Strathcarron, how they were the ones to stand up to the men when they came to evict them. But I don't remember the details."

Anna picked up Fiona's letters.

"I have a feeling we should try and find out more about the ladies of Greenyards. Fiona seems to have been inspired by them. I think they might be significant."

"The museum in Ullapool might have something. And we could try the archives of the local papers." He thought for a moment. "And there's an old guy in Achiltibuie – a neighbour of Aunt Sarah's. I'm pretty certain his family came from Strathcarron. He would definitely be worth a visit."

She leapt up.

"What are we waiting for?"

"You want to go now?" He glanced at his watch. "Well, why not. It's twelve thirty, we could do with a break. We could go to Achiltibuie and find out if the old guy is still around. And on our way back we'll stop in Ullapool and see what we can find in the museum. And then we'll go through this lot again. You never know we might have missed something."

There was a sound in the corridor. And a loud voice coming closer.

"Don't worry, Barbara. I know the way. Is this where she's hiding?"

A face in the doorway. It was Cameron. There was a flash of white teeth as he smiled at Anna. "Anna… dear girl." And then he caught sight of Fin and the smile disappeared.

"Fin… What are you doing here?"

He stepped into the room and was kissing Anna on both cheeks. Over his shoulder she was pleased to see Fin surreptitiously open the desk drawer and slide the letters inside, before locking it and pocketing the key.

"I heard that you were leaving so I popped in to say goodbye." Cameron held Anna's hands in his. "Now Barbara tells me that you're not going after all. So I thought I might be able to tempt you out for some lunch. Didn't realise you had company. I hope I haven't interrupted anything."

"Nothing important," said Anna. "We were just going through some of Charlie's things for Barbara. She wanted Fin's advice about some books she wants to sell."

Fin grinned broadly.

"Called in the expert. Glad to be of service."

Cameron looked him up and down.

"How very philanthropic of you, Fin. I thought you were hard at work on the next bestseller." Anna was fascinated by the way he could smile with his mouth, while his eyes were like chips of ice. "So how about lunch, Anna? Can I tempt you to join me?"

"That's really sweet of you, Cameron…"

"But she's got another date." Fin came round the desk and stood in front of it with his arms folded. "We're just off to see Sarah. We were on our way out when you arrived."

Barbara had followed Cameron down the corridor and was standing in the doorway.

"You two just off, are you?" she said calmly. "I didn't get the chance to explain to Cameron that you already had plans."

Anna could have hugged her. How ever was she going to manage without Barbara's intuition and wisdom when she finally got around to going home?

"I'll just get my bag," she told Fin. "See you outside. Bye Cameron." She kissed him quickly on the cheek and left the room. Barbara followed her.

"I couldn't stop him," she said in a low voice, her hand on Anna's arm. "He must have heard your voices, and he was down the corridor before I could say anything. I hope he didn't see anything important."

Anna took hold of her hand and gave it a squeeze.

"I'm sure he didn't. And thanks for covering for us. I owe you."

Barbara walked with Anna to the front door. "Just a thought," she said, letting go of Anna's hand. "You did hide those letters, didn't you? Cameron is still down in the study. You don't want him sniffing around and finding them."

"It's alright. I saw Fin lock them away in the desk drawer. We'll be back this afternoon to carry on."

"You can accuse me of being oversensitive if you like," said Fin, accelerating along the track towards the main road. "But I got the distinct impression that Cameron was less than delighted to see me. What do you reckon?"

Anna laughed.

"He's not a big fan of yours, is he?"

He glanced at her out of the corner of his eye.

"He's a big fan of yours though -"

Anna rolled her eyes.

"Cameron's alright," she said. "Just a bit pleased with himself sometimes."

Fin snorted.

"You can say that again."

"Let's not talk about Cameron. I'm much more interested in this man we're on our way to see."

"If he's there. We'll go and see if Aunt Sarah can help us track him down. And we'll stop and have some lunch while we're at it."

"Lunch? Do we have time?"

Her foot beat out an impatient rhythm on the floor, she drummed her fingertips against the edge of the seat. Fin reached out and laid a hand over hers.

"Relax," he told her. "Enjoy. This isn't a race, you know."

He wasn't to know it, but he was wrong.

CHAPTER SEVENTEEN

At Rowancross House Barbara was making coffee. She was doing it reluctantly. She had been hoping that when Fin and Anna left Cameron would go too. But he'd stayed – and made 'a drink would be nice' noises which had been impossible to ignore.

"Do you want milk and sugar, Cameron?"

He was prowling round the kitchen. Barbara poured boiling water onto a teaspoon of instant coffee in a mug. She was blowed if she was going to go to the effort of making the real thing. Cameron was clearly annoyed, presumably at the way Fin had swept Anna away from under his nose, and the last thing Barbara wanted was to get stuck with him while he offloaded his irritation onto her. Cameron on a good day was fine company. Cameron in the kind of mood he was in now was not.

The phone rang and Barbara picked up the receiver. Richard's voice said hello on the other end of the line. Barbara's heart sank.

He had just read Anna's text message. Was she there? She'd just popped out, had she? OK... Left her mobile behind... Again. Well, perhaps Barbara could clarify things for him. Had he got this right? His wife wouldn't be there to meet him when he arrived at the airport tomorrow? Barbara closed her eyes for a second. When she opened them she saw that Cameron was watching her. She made an apologetic face at him and went out into the hall to deal with Richard without an audience.

Left alone in the kitchen Cameron glared into his coffee mug. Finding Fin with Anna, the two of them all cosy together, was just plain aggravating. What were they up to? From the expression in their eyes when he interrupted them he was convinced that they were hiding something. He was pretty certain he had seen Fin slip something into the desk drawer when he came in.

He had a notion what it might be about. When he bumped into Fin that day outside the bookshop Fin had mentioned how Anna had been asking about whether Fiona and Iain would have known each other. At the time Cameron had been distracted by the satisfaction he felt when he heard that Fin and Anna hadn't hit it off. But, now that he thought about it, there had to be a reason for Anna to put the two of them together. She must have found something linking Fiona Gillespie with Iain Mackay.

She had been about to reveal something the day they walked up to the minister's house, and then decided not to at the last minute. And why was she was spending so much time with Fin MacLean when they didn't get on? There had to be something behind it.

From outside he could hear Barbara's muffled voice as she spoke on the phone. A thought occurred to him. Setting down his mug he went quietly out of the room and down the corridor to Charlie's study. With quick furtive steps he crossed to the desk and tried the drawer, rattling it with frustration when he found that it was locked. He looked around the room, opening drawers and cupboards, but could see nothing that looked as though it might be worth investigating. He was about to go back to the kitchen when, out of the corner of his eye, he caught a glimpse of something white on the floor under the leather armchair behind the desk. Looking over his shoulder, expecting Barbara to appear at any moment, he crossed over to the chair and picked up the letter that was lying there. He read it. Read it through again. Then put it back exactly as he had found it.

When Barbara returned to the kitchen Cameron was sitting at the table sipping his coffee.

"Everything OK?" he asked.

Barbara smiled sweetly at him as she picked up her cup. "Fine," she said. The last thing she was going to do was discuss Anna's marriage with Cameron.

"Anna's husband, was it? He must be wondering when she's coming home. Seems a very odd sort of relationship to me. They don't seem to spend much time together."

Barbara was putting the milk back in the fridge and pretended she didn't hear him. But Cameron wasn't going to leave it alone.

"I thought she was meant to be leaving us. What made her change her mind?"

Barbara shut the fridge door.

"She's enjoying herself," she said.

Cameron smiled.

"With Fin Maclean?" he murmured. "Really?"

Barbara had had enough.

"Look Cameron… I've got rather a lot on today. If you don't mind…"

At last he seemed to get the message. He stood up. Uttering a silent prayer of thanks Barbara walked with him to the front door. He paused on the doorstep.

"Is Anna still looking into the family history while she's up here? I haven't heard her mention it for a while. I hope she hasn't lost interest."

Barbara looked at him suspiciously.

"Why do you ask?"

"Because I've been thinking I'd really like to do something to help. I've got some letters that Robert Gillespie wrote to Fiona when he was away from home. I thought she might like to see them."

"Letters from Robert…?" It was the first she had heard of them.

"To be honest with you I haven't looked at them in years. But I know Anna's particularly interested in Fiona."

"Did Charlie ever see these letters?"

Cameron frowned.

"Do you know, I don't think he did."

Barbara clenched her fists.

"When Charlie was writing his book about Robert didn't it cross your mind that these letters might have been useful?"

Cameron shrugged.

"He never seemed terribly interested in the domestic side of Robert's life. Which is all these letters are."

Barbara stared at him.

"Did he know about them, Cameron?"

"Probably. I can't remember. I've had them for years. Never thought that much about them to be honest with you." He was avoiding Barbara's gaze.

"It was Anna showing so much interest in Fiona that made me think of them."

"Was it?" said Barbara through gritted teeth.

He stepped out through the front door. "You know, Barbara?" He glanced back at her. "A book about Fiona would be an interesting project. Maybe you should suggest it to Anna. Publishers would take her seriously, I'm sure of it."

"It's certainly a thought, Cameron."

Barbara held the door ready to close it on him.

"I know a thing or two about putting a book together, and I've got all the right connections. No doubt Fin could help. But he's really more use in North America. If Anna's found something interesting while she's been going through Fiona's stuff you would be doing her a real favour if you pointed her in my direction. And I'd like to help. Families should stick together, don't you think?"

Before she could reply he was gone. Barbara shut the front door and went along the corridor to the kitchen lost in thought. Cameron had left her with a sense of something being not quite right. But she couldn't put her finger on what it could possibly be.

Cameron drove away from Rowancross with his mind working overtime. That letter he had come across under the chair in Charlie's study had been quite an eye-opener. A letter to Fiona Gillespie from Iain Mackay, a letter that suggested a developing relationship between them. It was an intriguing discovery

Because now that he had time to consider it he remembered that there had been a rumour. His grandfather Cullum had mentioned it to him once. Something about a scandal narrowly averted. Something to do with Fiona going astray, disappearing for a period of time with no explanation as to where she might have been.

It had been hushed up at the time. Robert Gillespie had told nobody, and nothing had ever come out to explain what had really happened. Cullum had heard about it from his father Robert, Fiona's oldest son, and the only reason that Robert knew anything about it was because he was just old enough to remember the fuss at home when she disappeared.

Cameron pressed his foot on the accelerator and headed for home. He wanted to get back and take another look at the letters he'd mention to Barbara. Maybe they contained something to help shed light on the matter, some insignificant detail that might seem trivial on first reading but was packed with meaning when you knew the background. He had to find out. Because whatever it was that Fiona and Iain had got up to he was pretty certain that Anna and

Fin were onto it. And he wanted to get there before they did.

⇥ ⇤

After Cameron had gone Barbara couldn't relax until she had gone to Charlie's study to check that nothing important had been left lying around for him to stick his nose into. It was a relief to see that the desk was clear. She didn't notice the letter on the floor behind it.

She went back to the kitchen and cleared Cameron's empty mug into the dishwasher. He had been behaving very strangely. She didn't know how it had happened, but she was pretty certain that he had got wind of the fact that Anna had discovered something interesting and was following it up with Fin. All that stuff about helping her with her research. It hadn't rung true.

But there was one thing Cameron had said that had got her thinking. Barbara couldn't deny it. She loved the idea of Anna picking up where Charlie had left off and writing a book about Fiona. There were so many reasons why it would be a good thing for her to do. She would suggest to Anna that she should at least talk to Cameron, if for no other reason than to see these letters he had kept so quiet about. Because you never knew - they might contain something that would help in her pursuit of the truth. And if a book were to come out of it… Well that would be an unexpected bonus.

At that moment the last thing on Anna's mind was talking to Cameron. When Fin turned off the main road and headed towards Achiltibuie her impatience to get to the bottom of the mystery faded away in the face of the spectacular scenery. They were driving beside gleaming stretches of water with mountains soaring up and away from them. Clouds moved across the sky casting shadows over the purple hills, so that they were constantly changing colour and form in the shifting light. It was quite a thought that this landscape must have looked pretty much the same when the Vikings came.

"I've been thinking about what you said back there."

Fin's voice shook her into the present.

"About the women at Greenyards." He pulled into a passing place to allow a car coming in the opposite direction to go by. "I remember reading about the evictions that took place at Glencalvie. Which I'm pretty certain was just up the glen from Greenyards."

"Did the women at Glencalvie try to resist the evictions?

"I'm pretty certain they did… The women and the children."

"Did they succeed?"

He frowned.

"I don't think so. There was something about them taking shelter in the churchyard. That's what stuck in my mind. That's why I remember it."

"You think something similar happened at Greenyards?"

Fin shook his head.

"It's frustrating. I wish I could remember."

"Do you think that maybe Fiona heard about the women at Greenyards resisting eviction and got them to do the same thing at Kildorran?"

"It's possible I suppose. But like I said before, don't you think that if she had we would know about it. You couldn't keep something like that quiet."

"Perhaps Robert got involved in hushing the whole thing up. He was pretty influential wasn't he?"

"He was," said Fin. "But even so it would have been a hell of a thing to keep a lid on. Robert had too many enemies who would have been delighted to use his wife's actions against him. Something would have slipped out about it, I'm sure of it. And if it had your father would have been certain to pick up on it when he was doing his research. The one thing about Charlie was that he was incredibly thorough."

Anna stared out of the window.

"I hate the thought that I might have to leave before we find out what really happened."

Fin frowned.

"What's this about leaving? I thought you were staying."

"I am. But I've got to be realistic. God knows what Richard is going to say about all of this when he gets my text. And my youngest daughter is due back home at the end of next week. Whatever happens I have to be there to get her ready to go back to school."

"So how long have you got?"

"I don't really know. Three or four days -"

"Well," he said in a determined voice, "if all we've got is three or four days then we need to work fast. We're going to crack this before you have to go, if it's the last thing we do."

When they pulled up outside his aunt's house her car was parked in the drive, but there was no sign of her inside. She would be walking her dog, said Fin, and he took Anna down the road to The Summer Isles Hotel for a drink while they waited for her to return.

They sat on the terrace outside the hotel bar looking out across the view of the sea and scattered islands. The sun was warm on their faces. Anna sat back in the wooden chair and closed her eyes. Her legs were stretched out in front of her; she looked very much at home. Fin found it hard to imagine that she had another life, with a husband and daughters waiting for her to step back into their world.

As if she sensed him watching her she opened her eyes and met his gaze. Fin hadn't noticed before but the blue green of her irises was exactly the same colour as the sea.

"What is it? What's wrong? Have I got something on my face?"

"No... You're fine." He looked away, feeling caught out. It was a relief to see Sarah walking back along the road towards her cottage with her cocker spaniel at her heels. He stood up and waved, and called her over to join them. When she drew near Fin pulled up a chair for her, and she sat down beside Anna while he went inside to buy her a drink.

"I was sure Barbara told me you were flying home today," she said, motioning to her dog to sit beside her. "Did you change your mind?"

Anna smiled.

"Something like that."

"I hear you've been finding out about your great great grandmother. She sounds like quite a girl."

"She was." It was a novelty for Anna to have a family history she could be proud of.

"They were a tough lot, those Highland lasses," said Sarah, sitting back in her chair and smiling at

Anna. "When the men weren't sitting around drinking and singing songs about their bravery they were going off to war, or fighting with their neighbours, or hunting, or doing any of those other macho things that men seem to think are so important. It was the women who stayed put and got on with the hard work of looking after things at home. If you look at old photographs of life up here it's invariably the women you see carrying the heavy loads, digging the peat, even dragging the ploughs in place of the horses. But where are the songs to celebrate their heroic deeds? Nobody ever sang about washing the clothes and cooking the dinner, did they?"

Anna laughed.

"They were probably too busy doing the chores to find the time for writing songs about it."

"And of course history is written by men, isn't it?" Sarah called to the spaniel, which had begun to edge towards a child at the next table whose sandwich was at an accessible level. "Which is why they always get the starring roles. The only woman who gets much more than a mention in Scottish history - apart from poor old Mary Queen of Scots - is Flora MacDonald. And she's always irritated the hell out of me. She rows Bonnie Prince Charlie out of trouble, leaving his supporters to carry the can for him, and she's a heroine forever."

"Only because of the song…"

"My point exactly. But where does that leave all the others? Does anybody know about the women who were there at the '45, when the clans gathered to march on England? They went south with their men - often with their children in tow - in support of the Prince and his army. And suffered incredible hardship along the way. But who tells their story?

And what about the women who supplied him with the money and manpower to fight his cause? They tend to get mentioned in the history books as some sort of romantic appendage. As if the only reason they supported him was because they were all madly in love with him. I mean I ask you. What kind of press is that for the girls?"

"It does seem terribly one-sided in favour of the men."

"Doesn't it?"

Fin, returning with a drink for Sarah caught the tail end of their conversation. "What are you two getting so hot under the collar about?"

Anna and Sarah exchanged glances.

"Just girl talk, Fin dear. Nothing that would interest you," said Sarah amicably, taking the glass from him. "So what are your plans for the rest of the day? You haven't driven all the way out here just to see me, have you?"

"Actually we have," said Fin. "But we've got an ulterior motive. We're trying to find out about what happened during the Clearances over at Strathcarron. And I remembered that the old guy who lives up the road came from over that way. Am I right in thinking that he was a bit of an expert about the area?"

Sarah nodded.

"You mean James Munro. Such a charming man," she told Anna. "He's got to be well into his eighties by now. Used to walk miles across the hills every day. Said it kept him young. It certainly seemed to do the trick." She turned to Fin. "We spent an evening with him in the bar here, do you remember? When he told us all about his childhood."

Fin raised his eyebrows.

"Didn't he just."

Sarah laughed.

"Once he got started you couldn't stop him with a bullet. But most of it was fascinating."

Fin shook his head.

"He lost me after the first world war, I'm afraid I stopped paying attention. But I do remember him saying that he grew up in a cottage beside the river Carron. In the same glen as Glencalvie and Greenyards."

"He did. And he moved back that way to Dornoch a couple of years ago, to live with his daughter. Said she needed looking after, although I think it was the other way round. I had a Christmas card from him this year and he's still going strong. I'm sure he'd be delighted to talk to you. He always loved an audience. Do you want me to give him a call?"

Fin looked at Anna.

"What do you think? It could be useful. We could drive over and see him."

Anna nodded. She was willing to try anything.

"I'll go and ring him right away, if you like," said Sarah, standing up. "Have you eaten yet?" When they shook their heads she suggested they came back with her and have some lunch while she tried to get hold of James Munro.

They walked back to Sarah's house where she heated up some soup and set it out on a tray with a loaf of bread and some cheese and oatcakes. Fin and Anna took the tray outside onto the little terrace looking out over the bay, while Sarah rang Mr Munro. It turned out that he was delighted at the prospect of visitors interested in the Clearances. And, with time running out for Anna, it was agreed that they would visit him the following day. Sarah joined them in the garden, and they sat in the sun and spent a pleasant half an hour or so watching the sea change colour in accordance with the mood of the sky. The rest of the world seemed a long way away. Anna sat in the shade of Sarah's tamarisk tree and wished she could stop the clock.

But then she glanced at Fin, and saw that he was watching her, as he had been watching her on and off all day. And she thought that it was probably a very good thing that she only had a few days left. Because she had a feeling that otherwise things had the potential to get complicated. As if they weren't complicated enough already.

Fin must have noticed her noticing him, because he got up rather quickly and suggested he drive her home, so that she could get on with rereading the letters, while he went on into Ullapool to see what the museum and the bookshop had to offer. And it felt like a spell had been broken.

The sun was behind them as they headed back along the single-track road towards Ullapool. Anna leant back in her seat and watched the scenery roll by. In the shadow of the mountains, the comings and goings of human beings seemed irrelevant. These peaks and valleys, hills and lochs, that had been here for so many hundreds of thousands of years, made the one hundred and fifty that had passed since Iain wrote to Fiona seem like the merest blink of an eye.

Fin was naming the mountains for her. Ben More Coigach on their left, the foothills of Cul Beag rising up away to their right, the bizarrely shaped chimney that was Stac Pollaidh squatting darkly by the side of the road, and the mighty Suilven far off in the distance. Their outlines had become familiar to her, their brooding silhouettes shaping the horizon from many miles away. There was something wonderfully reassuring about their longevity.

Fin pointed to the climbers, black dots in the distance, clinging to the edge of Stac Pollaidh.

"You wouldn't believe the number of times the helicopters are called out to rescue people from the top," he said. "It might look like a relatively straightforward climb, but you'd be an idiot to underestimate this little mountain and tackle it unprepared."

He went on to tell Anna that, by comparison with the mountain ranges in Canada, Stac Pollaidh was an anthill. And that the winters over there made a January day in the Highlands seem like spring. After a while he stopped talking and reached out to switch on the radio. The fluid notes of a Bach violin concerto poured out of the speakers. And for a few precious miles, as they drove through the mountains, Anna felt complete contentment. And would not have changed one single thing.

They arrived at the junction with the main road to Ullapool. Fin waited as a lorry rolled by, belching out thick black fumes. It was a rude reminder of the real world that lay waiting for them. Fin pulled out and followed in the lorry's wake.

"He'll be stopped if he carries on like that."

He glanced over at Anna. Her eyes were closed and he wondered if she was asleep. But then she smiled.

"You're doing it again."

"What?"

"Staring at me."

He focused on the road ahead.

"I wasn't."

"Liar."

She turned her head and looked at him.

"Sorry." He reached out and took her hand and squeezed it. "I can't help myself. It's because you're beautiful."

"I am?"

"Of course you are."

"That's the nicest thing anyone's said to me in a long time."

She let her hand rest in his. When they drew up outside Rowancross House he still hadn't let go. He turned off the engine. And then he pulled her towards him and kissed her.

Barbara, walking down the staircase, paused on the mid landing to look out through the window at the car that had pulled up in the driveway. She recognised it as Sarah's and guessed that Fin must have brought Anna back. She sighed. She would have to tell Anna that Richard had called. She wondered if she should warn her about how angry he had sounded.

She peered through the window. Fin and Anna were sitting in the car. She could see their heads turn towards each other. When she saw them kiss she turned away, feeling uncomfortably like a voyeur. She continued on her way downstairs, wondering and anxious.

Anna got out of the car and shut the door behind her. Fin sat and watched as she walked away from him towards the house. She turned in the doorway and lifted a hand to wave goodbye. Then she was gone. He sat for a moment, not moving. Then he started the engine and backed up the car.

This was the last thing he had expected. And the last thing he needed. He would drive into Ullapool and see if there was anybody he knew at the Ferry. He needed a drink and some male company.

In Moscow Richard Sinclair sat on the edge of his bed in his overheated hotel room with his head in his hands. The hangover that had been tormenting him all day had finally begun to ease. But as it dwindled his guilt was ballooning to fill the gap. That woman… last night… What had he been thinking of? An image of slippery skin and peroxide hair tumbling across his face sneaked unwanted into his mind. He shook his head to try and erase the picture. But it stayed put, as sharp and clear as a snapshot, unwilling to allow him the luxury of pretending that nothing had happened.

He stood up and stumbled across to the window. As he looked out at the light fading across the grey city he told himself that this was all Anna's fault. None of it would have happened if she hadn't been behaving so strangely. She couldn't have any idea of how hard it was for him. Living out of a suitcase. Never at home for long enough to feel like he belonged there. Always out of step with the rest of his family. He felt like a stranger everywhere. He was tired of it, wanted it all to end. He had spent years and years fighting his corner, angling and working and strategising to get to where he was. Now he couldn't quite remember why.

He brushed a hand across his eyes. It was alright for Anna. She could choose what she wanted to do. He had rung earlier because more than anything he needed to hear the sound of her voice. But she had gone out. And what was it that Barbara had said on the phone? Anna was staying on a bit longer. Something unexpected had come up at the last minute. It was so unlike her. He wished he knew what she was playing at. Was she doing it to annoy him, to punish him for the fact that he wasn't up there with her?

If he had been a weaker man he would have cried. But tears were pointless. He had no choice but to keep going. Had always had to be strong. It wasn't a question of doing what he wanted. If it hadn't been for him the family would have fallen apart.

He thought of the woman, Yelena. She had made it clear from the start what she wanted. And again last night. He could still smell her perfume on his skin. Didn't seem able to get rid of it. It was sweet and strong, so different to Anna's. Yelena hadn't been too tired or too angry or too distant. But losing himself in her hadn't made him feel any better. In fact it had made him feel a very great deal worse.

Barbara was at her desk writing letters when Anna came in.

"Helpful trip?" she asked.

"Very. We saw Sarah. She sent her love."

Barbara looked up and saw that Anna's cheeks were flushed.

"There's tea in the pot if you want it. Just made -"

Anna turned towards the kitchen.

"Do you want one?"

Barbara glanced down at her letter.

"I've had one already, but I'd love another."

Anna backed out of the room.

"By the way," called Barbara after her. "Richard rang. Just after you left with Fin."

Anna head re-appeared through the doorway, her face even pinker than before.

"How did he sound?"

"Well, let's just say that it wasn't what you'd call the easiest of conversations."

Anna came all the way back into the room.

"Oh Barbara. I'm so sorry."

"It's fine, honey," said Barbara. "But I do think it might be a good idea if you rang and spoke to him yourself."

Anna nodded.

"I'll go and do it now."

She picked up her handbag and found her mobile. As she walked to the kitchen she was dialling Richard's number.

In his hotel room Richard saw her name come up on his phone. He stared at it. It rang for a while before switching to his messaging service. He picked up his jacket and left the room.

That evening Barbara and Anna ate together at the kitchen table. After failing to get hold of Richard Anna had gone off to her father's study alone and shut the door. She tried to settle down and reread the letters she had found that morning. But they raised almost as many questions as they answered. And she had a lot on her mind. What happened next between Fiona and Iain? Why wasn't Richard picking up his phone? And what was she going to do about Fin?

The feel of his lips against hers, the way he held her face between his hands as he kissed her – she couldn't stop herself from going back and reliving the moment. The memory of it made her catch her breath; with guilt, with pleasure, it was difficult to know. But she couldn't forget about it, no matter how hard she tried.

She had little appetite for food. Sat twisting spaghetti on her fork in a way that would have infuriated her if Ellie or Rose had done the same. It felt as if her old life had been shattered and the fragments thrown up into the air. Now they were spinning slowly above her, while she waited to see how they would fall.

Barbara ate quietly, watching as emotions chased each other across Anna's face like clouds across the sun. She said nothing, understanding that what Anna needed most was to be left in peace to work things out for herself. When they had finished Anna cleared the table while Barbara made tea for them. She handed Anna a mug, and they headed to the sitting room where they curled up at either end of one of the sofas.

"So what's the next step as far as Fiona is concerned?"

Barbara was hoping that focussing on the past might help Anna to stop worrying about the present for a while.

Anna sighed.

"It's frustrating. The letters leave us hanging in mid-air. It's possible that Fiona was planning some kind of resistance in response to Robert's plans to turn Kildorran into a sporting estate. We think she might have got the idea from Iain's sister at Greenyards. But so far we have no way of proving anything, no way of being certain." She looked Barbara in the eye for the first time since she had returned from her day out with Fin. "And I really have to go home. I can't stay on here much longer."

"No," agreed Barbara softly.

"Fin is taking me to Strathcarron tomorrow. He's going to text me and let me know what time he's picking me up. We're going to meet an old friend of Sarah's. Hopefully he might be able to come up with something to move us forward."

"And if he doesn't?"

Anna shrugged.

"Fin will have to carry on without me."

Barbara took their mugs back to the kitchen while Anna went to find her mobile to see if Fin had been in touch. She heard the house phone ring and, when she joined Barbara, found her having a conversation which ended with her handing the phone across to Anna. It was Cameron.

Barbara had told Anna about the chat she had had with him after Fin and Anna had left. And about how surprised she had been to hear of the existence of the hitherto undisclosed letters from Robert to Fiona, which she couldn't help feeling Cameron had intentionally withheld from Charlie. She hadn't wanted to give Anna more to worry about, so she didn't mention her concern that Cameron appeared to have got wind of Anna's discovery.

His voice on the phone was genial. He apologised for ringing so late in the evening.

"I didn't want to leave it until the morning in case I missed you," he said. "The thing is that I've just spoken with my cousin Hamish. Who is also your cousin Hamish. He and his wife Caroline have been fishing up on the Naver and are dropping in for dinner on their way back tomorrow night. When I mentioned that you were staying with Barbara he was particularly anxious to meet you. His father and your father were great mates when they were growing up but he couldn't make it to the memorial. So I suggested inviting you over for dinner and he jumped at the idea. He and Caroline would love to meet you."

Anna's heart sank. She didn't want to spend one of the few precious evenings she had left with strangers.

"It's sweet of you to ask, Cameron, but I think Barbara's got something planned for me -"

But Cameron wasn't going to give her the chance to refuse him.

"I just checked with her. She said she was pretty certain you were free."

"Did she?" Anna raised her eyebrows at Barbara who made an apologetic face at her.

"She's told you about my letters? I know you'd find them really interesting. If you came over for dinner I could show them to you."

"I would certainly love to see them".

"So say yes. You owe me. After blowing me out at lunchtime… And you can kill two birds with one stone. You can see the letters and meet Hamish and Caroline at the same time. You will like them, they're great fun. And they're family. Who knows when you will get another chance?"

He had a point. Anna thought to herself that if these letters of his contained anything useful it made sense to look at them sooner rather than later. And these cousins – it would be a shame not to meet them when they were so close by. So she said yes.

Later on her way to bed she decided to have another look at the letters she had found that morning. It had become a ritual, every night at bedtime, reading something Fiona had written. With only a few nights left she didn't want to stop now.

She went along the dark corridor to her father's study and flicked the light switch by the door. When she crossed over to the desk she noticed that one of the letters was lying on the floor behind the chair. She stared at it. How had it got there? Had someone been in and opened the drawer?

She bent to pick up the letter. When she tried the drawer it was a relief to find that it was still locked. Fin had given her the key and now she opened it to check that the other letters were where he had hidden them when Cameron turned up. They were all there. She tucked the one she had found back with the others. It must have fallen to the floor when Fin slid them into the drawer, and he hadn't noticed. She took them with her to her bedroom. Better to keep them all safe together. She would hate for any of them to get lost, or fall into the wrong hands.

CHAPTER EIGHTEEN

"Hey… Laura… Where the hell are you?"

It was morning and breakfast at The White Lodge was finished and cleared away. Laura was sitting at the kitchen table with a cup of coffee in her hand, reading Heat magazine, and wondering if she had enough money in her account to buy a copy of the handbag that all the celebrities seemed to be carrying this summer.

With a sigh she put her cup down and turned to see Cameron framed in the doorway, wearing nothing but a towel around his hips. His torso was still dripping from the shower. Usually when he appeared in this partially clothed state it was a precursor to something else. But Laura knew him well enough to know that sex after showering was a no-go as far as Cameron was concerned.

"What do you want?" Her voice was cool.

"Didn't you hear me call?"

"Yes."

"So why didn't you answer?"

"You knew where I was. Why didn't you come and find me?"

"I did. I'm here, aren't I?"

"So, what do you want?"

He raised his hands defensively.

"You don't have to bite my head off."

She frowned at him.

"What do you want, Cameron?"

"Just to let you know that Hamish and Caro should be here at about four. And I've invited Anna Sinclair to join us for dinner tonight. Thought you could do us something a bit special. You know, lobster, crab, some good champagne – push the boat out a little."

Laura looked down at her magazine. He stood in the doorway and waited for her to say something.

"It's not a problem, is it?"

"Why should it be?"

"I'll leave the details to you." He turned away. "You're good at that sort of thing."

She worked her lips into something resembling a smile.

"Thanks," she said. "Is it just the four of you?"

She didn't ask if she was going to be included.

"Just the four of us."

———✦✦———

"Anna. Fin's here."

Barbara, collecting the post from the mat by the front door, heard a car coming up the drive. She opened the door and stood watching as Fin pulled up and switched off the engine. He got out and turned towards her. He was dressed in his customary faded denim and cotton shirt with the sleeves rolled up. He was, she thought with a sigh, really very attractive..

"How are you doing, Barbara?"

Fin came over to join her on the doorstep.

"I'm good thanks, Fin. How about you?"

"I'm great... Fine. Doing well."

"Dear Fin," she said. "It's good of you to be so generous with your time. It means a great deal to Anna I know."

He dipped his head and didn't meet her eye. She had the feeling that he knew that she knew.

"It means a great deal to me too," he said.

———✦✦———

Anna sat beside Fin while he drove. They were heading across country, along a narrow road with passing places, with a river running alongside, and lush grassland stretching away on both sides. They met with little traffic. The only sign of life, apart from the usual scattering of sheep, were fishermen, and a couple of BMW's with German plates coming in the opposite direction.

"You're very quiet."

Anna sighed.

"Am I?"

He reached out and was going to take her hand. But she clasped both of hers in her lap and gave a quick shake of her head.

"Don't -"

"I'm sorry." He withdrew his hand. "Have I done something wrong?"

"I just think we should concentrate on finding out what we can about Fiona and Iain."

He put his hand back on the steering wheel. "Ok." He stared straight ahead. "If that's the way you want it."

At Rowancross House the phone rang. Barbara eyed it a little nervously. These days she was never quite sure who would be on the other end of the line. She picked up the receiver.

"Barbara. Hi. It's Sarah."

Relief. It was a friend.

"Sarah... Hello."

"I was hoping to catch Fin. Have I missed him?"

"You have. They left quite some time ago. Was it anything important?"

"Not really. It's just that I've had a call from Annie."

Annie was Sarah's daughter. She lived in Aberdeen with her husband and two young children and Barbara, knowing that she had recently been diagnosed with epilepsy, was immediately concerned.

"Is everything alright?"

Sarah sighed. "I think so. The baby has been taken ill with some mysterious infection, and Annie has got herself into a tizzy about it. I'm going to head over and give her a hand. I wanted to catch Fin to let him know that he will have to fend for himself for a couple of days."

"Oh Sarah, my dear, can I do anything to help?"

"Bless you, Barbara. We'll be fine. Just keep an eye on Fin for me, will you? He's been a little distracted recently. I'm a bit worried that he might be getting himself into a sticky situation, if you know what I mean."

If anything she sounded more anxious about her nephew than her daughter. Barbara understood exactly what she was talking about.

"I'll do my best to keep an eye on him," she promised.

After she had said goodbye to Sarah, Barbara sat at her desk and began to compile a list of things she needed to do after Anna was gone. She knew it was going to be important to keep herself busy.

It was a shame she couldn't offer Fin dinner that night. It would have been the perfect opportunity to spend some time with him, and try to get to the bottom of what was going on between him and Anna. But, after Anna had agreed to have dinner with Cameron, Barbara had got straight on the phone to a friend in Strathpeffer and invited herself for the night. It had come as a shock to discover that the prospect of an evening alone made her anxious as a nervous child, but she was trying to be kind to herself, and told herself there was no point in being brave for the sake of it. Anna had been perfectly happy to stay alone in the house for a night, and she would drive back early the next morning having caught up with Diana and her news.

She picked up her pen and wrote down a couple of the chores that she had been putting off since before Charlie died. The photo of him in a silver frame by the phone caught her eye. It had been taken in Paris when they were on their honeymoon, and she particularly loved it because it showed him at his most relaxed and happy. Now she picked it up.

"Hey old man. What d'ya reckon?"

But Charlie didn't reply, and Barbara put the photo back on the desk, and shuffled papers and made phone calls and filed bills. And tried very hard not to cry because he wasn't around to answer her questions any more.

When Sarah rang James Munro to ask if he would be willing to talk to Fin and Anna, the old man had been delighted to hear that the younger generation included individuals with an interest in a period of history that most people seemed to know nothing about. In fact he had been so delighted that he had insisted on inviting Fin and Anna to lunch. Sarah had accepted on their behalf, understanding that opportunities for James to discuss his favourite subject were few and far between, and that he wanted to make the most of it.

"He was so excited I couldn't say no," she had explained, when she told them what she had arranged for them. "I hope you don't mind. God knows what he will give you."

Fin had laughed and groaned and, remembering James's gift for verbosity, been afraid that they would never get away. But Anna hushed him, and said that she was very much looking forward to meeting Mr Munro, and that lunch was a lovely idea. But now, as they drove towards Dornoch, she couldn't help thinking about how little time she had before she had to leave, and how far away they still were from finding out what had really happened. She just hoped that something useful was going to come out of this meeting, and that they weren't wasting their time.

They reached the outskirts of Dornoch and made their way into the town centre. On either side of them the houses were built out of a soft, gold coloured stone that seemed to glow in the sunshine. Fin had already told her that the small town was unusual because it had its own cathedral. In the clear morning light it was more like a town in the Cotswolds than somewhere on the bleak north east coast of Scotland. Anna checked they had got the right address as Fin slowed before a pretty little house with a neat handkerchief of green lawn and a border stocked with late flowering hollyhocks and roses.

They walked up the path to the front door between hedges of lavender. The door of the house opened before they reached it, and they saw an old man in the doorway, bent over a metal frame. He looked frail enough to be blown away on the breeze, but beneath his bottle brush eyebrows his eyes shone brightly.

"Come in, come in." He beckoned to them, shuffling back to allow them to enter. Anna stepped across the threshold, and Fin bent his head behind her to go through the low doorway. The old man had taken Anna's hand in his and was peering at her.

"My dear," he said, "it is rare that this house is host to so charming a guest." He glanced at Fin, blue eyes twinkling. "You are a lucky man, sir."

Fin coughed, while Anna laughed and blushed and tried to explain that they were just friends. But James Munro beamed at her, and she could see that he wasn't really listening. They followed him across the flagstones of the narrow hall into the front room. The windows were open onto the garden, and the gentle hum of the bees could be heard from outside. A plump woman in her fifties appeared in the door.

"Betty," said the old man, "come and meet our guests. What do we have in the way of drinks to offer them? Sherry? Wine? Perhaps a beer for the young man."

Betty came into the room to say hello, helping her father to the chair by the fireplace, suggesting that Anna might be most comfortable on the sofa opposite. She was smiling and friendly, and gave no indication that the job of looking after her father and waiting upon his guests was anything other than a pleasure. Anna couldn't help thinking how bad tempered she had been after a fortnight of caring for her own mother when she fell and broke her ankle. Filled with guilt she stood up quickly.

"Can I do anything to help?"

Betty smiled and shook her head.

"You sit and talk to father. He has been so excited about your visit. He rarely gets the chance to meet people who have heard of Strathcarron, let along want to know more about what happened there."

She brought a beer for Fin, and a glass of chilled water for Anna, and left them to it while she prepared lunch. Fin and Anna sat side by side while the old man looked from one to the other with his bright, knowing eyes.

"She's made us one of her tarts for lunch." He nodded in the direction of the kitchen. "Onion I think it is - she's a fine cook."

"It's really kind of her."

"She enjoys doing it. She knows it's a treat for an old codger like me to have young visitors. I don't get out and about as much as I'd like to these days. My knees keep giving up on me. She's glad for me to have some company."

He leaned towards Anna.

"So, you're interested in the Clearances, my dear. I can't tell you how pleased I am to hear it. There's many know nothing whatsoever about that dark time." He shook his head. "You would think, wouldn't you, that man's inhumanity to man - particularly when it happens on native soil - would have had a greater impact. Left more of a trace."

Anna looked at the floor. She was uncomfortably aware that until a few weeks ago she was one of those who had never even heard of the Clearances. Beside her Fin spoke.

"We're particularly interested in the evictions at Greenyards, sir. We wondered if you might be able to tell us something of what happened there." He smiled in his frank way. "We are woefully ignorant I'm afraid."

"Hardly your fault, my boy. More the fault of those who wanted it hushed up. As if it had never happened. As if our people weren't betrayed by those in whom they had put their faith and trust. As if families weren't torn apart, lives destroyed."

He was staring straight ahead of him, his eyes cloudy. For a moment he seemed to have forgotten that they were there. Fin glanced sideways at Anna. She leant forward and laid a gentle hand on the old man's arm.

"We would be so grateful if you would tell us all about it," she said in a soft voice. "From what Fin's aunt was telling us, there is nobody who knows more about the evictions in this area than you."

James Munro looked into her eyes and smiled. He laid a wrinkled hand on top of hers.

"Flattery, my dear. But much appreciated nevertheless."

He told them that it was the evictions at Glencalvie, those that took place up the valley from Greenyards, which were his particular area of interest. This was because his grandfather's family had been amongst those to lose their homes, when the writs of removal were served on the tenants of the little glen. He explained that at the time the valley of Strathcarron was divided into two estates: Greenyards, which took up most of the lower valley, and Glencalvie a little higher up. Around five hundred in total lived on the land made up by the two estates; honest hardworking folk who paid their rents on time, were proud of the fact that they had no paupers on the poor roll, loved their land with a fierce passion, and found it hard to understand those who didn't have such a connection.

All around them, while the landowners of Sutherland sold their souls to the devil, they watched as the sheep flooded in. And, although they had managed to avoid the dreaded writs of removal for a lot longer than most, yet still they lived in fear as slowly but surely their traditional rights were taken away from them. First they were no longer allowed to graze their cattle and sheep and goats on the hills around them. Then fishing for salmon in the black waters of the Carron was prohibited. The deer and the grouse that had been the source of the meat on their tables from long before anybody could remember were forbidden to them. The woods were no longer a source of timber, so that those who had always used the trees of the neighbourhood to build their houses and bridges had to look further afield. Bit by bit their livelihoods were being taken away from them. And all they could do was watch and wait for it to get worse.

The land belonged the sixth laird of Kindeace, whose grandfather had brought it after Culloden from the original owner, a Munro who had lost out in the turmoil and gone bust. The laird spent most of his time in London, and was rarely seen in Strathcarron. But it was generally believed that he supported the people of the strath, and they were hopeful that he would not betray them. Until one fateful day an advertisement appeared in the Inverness Courier. It informed the people of Greenyards and Glencalvie that the farms they had lived in for generations were to be let on the open market.

There were nearly ninety people living at Glencalvie, eighteen families. And those eighteen families included the family of one Andrew Munro, a joiner by trade, with his wife Mary. They had four children, the youngest of whom was James Munro's grandfather. His great grandmother Mary was a beauty, a tall, strong woman with copper coloured hair and green eyes. Together with her husband she worked the land that their family had lived on for centuries, fed her animals, played with her children, sang and danced and went to church at the grey stone building at Croick beside the River Carron.

When she and the other inhabitants of Glencalvie found that their land, where they had resided for a great deal longer than the laird who was about to make them homeless, was to be put up for a higher rental, they offered to pay the increase. They wrote to the factor and asked for a meeting at which they would give him security that the increased rents would be paid without arrears. But, before any answer had been received, there were men riding into the glen to deliver the writs of removal that had been feared for so long.

Here the old man paused, shaking his head.

"Terrible. Quite terrible," he muttered. "The carelessness with which people treat those less fortunate than themselves. As if they are not entitled to the same basic human rights as the rest of us."

Fin and Anna waited quietly for him to continue.

"It was a dreadful thing." His voice trembled and he paused. Anna could see that he was getting tired.

"We heard something about the women getting involved," she said gently. "Would you know anything about that?"

James smiled and nodded his head.

"Ah yes," he said, "the women. They were a brave bunch. The sheriff's men arrived to deliver the eviction notices, and it was the women who went out to meet them. I suppose everyone was hoping that women might be more likely to persuade them to change their minds. Mary Munro, my great grand-mother, was one of them. They stood beside the bridge as the sheriff's men rode across, and smiled their sweetest smiles and called out in their most enticing voices, and asked the men for the papers. And the amazing thing was what happened next. Because the sheriff's men did just as they were asked. They handed over the papers, and stood by and watched while the women threw them onto the fire. And then they rode back to Tain."

"So it worked?"

"Temporarily, my dear. The Sherriff and his men came back again. And again they were met by a group of townsfolk, and again most of them were women. Things got a little more heated this time. But nothing too serious."

"And they managed to stop them?"

"They did. And this time the people of Glencalvie must have been pretty confident they had seen them off once and for all, because they were left in peace for over a year."

"But it didn't last?"

"It was some time towards the end of 1844 that they were told they had until the following spring to remove themselves from their homes. They were paid to leave peacefully. But only a handful of them were offered any alternative housing. The others found out from the law agent at Tain that they would get the rest of the money promised to them only if they agreed to emigrate. It was the first they had heard of it. That not only were they expected to leave their homes, but their country as well.

Ninety people spent a week in the churchyard at Croick. Twenty three of them were children under the age of ten. They put up tarpaulins and sheltered from the wind and the rain - men, women and children, young and old. And then, when it became clear that nobody was going to help them, they drifted away like leaves in the wind."

"Where did they go?"

"South, some of them. To the industrial towns that were hungry for labour - to places like Glasgow and Liverpool. My great grandparents ended up in Glasgow. It was my grandfather who moved back up here after the war.

And presumably some did what was demanded of them, and took the money and emigrated." He shook his head sadly. "There was a great fuss made about it. In the papers, I mean. A chap from The Times came up. He was there to see what happened, and he wrote some pretty stirring reports about the whole thing. But, in the end, what good did it do?"

At that moment his daughter came back into the room. She bent down to look at him and patted his hand. "Are you alright, Dad?" she asked him gently.

He waved away her question with an impatient hand, but his eyes were wet.

"I'm sure you could all do with something to eat," she said, and she helped her father to his feet and led him from the room. Fin and Anna followed. Neither of them spoke.

Lunch was served on rose patterned plates, with cut glass tumblers for their water, neatly folded napkins in enamelled napkin rings, and a bowl full of roses in the centre of the table. An onion tart with crisp golden pastry took pride of place, next to a bowl of salad leaves, and a basket of white rolls sprinkled with poppy seeds. It seemed to Anna that Betty Munro had gone to a considerable amount of trouble to feed her father's guests.

"Everything alright, Dad?" Betty said as she sliced the tart and handed it out to each of them.

"Yes. Yes," he said, with a touch of irritation. "Don't fuss, Betty."

Anna heard her sigh. "This is so kind of you," she said, smiling at her.

Betty nodded her head at her father. "It's nice for him to have guests. You'll have noticed he likes to talk. But he tires easily these days. I have to keep a close eye on him."

They ate the onion tart and discussed the extraordinary summer weather. And Betty watched her father, and cleared the plates, and brought in lemon syllabub with raspberries from the garden. As Anna was scraping the last traces of the syllabub from the bottom of her glass bowl she noticed the old man's head drooping beside her, and his chin sank upon his chest.

"Dad." Betty touched his arm. "Everything OK?"

He lifted his head. His eyes were unfocussed, and he looked at her for a moment as if he didn't recognise her.

"I hope we haven't worn him out," Anna whispered anxiously.

There was nothing wrong with James Munro's hearing.

"I'm fine," he growled. "Absolutely fine." He smiled across the table at Anna, his false teeth gleaming whitely. "Of course, my dear," he said, "you probably know that it all happened again. Nine years later. At Greenyards. Only this time the women were more determined."

Anna leant towards him, her face eager.

"And were they any more successful?"

"I wish I could tell you that they were. But I would be lying if I did. The poor lasses met with such brutality it doesn't bear thinking about. And to make matters even worse a handful of them landed up in jail."

Beside her Anna heard Fin draw in his breath.

"It didn't get reported in any detail though, did it, sir? Not in the same way as at Glencalvie. I found a reference to it at the museum in Ullapool. It said that the only report of what happened at Greenyards came from a lawyer from Glasgow, who wrote to the papers but got little response. In the end he published an account of what happened himself."

James nodded his head.

"You'll be talking about Donald Ross. If it hadn't been for him the truth of what really happened at Greenyards would have been buried." He drew in a shallow rasping breath. "The rest of the country was more interested in what was going on in the Crimea than in the brutal treatment being meted out to a handful of women in the Highlands."

He reached out for his glass with a trembling hand. Betty leant across to guide it to his lips, glancing at Fin and Anna. It was obvious that their time was running out.

"Would you happen to know?" asked Fin. "Were there any other incidents similar to Greenyards? Where it was the women who got involved and ended up getting beaten for it?"

James turned his watery gaze upon Fin.

"Well, of course, there were the ladies from your neck of the woods." Anna held her breath. "From Coigach, right by the mouth of Loch Broom." So not at Kildorran.

"But they were a deal more successful. And, thankfully, there was no violence involved. The Sheriff and his men came by boat and arrived on the shore accompanied by the leaseholders of the land to be cleared. They found a group of women and children waiting for them. It seems that the prospect of violence, and the negative reaction this would cause, was enough to persuade them to change their minds and head back to Ullapool. That was in 1852. One of the rare occasions when the people were successful in the defence of their homes."

He paused again and closed his eyes. Fin glanced at Anna.

"Dad?"

Betty patted her father's arm. He opened his eyes.

"We were wondering if there might have been anything similar at Kildorran?" Fin spoke quickly. "Around about the same sort of time as the Greenyards evictions?"

"We think that the daughter of one of the local Mackenzie chiefs might have been involved," said Anna. "Her name was Fiona Gillespie. Her husband was a well known politician."

James gazed at Anna as if deep in thought. He blinked a couple of times, looking rather like a dishevelled owl. And then his eyes closed again, and this time they stayed shut.

"Dad," said Betty.

He had slumped down in his chair. Anna looked at his daughter.

"Is he alright?"

"He's dropped off. It's nothing to worry about."

"We've worn him out."

Betty shook her head.

"It's really not your fault. He's been a little under the weather lately, and I thought that your visit would do him good. Which it will. He'll be talking about it for days. But, if you don't mind, it might be better to be getting on. He really needs to rest now."

Anna could have cried with frustration. But there was nothing to be done. In his chair at the table the old man was dropping in and out of sleep. They had outstayed their welcome. She pushed her chair back. Opposite her Fin was already standing, making polite noises to Betty about the meal and thanking her for her kindness. Betty led them out into the narrow hall.

"I hope it's been useful," she said. "I always told him he should write it all down, but he prefers talking. It's a shame really. When he goes a lot of what he remembers will go with him." She walked with them to the front door. "One thing - " She stopped with her hand on the latch. "You were asking Dad about the politician's wife. The one who was there at the Greenyards evictions. You're the first person I've heard mention it. Apart from Dad that is…"

They both stared at her.

"I remember Dad telling me about it. She wasn't from the village, but for some reason she was involved. She was one of the women who ended up in prison."

With her heart in her mouth Anna begged Betty to tell them everything she knew. They stood in the hallway while she told them about her great grandfather, who, when he was a boy and still living in Glencalvie, had been friendly with a lad from down the valley at Greenyards. Years later, long after their families had left the area, they came across each other while serving in the same regiment. It seems that they spent an evening together drinking whisky and reminiscing. The lad from Greenyards told William Munro about a young woman who stood up and fought with the others when the eviction officers came. But here was the thing. Because she wasn't from the strath. She had come from somewhere over near Inchbae. But, although she wasn't local, she stood her ground with the best of them. Got badly beaten according to this fellow. And she was among the unfortunates who got arrested and dragged off to jail in Tain.

Here Betty shook her head. "It seems that it was something of a mystery. Because of her background. If the papers had got hold of it there would have be no stopping them. Because the story was that she was some high-class lady from over the hill, the wife of a big shot politician. But no one ever spoke about it. It was completely hushed up."

CHAPTER NINETEEN

At the same time that Anna and Fin were eating onion tart with James Munro, Cameron was sitting at the desk in his office, sipping whisky, and wondering about the best way to go about persuading Anna to take him into her confidence and tell him what she had discovered to connect Fiona Gillespie with Iain Mackay.

Cameron's office was a wood-panelled room just off the entrance hall of his house, with a picture window looking out across Little Loch Broom. It was where he went to ponder and plan. There was a sketch by Landseer on the wall, which Cameron had chanced upon in the house of a deceased relative, and which he had 'saved' on the basis that his cousin Edward, who by rights should have had it, wouldn't know enough about it to look after it properly.

The Landseer sketch hung above the fireplace opposite his desk, so that he could look at it whenever he sought inspiration. Now he sat back in the black leather chair and considered the fine rendition of the stag's majestic head. In front of him on the desk was a folder containing the letters from Robert Gillespie that he had used as a lure to tempt Anna to join him. That morning he had gone to his safe and taken them out. It had been a while since he had looked at them.

The last time had been after Charlie had called round to ask whether Cameron might have any material that would be useful for his research. Cameron had failed to mention the letters. But, after seeing Charlie on his way, he had taken them out and read them through. The truth was that they contained little of interest. Most of them had been written while Robert was away from home on business, and they amounted to little more than an itinerary of his movements. Sprinkled amongst the practical details were expressions of love and affection for his wife and his sons. Charlie would have found them dull, Cameron was sure. But Anna might like them. Women were far more interested in this sort of thing. And his plan was that, as a quid pro quo, she would share her own discovery with him. After all it was only fair.

The phone rang. Cameron leant across the desk and picked up the receiver.

"Could I speak to Laura MacBride, please?"

"She's not here at the moment."

Laura was out shopping for the evening's meal with strict instructions from the usually tight-fisted Cameron not to spare any expense.

"Might I leave her a message?"

"Of course."

"This is Elizabeth Montgomery. I'm the manager at Grey Gables. Miss MacBride's great grandmother, Jean, is one of our ladies."

"Oh yes –"

Cameron gazed out of the window as a small wooden boat, with a dark figure manning the outboard engine at the rear, puttered across the surface of the loch.

"She's been taken rather poorly, I'm afraid. We're rather worried about her."

"I'm sorry to hear that."

The boat was heading towards the circular nets where the farmed salmon thrashed and leapt. Cameron wondered if it was John at the helm. John owed Cameron a not inconsiderable amount of money, after a late night poker game that got a little out of hand. He had been conspicuous by his absence for the last few sessions. Cameron stood up and went to the window.

"Would you ask Miss MacBride to call," said the voice on the phone.

"Of course," said Cameron distractedly.

"As soon as she returns. Jean is asking for her. She keeps on about wanting to see somebody called Anna Gillespie. Miss MacBride is meant to be bringing her to visit. Apparently she has something important she wants to give her. But she won't let us take care of it for her. And it seems to be causing her a deal of anxiety. We'd appreciate Miss MacBride calling in as soon as possible."

Cameron had turned away from the window. Suddenly John was no longer so interesting.

"You say she's asking for someone called Anna Gillespie? You're sure that was the name?"

The woman hesitated. Cameron guessed she had realised she might have given away too much information about a private concern.

"If you would pass on the message to Miss Macbride, I would be most grateful. Will you ask her to ring us as soon as possible? And suggest that she brings this Anna to visit as soon as she can."

"Absolutely," said Cameron. "Leave it with me."

Fin and Anna said goodbye to Betty and went to the car. As they headed back into the centre of Dornoch they were both thinking the same thing - that at last it seemed that they were getting close to discovering what it was that Fiona had got herself involved in. Anna frowned through the windscreen at the road ahead.

"It's got to be her, don't you think? The high class lady from over the hill?"

"It's hard to believe it was anyone else." Fin slowed to allow a woman to cross the high street in front of them. "The date is spot on - the Greenyards evictions took place in 1854, which is the same year Fiona's letter was written. We know she was beaten up and arrested. And you heard what Betty said. The wife of a politician."

"So how are we going to prove it?"

He pulled away from the crossing.

"That," he said, "is where it gets difficult."

As they left the outskirts of Dornoch he suggested that they take the opportunity, while they were in the area, to drive up through Strathcarron and take a look at the site where it had all happened. Anna was excited at the thought of visiting Greenyards, but when they got there there was little to see – just fields and trees and a few scattered houses built long after the evictions would have taken place. So they continued on up the strath to the church at Croick, parked the car on the side of the road, and went to take a closer look.

They had driven up the valley towards what appeared to be nothing more than a stand of tall trees on the hillside. As they drew nearer they caught a glimpse of a square grey building. When they arrived they found a simple place of worship, built by somebody who clearly understood that functionality had its own beauty, and that the people who would use it had no need of show, even if they could have afforded it.

"It's one of the Telford churches," said Fin, reading the words on a small stone plaque by the roadside. "I thought it must be. Thomas Telford was commissioned to build them for communities that didn't have any church buildings. The budget for each one was about £1500. He designed the one in Ullapool as well – it's the museum now. All together there are about thirty or so of his churches in the Highlands."

They walked down to the small wooden gate and passed through. The church stood solid and square in front of them, shadowed by the trees which guarded the boundary of the graveyard. Anna walked along the gravel path that ran along the side of the building. Around the corner the graveyard spread out in front of her, bounded by a low stone wall, and scattered with headstones rising out of the soft grass. She wandered between them, stopping to read dates and names, Ross and Macleod and Munro, family members buried here going back generations.

Fin had taken a sheet of paper out of his pocket and was reading it. Leaving him, Anna went round the next corner and found a small wooden platform pushed up against the wall, beneath an arched window with diamond patterned glass. It was a very simple structure, with two steps and a wooden hand rail on either side. Many hands had worn the rail to a smooth finish, the steps were scuffed by the tread of many feet. Anna thought that perhaps it was some kind of scaffolding for workmen to repair the window. There was a sheet of clear plastic tacked over the window, and several of the diamond shaped panes behind it were scratched and broken. Perhaps this was work in progress. And yet the platform looked as if it was a permanent feature. Anna stepped up onto it and peered through the leaded lights into the interior of the church.

Inside she could see wooden pews and plain white walls, and an altar with a cross at the far end. Anna craned her neck to get a better view. But she was conscious of a feeling of disappointment. The interior of the church was unremarkable. She had been expecting something more. She was aware that Fin had joined her and was standing on the platform beside her.

"Isn't this amazing?" said his voice in her ear.

She turned to look at him, wondering what it was that she had missed. But he wasn't looking through the window. He was looking at the window. Anna took a step backwards.

"What is it? What have you seen?"

And then she realised what she had failed to notice the first time. The marks in the glass, that she had thought were cracks and scratches, were more than that. On the diamond shaped panes words had been etched into the glass. Scrawled in misshapen letters were names and dates and messages - as clear as if they had been written yesterday.

Someone had written:

John Ross shepherd... Amy Ross... The Glencalvie Rosses...

Someone else:

Glencalvie people was here...

And:

Glencalvie people was in the church here May 24 1845.

In another hand:

Glencalvie people the wicked generation...

Anna gripped Fin's arm.

"Who did this? What is it?"

"The people of Glencalvie... You remember. James Munro told us about them. They were the ones who came here after being evicted. They spent a week in this churchyard. They stayed here because they had nowhere else to go."

Anna stared at the glass.

"And this is all that is left of them -"

There was a catch in her voice. These names scratched in the glass, the words left behind by a forgotten generation, had a terrible poignancy about them that brought tears into her eyes.

"Come on." Fin took her hand and helped her down from the wooden platform.

"It seems so peaceful now," she said looking around. "It's hard to imagine what it must have been like."

"Maybe this will help," he said, letting go of her hand and passing her the sheet of paper he had been reading. "James Munro gave it to me while you were talking to Betty. It's a copy of the report from The Times journalist who came to Glencalvie and wrote about what happened."

She sat down on the bottom step of the wooden platform and read:

Behind the church, a long kind of booth was erected, the roof formed of tarpaulin stretched over poles, the sides closed in with horsecloths, rugs, blankets and plaids... Their furniture, excepting their bedding, they got distributed amongst the cottages of their neighbours; and with their bedding and their children they all removed on Saturday afternoon to this place...

I am told it was a most wretched spectacle to see these poor people march out of the glen in a body, with two or three carts filled with children, many of them mere infants; and other carts containing their bedding and their requisites. The whole countryside was up on the hills watching them as they silently took possession of their tent.

A fire was kindled in the churchyard, round which the poor children clustered. Two cradles with infants in them, were placed close to the fire, and sheltered round by the dejected-looking mothers. Others busied themselves into dividing the tent into compartments by means of blankets for the different families. Contrasted with the gloomy dejection of the grown-up and the aged was the, perhaps, not less melancholy picture of the poor children thoughtlessly playing round the fire, pleased with the novelty of all around them.

Anna looked up at Fin. "How could this be allowed to happen? It seems so terribly wrong."

Fin held out his hand to her.

"At least they didn't give up without a fight. Certainly not at Greenyards anyway –"

"But it didn't stop them losing everything, did it?"

"No, it didn't."

They stood in silence in the shade of the little church. Then Fin pulled Anna to her feet. "Come on.

We should be thinking about getting back. Barbara will think I've kidnapped you."

By the time Fin dropped Anna back at Rowancross House it was nearly six o'clock. Barbara had been keeping an eye out for them and came out onto the driveway as Fin pulled up in front of the house.

"How did you get on?" she called as Anna opened the car door.

"We've had a good day," said Anna, "really useful." She went up to join Barbara with Fin following behind her. "We're pretty certain that Fiona was involved in the evictions at Greenyards. We just don't know how or why."

Barbara put an arm around her waist. "Sounds intriguing."

"It is," said Anna. "But frustrating too. We don't really know how we're going to go about proving it."

"I'm sure you'll come up with something." Barbara gave Anna's waist a squeeze. "Richard called this morning. He's home. Wants you to ring him." She felt Anna stiffen under her embrace.

"How did he sound?"

Barbara hesitated.

"Don't tell me. I can guess." Anna turned to Fin. "I'd better go in and ring him. Shall we talk in the morning? Then we can decide the best way to move this forward."

"OK."

Barbara thought they seemed uncertain of how to take their leave of each other.

"Right…" said Anna, hoisting her bag onto her shoulder.

"I'll be going then," said Fin awkwardly.

Anna walked away from him across the gravel to the front door. Barbara watched him watching her.

"Sarah rang," she said to him. "She asked me to let you know that she's had to go down to Aberdeen for a couple of nights. To help Annie. I think she's worried you won't be able to manage on your own. I'd cook dinner for you myself, but I'm off to Strathpeffer for the evening."

Fin uttered a short laugh.

"You don't have to worry about me, Barbara." His eyes were following Anna as she went in through the front door. "I'm quite capable of looking after myself."

Are you, thought Barbara, seeing the expression on his face? She wasn't so sure.

The taxi taking Anna to Cameron's house followed Barbara's Volvo as far as the Braemore junction, where it turned right onto the road to Gairloch while Barbara headed south. The taxi driver kept trying to start up a conversation. But Anna was in no mood to be friendly. Her day out with Fin had been a long one. And she was unsettled by the tension that was growing between the two of them, which might be unacknowledged, but was becoming increasingly difficult to ignore. All she really wanted was to curl up on the sofa at Rowancross House, with a glass of wine, and something mindless on the television. The last thing she felt like doing was making an effort with people she didn't know, even if they were family. To make matters worse, she couldn't stop thinking about her phone call with Richard.

"I wish I could understand what you're still doing up there," he had said to her.

"It's hard to explain…"

"So try."

He was using his best 'trying to be reasonable but losing his patience' voice. She knew it well. It made her feel like doing the exact opposite of what he was asking for.

"There are a few things I have to sort out before I leave."

"What things?"

"I've got to tie up a few loose ends."

"You're being very secretive."

"I don't mean to be."

For a moment he was silent.

"Look here, Anna." She could hear that he was beginning to lose his temper. "I would appreciate it if you would tell me when exactly you are planning on coming home. Or are you expecting your daughter to return to an empty house?"

Anna had every intention of booking a flight for the weekend. But she was damned if she was going to make it easy for him.

"You don't have to worry," she had said in a non-committal way. "I'll be back in plenty of time,"

They said goodbye to each other in the cold voices of strangers.

When she arrived at The White Lodge Cameron was waiting for her. As Anna raised her hand to the polished brass door knocker, at the slightly too grand entrance to his house, the door swung open. He stood in the doorway smiling down at her. He was wearing soft grey trousers and an expensively tailored shirt. On his feet were polished leather brogues. His skin glowed, his teeth shone, his hair was brushed and gleaming. He looked, thought Anna, exactly what he was - an impostor disguised as the perfect country gentleman.

"Welcome," he said expansively, beckoning her inside. She was surprised that he didn't add 'to my humble abode.' When he leant forward to kiss her cheek she could smell his aftershave, a subtle, tricky aroma that was hard to pin down, and in her reluctant state of mind seemed to sum up all that she mistrusted about him. The jet black eyes of a stag's head over the fireplace seemed to be watching her as she followed him into the entrance hall. Cameron helped her out of her jacket and stepped back.

"Wow," he said, "don't you look sensational."

The prospect of dinner at Cameron's house had posed something of a problem when it came to deciding what to wear. Barbara had warned her that Cameron tended towards the formal when it came to entertaining, and Anna had been worried that her wardrobe was inadequate for such an evening. She had – at Barbara's suggestion – looked through her stepmother's clothes for something suitable. But in the end she stuck with one of the outfits she had brought with her to wear for dinner at the hotel near Fort William, where she and Richard had originally planned to spend a few days. It was strange to think how differently things had turned out.

She picked out a pair of wide coffee coloured trousers in a mix of heavy silk and linen, which she paired with a chocolate brown vest top in soft jersey and a wide leather belt. She put on make up for the first time in weeks; blusher, eyeliner, mascara and lipstick; and was surprised at the face that looked back at her from her mirror. But she was pleased with what she saw. She hadn't made much of an effort with her appearance since the memorial service and it made a nice change to get dressed up.

From downstairs she heard the front doorbell ring and, assuming it was her taxi, she picked up her jacket and bag and made her way slowly downstairs. For the first time in weeks she was wearing high heels, and it was taking a while to get used to the unfamiliar sensation of height and altered balance. She saw Barbara passing the bottom of the stairs on her way to answer the door. Pausing on the landing to check her reflection Anna was surprised to hear Fin's voice. She heard him explaining that he was on his way into Ullapool for a drink at the Ferry and had called in to pick up the jacket he had left in the kitchen that morning. Anna turned the corner into the hall as he came in.

For a moment Fin didn't recognise her. This elegant creature with the smoky eyes and mane of chestnut hair couldn't be the same woman who had sat beside him all day in her denim jeans and loafers. The look she gave him was uncertain.

"I've overdone it, haven't I?"

Fin blinked.

"What... No... Not at all. You look great."

She had told him about her dinner date with Cameron while they were driving along the side of the Dornoch Firth on their way to visit James Munro earlier that day. Knowing Cameron as he did he had been instantly suspicious, but she had been quick to reassure him. There would be other guests, family members she was looking forward to meeting. It was not going to be just the two of them. And if there was a chance that Cameron's letters contained information that might be of help to them, it would have been foolish of her to turn down his invitation.

Now Fin looked at her and wished he could stop her from going. He hated the thought of her having dinner with Cameron, particularly looking this good.

"You're making me really nervous," she said, screwing up her face. "Is it the makeup?"

Her lips were stained a rich pink. He remembered how they had felt against his own when he kissed her. He was seized by the strong desire to kiss her again.

"You look very nice," he said mechanically.

Barbara rescued him.

"Come on," she said to Anna. "The taxi's here. You should be going. Cameron hates people to be late."

CHAPTER TWENTY

Cameron led Anna across the parquet floor into his drawing room, where the walls were hung with so many paintings that it was hard to spot a patch of bare wall. A long oak sideboard in the corner displayed a collection of enamel boxes. In the bay window a model tea clipper with a polished hull sailed across a marble table top. There wasn't a surface that didn't display one of Cameron's possessions. Anna first thought was that it must be a nightmare for Laura to keep everything clean.

There was a bottle of champagne on a silver tray, with crystal champagne flutes. Anna looked at the glasses. There were only two of them.

"I'm really looking forward to meeting Hamish and Caroline," she said, looking around her. "When are you expecting them?"

Cameron was filling the glasses with champagne. He handed one over to her.

"Such a shame," he said. "They rang a couple of hours ago. Caroline's mother is unwell. They've had to head south without stopping. Sent their apologies. Hope to meet you some other time."

Anna's heart sank. An evening alone with Cameron… It was the last thing she wanted. She looked at him over the rim of her champagne glass. He was staring at her with a kind of acquisitorial eagerness. She had the uncomfortable feeling that, if she weren't careful, it would be her head that was the next thing to go up on the wall alongside his other trophies. There was something about his eyes, an odd glimmer, which suggested that this was not the first bottle he had opened this evening.

"We don't need them to enjoy ourselves," he said, waving her over to a mulberry coloured sofa. "Why don't you sit down? Make yourself comfortable."

Anna squared her shoulders and did as she was bid. She told herself she was more than capable of handling Cameron Gillespie, drunk or sober.

Cameron sat opposite her in a wing backed chair covered in tartan. He crossed one elegant ankle over his knee and sipped his champagne.

"So, I hear you and Fin were out and about again today?"

Anna stared at him. "How did you know?"

He smiled.

"I have my spies…."

"Really?"

"I'm teasing you. Laura was driving behind you. On her way back from Inverness. You certainly seem to be seeing a fair bit of each other. I must have got the wrong end of the stick. I thought you weren't too keen on him."

Anna shrugged. "He's OK." She wasn't there to talk about Fin. She wanted to get to the point of the evening. "So what about these letters? I'd really like to see them."

"There's no hurry is there?" He stood up and went over to refill his glass. "I thought we'd have dinner first. Relax, enjoy ourselves, get to know each other a little better."

Anna felt she already knew Cameron quite well enough.

"So how are you getting on with Fiona?" he said, coming back and sitting down. "Such an interesting woman – I've often wondered about her?"

Anna narrowed her eyes at him. This evening he was like a snake. She felt as if she was waiting for him to strike.

"There was a rumour, you know. That she did a vanishing act for a few days. A bit like Agatha Christie… Nobody could track her down."

Anna sat bolt upright. Then forced herself to lean back against the cushions.

"Really?" She did her best to keep her voice level. "It sounds very mysterious -"

"Doesn't it?" She was aware that he was watching her closely. "It was hushed up at the time. The family wanted it kept quiet. I only know because my father told me about it." He sipped his champagne. "You've been digging around a bit in her things, haven't you? I don't suppose you've come across anything that might explain what she got up to when she went missing?"

"There's nothing about it in any of her journals," she said, meeting his gaze.

"So what about her letters? Barbara was telling me that you and Fin have been hot on the trail of something really interesting."

Anna dropped her eyes. He knew something. She was sure of it. But Barbara wouldn't have let slip anything important. So what had he found out? And how?

"You must have misunderstood," she said in as nonchalant a tone as she could manage. "Fin's been showing me some of the sites where the Clearances took place. It was Barbara's suggestion." She looked up at him with what she hoped was a frank expression. "Between you and me I've begun to get rather tired of the whole thing. I'm really only keeping up with it for Barbara's sake."

He got up to fill her glass. She couldn't tell if he believed her or not.

—·—

In the kitchen Laura was putting the finishing touches to the starter. She had persuaded Cameron not to sit down for dinner in the rather austere dining room, but to set up a table in the Edwardian conservatory with its views out to sea. Although why she had bothered was beyond her. The last thing she wanted was for the evening to go well.

Usually, when Cameron had guests, Laura prepared and served the meal, and then sat down at the table like any other hostess. So she had been angry enough when Cameron made it clear that this time it was going to be different, that this time she was only there to serve. When it turned out that Anna Sinclair was to be the only guest, she was on the verge of going on strike. Until Cameron sat her down and explained that the only reason he had invited Anna was because she had something he wanted, something that would make it possible for him to achieve his goal and finally get a book published. The dinner was part of his plan. What Cameron wanted Cameron must have. So Laura found herself in the position of doing her utmost to make sure that the evening went well, when what she really wanted was to do everything in her power to sabotage it.

She finished dressing the lobster salad, carried it along the corridor, and set it down on the table in the conservatory. She lit the candles and checked that the white wine in the ice bucket was the right temperature. Outside dusk was gathering, the last of the light glimmering on the edge of the far horizon. It was a perfect evening, still and clear. Laura stood and stared out across the loch and imagined for a moment that she was the one sitting opposite Cameron at the table tonight, catching his eye through the candlelight, waiting for the moment when he leaned across and took her hands and told her that he had always loved her and that she was the only one for him.

She turned abruptly on her heel and headed back to the kitchen to check that the potatoes hadn't boiled over.

In the bar of the Ferry Boat Inn Fin put his empty glass down and rummaged in his pocket for change.

"Do you want another one?" he asked the man sitting beside him.

"If you're buying…"

Fergus Grant, lobster fisherman and part time photographer, had known Fin since they were boys. His father was a carpenter in Achiltibuie and his mother did the books for the Smokery. When Fin used to stay with his aunt in the school holidays he and Fergus fished for trout together in the lochans, stalked deer in the hills, and haunted the camp site at the back of Ullapool in the hope of persuading the nubile Swedish girls to unleash their legendary liberal sexuality on a couple of desperate teenagers. Unlike so many of his contemporaries Fergus did not head south as soon as he was able. The pace of life on the west coast suited him, so he stayed put and was perfectly content with his lot. Fin envied him.

"So what's up, mate? Nothing to do with a woman, is it?"

Fin's head shot round.

"What makes you say that?"

Fergus shrugged. "How long have I known you?"

Fin called the barman over.

"Am I really that predictable?"

"Yup" said Fergus. "But if you need to drown your sorrows it's fine with me. How about we make an evening of it and share a taxi back?"

But Fin shook his head.

"One more, but that's it. I've got to drive myself home."

"Ok – but why not come back to mine for something to eat. Sally will be pleased to see you. She was only just asking about you."

"Why not." He could do with the company. Distraction was what he needed most.

Anna sat opposite Cameron in the conservatory and watched him finish off another glass of champagne. She bent her head to look at the plate of food in front of her. It looked delicious, but she wasn't feeling very hungry. When Cameron had invited her to dinner he had promised to drive her home. Now she was wishing that she had asked the taxi driver to come back for her.

Cameron reached across for the bottle of wine in the ice bucket and offered it to her. She shook her head.

"So how is Fin getting on with his book?" he said, filling his own glass.

"Fine, I think," she said wishing that he would stop steering the conversation back to Fin.

"So what's he got that I haven't?"

Anna stared at him.

"What are you talking about?"

"Well, you haven't been avoiding him, have you?"

"I haven't been avoiding anyone…"

"You've been avoiding me."

She sighed.

"I haven't, Cameron."

"So, what's the big attraction then?"

"What do you mean?"

"Fin. You were looking pretty cosy when I caught you together in Charlie's study."

"What do you mean – 'caught us'?"

"Come on. What are you two up to? Or can I guess?"

Anna put down her fork. "It's really none of your business, Cameron." She was tempted to ask him to take her home right away. But he must have realised that he had gone too far.

"You're right… I'm sorry… I'll shut up" He waved his glass at her. "How's the lobster?"

"It's delicious. Laura's a very good cook."

Anna had been wondering if Laura would appear to clear the starter away, but it was Cameron who got up and bent over her to take her plate. He left the room, and she heard his footsteps retreat down the hall. Had he asked Laura to stay out of the way? At that moment she would have welcomed the sight of her unfriendly face.

He returned carrying plates of pink lamb cutlets, and went across to the dresser where he lifted the lid on a heated tray to reveal bowls of new potatoes ands sliced courgettes in butter and garlic. So, no Laura then. It made her feel even more uncomfortable, the thought that, somewhere in the house, Laura was hiding. She glanced surreptitiously at her watch. It was only nine fifteen. She wondered at what point she could ring for a taxi.

The meal finished with a raspberry and peach Pavlova served with the cream whipped into peaks. It looked very tempting, but Anna had completely lost her appetite. She struggled to finish hers, and was relieved when Cameron laid down his napkin and pushed back his chair.

"Shall we?"

Anna was delighted to follow his example. The sooner he showed her the letters, the sooner she could leave. He stood back to allow her to go out of the room in front of him. From somewhere in another part of the house she could hear the sound of plates clattering and the muffled hum of music from a radio. It was reassuring to hear. A reminder that they weren't completely alone. She walked along the corridor with Cameron close behind her.

"Here we are -"

He pushed open the door into a room lined with books. A mahogany desk was placed by the window, with a brass reading lamp casting a pool of light on the green leather surface. In the dim light Anna could make out a framed sketch of a stag on the wall above the fireplace. Cameron walked across to the desk and pulled back the chair.

"Here you go," he said, indicating that she should sit.

She settled herself in the chair and watched while Cameron went over to the stag and lifted it from the wall. Hidden behind it was a safe. Cameron punched in the code and pulled the handle to open the door. Reaching his hand inside, he took out a bundle of papers, and pushed the door shut so that she couldn't see what else he had stashed away in there.

"Is the light good enough? Can you see?" He had come back to the desk, and now he leant over to set the letters down in front of her. He was so close that the sleeve of his shirt brushed her cheek. He twisted the head of the reading light. "Is that any better?"

She glanced up at him.

"That's fine… Really."

He was too close. She could feel his breath on her cheek. She read the first letter.

June 7th 1853

My dear,

Another busy day. Rogers was delayed by several hours which threw everything out and now I am working late to make up for it. If everything goes according to plan I will be back on Thursday. I hope the boys are behaving themselves.

Your devoted husband,

Robert

She looked at the next.

September 12ᵗʰ

My dear,

How are things at home? I hope that everything is running smoothly. I have arranged for a Mr Duncan from Gairloch to come and look at the thatch on the barns. If he arrives before my return would you remind John that we will require a detailed breakdown of the costs involved before I am prepared to commission the work.

I think it unlikely that I will be back before the end of the week. The business I have with Davis and Son is taking a little longer than I had anticipated. I have invited Mr Davis and his wife for a visit. They are particularly taken with the notion of visiting the Highlands. I thought we might combine their trip with that of the Johnsons which should make the arrangements easier for you, my dear.

I remain your loving husband,

Robert

Anna glanced quickly through the other letters. From what she could see there seemed to be more of the same. It was hard to believe that there was anything useful here. She couldn't help feeling that if there had been Cameron would have done something about it a long time ago.

Behind her he seemed to have noticed her loss of interest. He leaned forward and rested a hand heavily on her shoulder.

"You seem disappointed. You were hoping for something more?"

She glanced up at him.

"They're very interesting. Really -"

He laughed.

"You don't have to be polite. I only keep them in the safe out of a misplaced sense of family loyalty. They're hardly worth hanging on to."

Anna stared back at the letters.

"That's not what you said when you told me about them."

"No. But if I had told you the truth you might not have come."

"So what exactly *am* I doing here, Cameron?"

He leant closer. And his hand tightened on her shoulder.

"I think you've discovered something. Something important," he said in her ear. "Fin Mackay clearly knows all about it. I think it's only fair that you tell me."

Anna's heart was beating fast. She tried to stand up, but he twisted her chair around to face him and put a hand on each arm so that she was trapped.

"Come on Anna… Spill the beans."

"I don't know what you're talking about."

"I think you do."

He was a lot more drunk than she had suspected.

"It's getting rather late, Cameron," she said. "I think it might be a good idea if I called a taxi. Do you have the number?"

But it was as if he hadn't heard her. He lowered his face so that he was staring into her eyes. "Come on… What have you found out? It's got to be something to do with a relationship between Fiona and Iain Mackay. And I wouldn't mind betting that there's an explanation floating around for Fiona disappearing the way she did."

Anna pulled her head back. How had he guessed?

"I really don't know what you're talking about."

He shook his head and smiled. "Oh I think you do…" And then he bent down and tried to kiss her. She stood up.

"Come on Cameron. Don't be ridiculous."

But he took her by the shoulders.

"Please Cameron…" She tried to push him away, but all he said was, "Don't be a pain, Anna," and tightened his grip on her. Now he was pushing her backwards, and she felt the arm of a sofa at the back of her legs.

"Cameron…"

"You're giving it up for Fin so you can give it up for me too," he said in an ugly voice, and he tipped her back so that she fell and he came down on top of her, and they were both of them sprawled across a leather sofa in the corner of the room.

"Cameron," she said angrily, pushing at his chest, "what the hell are you doing?"

But he wasn't listening. He was too busy fumbling at her waistband with one hand, while he held her face with the other. Now she began to feel alarmed. Cameron was drunk and strong and capable of anything. She struggled to escape from beneath him and saw an ugly light come into his eyes.

"Jesus Christ, Cameron."

Suddenly the room was filled with light from the spotlights in the ceiling. Over Cameron's shoulder Anna could see Laura's face staring down at them with an expression of disgust.

"Get up, Cameron."

Her voice was wintry. For a moment all the energy in Cameron's body drained away, and he slumped down on top of Anna, a dead weight pinning her against the soft leather. Then he turned his head and looked up.

"Christ, Laura," he said.

She gazed back at him, unblinking. He pulled himself up and away from Anna and slowly got to his feet. Anna tugged the waistband of her trousers back into place. Then she sat up.

"I'm going to leave now," she said in a voice tight with anger.

Neither Laura nor Cameron said anything. Then Cameron took a deep breath, and with slow careful footsteps walked past Laura and out of the room.

"Would you like me to give you a lift home?" asked Laura in a flat voice.

Anna shook her head. It was absolutely the last thing she wanted. Instead she asked Laura to find her the number of a local taxi. She perched on the edge of one of the oak chairs by the front door and dialled the number with hands that shook. The phone rang and rang but nobody answered it. So she rang Fin instead.

"Hello."

"It's me... Anna."

"Is something wrong?"

"Yes... no... not really." She paused. "Where are you? Could you come and get me? As soon as possible... Please..."

"I'm in Ullapool. I was just about to go home. What's wrong? What's happened?"

"I'll explain when you get here. I'll be waiting outside. You don't have to come in."

With Anna on the phone in the hall, Laura went to find Cameron. She found him in the drawing room, lying sprawled against the cushions with his head back and his mouth open. He was unconscious. She walked across the room to the sofa and looked down at him. In the light from the table lamp, with his mottled face and gaping mouth, he was an ugly sight. She realised that for the first time she was seeing him for what he really was, an arrogant bully with an uncertain temper and a selfish heart. She was filled with a sense of disgust - for herself - for him - for the whole sleazy set up.

She left him and went down the corridor to the hall. There was nobody there; Anna must have left already. But Laura hadn't heard a car arriving. She stood uncertainly under the glassy eyes of the stag. She felt bad about Anna.

Laura thought for a moment. Then she pulled open the front door and looked outside. In the twilight she could just make out a figure standing on the edge of the drive. She lifted a jacket from a rack inside the cupboard by the stairs and stepped outside, pulling the door shut behind her. She walked across the drive towards the silent figure. Dew was settling on the grass and the night air was cool. When she reached Anna she stopped.

"Here." She offered the jacket to Anna. "You'll catch cold."

There was no reply. Laura stood beside her uncertainly.

"I'm sorry," she said hesitantly. "I know what he's like."

Again no reply from Anna.

"I should leave him really," said Laura. "I know I should. I just can't bring myself to do it. I'm all he has."

Now Anna spoke.

"You don't have to explain, Laura. It's not your fault. He's lucky to have you."

Laura let out her breath with a sigh.

"That's what my great grandmother says. She's never liked him." She hesitated. "By the way... I've got a message to give you from her. From my great grandmother, that is -"

In the darkness Anna turned her head to look at Laura.

"For me...?"

"She wants you to go and see her. She says she's got something to give you. I've no idea what it is. But last time I saw her she kept on going on about it. I feel bad. I wasn't going to bother... I was annoyed."

Anna was staring at her.

"Why on earth would your great grandmother want to see me?"

Laura shook her head.

"I really don't know. I've got a feeling that it might be something to do with Fiona Gillespie. But don't tell her I said so."

In the distance, out on the main road, headlights flared and the murmur of a car engine came to them through the night air. Laura turned to Anna a little stiffly.

"That will be your lift. I really am so sorry about tonight.

CHAPTER TWENTY ONE

"How is Jean this morning?"

The clock was showing six o'clock. Outside in the garden of the nursing home the grass was sparkling with dew. A pretty girl with a crown of tight brown curls stirred a spoonful of instant coffee into a mug for the night duty nurse in the cramped room off the back corridor that served as a lounge for the staff.

"She seems a little more settled." The night nurse took the mug with a grateful sigh. "But we had to call the doctor at four this morning. She was having trouble breathing."

"Did you get hold of the granddaughter? Is she coming?"

"Elizabeth rang yesterday. Had to leave a message. I hope she'll be here soon. And that she brings this woman that Jean keeps on about. I reckon she won't rest until she's seen her."

"It's still bothering her?"

The night nurse nodded. "Whoever she is, she better come soon. From the way the doctor was talking…"

In the whitewashed bedroom under the eaves of the house in Achiltibuie Anna turned away from the sleeping body lying next to her and slipped noiselessly out of bed. She tiptoed across the knotted rug that covered the whitewashed floorboards, picking up her clothes as she went. Silently she went into the bathroom, where she dressed quickly and ran her fingers through her hair. In the mirror above the sink her eyes met with those of her reflection. She stared at herself for a moment, wondering if it was possible to tell from her face that everything had changed.

As she crept back into the bedroom Fin muttered in his sleep and flung out an arm across the pillow. She sped past him and went downstairs, hoping it wasn't too early to phone for a taxi. She wanted to get back to Rowancross House before Barbara returned from Strathpeffer. She needed time to think.

By the time Fin had turned in through the gates and accelerated up the drive to Cameron's house Laura had returned inside, and Anna was standing alone, a hunched figure on the edge of the lawn. She stepped back as the headlights swept across her. In that moment Fin caught a glimpse of her face. He slammed his foot on the brake and leapt out of the car.

"What the hell - ?"

He tried to take hold of her, but she held up her hands to stop him.

"I'm fine… It's fine." But her voice was hoarse. "I just want to go home."

He badly wanted to wrap his arms around her and hold her close. He wanted to shake her and make her tell him what had happened. But she had turned away from him and was getting into the car. He glanced up at the house. A light shone out onto the drive from a room at the far corner. He fought with the desire to go up and batter his fists on the front door, to drag Cameron outside and demand to know what had been going on. But then he looked back at Anna. She was slumped down in the passenger seat with her arms folded tightly across her chest, staring ahead of her. He realised the best thing was to do as she asked and take her home. He got back into the car.

"OK?" he asked her.

She nodded. He backed the car at speed, deriving satisfaction from the way the back wheels span on Cameron's lawn as he drove away.

"Do you want to tell me about it?"

They were heading back towards Ullapool. The headlights bounced off trees and rocks as the road rose steeply in front of them.

"There's nothing much to tell. Cameron was drunk and got a little over amorous. That's all."

Fin thumped the steering wheel with his fist and swore.

"That's more than enough. I feel like going back and sorting him out."

Anna put out her hand towards him.

"It really wasn't that big a deal. He was far too drunk to get very far. And Laura came in and interrupted us before anything could happen."

Fin glared at the road in front of him.

"I always knew he was a shit."

"What was more worrying is that it appears he knows that we're onto something with Fiona and Iain. He seems to have guessed about their relationship."

"How the hell did that happen?"

Anna shook her head.

"I've got no idea."

Fin was racking his brains, wondering how Cameron had got wind of their secret. He hated the thought that he might get to the truth before they did. Anna made a muffled sound, and he looked across and saw that she was shivering.

"You're cold… Have my jacket."

He reached behind him and lifted it from the back seat. She took it and pulled it round her shoulders, huddling under it. He glanced at her.

"Are you OK?

"I'm fine."

"You don't sound very sure."

"It's silly… I'm a grown woman. But I can't help wishing that Barbara hadn't chosen tonight of all nights to be away."

He thought for a moment.

"Why don't you come back with me?"

She frowned.

"What are you talking about?"

"To Sarah's. There's a spare room. It's very comfortable."

She was looking uncertainly at him.

"Are you sure? Won't Sarah mind?""

"Of course not. In fact - after what you've been through tonight - I know she would be really cross with me if I didn't insist."

He drove her to Achiltibuie. Once they were inside his aunt's house he settled her in the most comfortable armchair and went to find out if Sarah had any brandy. Anna curled her knees up under her, rested her head back against the cushions, and closed her eyes. Now that the evening was over she couldn't help wondering if she had overreacted. But then the memory of Cameron's weight on top of her and the smell of his breath on her face came back to her, making her feel sick and angry at the same time, and she was glad she wasn't spending the night at Rowancross alone.

"Here… Drink this."

Fin was standing over her with a glass of brandy in his hand.

"I don't think I like brandy," she said, taking it from him.

"It's good for you," he told her.

She took a tentative sip. He sat down opposite her.

"Are you sure you're alright?"

The brandy burnt its way down her throat. "I just want to forget about the entire evening," she said. "Distract me. Tell me about your travels. I want to hear about somewhere warm and wonderful and completely different to here."

So he told her about a recent trip to Spain, when he had hired a car and driven from north to south, staying in the Paradors along his way. He told her of the sunsets across the high mountains, of nights sitting under the stars in Seville, of the ghosts from the Civil War that still haunted the villages, of bull-fights and flamenco dancers, and the gardens of the Alhambra in Granada. As he spoke the tension in her limbs subsided and she began to feel human again.

He went to find sheets for the bed in the spare room and made it up for her. When he came back she had risen to her feet and was looking out of the window to where the dark outline of the island in the bay rose out of the sea. He stood beside her.

"Are you ready to go to bed?" he asked her. "Will you be alright?"

She turned and looked at him and nodded her head. He held out his hand. When she took it in her own he curled his fingers through hers. And she leaned towards him and lifted her face to his, thinking that this wasn't what either of them had planned. But it was what she wanted.

He bent his head and kissed her. Then, without speaking, he led her out of the room and up the staircase. She followed him past an open door where lamplight shone on a freshly made bed, and up another flight of stairs to his own room at the top of the house. She stood in the doorway and watched him while he switched on the light beside the bed and pulled the curtains. Then he came back to her.

"Are you sure this is what you want?" he said.

For an answer she lifted her arms and pulled the jersey vest over her head.

⊱ ⊰

Barbara arrived back at Rowancross House just after nine. Anna was still in the shower. Barbara could hear the hiss of water from down the landing as she took her overnight bag up to her bedroom. She was in the kitchen filling the fridge with tayberries from her friend's garden when she heard Anna come in, and she shut the fridge door and turned to look at her stepdaughter.

"So how was last night? Were the letters any help?"

"No… Not really… Not at all."

Anna crossed quickly to the breadbin, took out a loaf, and began to cut slices for toast. Her head was bent over the task, she seemed distracted. There was a restlessness about her that Barbara couldn't put a finger on.

When she came to sit down at the table Barbara could see that her face was pale and she seemed unwilling to meet Barbara's gaze. For a moment Barbara was inclined to be worried. She was about to ask if everything was alright when Anna looked up and caught Barbara watching her. The green eyes that were so like her father's were shining, illuminated by an inner glow that Barbara hadn't seen before. Was this a good sign or a bad sign? It couldn't be anything to do with Cameron, she was certain of that. Maybe Anna had patched things up with Richard and this was why she looked so radiant. She hoped so.

"I was wondering if I might use the car this morning." Anna spoke quickly, spreading honey onto her toast. "Laura gave me a rather curious message last night. It appears that her great grandmother has something she wants to give me. I can't imagine what it might be. But I ought to go and see her and find out."

Barbara was intrigued. But Anna's odd mood did not seem to allow for discussion. So Barbara handed her the car keys and, half an hour later, watched her stepdaughter drive away, wondering what had happened the night before to put Anna into such an enigmatic frame of mind.

"Amy… Have we heard anything from Jean's granddaughter yet?"

Elizabeth Montgomery, manageress of Grey Gables, popped her head round the office door to find the curly headed helper sorting through the post. Amy shook her head.

"Not yet –"

Elizabeth came into the room.

"Now that is strange. I left a message for her yesterday afternoon. I was expecting to hear from her last night."

"Perhaps she's on her way over."

Elizabeth frowned.

"Maybe… I'll give her another try. It's possible she didn't get the message. I made it very clear that it was urgent." She checked her watch. "I'll go and ring her now."

At the door she stopped. "How is Jean this morning? Have you been in to see her? Miss McBride will want to know."

"I just checked with Marie. Apparently she didn't want any breakfast. It's been a few days now she hasn't really had any appetite. But she's asking for her great granddaughter. And she wants to know when this Anna person is going to visit her."

"I'll mention it again to Miss MacBride," said Mrs Montgomery. "If I can get hold of her, that is."

She left Amy and went through reception on her way back to her own office. As she went past the dining room she noticed a tall man with dark hair standing by the glass doors of the resident's sitting room, peering inside.

"Can I help you?"

He turned and smiled.

"I hope so," he said. "I'm looking for Mrs MacBride. I wonder if you could tell me where I might find her."

The manageress looked surprised.

"I'm sorry," she said politely. "Are you a relative?"

The man smiled again.

"Not exactly a relative. But a close friend of her granddaughter. There was a message to say that Mrs MacBride wasn't feeling too good. Laura asked me to come and see how she was getting on. She would have come herself, but she's been unavoidably called away. Won't be able to make it until tomorrow, at the very earliest."

Mrs Montgomery frowned.

"I see," she said slowly. "That is most unfortunate." She hesitated. "I'm not sure that Mrs MacBride should be receiving visitors. She really isn't in very good shape."

The man looked concerned.

"But that's exactly why I'm here. Laura is terribly worried. Couldn't rest until I promised to come over straight away and see how Jean was getting on."

"We don't make it a policy of allowing strangers in to see our residents."

"I'm hardly a stranger," he said. "Laura… Miss MacBride that is… works for me. And I've know Jean since I was a little boy."

He sounded genuinely upset. Mrs Montgomery softened.

"She's had a bad night, but she's hanging on. She's made of strong stuff. I'm sure it wouldn't do any harm if you saw her for a few minutes. Then you can report back to Miss MacBride. Suggest she visits as soon as possible."

"Thank you," he said. "You're very kind."

Mrs Montgomery led him along a corridor lined with prints of poppy fields and lavender. Outside the room at the far end she hesitated.

"Only a few minutes. She tires very easily."

Jean lay in her bed propped up against the pillows. She could hear voices outside and lifted her head to watch the doorway. She hoped it was Charlie's daughter come to see her at last.

But it was Cameron Gillespie who walked into the room. Jean's eyes flared.

"Hello Jean -"

"Cameron?"

On the other side of the door Mrs Montgomery nodded to herself. It was alright, Jean did know the man. She turned away. There was no need to ring Miss MacBride now. Cameron would make sure she knew what was going on.

"What are you doing here, Cameron?"

Jean looked at her unexpected visitor with no attempt to disguise her dislike. He had settled himself in the chair beside the bed and was looking at her with a solicitous expression in his eyes that was a false as his smile.

"I've come to see how you are getting on, Jean. I heard you weren't feeling too good."

She sighed, wishing she was feeling stronger.

"I don't see what business that is of yours."

"Now Jean – " He rested his hand on the side of the bed. "That's no way to go on. You know how fond I am of you."

She stared at him.

"I know no such thing."

He was holding a bunch of flowers and he waved them at her.

"I bought you these."

She ignored the limp offering.

"What are you doing here, Cameron?" she repeated.

He seemed to realised there was no point in pretending. He put the flowers down on the bedcover.

"Well you know, Jean," he said slowly. "I heard something yesterday that got my curiosity working overtime. And I thought I would drop by and find out what it was all about."

"What was that then?" she said in a tired voice.

"A little bird told me that that for some inexplicable reason you were rather anxious for Charlie Gillespie's daughter to visit you. Something about you having something to give her. Now what's that all about, Jean? What on earth would you have to give to a woman you've never even met?"

Jean turned her head away.

"That is none of your business, Cameron."

He leant forward on the edge of his chair.

"Come on," he said in a wheedling tone of voice. "I'm guessing it's got something to do with Fiona Gillespie. From what I hear she and your grandmother were thick as thieves. There was some scandal, wasn't there? Something that was hushed up at the time? Did Fiona give her something to pass on to you? Come on Jeanie, you can tell me?"

Jean looked back at him with frightened eyes. If she could have risen and left the room she would have done so.

"Come on, Jeanie. Spill the beans. What's the big secret? You don't want to waste your time with Charlie's daughter. She's as unreliable as he was."

Jean gazed at him with dislike, anger fuelling a surge in her strength.

"You always were a nasty piece of work, Cameron."

"That's not very kind of you, Jean," he said, looking around the room as he did so. "Come on, what have you got to tell me? Where is your little secret hidden?"

He had risen and was walking towards the cupboard in the corner.

"Is it in here?"

"Cameron... No."

Jean tried to lift herself up from the bed. Cameron saw and he smiled.

"I'm guessing it is. Let's have a look, shall we?"

Jean's breathing had quickened and her heart was racing. She reached for the panic button beside her bed. But before she could press it the door opened and Amy's curly head appeared around the door.

"Sorry to interrupt," she said brightly. She caught sight of Jean's anguished face and her expression changed. She stepped into the room. "I'm sorry, sir," she said to Cameron in a voice of icy politeness. "Mrs Montgomery asked me to pop in and check that everything was OK." She glanced pointedly at the door. "Jean isn't looking too good. I think it would be a good idea if you were to leave."

Cameron opened his mouth to protest. But the young woman was looking at him so fiercely that he shut it again.

"Of course," he said in a placatory tone. "I'm sorry if I've outstayed my welcome." He looked at Jean in the bed. "Maybe I'll pop in another time, Jean."

The old woman was pale and her breathing was laboured. But still she found the energy to glare at him.

"Don't bother, Cameron," she managed to spit out at him. "You won't be welcome."

━┿ ┿━

When Anna arrived at Grey Gables, an hour after Cameron's hasty departure, she met with a frosty reception from the woman in the office.

"Mrs MacBride is not well enough to receive visitors," she was informed. "You should have rung first to check and we could have saved you the journey."

"I'm sorry," said Anna uncertainly. "I was told she had asked to see me."

The woman glanced up from the form she was filling in.

"What did you say your name was?"

When Anna told her the woman's expression changed. She rose from the desk and came out to apologise.

"I'm so sorry," she said. "Jean has had another visitor this morning. Uninvited and unwelcome from what we can make out. It's left her very weak. We've had to call the doctor again."

"I'm sorry," said Anna, turning towards the door. "I'll go. I don't want to make things worse. I only came because I got a message that she wanted to see me."

Mrs Montgomery put a hand on her arm.

"She does… Very much. Give me a minute and I'll just go and make sure she's up to seeing you. It will upset her even more if she hears that you were here and we sent you away."

Anna watched her walk away. She couldn't imagine why an old woman she had never met should be so anxious to see her. She hitched her bag up on her shoulder, feeling uncomfortable and a little embarrassed by the whole thing. The woman reappeared and beckoned to her. Reluctantly Anna went to join her.

Mrs Montgomery stopped outside a closed door and tapped on it gently. When Anna went in she found an old woman with a lined face as pale as the pillowcases she was resting against. Her eyes were closed. Anna stood beside the bed while Mrs Montgomery bent over and placed a hand on the old woman's arm.

"Jean, dear," she said softly. "The lady you wanted to see has come to visit you."

Jean opened her eyes and peered at Anna.

"Who is it?" she said in a weak voice.

"It's Mrs Sinclair... Anna. You've been asking to see her."

The old woman's eyes widened in comprehension.

"Oh yes," she whispered. "She's here. That's good."

She lifted her head from the pillow and looked at Anna.

"I'm so glad to see you, my dear."

CHAPTER TWENTY TWO

When Anna got back to Rowancross House there was a strange car in the driveway. She parked the Volvo beside it and went inside. As she took off her jacket and hung it in the hall cupboard she heard Barbara calling to her.

"Anna... We're in here..."

A little reluctantly Anna put the package that Jean MacBride had given her on the hall table and followed the sound of Barbara's voice into the sitting room. She was hoping that the 'we', whoever the 'we' was, wasn't going to take up too much time. Jean MacBride's mysterious gift was demanding her attention.

The other half of the 'we', sitting on the sofa opposite Barbara, was Richard. He stood up as she came in.

"Hello, Anna," he said.

She stood in the doorway and stared at him. The colour drained from his face as he waited for her to say something. Barbara, looking from one to the other, intervened.

"What a lovely surprise this is, isn't it, Anna? Richard caught the early flight this morning. He arrived about fifteen minutes ago. You must have been following him all the way back from Inverness."

Barbara had been checking her emails, and wondering what could possibly have happened to put Anna into such an odd mood, when the doorbell rang and she went to the front door and opened it to find Richard standing there.

"Richard… Good heavens…"

It took a brief awkward moment for her to register his presence before she stepped forward and hugged him.

"What a surprise."

He hugged her back with unexpected warmth.

"Is Anna expecting you?" Barbara was uncomfortably aware that he was there with no wife to greet him. "I'm afraid she's not here at the moment."

He stepped backwards off the doorstep and stood on the drive. "Not here. Right…"

Barbara felt dreadful.

"She shouldn't be too long. Back any moment I should think."

Now that she was able to get a proper look at him she couldn't help noticing that he looked terrible. His skin was an unhealthy shade of grey and there were dark circles around his eyes. Seeing him looking so rough made her feel even worse.

"She's gone to Inverness. Such a shame… If you had let us know you were coming she could have picked you up on her way back."

"Sorry –"

"You don't have to be sorry."

She hadn't meant it to sound like a rebuke.

"Sod's law really." He sighed. "I need to see her. I just want to know when she's going to come home." He didn't say 'if she's going to come home', but it hung unspoken in the air between them. "Things have been a little difficult recently. I thought it might be better if we discussed it face to face." He glanced at her uncertainly. "I hope you don't mind putting me up for the night."

Barbara reached out for his arm. "Of course I don't mind."

She wasn't sure how Anna was going to react. But what else could she do?

Now, standing between the two of them while they eyed each other like boxers preparing for a fight, she decided she didn't want to be the referee.

"I was about to heat up some soup for lunch," she said. "I'll go and do it now." And she walked past Anna, still motionless in the doorway, and left them alone.

As if Barbara's going had broken a spell, Anna came properly into the room. Richard was staring at her as if he didn't recognise her. The truth was that it felt as though he didn't. She was like a different person compared to the one he had said goodbye to at the airport all those weeks ago. Her skin was tanned and her hair had picked up highlights from days in the sun, as if the weeks she had been away from him had been spent on a tropical beach rather than on the west coast of the Highlands. There was an ease about her, an air of relaxation, that reminded him of when they were first married. She looked amazing.

She perched on the arm of one of the sofas.

"So, what are you doing here?"

Her was taken aback by her blunt approach.

"I rather hoped you might be pleased to see me. After all, the plan was for me to join you up here."

She gave him an appraising look.

"But the plan changed. You were the one who changed it. If you remember…"

He bit his lip.

"I just want to know what's going on. And when you're planning on coming home?"

She frowned.

"I told you on the phone. I'll be home in time for Ellie."

"And when will that be?"

"I haven't decided the exact day."

He looked at her, and wondered who she was, and if he had ever really known her.

"I thought you might like to come home with me."

"When are you going back?"

"I've booked a flight for tomorrow morning."

She shook her head. "That's no good for me," she said. "There are some things I have to do."

He didn't dare ask her what they might be.

There was an afternoon and an evening for them to get through. She didn't know what to do with him. In the end she took him to Inverewe Gardens. He wasn't much interested in the gardens themselves, but he was attracted by the idea of the original owner, Osgood Mackenzie, scouring the planet to bring back shrubs and trees for a garden built out of the rock in one of the most inhospitable places in the world, and was happy to pass a couple of hours there.

Side by side they wandered the hidden paths and sheltered corners, and she asked him about Moscow and told him a little of how she had been spending the summer. It was as if they were business associates meeting up for an appraisal, rather than husband and wife reunited after weeks apart.

They ate dinner together in Ullapool, at The Ceilidh Place. Barbara had booked a table for them while they were visiting the gardens, but refused to accompany them, even though both Anna and Richard tried, separately, to persuade her to change her mind.

"You need to talk," she told Anna a little sternly, when Anna pleaded with her to go with them. "It's not fair on him. He's come all the way up here for a reason. The least you can do is have dinner with the poor man."

"But it feels like we've got nothing to say to each other."

Barbara frowned.

"You've been married to each other for twenty years. There's plenty to talk about." She looked at her stepdaughter. "Give him a chance, Anna. He deserves it. You both do."

With Richard she was less blunt.

"It's very sweet of you," she said to him. "But don't you think that you and Anna might benefit from spending some time alone together. There must be a whole lot to catch up on."

Her face was sympathetic. She seemed to understand how difficult it was for him. Richard was
overtaken by the desire to throw himself on her
shoulder and weep and say that this wasn't how he
had planned it, that he was tired of working and
travelling but didn't know what else to do. And that,
more than anything else, he was frightened to spend
time with a wife who had turned into a stranger over
the summer. He managed to restrain himself.

Barbara saw his anguished expression and patted
him on the shoulder.

"Why don't you ask her about Fiona Gillespie,"
she suggested gently, looking at the grey strands
threading through the dark hair that curled back
from his temples, and wondering about that elusive
stage of life one had always believed in where things
were supposed to get easier.

"And don't let her fob you off with small talk," she
told him fiercely.

They faced each other over candlelight in the busy
restaurant. Richard watched her as she read the
menu. She was looking, he thought, utterly beautiful and maddeningly composed. He had to sit on his
hands to stop himself from reaching across the table
and shaking her. He wanted to tell her that she was

his wife and she was coming home with him the next day whether she wanted to or not. But he remembered Barbara's advice and, after they had ordered their meal, he filled their glasses with wine and asked her to tell him about Fiona Gillespie.

She began, a little woodenly at first, to fill him in on the family history. About Fiona and Robert, about Kildorran, and about the Highland Clearances. She told him how - much to her surprise - she had found herself growing more and more involved. She didn't mention Iain Mackay. Or Fin MacLean.

He watched and listened, sipping his wine and asking the occasional question, while she grew progressively more animated as she told him of her increasing fascination in a period of history she hadn't even heard of until she visited her father's house.

"You know the other thing about it," she said, looking at him properly for what seemed like the first time that evening. "I feel that I know my father so much better than I ever did before. Even though he's not around any more. Before I came here it was like I had no background, no history. Now it feels like I have a much clearer understanding of who I really am." She glanced at him. "That probably sounds ridiculous to you."

He shook his head.

"Not at all," he said. "We all share the need to make our stories complete."

She looked at him in surprise. As if she hadn't expected him to be so perceptive.

"We do," she agreed. "I didn't realise how important it was until I came here."

The most awkward moment of the evening came when they got back to the house. When Richard followed her into the bedroom for a moment she wondered what on earth he was doing. Over the past few weeks this room had become her sanctuary. The idea of a man intruding, putting his things in the bathroom, his clothes on the chair - even when that man happened to be her husband – was unsettling.

He must have seen that something was wrong. As he sat on the edge of the bed to remove a shoe he looked up at her, and saw her face.

"What…?" he said. "What is it?" His brow furrowed as the light dawned. "You think I should sleep somewhere else? Is that what it is? You don't want me in here with you?"

She felt her face grow hot.

"Of course I do. Where else would you sleep?"

But he had seen, and he knew.

They slept in separate zones in the wide bed, delineated by invisible boundaries. In the morning she waved him off down the drive. When he raised a hand to wave back he didn't know whether he was waving goodbye to what was left of his marriage.

After he had gone Anna rang Fin.

"Fin… Hi… It's me."

There was silence on the other end of the line.

"Fin… I'm so sorry."

She heard a sharp intake of breath.

"What exactly are you sorry for?" he said.

"For creeping out yesterday morning. For not getting in touch until now. Something came up… I had to deal with it… I couldn't ring…"

He let out his breath in a sigh.

"Do you want to tell me about it?"

"Not really… It's a family thing. It's not why I rang. I really need to see you. As soon as possible. I've got something really exciting to show you. I've been saving it up so that we could look at it together." Her words were tumbling over each other. "I didn't want to open it without you."

"Open what? What have you found?"

"Not found. It's something I've been given. You've got to come -"

"I'm on my way."

He was on the doorstep in twenty minutes. She opened the door to him. When he saw her standing in front of him, her eyes shining with excitement, he had to stop himself from taking hold of her and kissing her right there and then in front of anyone who might be passing. Not, he told himself - trying to think sensibly - that in this part of the world anyone would be likely to be passing, but there was Barbara to consider, and anyway Anna had grabbed his hand and was dragging him through the hall and down the corridor to her father's study.

"There…" She went into the room ahead of him and gestured towards the desk. Resting upon it was a small book bound in navy blue leather. Fin glanced from it to Anna and back again.

"So? What is it?"

She picked the book up and handed it to him.

"It's hers… Fiona's… It's the last one… I'm not absolutely sure, but I think it's going to tell us the whole story."

He stared at her.

"Where did you get it?"

"Laura MacBride's grandmother gave it to me. She's been keeping it for the right person. Apparently I'm the right person."

CHAPTER
TWENTY THREE

After Mrs Montgomery had left the room with a request to Anna to call if Jean's condition seemed to be getting any worse, Anna had sat herself down in the chair beside the bed. Jean's eyes had closed again and the breath in her chest rattled softly in and out. Her small hands, speckled with age, clasped the bed cover. The skin on her face was wrinkled and dry like parchment, coated with a feathering of soft white hairs.

Anna coughed gently. Jean opened her eyes and blinked a couple of times, and stared at Anna as if she wasn't quite sure where she was.

"It's Anna." Anna leant forward. "I'm Charlie Gillespie's daughter. You wanted to see me."

The eyes focussed. A connection was made somewhere in the old woman's brain. She smiled and nodded, her dentures showing white between frayed lips.

"Charlie's daughter?" she said faintly. "Such a good boy. He was always one of my favourites. Always so kind hearted. Never had any airs and graces. Not like some."

She peered at Anna.

"You have the look of him, my dear. He was a fine looking man." Tears sprung into the corners of her eyes. "I was sad to hear of his passing."

She sighed and her eyelids slid shut again. Anna was about to stand up and slip away when the blue eyes opened and focussed on her.

"I have something for you," said Jean in a stronger voice. "Would you mind going to the cupboard for me and opening the drawer on the right."

Anna stood up and crossed to where Jean was pointing. She opened the cupboard door and tugged at the drawer.

"There's a parcel inside," said Jean behind her. "Do you see it?"

The drawer was lined with faded lining paper. Inside was a bible, a packet of hairpins, a wooden box that looked like it might contain jewellery, and a sheaf of documents tied with a red ribbon. There was also a small flat square parcel wrapped in thick brown paper and tied up with string.

"Is this it?" asked Anna, lifting it out and showing it to Jean.

"That's the one."

Anna took it across to the bed and handed it to the old lady.

"No," she said. "It's for you, dear."

Anna frowned at the package in her hand.

"But what is it? And why me?"

So Jean MacBride, with many stops and starts and pauses for breath, explained.

"The women in my family have always worked for the Gillespies. My grandmother was the first. Her father was a tenant at Kildorran, and she went to the big house to be nursemaid to your great grandfather, Neil, when he was a baby, and moved with your great great grandmother to Rowancross House when the family went there. My mother took over from her. And, when Neil grew up, mother stayed with Mrs Gillespie and became her personal maid. She looked after her right up until the day she died."

Jean's eyes grew misty with memories of her mother. "She was a good woman, my mother, hard working, nothing was too much trouble for those she cared for. And she loved your great great grandmother. I reckon she would have done anything for her. She told me that Mrs Gillespie was the most kind hearted, the bravest, most honourable, most spirited lady she had ever known. She nursed her to the end, when she was too sick even to go to the bathroom by herself. And Mrs Gillespie must have loved her back, she certainly trusted her. Because the night before she died she gave my mother a book." Her gaze rested on the parcel in Anna's hand. "A diary it was. Full of memories she wrote down when she was an old lady." Jean pursed her lips. "Although nothing like as old as I am now.

Anyway the point is that she told my mother to keep the journal safe, and to show it to no-one, until the right person came along. It had to be given to a female descendant of Neil's. She insisted that it was for a woman to read. Only a woman would be able to understand.

She didn't want it to go to any of her three sons. And she particularly didn't want it opened in the lifetime of her favourite, Neil. She said that he wouldn't be able to understand, and that it would break her heart to consider that he might think less of her for what she had done.

Well, my poor mother was put into a right pickle over the whole thing. Because not only did Neil not have any daughters. But neither did his son, your grandfather, Charles. So mother had to hand the job on to me. And it took your father, Mr Charlie, to come up with the daughter we had been waiting for. And then the silly boy went and got divorced from your mother, and you never appeared up here, and I thought the opportunity would never arise."

"But now, here you are. And it's in your hands." She smiled at Anna. "My duty is done."

═╼ ╾═

Anna sat in her father's leather chair. Beside her Fin had pulled up the armchair. She opened the cover of the blue journal and turned to the first page.

"I'll read it aloud, shall I?"

He nodded. She cleared her throat.

I*t all seems such a long time ago now. Sometimes I wonder if it really happened at all. Or if it is just the foolish meanderings of an old woman who spends too much time in her bed, with nothing to do but stare at the wall and think about the past. That is why I am determined to write it down before I forget, or before I am unable to hold a pen, whichever comes first.*

I do not wish for what happened to be made known to anyone, apart from the one to whom this journal is given. Robert was old enough to remember that his mother went away for a while, but he never knew what happened, and he would struggle with the truth. I have no doubt that his brother Angus, had he survived, would have felt the same way. As for Neil – well, he has always been a very different kettle of fish. I have asked myself on many occasions whether it would be right to tell him the truth – whether he would understand. But I always stopped myself, because what good would it do? It would cause nothing but pain and unhappiness.

It is difficult to know where to start, how far back to go. I do not intend to write my life story, but nor do I wish to leave anything out. For I do this for myself as much as for anybody else. And I want to go back to that time. I want to relive the past.

I suppose it started when Robert went away to London. We parted on bad terms. From the moment I learned of his plans for our tenants we had not spoken. Was betrayal too strong a word for what he had done? I did not think so. My husband had betrayed my people, and in doing so he had betrayed me. And, although he kept on trying to explain, I was having none of it.

When he was preparing to leave I remember that I was in the kitchen with Mary, helping to make butter with the boys. Robert called me out to bid him farewell, but I pretended I did not hear him. He was angry with me, I could tell. He stood in the doorway to the kitchen and spoke my name. Mary looked at me and frowned and shook her head at me, and I knew that she thought it was wrong of me to let him go like that. But I turned my back on him and he left for the South without a kiss from his wife, without so much as a goodbye.

Three days later Iain Mackay came to Kildorran. I caught sight of him in the distance when I was out riding. He was cantering his black horse in the direction of *his sister's house. I do not think that he saw me. But I very much hoped that he would find the opportunity to call on me so that I could tell him in person that Robert's plans for the estate had nothing to do with me.*

He did not come for several days, and I began to think I would not see him until one evening there was a knock upon the door, and he came in and stood in the great hall with his plaid tied across his shoulders, and he looked at me with his fierce eyes and told me that he was set to leave Kildorran early the next morning, and did not want to go without saying goodbye.

I asked him what it could be that took him away from his family at such a time. For I had heard the day before that his father was very unwell, and that the family feared the worst. I said that I hoped his father's condition had improved, but Mr Mackay shook his head and explained that his father was no better, but that - considering the mission upon which he embarked - he had his father's blessing to leave. At first he would not tell me where he was going. But I pressed him, and eventually he explained what had happened.

A couple of weeks previously an attempt had been made to deliver writs of eviction upon the residents of Greenyards. His sister, Maggie, had been amongst those who had been successful in persuading the cowardly fellows to turn back. Now it appeared that a strong force of police was set to arrive at any moment to carry out the intended removal, and the women of the district were preparing themselves to stand up against those who came to turn them out of their homes. Maggie had every intention of being there in the front line with the others. And Iain was not going to stand by and let his sister face danger without his support.

The women of Greenyards were an inspiration to me. Encouraged by the recent success of the woman of Coigach - and mindful of the fate of those further up the valley at Glencalvie - they were committed to standing firm, and I was wholehearted in my support of their refusal to back down. I was angry beyond words with my husband, and desperate to demonstrate my solidarity with those who suffered at the hands of the callous and unfeeling landowners. So I demanded to go with him.

His response was exactly as you would expect. He didn't laugh - he was too polite for that. But he told me - in the tone of voice he might have used when speaking to a child – that it was too challenging, it was too dangerous. And here was the heart of it - it was not my fight.

How was it not my fight? These women were my sisters. We were all Highlanders. They were standing up for what mattered most - their homes. Did the soldiers who marched away to do battle in far off lands turn back and say it is not my fight? What could count for more than home and hearth, family, and the ties of blood and friendship? I could not rest while these brave women stood up to those who would take away from them everything that they had worked so hard to establish. I was determined to go with him, but he would have none of it. Even though I cajoled and begged him. He just grew more implacable and would not be persuaded.

So another parting on bad terms. I was angry with him, angry at the situation - helpless, useless woman, left at home while others got on with the things that really mattered. This time those others were of my own sex; women were preparing to mobilise and act, and I wanted to be there with them. But he grew impatient and would not listen. And he went away then, and I did not think I would see him again.

I could not sleep that night. It felt as if my world was crumbling around my ears; everything was changing. In the middle of the night, while the house slept around me, I rose from my bed and went downstairs with a candle to light my way. I wandered in the great hall, and spoke to the portraits of my ancestors, and asked them what I should do. When I lifted the candle to their faces I saw that they were looking at me with eyes that were fierce with the light of battle. And it seemed that they said to me that I should go and do what I felt was right, for action is the way of this family.

So, I went back to my room, and found the boy's garments I had worn the day that Iain Mackay found me by his sister's gate. I left a note for Mary telling her that a messenger had arrived in the night and that I had been called away to tend Flora's mother who had been taken ill. Aunt Margaret has been unwell for some time, and Flora is away down south, so Mary would expect me to go and help. Although possibly not in the middle of the night. So I crept from the house, and saddled up my horse, and took the track across the hills.

Iain must have left his sister's house soon after, for he caught up with me as I went along the path that ran by the edge of Loch Vaich. At first my disguise fooled him, for he glanced across and bade me good morning, and for a moment there was no sign of recognition. But then he looked and looked again. And his eyes grew wide with disbelief, and his face was full of thunder.

I think he would have sent me back, but the clouds had begun to roll in, and behind us the weather was turning to rain, and we could not see beyond the loch. So I went with him, but he was so angry with me that he made me ride behind him and would not speak to me. By the time we reached Glencalvie Forest we had exchanged no more than a few words.

He rode his horse easily with his great black dog following at his heels, and did not look back at me. Thunder was rumbling in the mountains, and lightning flashed across the black sky; the storm had caught us up. We rode as fast as we could over the rough ground. I do not think he could have gone any faster had he been alone, and I was pleased not to be the burden he was so clearly expecting me to be.

We reached his sister's house with the skies above us as dark as if night had fallen early. The dogs began such a barking, as we rode down the strath on the south bank of the Carron River, that several people came rushing from their homes as if they thought it was the police come early to evict them. As we drew near Maggie came out from her house with her husband Donald beside her. Iain climbed down from his horse and embraced his sister. In the glow from the lighted doorway I could see that her face was pale and drawn as she greeted her brother, and they spoke in low, hurried sentences so that I could not hear. I stood with my hand stroking the head of Iain's dog, and he leant his weight against me as if to comfort me. They turned to look in my direction and their faces were stern. I knew they were talking about me, and I thought they might be about to send me home. But then, to my great relief, Maggie left her brother and came to welcome me with her hands held out and a warm smile.

She was a tall woman, with a strong face and her brother's dark eyes. I told her that I had come to offer my support to the women of Greenyards, and she squeezed both of my hands tightly with her own, and thanked me, and said that they needed all the help they could get. At that moment I could have fallen on her neck and embraced her, for I had been feeling so nervous and foolish and out of place, and I was waiting for her to follow her brother's example and scold me. Now he came walking across to join us, and, for the first time that day, I saw the glimmer of a smile in his eyes.

We were taken in and ate a simple meal of mutton with potatoes. I sat at the table in the dimly lit room with smoke from the fire stinging my eyes, and listened while they talked. Iain was questioning his brother-in-law, suggesting that the men of Greenyards should support the women in their action. Donald shrugged his shoulders, and nodded his head in the direction of his wife, and muttered something about nothing being as hard as trying to convince a woman.

Now Maggie leaned across the table and laid a hand on her brother's arm and looked in him the eye. She told him in a steady voice that it had been agreed that the women would have a better chance of persuading the police to turn back. With the men present it became a confrontation that would in all likelihood end in violence. This time the women would not give way, but they were confident that no man - no matter how he had been instructed - would wish to inflict serious harm upon women and children.

Iain looked doubtful. I could see that he was worried. But Maggie was having none of it. She reminded him of the women of Coigach, who had achieved a great victory for their people only a year previously. It was the women with their boys who stood in the foreground, with their menfolk bringing up the rear, as the Sherriff arrived by boat to deliver his unwelcome demands. The women were civil, but they stood firm. And the men saw that they would not be persuaded and, unwilling to embark upon a course of action that could lead to injury, withdrew.

Iain shook his head and reminded her of what had happened closer to home, just up the strath at Glencalvie. But Maggie looked haughtily upon him and said that the people of Glencalvie had failed to organise themselves properly, because they were unwilling to face the reality of what would happen if they did not. They were unprepared. And as a result went quietly in the end. This time, said Maggie, with a determined glint in her eye, it would be different. This time they knew what to expect.

I was impressed by her words. I was glad to be there. These women had worked too long and too hard to stand by while their homes were taken away from them. They might not have strength on their side, but they had wit and cunning and these would serve them well. While the men talked of honour and revenge, the women would act. And they would win.

I saw Iain turn away and shake his head. When the opportunity came I spoke quietly to him, asking him why he looked so troubled. He told me that he was gravely concerned that his sister did not appreciate that these men had a job to do and would not tolerate any obstacles in their way. There was the potential for things to get unpleasant, and he wanted to be there if they did.

Maggie would not allow him to accompany her and the other women. She said that he could stay back and wait with the rest of the men, so that they were ready if they were needed. I saw Iain look to his brother in law for support, but Donald's face was resigned. There was none of the fire that burned in his wife's eyes; he looked exhausted, as if he was beaten already. He was a man of honour who knew in his heart that he was unable do the one thing that really mattered, he could not protect and provide for his family. I saw this in his face, and I wanted to weep for the tragedy being inflicted upon these people.

When the time came for sleep I was given a mattress stuffed with chaff, on a rough bed pushed up against the stone wall of the house, with a curtain for privacy. Iain slept in a box bed in the kitchen. I do not think I closed my eyes for more than a minute. The bed was not comfortable, but had it been the finest horsehair mattress, made up with silk and satin, I think that I would not have slept. It seemed that Iain too was unable to rest. I could hear the rustling of his mattress as he turned in the night, the slow quiet hush of his breathing. I lay and stared into the darkness, and his presence filled the space behind my eyes. Was he aware of it? At one point I could swear he said my name. I sat bolt upright in bed, and waited for him to repeat it. But he did not, and I could not be sure that I had really heard him at all.

The household was awake well before dawn. A neighbour had tapped on the door, with a muttered warning that a large body of men had come over the hills from Alness and was gathering up the strath, awaiting the arrival of the Sheriff Substitute and the law agent before they advanced. It was worrying to hear that the men were taking alcohol to prepare themselves for the fray, to steady their nerves.

When we left the house the sky above our heads was a dull grey, streaked with pink. The air was chilly, and Maggie and I wrapped shawls about us for warmth. Chickens were clucking, a cockerel's cry sounded unnaturally loud in the still air. There was a hush across the strath, a holding in of breath, a quiet sense of anticipation. As we walked along the road we were joined by others, women with their heads bowed, who left their houses without looking back.

Maggie walked beside me. When I glanced across at her I saw that there was a smile on her lips, and her stride was full of vigour and energy. A handsome woman, tall and proud, fell in step beside us. Maggie introduced her to me. Her name was Margaret Ross. On the other side of her two others turned their heads towards us and smiled; Margaret was marching with her sisters Elizabeth and Janet. By the time we got to the edge of the wood there must have been at least sixty or seventy women. But there was none of the chatter you might expect. We stood in the shelter of the trees in silence and waited.

It was dark under the pines; the needles underfoot muffled the sound. Then, with a crack like a branch breaking above our heads, a gunshot rang out from the hills, and we heard the dull tramp of many footsteps. Along the road beyond the wood appeared a great party of men, marching together. It was impossible to say how many there were, but we could see that they had clubs in their hands, and, even in the dim light of dawn, it was possible to see that their faces were set and there was no pity in their eyes.

When they saw that we were waiting for them they stopped, and I saw that there was a carriage drawn up behind them, and a heavily built fellow with a fringe of black hair and a sick sallow complexion stepped down, with a small man following in his wake, and came round to the front of his little army.

The Sherriff Substitute scanned the crowd of women with cold eyes. I noticed that the men with him did not look at us, but stared at their leader as they waited for his command. Then he shouted out in Gaelic that we must clear out of the way so that the officers of the law could carry out their duty.

Maggie and I were standing to the left of the crowd. The woman in front of me was taller than I, and I had to lean on tiptoe to see over her shoulder. Nobody moved. Then the man took a scroll of parchment from his left pocket and began to read the Riot Act. Beside us a woman in her early forties squared her shoulders and stepped forward. I heard Maggie mutter under her breath, "Go to it, Ann."

This was Ann Ross. She stood in front of us and told the man in a strong voice that Alexander Munro, the tacksman of Greenyards, had denied that warrants had been issued in his name, and that they were consequently illegal. The Sherriff Substitute looked at her with contempt and shook his head. Seeing this, several of the women stepped forward to stand shoulder to shoulder with Ann. He stared at them all for a moment, and then he spat on the ground at their feet and cursed, and thrust the parchment back into his pocket. Then he looked over his shoulder and shouted an order to the assembled force. "Clear them out of the way," he said. And although his face was turned away I distinctly heard when he added.

"If you have to, knock them down."

And so it began. In one ferocious move the men raised their truncheons above their heads, and with a great shout they came forward in unison. Then I was afraid. For there was something inhuman about their readiness to threaten us in such a way. Was it the alcohol that turned these men into animals? What did it take to find the willingness to attack a crowd of defenceless women? I had never seen such faces before. That they meant to harm us was in no doubt.

I think at first we did not know what to do. What woman would? Who amongst us had any experience of waging war? There was a moment when we stood and watched as they came upon us. Then one of the women threw back her shawl to reveal her grey hair, and stood forward. She waved a sheet of white paper in front of her, as if it were some kind of magic charm, and called out to the men. "See here. I have a letter. From Mr Munro. He writes that he has not authorised this action. You cannot proceed."

You will not believe what I tell you now; I could not believe what I saw. She was not a big woman, considerably smaller than I. And she was old, fifty or more at least. They struck her with their sticks. Not one of them, not two, but three together. Three men joined forces against this one grey haired woman. I watched as they knocked her down. And I saw one of them raise a boot, and stamp down upon her poor defenceless head, and she rolled on the ground and tried to crawl away as they laid into her, kicking her again and again, as if she were no better than a dog.

I don't know if I cried out. I think I must have done, for a young woman beside me turned and looked at me, and I saw the shock on her face at what was happening. As she turned back a red faced man bore down on her, with his truncheon raised above his head and a murderous look in his eyes. She raised her hands, her small fists clenched. He brought down his truncheon and I heard it crack against her shoulder bone. He raised it again, bringing it down against her breast, and she cried out and began to stagger away, seeking to escape. He followed her. I tell you he followed her. She tried to hide from him, pushing herself against a thorn bush, the jagged thorns tearing at her flesh, so that I could see the blood gushing from her wounds. And the man kicked out at her as he pulled her from her hiding place. Another man joined him and produced a pair of handcuffs, while his companion threw her to the ground. And then he bent down to her, and put his knees on her chest, pinning her to the earth while he wrapped the cuffs about her wrists.

It was hell on earth. All about us women were crying out. Again and again I heard the sickening crunch as wood met with skin and bone. I could hear children screaming for their mothers. Dodging between falling bodies and the rushing advance of angry men, I bent to help a girl who lay on the ground, her left arm bent under her, her face bruised and bloody. On the far bank of the river a woman flung herself into the water and began to wade towards us, dragging off her apron as she did so, and commencing to tear it into strips, preparing bandages for the wounded as she struggled through the rushing water. She could not see what I saw. A pair of constables stood and waited for her. As she approached the bank they began to wade through the water towards her. I screamed out a warning. She raised her head and her eyes grew wide as she saw them waiting for her, water swirling around their ankles. She tried to run, but her long skirts were heavy with water, and she stumbled. They were nearly upon her. She picked herself up and struggled away from them, looking at them with the eyes of a hunted beast. They caught up with her, and they beat her as she struggled through the water, until she slipped and fell and slid into the river.

Where were our men? Apart from Iain Mackay and a few others, help did not come. Why did they not come forward in support of their wives? In the confusion of that terrible day I can't say what happened to them. Only that they were noticeable by their absence. Did they not realise what was happening to their womenfolk? Or maybe they thought it was beneath them, the warrior race of the Highlands, to fight with policemen.

There was one, an old soldier, in his sixties, I should say. I came upon him as he lay on the ground. He had been badly beaten. I bent down to offer him assistance, and he looked up at me, and waved me on, and told me that there were others who needed help more than he. I could not help noticing that his eyes were full of tears.

"It's a terrible business," he said to me in a voice of great sorrow. "I was there when we got the better of Bonaparte, at Waterloo. I never thought I would see the like of today." And he shook my hand and urged me on.

When I look back, it seems that it went on for ever, the slow motion agony of terrible events unfolding. But the reality was that it lasted only a short space of time. In the few minutes it took for us to understand the full impact of what these men were willing to do to achieve their ends, the women of Greenyards began to turn away and try to escape. But the evil creatures would not allow this. They followed us up the brae, cursing and swearing, grabbing at hair, at skirts, legs, arms, whatever they could lay their hands on; seizing the poor women, flinging them to the ground and beating them where they lay.

I lost Maggie for a while in the turmoil. We had seen the three Ross sisters felled beside us, like young trees cut off in their prime. Margaret received such a blow to the head that it gaped open and blood spurted from the wound. Beside her, her sister, Elizabeth, was knocked to the ground. A man was stamping on her, leaving the imprint of his metal rimmed boots on her poor broken body.

Then we were running together, stumbling across the stony ground. One moment Maggie was beside me, and I saw her face full of bewilderment and disbelief. And then she was jerked backwards, her head snapping back on her neck, as a man behind us seized her and yanked her back, tearing a handful of her long dark hair out by its roots. I screamed and stopped running. And was grabbed around the neck by a man with veins that stood out on his face like ropes. I managed to pull myself out of his grasp, and made to escape, until I saw Maggie on the ground. She was surrounded by men laying into her with their boots without mercy.

Out of nowhere came a figure, hurtling into the men like a cannonball, scattering them across the heather. Iain had come to save his sister. He fought like a tiger, his fists bare, his face grim as death. And he was getting the better of them. One against three, and he looked likely to beat them. Until two others saw what was happening, and came to join in. One of them stood behind Iain and was lifting something above his head. I saw that it was great piece of rock. I sprang at the man, clawing at his face with my nails, screaming in his ear all the curses and oaths and terrible words I could think of. The man with the bulging veins seized me and tore me off his companion, and I could see that there was murder in his eyes. He swore at me and drew back his cudgel. There was a jolt of intense pain, a blinding flash, and then darkness.

CHAPTER
TWENTY FOUR

S itting at her desk, Barbara was aware that silence had fallen at the other end of the house. She had been attempting to get on with the thank you letters she still owed to people who had written so kindly after the memorial service. The sound of Anna's voice reading to Fin had provided a comforting backdrop. Barbara's hand hovered over the page as she waited for it to restart.

She wished she knew what was going on with Anna. Something had happened, but her stepdaughter was giving nothing away; her customary openness had been replaced by a reserve that Barbara couldn't penetrate. Now, with all the comings and goings of the past twenty four hours, Barbara felt as if she was taking part in a play where she hadn't been given the script.

Her evening in Strathpeffer had given her a lot to think about. She had known Diana Grant from the early years of her marriage, when she and Charlie were renting a house while Rowancross House was being renovated. Diana and her husband Hugo were next door neighbours who became close friends. Born on the Black Isle, Hugo couldn't imagine living anywhere else, and his passion for the Highlands helped Barbara to view the prospect of life in the north in a more positive light, putting Charlie Gillespie forever in his debt. Diana and Barbara had found that they shared more in common than their initial reluctance to live so far away from what they both saw as civilisation, and were soon great friends.

When Hugo died of liver cancer Diana had taken over the running of the second hand bookshop that had been his passion and hobby. But the truth was that he had left her with a house that was too big for her, and a business that wasn't big enough. Originally from Hampshire, Diana had been happy enough to embrace life in the north while she had her husband at her side. And for three years she had continued without him. But the reality was, as she admitted to Barbara, that she was lonely. And, at the age of sixty three, couldn't help thinking that it was time to make a change before it was too late.

She and Barbara had stayed up late into the night discussing how they felt about facing life without a husband beside them. Both women were quick to agree that they loved the Highlands. But both were of the opinion that it was not the place in which either of them would choose to grow old alone.

Diana told Barbara that she was thinking of moving south, of buying a flat in Winchester so that she could see more of her grandchildren, and a house somewhere in the South of France.

"So that I can soak my bones in the sun, and pretend to myself that I'm not really getting any older. That it's just the people around me who are getting younger."

Barbara had laughed and told her not to be ridiculous, that she looked no different to when they first met. But later that night, lying in bed alone, she began to wonder if Diana might have a point.

Richard had turned up on the doorstep within hours of her returning home, and since then she had not had much time to think. Now, as she sat and waited, and wondered if Anna was going to start reading again, the silence in the house sounded loud in her ears. She stared across the garden without seeing it. Perhaps the time had come to visit the cousin in Italy who kept on inviting her, and see what the rest of the world had been getting up to while she had been hidden away in the Highlands. She reached for her phone to look up Sheila's number in Tuscany.

At the other end of the house Fin was watching Anna. She was sitting back in her father's chair, staring out of the window.

"You OK?"

Anna turned to look at him.

"I'm struggling to get my head round what happened to those women. To Fiona. It's hard to take in."

"Do you want me to take over?"

She leant forwards and picked up Fiona's journal.

"No. It's fine. I'm happy to carry on. I want to…"

I woke with black earth against my face, and the sharp taste of blood in my mouth. My head was pounding, and my arms ached as though they had been twisted off my body. Somebody was dragging me to my feet. I think I must have moaned, for a rough voice told me to be quiet, and I was pushed into standing, and found that the pain in my arms was because there were handcuffs on my wrists.

I was standing with four others against the stone wall of one of the houses. We were surrounded by a sea of men's faces, all angry and closed, full of bitterness. It was hard to see that the creatures who stood alongside me were human. When I looked I saw that one of them was the woman, Christy Ross, who had tried to read out her letter. Only now her grey hair was caked with mud and dried blood, and her face was a mass of purple bruises.

Next to Christy was a girl who could have been no more than eighteen. Her face was puffed up with one eye completely shut. She was weeping silently. I realised it was the girl who had tried to hide in the thornbush. Beside her I saw another girl, not much older. She stood proud and tall and would not weep, although I could see the marks of boots on her cheek and blood in her hair. There was another woman, in her forties maybe, and she spat at the men and made the evil eye and they pulled back from her as if they were afraid.

We were marched in single file to the gaol in Tain. I saw a pack of dogs licking the earth where our blood had fallen. The men laughed and shooed them away, but I think that they had more respect for the dogs than for us.

Why did they choose us? They accused us of being the ringleaders, but I think they just took whoever came to hand first. We were thrown into a filthy cell, with nothing but a pail of foul water to quench our thirst. The straw on the earth floor was soiled and evil smelling, the stone walls dripped with water. The young girl, whose name was Margaret, was suffering badly from her injuries. She needed to see a doctor. We called out to our jailers, begging and pleading with them for assistance, but, although we know they heard us for we heard them laughing, nobody came to help.

It was the longest night of my life. The other women sat slumped around me, nobody sleeping, Margaret Ross muttering and crying out with the fever that had set in from her wounds. I sat on the floor with my legs stretched out in front of me, nursing my injuries, and wondering what was to become of us all. I thought of my little boys, of what they would do if they could see their mother in such a state. I thought about Robert, and what it would do to him when this story came out, as it surely would. But mostly I thought about Iain Mackay. About whether I would ever see him again. About the way he had whispered my name in the darkness. About whether he was dead.

In the morning they brought us a pail of grey porridge. It was full of grit and bugs, and nobody felt like eating it. Christy Ross banged on the bars of our cell with the pail, and shouted for somebody to bring a doctor for Margaret, but nobody came. When we had given up all hope of being heard, a man came in and stood by the bars, peering in at us as if we were a pack of exotic animals in a cage brought back from the other side of the world.

"Is there a woman by the name of Fiona Mackay among you?" he said abruptly. We all stared at each other, for there was nobody of that name. Then I stepped forward. "I am the only Fiona here," I said. "Although my name is not Mackay." He looked hard at me with suspicious eyes.

"You'll do," he said. He unlocked the door and held it back for me to go through. I looked at the others. I did not know what was in store for me. Christy made a slight motion with her head. "Go on with you," she said softly.

It was difficult to walk. Each step set a ringing pain clattering in my head, so that I thought I might faint. But I was determined not to show my weakness, and, with the eye of my jailer upon me, I held up my head and made my way out through the heavy wooden door at the far end of the room with the other women calling to me to take good care.

There was a man in the outer room. He had his back turned to me as I entered, but I knew instantly that it was he, and that he had come for me. When he turned and I saw those eyes, black and fierce and full of passion, I had to stop myself from running into his arms, in spite of my wounds.

He took me from that terrible place, and rode with me back across the hills. But he did not take me home to Kildorran. Instead he took me to a stone cottage with rowan trees growing all around it, by the shores of Loch Broom.

I stayed there with Iain Mackay for several days, while he nursed me and cared for me, until my wounds began to heal and the bruises faded. The cottage was no more than one room, with a floor of bare earth, and a bed fashioned out of bracken and heather. He covered me with blankets and built a fire in the hearth. And he made a poultice out of bran for the bruises on my face, and bathed the cuts on my body with salt water. On the first morning he went out with a gun and returned with a rabbit slung on a piece of rope, and he made a stew out of it and set it to cook on the fire, and he brought me water to drink from a wooden cup. He sat beside me while I slept, and was there when I opened my eyes.

At first I was confused, and could not remember clearly what had happened. I drifted in and out of consciousness, thinking that I was at home in bed at Kildorran, or that I was with John in the bothy in the hills hunting for deer, or that I was still in the cell at Tain. When I knew where I was I would not rest until he told me how it was that he had been able to rescue me.

He sat beside me and told me that he had done a deal with the Sheriff at Tain. That, in return for his promise that he would write nothing of the events that had taken place at Greenyards, they would release the woman called Fiona with no questions asked. When I heard this I was angry with him. What of the others? As weak as I was, I rose from my bed, insisting that he had to take me back. He would not hear of it. He watched me while I raged and carried on, until I was too weak to continue and would have fainted, had he not come to me and put his arms around my waist, and carried me back to my bed.

Then he sat down beside me again and told me that it was for the best. That no good would come from the world discovering that the wife of Robert Gillespie was present at Greenyards on that terrible day. My sons and my husband would suffer. The publicity would cause great damage to the family. And it wouldn't help the people of Greenyards. The deed was done and nothing could change it. It was already too late for them. They would go from their homes, and nothing could be done to stop it now.

He was right. I knew it. But still I wept. For it seemed to me then that it had all been for nothing; the truth would never come out. Nobody would know what had really happened that day.

He waited until the weeping stopped, and then reached out and touched my face where the tears had fallen. His fingers were cool against my skin, and I couldn't help myself. I lifted my hand to his face and pressed my thumb against his chin. He leant forward and took a handful of my hair from where it lay across my shoulder and twisted it around his hand. Then he let it drop and his hand moved down my neck, and he moved onto his knees so that his face was next to mine and I could feel his soft breath against my cheek. I moved against him so that our bodies were touching, and very gently he slid onto the bed and stretched out beside me.

He told me about the first time he saw me, of how the world had spun on a different axis from that moment on. And then he asked if he might be allowed to do the one thing he had been wanting to do from the moment we met, which was to kiss me. I couldn't speak, but I think I must have nodded for he leaned into me and touched my lips with his own. And he didn't have to ask again.

We stayed in the cottage by the rowan tree for two more days. We knew nothing but our passion for each other and for those brief intense hours the rest of the world ceased to exist. My baby, my little boy, was conceived in the bed of bracken and heather. I built up a store of memories that have stayed with me through the years, as fresh and bright as if I was still there with him, and the time hadn't passed, and we were still young and in love and free of all thought but for each other.

But it could not go on. On the sixth day after he brought me there, he put me upon his horse and took me back to Kildorran.

CHAPTER TWENTY FIVE

The door to Charlie's study opened and Barbara heard footsteps and Anna calling out to her. She put down the phone without dialling Sheila's number. There was plenty of time to plan and explore options. In the immediate future there were things on the doorstep that needed her attention. She called back to Anna that she was in the sitting room and heard her stepdaughter's light tread as she ran down the hall.

"Here you are."

Anna came quickly into the room. Her eyes were bright with excitement. Barbara raised her eyebrows.

"I'm guessing from your expression that it was worth the drive to Inverness."

"It's what we thought… Fiona was at Greenyards. And she and Iain Mackay were lovers."

Fin's lean frame appeared in the doorway.

"Exciting, huh?" said Barbara including him in her smile.

"It certainly is."

He came into the room behind Anna. When their eyes met it was as if the temperature in the room was raised by several degrees. So that's how it is, thought Barbara. I should have guessed. She felt sorry for Richard.

"We're taking a breather," announced Anna. "Aren't we, Fin?" She took him by the arm. "My voice is getting tired. I've been reading all morning." She began to drag him towards the door. "We thought we'd make some sandwiches and take them outside. Is that alright? Do you want anything?"

The discovery had left her exhilarated, breathless, full of fire. Barbara noticed that Fin couldn't take his eyes from her face. When they left the room it was as if somebody had sucked all the life out of it. Barbara sat back down at the desk and sighed.

Fin and Anna sat on the old bench in the garden, sheltered from the wind blowing off the water by the pine trees. On the grass beside them were the remains of their sandwiches and a glass bowl containing a few bruised raspberries. Anna leant forward and put her glass down.

"Shall we carry on?"

"Give it another minute or two," said Fin easily, reaching out to pull her back so that she was leaning against him. She allowed herself to be pulled, and they sat in comfortable silence. Then suddenly she was leaning away from him and sitting bolt upright, hands gripping the seat on either side of her. He stared at her.

"What's the matter?"

"It's just clicked."

"What?"

"The baby…"

"What about the baby?"

"It's Neil."

"What do you mean?"

"I mean it's Neil. I can't believe I didn't make the connection before. Fiona had three sons. The youngest was Neil. He was born in 1854. Don't you see?"

Fin whistled slowly through his teeth.

"You're saying Iain Mackay was Neil's father?"

Anna stared at him.

"He has to be." She drew in her breath. "Which means that Iain Mackay is my great great grandfather."

Fin stared back at her. Then he leapt up and grabbed both of her hands, pulling her to her feet. "You realise what *that* means?"

He put his arms around her and swung her round, so that her heels kicked out behind her, and she laughed and begged him to put her down.

"What does it mean?"

He put his hands on her neck and pulled her towards him, so that their foreheads met.

"OK," he said. "So here's the thing. Iain Mackay never married, he didn't have any children. Or at least that's what everybody believed until now. Right?"

"Right," she agreed.

"So now we find out that he did have a child – Neil. And Neil had three children. But one of them died and the other never married. So the third son, Charles, was the only one to produce an heir."

"My father?"

"Absolutely. Neil Gillespie's only grandchild. And he goes on to have just the one child, a daughter."

"Me?"

"So what does that make you?"

Anna screwed up her face.

"I suppose it means I must be related to you in some way," she said.

He paused.

"Hadn't thought of that," he said, frowning. "But that's not my point." He grabbed her hands again. "My point is that you are a direct descendant of Iain MacKay. Which must give you a pretty good claim to a sizeable chunk of the Mackay publishing empire."

Anna sat down again on the bench and stared up at him. He stood in front of her with his hands on his hips and a big smile on his face.

"Quite a thought, huh?"

She wasn't sure how to react.

"I suppose so."

"Come on, Anna." He sat down beside her. "It's fantastic. Amazing. The long lost heir to a publishing phenomenon. It's one hell of a story."

Anna looked at her feet.

"I don't think I want to be one hell of a story," she said slowly. "That's not what this is all about. It isn't about me." She glanced up at him. "It's about Fiona."

Fin took her hand.

"Of course it's about Fiona," he said. "But it's also about you being the possible heir to a massive fortune."

Anna smiled at him.

"You know what," she said, "let's go and finish reading. I don't really care about heirs and fortunes. I just want to know how it ends."

The pain of losing someone you love is unlike physical pain. Physical pain goes away. You remember that you felt it, but not what it felt like. Losing someone you love is different; the loss endures. You might forget it for a while. You might

grow accustomed to being without that which you have lost. You might even learn how to be happy again. But when you revisit it, the pain is still there, as strong as ever, unabated. It never leaves you.

He stopped at the bridge, and I carried on up to the house alone. Dawn was breaking across the mountains, and I looked back and saw his silhouette, standing on the hillside watching me. It felt as though something was tearing out my heart. I could not admit to myself that it was the last time I would see him. But deep inside I knew.

What did I expect when I got home? That I would be able to creep in without anyone noticing that I had gone? That nobody would have paid much attention to the fact that I had been absent for more than a week? That there would be no repercussions? To be honest I'm not sure what I expected. I was numb.

I came up through the garden and pushed open the door to the back hall. All was quiet. I presumed that the household must still be sleeping, although it seemed odd that no sound came from the kitchen, when surely fires should be lit for the start of the day. I tiptoed up the back staircase and slipped into the boys' room. Their curly heads lay on the pillows, and I stood and gazed at them, and told myself that in the end this was what it was all about. Then I crept along the hallway to my own room and closed the door behind me.

Now there I was and what was I to do? How was I supposed to manage my reappearance? I had not thought this through, and stood with my back against the door, and felt like a fool. There was only one thing for it. I changed my clothes and left the room to look for my husband.

The only person I could find was one of the house-maids. I came upon her in the pantry. She nearly jumped through the window with shock when I spoke her name, and she looked at me out of wide eyes as if I were a ghost. When I asked where everybody was she stared at me as if I was insane, and told me that they were all out looking for me. She said that the master had come home earlier than expected, and sent a messenger to my aunt's, and, when he learnt that I was not there, he had gone out into the hills to search for me. He had not slept, had not rested, had kept the entire household in a state of constant alert until I was found.

John returned by late morning, and I heard his boots ringing out on the flagstones in the hall as he came to find me. At first I thought he might sweep me into his arms and hug me, such was the relief in his anxious face, but then the thunderclouds rolled in, and he was as angry as I have ever seen him. I think he wished that he could have scolded me in the way he would have done if I was still a child, and had done something dangerous or foolish. Now all he could do was look at me with a sorrowful expression in his eyes, and shake his head and mutter into his beard. He told me that my husband had gone away across the hills to Gleann Beag and Gleann Mor to search for me.

I played with my boys, and told them stories, and waited all that long afternoon, while my husband was out in the hills looking for me. I thought of the other one who would also be worrying for me. And I did not know what to do.

It was dark by the time Robert came home. I heard the sound of horse's hooves coming up the drive, and then voices. The great door in the hall creaks when it swings open, and the sound of it was like a cry. How can I begin to describe the force of his anger when he laid his eyes upon me? For it was like nothing I had ever seen before. This man who never lost his temper, who kept such a tight rein on his emotions, so that most of the time it was impossible to know what he was thinking, now he strode towards me with his eyes blazing and a storm raging within. I think he would have seized me, but he turned away at the last moment. Now he flung himself across the room, slamming the fist of one hand into the palm of the other, as if it were my face that he was battering.

All I could do was watch him. I had never seen him like this. Gradually, as a ferocious storm blows itself out, his anger subsided. Finally, he began to grow calm. Now the pacing and swearing ceased, but what was left was even worse. For now he turned his eyes upon me, and in them I saw such pain that it was like an arrow in my chest, and I felt my eyes filling with tears. For it was as if I had delivered the fatal wound to a ferocious beast, and was being forced to watch him fade away and die.

Only then did I realise that I had got it wrong. I believed that he had grown indifferent to me. I had convinced myself that the more time he spent in the ballrooms and salons of Edinburgh and London, mixing with the kind of sophisticated people who made me feel so out of place, the less time he had for his wife. I thought that his heart had turned to stone, and that he put me into the same category as the people of Kildorran whose homes he was intending to take away. I thought that he had turned into the enemy.

Now he stood with his back turned towards me. He leant against the stone mantle above the fire with his head on his arms, pushing at the burning logs with the toe of his leather riding boot. His shoulders sagged in a way that spoke to me of desolation. I was frightened of rekindling his anger but there was nothing for it. I spoke to him quietly, as if he were an animal to be gentled.

I told him that I knew how worried he had been about me. And that I appreciated that I owed him an explanation for my absence. But I told him that if he loved me, as I believed he did, then he would be prepared to leave me alone for a few days and not ask any questions of me.

When he turned from the fire his face was grey and drawn.

"If I do as you ask, then you will stay?"

I could not face those eyes. I bent my head in front of his gaze.

He did as I asked. For two days and two nights I spent the time alone in my room or riding out on my horse. I played with my boys in the afternoons, and put them to bed at night. On the third day I went to find my husband.

He was standing in front of the mirror in his bedchamber, tying his collar at his neck. When I stood behind him I could see my reflection over his shoulder, and my face was pale and ghostly in the silver glass. He looked into the mirror and his eyes met mine.

"Well?" he said quietly.

For a reply I stepped forward and put my arms around his waist, and laid my head against his broad back. He twisted in my embrace, so that he was facing me, and he took my face between his hands and the light in his eyes burnt brightly. I knew he had forgiven me.

In the end it wasn't a difficult decision to make. Painful, but not difficult. When I stood alongside the women of Greenyards and saw the way they fought for what was important to them, it made me think about everything I had put into my own family, the time, the effort, the love. I had invested too much in it to simply walk away. Through my husband and my sons I forged my link with the past and built my bridge into the future. Although with Iain Mackay I felt more alive than I had ever felt before, if I were to go away with him as he had asked I would be leaving part of myself behind, the person who was a wife and a mother. And I could not do that.

I think that Robert knew how close he had come to losing me. For the kind of man he was, it was hard for him to bear. In those days I grew to understand the depth of his love for me. That he was prepared to be silent, to accept that there was a part of my life that would remain forever my secret, was all the evidence I needed.

There was one thing I made him promise me. I could not sit back and watch while he destroyed an entire way of life, no matter how honourable his intentions. I told him that while I understood that change was inevitable and necessary, there had to be a way of achieving it so as to be of benefit to the people whose lives would be most affected by it. If he persisted in his current approach with regard to Kildorran then - although I could not stop him - I would not stay and be a witness to the destruction of the lives of people who had as much right to the land as I did. So I offered my husband an ultimatum. Change his plans, or lose his wife.

Robert changed his plans. We never discussed where I had been and what had happened in the week that I went missing. I suspect that he must have had some inkling of what had taken place, for there were rumours circulating for long after the people of Greenyards were gone from the valley of Strathcarron. But he never said anything. Sometimes I would catch him watching me, as if I was some kind of alien creature that he was struggling to understand, but he treated me with a degree of care and consideration that had been missing in the early years of our marriage.

Neil was born on November 12th. Everybody said that he took after me. Only his eyes, the dark intense brown, could be considered to have come from his father. It was a matter of great relief to me that so many people made the connection and congratulated Robert on his fine new son. I was secretly full of joy to see that there was something of his father in his face.

I heard from Iain MacKay's sister that, out of the women arrested with me that day, only one was charged. Ann Ross, who was beaten while she lay on the ground, and who had comforted me in the cell, was identified as a troublemaker. But since it seemed that the magistrates couldn't bring themselves to admit that the fair sex was capable of delivering such a massive blow to male pride and dignity, they brought in her husband, Peter, and arrested him as the ringleader. Which was the ultimate insult.

Ann Ross spent a year in prison, while her husband got eighteen months hard labour. In his summary the judge told the jury that 'there exists a singular and perverted feeling of insubordination in some districts of the Highlands against the execution of civil processes in the removal of tenants. This feeling is most prejudicial to the interest of all, and it is absolutely necessary to suppress it.'

Two years after Neil was born Robert built the house at Rowancross for me. On the day they demolished the old stone cottage on the site where the house was to be built I made sure to be busy with preparations for Robbie's sixth birthday and could not go and watch, even thought the boys begged for me to go with them.

In later years I spent most of my time at Rowancross. Robert travelled between the shores of Loch Broom and the house in Dundee, where he managed his business. It was an arrangement that suited us well. We were good companions.

I didn't see Iain Mackay again. I thought that he might try and get in touch with me, but he did not. I knew that the terrible events he witnessed at Greenyards had changed everything for him. In the days we spent together he told me that never again would he be able to look upon the glens and mountains of the country of his birth without seeing the bloody scenes, the beaten women, the bloodstained hands of the men who had wrought such uncalled for damage on such undeserving heads. He said that if Upper Canada was good enough for the many Highlanders who had either chosen to go or been sent, then Upper Canada was good enough for him. He asked me to go with him. I remember that I clung to him, and kissed his dear lips and stroked his face, and believed that I could forget my children and my duty and do as he asked.

When he left me at the bridge, with the mist rising from the valley and the sun lifting over the peaks of the mountains, I told him to try and forget all about me. When I didn't hear from him again I tried to convince myself that it was for the best. Several weeks afterwards Iain's sister, Ann, slipped in to see me under the cover of returning the new puppy that had escaped again from its kennel in the back yard. Ann brought news of the family. She told me that her father - now completely bedridden and unable to speak - still clung to life with a determination that would be admirable if it wasn't so sad. For her sister Maggie emigration had been too great a step. Instead she and Donald had taken their children and made their way to Glasgow, and were looking for work in the factories there. That Ann was fearful for her sister was evident. It was a hard life on which they embarked.

I didn't ask about her brother, and she didn't mention his name. Until, as she was leaving, she told me in a casual manner that he was set to leave Ullapool at the end of the month, to join a boat out of Liverpool bound for Canada. Before I could say anything she was gone.

The day that Iain's ship was due to sail I took my horse and rode the track across the hills to the empty cottage on the shores of Loch Broom. I watched as the little ship sailed out through the mouth of the loch towards the open sea. There was a figure at the stern, hands thrust into pockets, hat pulled down low. I thought it might be him. I watched until the little boat was a speck on the distant horizon. Then I rode home to bathe my boys and discuss the outrageous price of candles with my husband over dinner.

Years later when Jane - who had been kitchen maid at Kildorran at the time of which I write - was leaving the household to move south with her husband, she came to see me. She stood before me in the morning room and would not look me in the eye. Her honest, homely face was troubled. She said that there was something on her conscience that had been bothering her these past years, and she couldn't leave without owning up to it. I stared at her in surprise, and couldn't begin to imagine what she was talking about.

She told me that it was a couple of weeks or so after the time that I went missing that a man had come to the back-door with a letter. He was a tall man, with the collar of his coat turned up and his hat pulled low across his face, so that she was unable to recognise him. I had taken the boys to visit Flora for the day. On being told that I was away from home the man had given Jane strict instructions that the letter should be given into the hands of the mistress and nobody else. He made her promise to do as he asked. She remembered that he had taken her by the hand, and that he spoke to her in a fierce desperate voice.

Now Jane looked ashamed. She told me that she was a foolish girl in those days, and forever getting into trouble for failing to carry out her tasks as she should, and that, what with one thing and another, she forgot all about the letter. Then, when she remembered her promise, she was worried that I would be angry with her for leaving it for so long before making the delivery. So rather than give it into my hand, she left the letter on my pillow when she was tidying my room, believing that I would be the first to find it. But then the master had come home, and went upstairs to look for me, and he must have found the letter. Because when Jane went back to check there was no sign of it.

I heard from him only once. Many years later a letter arrived for me, with the postmark of Canada on the envelope. I recognised the writing immediately. Inside was a sheet of paper with a poem by Robert Louis Stevenson written out upon it. There was no note to accompany it, no indication as to the identity of the sender. But I knew.

Blows the wind today, and the sun and the rain are flying,
Blows the wind on the moors today and now,

Where about the graves of the martyrs the whaups
are crying,
    My heart remembers how!
    Grey recumbent tombs of the dead in desert places,
    Standing stones on the vacant wine-red moor,
    Hills of sheep, and the homes of the silent vanished
races,
    And winds, austere and pure;
    Be it granted me to behold you again in dying,
    Hills of home! And hear again the call,
    Hear about the graves of the martyrs the peewees
crying,
    And hear no more at all.

Anna finished reading, closed the cover of the little book and sat with her head bowed. For a few moments neither she nor Fin spoke. The clock on the mantel-piece ticked softly. He was the one to break the silence.

"So do you think they were happy together?"

"Robert and Fiona?"

"Yes."

"In their way…"

He sprang up from his chair and strode across to the window, and banged his fist against the window frame.

"It seems such a waste -"

She looked at her hands in her lap and didn't say anything.

"You're going back, aren't you?" He spoke without turning his head to look at her.

"Yes."

"Is there nothing I can say to make you stay?"

She answered softly. "No."

"What if I were to tell you that I love you? Would that make a difference?"

She twisted her fingers together.

"Oh Fin," was all she said.

He turned abruptly and came and stood in front of her.

"And what about Fiona? Are you going to walk out on her as well?"

She lifted her head. "What do you mean? I'm not walking out on her. We know what we need to know."

He sighed.

"So you're happy to leave it at that?"

"Yes," she said quietly. "I've got no other choice."

Inverness Airport was busy with holidaymakers flying south at the end of the summer. Mothers with children heading home for the start of the school term herded their offspring through the barriers, like sheepdogs driving sheep into their pens. Red faced men in Barbours, with their guns and their fishing rods in canvas bags at their feet, stood and scanned the boards for their flight numbers. In the coffee shop at the far end of the airport Anna and Barbara sat opposite each other across a table.

They had arrived in plenty of time for Anna's flight to Gatwick, and Barbara had insisted on waiting with her until it was called, despite Anna telling her that she would be fine on her own.

"Sure you don't want another coffee?" Barbara asked for the fourth time. "I'm having one."

"No thanks," replied Anna. She was staring into her empty cappuccino cup, as if the answer to all her problems lay in the bottom of it. Barbara wished she could think of something to say to help, but failed to come up with anything. So she got up and went to the counter to order another coffee for herself, checking the departure board on her way back.

"Your flight isn't boarding yet."

"No?"

"Will somebody be there to meet you at the other end?"

"Richard said he would."

Barbara nodded.

"Good."

Anna looked up as Barbara sat down opposite her. The bleak expression in her green eyes was heartbreaking to see. At the table next to them a girl was talking loudly into her mobile phone. Barbara leant over and put her hand on Anna's arm.

"Are you absolutely sure this is what you want?" said Barbara quietly.

She hadn't dared ask before. Even when Anna came and found her - after Barbara heard Fin's car speeding away up the drive - and told her that she had to go home. Anna's face had worn the same stricken expression it wore now. Barbara hadn't asked any questions. Instead she had stood up and gone across the room to where Anna was standing and taken her stepdaughter in her arms. Anna had cried bitter angry tears that ran down her cheeks and dropped unchecked onto Barbara's sleeve.

"I don't want to give this up," she said bitterly. And Barbara had held her and said nothing.

Now Anna looked Barbara in the eye.

"This is the only way," she said. "We both know that."

Barbara nodded. Over the tannoy a woman's voice was reminding people not to leave their bags unattended.

"Will you see him again?"

Anna closed her eyes.

"No," she said.

Anna's flight was being called. Barbara stretched her arms across the table and took Anna's hands in hers.

"Do you think Richard has any idea about Fin?"

Anna shook her head.

"I don't think so."

"I want you to know that I think you are doing absolutely the right thing," said Barbara forcefully.

Anna nodded.

"Yes."

"Richard loves you so much."

"I know."

Arm in arm they walked through the airport to the barrier. When they could go no further together Barbara put her arms around Anna for the last time and hugged her.

"Good luck, my dear," she whispered in her ear, holding her tightly.

CHAPTER TWENTY SIX

On Christmas Eve Barbara took the same flight from Inverness to Gatwick as Anna had at the end of the summer. Richard was waiting for her as she came through the barrier. She wheeled her trolley towards him, smiling and waving.

"You look great," he said, and he hugged her.

"You too," she said, meaning it. He looked very different from the last time she had seen him.

"Anna was going to come," he said over his shoulder, taking the trolley from her and negotiating a passage through the Christmas travellers. "But Ellie had a load of friends staying over last night, and

Anna wanted to make sure they all got to where they were supposed to be in time for Christmas."

"I would have been happy to take a taxi."

He was loading her luggage into the back of the car, the smart leather suitcase, a Mulberry overnight bag, and several carrier bags crammed full of presents all beautifully wrapped in silver paper tied with silver mesh ribbon. He laughed.

"You would have had to hire a van for this lot," he said.

Once they had found their way out of the airport, and were speeding along the fast lane of the motorway, Barbara turned to him.

"So, how is everything?"

He looked at her out of the corner of his eye.

"Good," he said. "Things are really good."

"How are the girls?"

He told her that Ellie had started boarding school after the summer and it was hard to persuade her to come home. Rose was flying in from Australia later that day, with a new boyfriend in tow. With Anna's mother and his father they would be quite a party for Christmas Day.

"Brave of Anna," said Barbara. "Inviting the old fogeys when she must be dying to spend time with her girls."

"What about me?" he laughed. "Isn't it brave of me as well?" Then added quickly, "Not that anybody could call you an old fogey, Barbara."

Barbara nodded to herself. He was a nice man. What made his charm so appealing was that it was genuine.

"And Anna? How is she?"

She waited almost anxiously for his reply.

"She's fine."

He was negotiating his way through heavy traffic going through roadworks on the motorway. Barbara wondered if he was going to elaborate. "How was your flight?" he asked cheerfully. Barbara sighed. Obviously not.

"Very straightforward," she said. She was going to have to wait until she saw Anna to find out how she really was.

Richard rang Anna to let her know they were nearly home and she was waiting for Barbara in the doorway when the car turned into the drive. She came out to greet them. Barbara opened the passenger door.

"There you are."

They put their arms out and held each other tightly.

"How are you getting on?" said Barbara.

Richard had left them to carry her bags inside. Anna glanced towards the house.

"I'm fine," she said. "Really... I miss you though. At times I've felt very lonely."

Barbara squeezed her arm.

"I'm here now."

Nobody went to bed that night until past midnight. Rose arrived in time for supper with her surfer boyfriend in tow, and Barbara made Anna sit down with her daughter at the kitchen table while she and Richard laid the table around them, heated lasagne and made salad. She tried to help with serving dinner as well, but Anna insisted that she sit down with Richard and behave like a guest.

The conversation ebbed and flowed around the table like the sea. During the course of the evening Barbara was able to observe all of them. Ellie was suffering from the effects of an overabundance of parties in the run up to Christmas and, after an initial burst of energy when her sister arrived home, said little, but sat yawning with her chin resting on her hand and her eyes sliding shut. Rose barely stopped talking for long enough to eat. She was full of her adventures. Anna sat next to her daughter, reaching out a hand from time to time to pat her arm or stroke her hair, as if she didn't quite believe that she was real.

Richard was the original human dynamo. Topping up wine glasses, clearing the table, loading the dishwasher;

he didn't stop. When Barbara got up to help he told her firmly to sit down. Barbara watched Anna with her family around her. She noticed the way Richard and Anna exchanged smiles over their younger daughter's head as she nodded off in her chair. When Anna got up from the table to refill the water jug she saw her wipe a trail of soap suds from his cheek where he had rubbed his face while he was washing up. It was a relief to Barbara to see that their relationship appeared to be holding together in spite of – or maybe because of - the turmoil they had been through.

By mid morning on Christmas Day the kitchen was quiet. Breakfast had been eaten and cleared, away and now Anna was moving saucepans around on the hob and checking that the water surrounding the Christmas pudding hadn't boiled dry.

Barbara sat on the sofa in the living room, tying the linen napkins with velvet ribbon for Anna's table. In the dining room she could hear Rose and Ellie talking while they laid the table. Although they spoke softly to each other their voices carried to where Barbara was sitting.

"So, how's Mum been?" asked Rose.

Barbara stiffened. She thought about getting up to shut the door. She didn't want to eavesdrop.

Then Ellie's voice: "What do you mean?"

"You know," said Rose. "After the summer? When she got back after grandfather's funeral?"

There was a moment's silence. Then Ellie spoke again.

"What do you mean?" she repeated.

Barbara heard Rose sighing.

"Come on, Ells. Staying on in Scotland all that time. The whole thing about being obsessed with the family history, when she's never shown the slightest bit of interest before. Not being there when Dad came back from Moscow. It's just so unlike her."

Barbara put the ribbon down and stood up.

"You make it sound a bit mad," Ellie's voice said, beginning to sound anxious. "I just thought she was having a nice time up there. Dad was away. We weren't around." She hesitated. "I suppose I didn't really think that much about it."

Rose wasn't giving up.

"So, how was she when you got back from the States? Was everything OK?"

"Bloody hell, Rose." Ellie was protesting now. "I don't know. She was like she always is. Sorting stuff out, buying the wrong sort of tights, complaining about having to sew on all the name tapes, nagging me about being organised. You know what she's like."

Barbara tiptoed to the door and began to push it shut.

"But that's the point," she heard Rose say. "I don't know if I do anymore. There's something different about her."

⚊⟨⋅ ⋅⟩⚊

In the kitchen Anna bent down in front of the range to pull out a tray of potatoes. Had she done enough? Jim looked like he could eat an entire field's worth without drawing breath. Behind her she heard footsteps, and Richard came into the room and began opening and closing drawers. She closed the oven door and stood up. He was wearing the denim shirt that Ellie had given him, and a beaded necklace that Rose had brought back from Australia. Not something he would have chosen for himself in a million years, but in a bizarre way it suited him. He looked across and caught her watching him and he grinned at her and waved a corkscrew in the air.

"Going to open the red wine. Give it time to breathe. Everything going OK, darling? Anything you need?"

She smiled and shook her head. She couldn't fault him for effort. He was trying so hard.

The tension between them when she came home from the Highlands was camouflaged, but not diminished, by the return of Ellie from America. And by the subsequent bustle and business of getting her off to school. When she was gone the house with just the two of them in it seemed unnaturally quiet. Whether by chance or design, Richard was working out of his London office and came home every night. He bought a monthly season ticket for the train. He even put his suitcase away in the attic. Anna used to envy her friends whose husbands were always home by seven. Now she wasn't sure how she felt about having him around the house so much.

For several weeks they trod carefully around each other, as if afraid that any sudden movement might spark off a row. Anna returned to her job as classroom assistant at the local primary school, but found it hard to summon up the enthusiasm required to deal, not with the children, but with the parents, whose requests and demands seemed ever more ridiculous. At night they ate supper together at the kitchen table, and conversation flowed relatively freely. But Anna couldn't shake off the feeling that she was treading water, waiting for something to happen.

And then one morning, when he was shaving in their bathroom, she came in and he looked at her reflection in the mirror and set his razor down on the edge of the basin, and said in a tight, strained voice, "So, what are you going to do?"

Anna was rummaging through a drawer, and she stopped what she was doing and looked at him in the mirror.

"What do you mean?"

His eyes stared at her.

"Are you going to stay?"

She gazed at him and - to give herself time more than anything else - said again, "What do you mean?"

"Jesus Christ, Anna." He swung around to face her. "Do you want me to spell it out? Are you planning on leaving me? It's not that difficult, is it?"

She gazed at him in amazement. It occurred to her that it had been a long time since either of them had said what they really thought. Very carefully, looking him in the eye, she said that she had absolutely no intention of leaving him. That they had both invested far too much time and effort into the family for her to walk away from it now. They had grown apart, and stopped talking to each other, and that was very dangerous. But hopefully the damage wasn't permanent. And, if they both tried really hard, they would make a go of it.

She knew she was talking in clichés and wondered if he could hear through them. It was hard for her to read his expression. Was it relieved, thankful, defiant? She didn't know. But the point was that she was talking, and he was listening. And now it would be his turn to talk, and her turn to listen. And maybe, between the two of them, they would be able to find a way through this and make it work. And be glad that they had.

It had been Richard who had suggested an extended family Christmas. He had thrown himself into it with enthusiasm, taking Ellie off to choose the tree when she came home for the holidays, spending hours in the wine merchants tasting and choosing, chopping enough logs to have open fires for the next few years. And getting so wired up Anna was worried that there was no way it could live up to his expectations.

They invited Richard's father, Douglas. Anna's mother would be there adding her particular brand of strident humour to the mix. There were both girls, plus one boyfriend. And there was Barbara. Anna had been delighted when Richard, without prompting, suggested that it would be nice if they invited her to join them. She had been thinking it herself, but had been unable to bring herself to mention it. There was a residue of touchiness when Barbara's name was mentioned, as if in some way Richard held her to blame for nearly losing his wife for him. But when he arrived back from the airport with Barbara, weighed down with bags full of the gifts she had brought for them all, chocolates from Brussels, fruit cake from Scotland, sweet wine and nuts from Italy, he ushered her into the house with such a proprietorial air it was as if he had invented her himself.

It didn't take Ellie and Rose long to fall in love with their step grandmother, helped along by her announcement that in her book Christmas Eve gifts were a must. She produced a hand painted scarf from Venice for Rose and a brooch in the shape of a stalking panther with glittering eyes for Ellie. Then she sat down with the pair of them on the sofa in the family room and, within half an hour, both were convinced that they had never met anybody who understood their lives half the way that she did.

Richard, although on the face of it one of her biggest fans, took a little longer to fall under her spell. Anna hadn't been wrong when she suspected that he regarded Barbara as a threat. But her kindness and sympathetic ear were irresistible. Before she had been with them a day he was seeking her out to tell her how bad he felt about the fact that he didn't go to visit his mother in the home as often as he should. When they had finished talking he went to find Anna to tell her, as if she didn't know it already, that Barbara was, in his experience, the most intelligent and intuitive American he had met in a long time.

Now the intelligent and intuitive American was doing her bit with Anna's mother and Richard's father in the living room, having recognised that the best help she could give Anna with the last stages of the Christmas lunch was to keep the older generation, and Jennifer in particular, out of the way.

Jennifer, dressed in an A-line tweed skirt with a cashmere cardigan and pearls, was sitting next to Barbara on the sofa by the fire, with Douglas's labrador snoring at her feet, and a glass of champagne in her hand. She looked up as Jim - who had finished opening the wine with Richard and was anxious to retie the invisible bond with Rose - peered in through the door. She beckoned him in with an imperious wave of her hand, but he had seen that Rose was absent, and he backed away and they heard him thunder down the hall.

"That boy is a ridiculous height," said Jennifer sounding indignant. "Is it an Australian thing, do you think? Or are the young of today all turning into giants?"

Barbara smiled and wrapped the end of her shawl across her shoulder.

"Must be something to do with the diet, don't you think Douglas?"

Richard's father, sitting in the arm chair opposite, smiled.

"I'm sorry, Barbara," he said in a courteous voice. "I missed that. What was it you asked me?"

She drew them into a conversation about modern diet compared to the food they ate when they were young, and was pleased with herself for managing to find a subject that distracted Jennifer from talking about Anna and how much she was worrying about her.

Jennifer hadn't been in Barbara's company two minutes before she had laid a hand on her arm and drew her to one side.

"Now perhaps you can tell me," she said in a loud whisper, "whatever is the matter with Anna?"

Barbara looked startled and asked what she meant.

"Dear Barbara," said Jennifer with a touch of impatience, "you must have noticed. I appreciate that you haven't known my daughter very long, but she did spend most of the summer hiding away with you in the wilds of Scotland. And she's come back in the most peculiar mood."

Barbara wasn't sure that she wanted this conversation to continue. She still hadn't had a proper chance to speak to Anna in private.

"Well Jennifer, you've got me there," she said slowly. "Anna seems fine to me."

"You think so?" Jennifer sniffed. "Well to my mind she's a different person."

"How do you mean exactly?" asked Barbara carefully.

Jennifer was only too eager to elaborate.

"I'm really rather worried that she seems to be developing something of a selfish streak," she said. "She is my daughter. And the last thing I want to do is criticize. But there have been a number of occasions recently when she has been incredibly tactless, and

I have had to say something about it to her. Do you know that she actually suggested that I might think about apologizing to the Baileys next door? When she knows how difficult they are. And she has asked me to stop ringing her when she is working. Which I have to do because she doesn't always pick up when she's at home, so I can't get hold of her." Barbara was biting her lip. "And then the last straw was on Friday, when she told me she didn't have time to buy my Christmas presents for Rose and Ellie, when she always has done in the past, and she knows how difficult I find it."

Barbara fought the temptation to tell Jennifer that if anybody was being selfish it was her, and that she didn't deserve a daughter like Anna. But she had resisted the urge and steered Jennifer into calmer waters.

⚍⚌

In the corner of the kitchen there was a soft pop as Richard eased the cork from a bottle of champagne. He took a pair of champagne flutes from the cupboard and filled them. Setting down the bottle, he brought a glass over to Anna and handed it to her.

"Can you stop what you're doing for a minute?" he said. "I've got something to give you."

Anna took the glass he offered her with a look of surprise. The family custom was to give presents after lunch. What was he up to? He took her hand and placed an envelope into it. She looked from it to his face with a puzzled expression. He was not usually one for surprises. Didn't like to risk getting it wrong.

"Aren't you going to open it?"

She put down her glass and opened the envelope. The letter inside was typed on headed notepaper with their home address at the top. It was addressed to Peter MacGregor, Richard's boss. She glanced at him.

"What is this?"

"Read it."

She read. It was a letter of resignation. She stared at him.

"But I don't understand…"

He took her hand and led her over to the kitchen table and sat her down and explained. He told her that if he had learnt anything from the events of the past year, it was that if you spend all your time working for the things that matter, but in the meantime you neglect the things that matter, the danger is that one day you wake up and find that the things that matter have gone while you were too busy to notice.

At this point he paused and said, "You get what I'm saying?"

He told her that he had always loved her, from when he first saw her. But he realised that maybe it hadn't been that obvious over the past few years, and that spending so little time with her had made it difficult for him to show it. She opened her mouth to say that she understood and he didn't have to explain, but now he took hold of her other hand and pulled her round so that she was facing him, and he hushed her and carried on.

"The thing is," he said. "I want to make it up to you. I've spent too much time away from you and the girls. I've been an absentee husband for too long. So." He took a deep breath. "I've resigned."

"OK," she said slowly, feeling a little dazed.

He gripped her hands tightly. "The deed is done. This is a copy of the letter I gave to Peter last week. We've got to work out the final details, but they've accepted my resignation, and as of the New Year I'm out of there."

Anna bit her lip. "Good heavens," she said.

"Anna, Anna…"

She could feel his exhilaration. He let go of her hands and lifted her up in his arms and swung her round. She had a sudden painful vision of Fin doing exactly the same thing. Richard set her down.

"I know it might make things a bit difficult for a while. Money isn't going to flow as freely as we might like, what with Ellie's school fees and both of them going to university. But I reckon with careful management we should be able to manage. And if it's not too late for me, I'm going to retrain. I want to be a teacher…"

He looked into her face. "You're shocked."

Anna's head was spinning. It was too much to take on board. She opened her mouth to ask him why the hell he had gone ahead with this huge decision without discussing it with her first. But then she stopped herself. At least he recognised that things needed to change. Which was a start.

She raised her glass to him.

"I'm really happy for you," she told him. "Let's drink to new beginnings."

Lunch was a noisy, good humoured affair. It turned out that Jim was something of a comedian, and he told several outrageous jokes - just the right side of tasteless - that had the whole table roaring, even Jennifer. The girls sat either side of their father and spoilt him as only they knew how. Barbara took Richard's father under her wing to the extent that he was able to forget for a few hours that this was the first Christmas without his wife. When Richard raised his glass to toast absent friends, Anna found that not only was she thinking of his mother, but for the first time she included Charlie in her thoughts, and wished he could have been there with them, and was sorry for all the times that they had celebrated Christmas and hadn't invited him.

With her glass raised, she looked across the table at Barbara and their eyes met. Barbara smiled and raised her glass in acknowledgement, and Anna had the strangest feeling that she could read her mind, that she understood and that it was the best Christmas present Anna could have given her, to know that finally Charlie's daughter understood and appreciated her father as she had never done before.

After lunch they moved into the drawing room, and the girls did as they had done since they were little, and handed out the presents from under the tree. There was the crackle of paper being unwrapped, combined with expressions of gratitude and exclamations of delight. When all the presents were opened Barbara came across the room and drew Anna to one side.

"I have something for you," she said.

Anna, who had already unwrapped an exquisite Hermes scarf from her, looked surprised. Barbara was reaching into her handbag, and she drew out a large brown envelope. She handed it to Anna, who took it from her, wondering about a day that had seen not one but two envelopes as presents. She hoped that the contents of this one weren't going to be such a shock as the last.

In the envelope were the deeds to Rowancross House. Anna pulled them out and looked at them without comprehending what they meant. Then her mouth fell open, and for the second time that day she said, "But I don't understand -"

"Rowancross... It's yours," said Barbara, resting her hand on Anna's arm.

Anna stared at her. "But it's your home."

Barbara drew her down to sit beside her on the sofa. She said that she had just come back from Italy, where she had brought a recently renovated farmhouse just north of Sienna. She had found that without Charlie she couldn't be happy in the Highlands. It was his place; there were too many memories. She had loved living at Rowancross House because of him, because it meant so much to him. So it wasn't really her gift. It was his. To the daughter he had loved.

"What have you got there, Mum?"

Ellie came over to sit beside her. Anna turned to her daughter with eyes that glistened with tears.

"Barbara is giving me the house. She's giving me Rowancross."

Ellie raised her eyebrows.

"Wow... That's great," she said a little uncertainly. "Does that mean we're moving?"

Anna laughed.

"No, of course not," she said. "But it does mean we – or more likely me and your father - might spend quite a bit of time up there." Suddenly Richard's resignation took on a new light. She held her daughter's hands in her own. "Oh Ellie, you will love it. I can't wait to take you there. There's nowhere else like it."

Ellie, reassured by her mother's enthusiasm, laughed.

"I can't wait to see it," she said.

With the presents all opened Douglas and Jennifer settled themselves in opposite corners of the sofa, Douglas already dozing after a couple more glasses of wine that he was used to, and Jennifer about to embark on the giant Christmas quiz in the newspaper. In the kitchen Richard and Jim were taking male bonding to new heights, making a show of donning rubber gloves and squirting too much washing up liquid under the running tap in the sink. Rose and Ellie, both trying to pretend that they weren't suffering from the after effects of a late Christmas Eve and too much wine at lunchtime, disappeared, ostensibly to watch a film, although Anna was willing to bet money that both would be asleep by the time the opening credits had rolled. She and Barbara put on waterproofs and Wellingtons, and took Douglas's dog out for some fresh air.

Over the hills to the west the setting sun had broken through the clouds and was casting long shadows across the ploughed fields, throwing the skeleton branches of the trees into sharp relief. The labrador ran wildly in ever increasing circles, sending a flock of pigeons flapping into the air. Barbara tucked her hand under Anna's arm, and they walked together in comfortable silence.

"You will come back and stay at Rowancross, won't you?" said Anna.

Barbara squeezed her arm.

"Try keeping me away."

They turned into a path that ran along the side of a deserted golf course. Barbara took a deep breath.

"So, how is everything?"

Anna continued walking and didn't reply for a moment. Then she said, "There's no-one else I could say this to, but I didn't realise it was going to be this hard."

Barbara looked at her.

"My dear..."

"I suppose I thought that because I had changed so much I would come home and find that everything else had changed as well. But nothing has. Or not really."

"Richard certainly seems to be trying very hard to do the right thing."

Anna sighed.

"He is. Almost too hard. I don't know what's wrong with me. I suppose I just wanted somebody to notice. To understand."

Barbara linked arms with her.

"I think he probably understands more than you give him credit for. Maybe he's just not very good at expressing it. He's a good man you know."

"I know he is," said Anna. "And I know that all of this has been as difficult for him as it has for me. I think we'll get through it. We'll probably look back and see this summer as the best thing that could have happened to us."

"I'm sure you're right."

They headed across the fields with the sun setting in the hills behind them.

"So, have you given any more thought to the idea of writing a book about Fiona?" said Barbara. "I know it was Cameron's suggestion originally, but that doesn't necessarily make it a bad one."

Anna shook her head.

"There are enough writers in this family, without adding another one. And it would have been the last thing Fiona would have wanted, for her life to be made public. That wasn't the point at all." She hesitated. "No," she said, "I'm going to keep Fiona's secret for her. When the girls are old enough to understand I'll show them the diaries and the letters. And they can pass them on to their daughters in turn."

Barbara thought about this for a moment. "You're right," she said. "I think that's a lovely idea."

Anna glanced at her. "Speaking of Cameron... How's he getting on?"

Barbara chuckled. "He's in a bit of a state at the moment from what I hear. Laura's found herself a job in Edinburgh, and he's completely gone to pieces without her."

"So she finally found the balls to dump him."

Anna's voice was full of satisfaction. Barbara told her that, after Laura had gone, Cameron had followed her and proposed marriage. And Laura had told him exactly what to do with his proposal and sent him packing.

"Good for her," said Anna.

Dusk was falling and, as they walked past, lights came on in the windows of the houses in the lane. Barbara wondered if Anna was going to ask about Fin. They were drawing near to home and she hadn't mentioned his name. And there was another thing she was curious about.

"You wouldn't think of getting in touch with the people at the Mackay Group?"

Anna screwed up her nose.

"Why would I want to do that?"

"To introduce yourself?"

Anna shook her head and Barbara laughed

"Not tempted by the thought that you might be an heiress, then?"

"It's the last thing I care about," said Anna vehemently. "My summer with you gave me so much – a father, a family history, a past. And it gave me Fiona. And Iain Mackay. I love the thought that their blood runs in my veins. That's worth more to me than money could ever be."

She had her hand on the gate into the front garden when Barbara stopped her.

"By the way," she said, deliberately casual. "There was something else… I forgot to mention." She hesitated. "I saw Fin MacLean a few weeks ago. He was visiting Sarah before he left to spend Christmas in Toronto. He called round to ask me a favour, he asked me to give you this. Said it was his Christmas present to you."

It was the third envelope Anna had received on that extraordinary day. This one was A4, white, with a cardboard backing. There was no address on the front, no name. Anna slid a finger under the flap. Inside there was a single sheet of paper. She took off her gloves so that she could ease it out. Standing under the light from a street lamp she saw in the middle of the page, in large black type, three words:

THE UNSUNG HEROINES

Anna turned to Barbara with puzzled eyes. "What is this?"

So Barbara explained. This sheet of paper, she said, was the title page to a book that Fin was in the process of writing. He already had a publisher for it. Was hoping to finish it by the middle of the year, and see it on the shelves within the next eighteen months.

"You're talking about his novel?" said Anna, unsure of the significance to her.

But it wasn't his novel. He had put that to one side for the time being. Barbara told her to turn over the sheet of paper. On the back was a short paragraph. The blurb, explained Barbara. It said:

The Unsung Heroines is the story of the women of the Scottish Highlands, the women who were the backbone of a society that prided itself on its warriors, but overlooked the fact that many of those happened to be female rather than male. While the men were recognised for their bravery, the women went unnoticed. Until now. This book redresses the balance.

ABOUT THE AUTHOR

Jane King graduated with a law degree from Warwick University in 1980, and went on to qualify as a barrister before moving into advertising in 1983. After reaching board level at a London advertising agency she gave up work to spend more time with her three children. A garden designer and blogger who writes about gardening and travel, she has drawn on her Scottish roots and regular trips to the Highlands to write The Greenyards Legacy. Jane lives in Surrey with one well-behaved husband and two badly-behaved dogs.

Printed in Great Britain
by Amazon